THE

ENDLESS

FALL

DEADWOOD DUET BOOK ONE

EMMERSON HOYT

Most of us will never tame a dragon or save a kingdom. Our beauty and cleverness won't bring an empire to its knees and our sacrifices won't stop the world from ending—but all of us will make a mistake.

To my fellow fuck-ups, there's still so much of our stories left to tell.

Authors Note

The Endless Fall is a small town,
southern gothic contemporary romance with dark themes.
Book one will read a little bit like a prequel, concentrating heavily on
the romance between the two main characters while laying the
foundation for book two.
You can expect atmospheric dread, melancholy,
uneasy character relationships, and a cliffhanger.
The second book in the duet will be darker than the first.

This story contains heavy subject matter. For a list of content
warnings, please visit the back of the book.

Prologue

Willa, Age 25

The distinct sensation of being watched whispers across my skin like an unseen caress. I might've spent the last five hours tracking down a rogue mountain lion, but something—or *someone*—is hunting me.

Scalp prickling with awareness, I train my rifle on the stream of sand trickling over the rocky face of the red canyon wall in front of me. Little spirals of heat rise into the air off of sunbaked boulders and sweat drips down my spine while I wait with bated breath for whatever's been following me to make itself known.

The sand stops, a gust of hot, dry wind lifting the damp hair off my neck and flooding my nostrils with desert sage and arid dirt. I wait another moment, and when nothing moves, I relax my shoulders and let loose an annoyed puff of air.

After four years of working undercover to investigate wildlife crimes across the southern United States, this assignment is so far outside my normal scope of duty it's almost comical. But of course, I was the only available agent when the call for assistance came from local rangers.

I never should've picked up my damn phone. Especially since this is my last weekend off before reporting for my next job.

1

As a special agent for the U.S. Fish and Wildlife Service, I'm usually charming my way into a smuggler's confidence or staking out the latest shipment of trafficked goods. More often than not, this means I spend my days in a dusty warehouse, dingy dive bar, or— *when I'm really lucky*—on a kingpin's yacht down in the Gulf of Mexico. Not in the desert, sweating my tits off under the blazing Texas sun while something stalks my every step.

I haven't had to do shit like this since—

A twig snaps somewhere inside the mouth of the canyon, and my body tenses.

Chances are whatever's trailing me is an animal, but I've pissed off too many scumbag traffickers not to at least consider that one of them might've tracked me down looking for retribution.

Despite the scorching temperature, I shiver—the scars stamped up and down the length of my back tightening with a sudden ferocity as the breeze causes loose strands of my white-streaked hair to lash across my neck and cheeks.

It's an animal, I say to myself for the nine hundredth time, keeping my head on a swivel. *It's not a murderous convict seeking payback, or a skinwalker, or any of the other horrifying creatures Mrs. Crowe told you about when you were a teenager.*

It's *just* an animal.

Sweaty palms clutching my rifle, I approach the entrance of the box canyon on soft feet while scanning the crevices in the rock walls for any sign of movement. Apart from the blood *whooshing* violently in my ears, nothing stirs.

Sweat and sunscreen drip into my eyes and down my neck, my rapid pulse drowning out all other sounds. I'll need to stop for a water break soon if I want to avoid passing out, but for now, I settle for readjusting the red bandana around my neck and swiping my sleeve across my face.

Five hours on the trail and there's been no sign of another human and only rare evidence of the well-camouflaged creatures calling Big

Bend National Park their home. I did find a putrefying section of a half-eaten Bighorn sheep leg about a quarter mile back, as well as quite a bit of sun-bleached scat in a dried riverbed that I suspect the mountain lion's been using as an oversized kitty litter box, but no fresh tracks.

Another twig snaps and my chest hitches.

Whatever made that noise is close. *Too* close.

Slowing my steps, I drop to one knee. The hairs on my neck stand on end as I silently switch out my rifle for my sidearm and rise to my feet.

It's the mountain lion. It has to be. I click off the safety on my handgun. *She's looking for her next meal, and if I'm not careful, it's going to be me.*

My knuckles blanch as I grip my gun tighter.

This feels wasteful and wrong. We're the ones who encroached on *her* territory. It's not the cougar's fault she doesn't know the difference between prey and hikers... Unfortunately for both of us, her fate was sealed the second she took down that birdwatcher.

In the past week alone, there've been three more attacks, and if my suspicions are correct, there's a very real possibility I'm seconds away from being the fourth.

The breeze picks up, and I inhale deeply, trying to scent anything on the wind that might give me an idea of what direction she'll come at me from. When I was growing up, my hyperosmia was a nuisance, but out here on the job, my heightened sense of smell has saved my life more than a time or two.

Right now, all I can smell is juniper and bits of dry Texas earth caked on the inside of my nose. But when I inhale again, my spine stiffens at the faint note of cheap whiskey and black-pepper aftershave riding the wind—a scent that doesn't belong anywhere near this mountainside.

I draw in another breath, trying to make sure I'm not imagining it or catching a whiff of something lingering in my hair from the cantina I stopped at last night for dinner... *There it is again.* My nose scrunches at the underlying musky aroma of an unwashed male body.

Pulse racing, I scan my surroundings, a snarl forming on my lips when a shadow steps out from behind a boulder barely twenty feet away. Even from this distance, I can see the saccharine smile plastered across his leathery cheeks and something black and shiny tucked into his intricate belt.

Motherfucker.

I raise my gun, the polymer grip biting painfully into my palm as my blood runs cold.

Of all the people who could've come after me, I never imagined it would be *him*. Not after all this time.

"You're a hard woman to track down," he says in a once familiar East Texas drawl.

His grating voice echoes off the canyon walls, the vibration unearthing memories long since buried and awakening a slumbering well of deep hatred in my blood.

Aiming my pistol at the center of his chest, I take a single step forward. "Why are you here? I warned you what would happen if I ever saw you again."

My voice quavers the tiniest bit, and he shakes his head, eyes narrowing in mock disappointment as he clicks his tongue. "Don't play dumb, Willa Dunn. You know why, the same way you know what I'm about to do."

Unease skitters up my spine in the sweltering heat, like a lizard fleeing from danger, but I harden my jaw, refusing to let him see how unnerved I am. "You're going to have to be a bit more specific."

"I lost everything because of *you*," he spits, a hint of tobacco accosting my senses when he steps closer. "Figured it was about time I repay the favor and finish what your mother started all those years ago."

I belt out an unexpected laugh, the sharp sound surprisingly loud and a little unhinged. If I had a nickel for every time I've heard that phrase...well, I'd have two or three nickels, but still. These idiots really need some new material.

"You waited seven years and came all this way just to kill me?" I laugh again at the ridiculousness. "God, you really are pathetic."

The man's smile fades, his fingers inching toward the gun tucked into his waistband. "Watch your mouth, girl—"

A piercing scream splits the air, high-pitched and everywhere all at once as it ricochets off the dusty canyon walls. I can't pinpoint where it's coming from, but there's only one animal that screams like that, and this one already has a taste for blood...

My hackles rise, and my head snaps right and then left, up and then down in search of danger, barely catching a blur of movement before the cougar springs out from a crevice in the rocks, landing on top of the man before he can draw his gun.

He screams—at least, that's what I think that choking croak was meant to be—but the sound quickly cuts off when her teeth clamp onto his throat. Doubling down on her assault, the cougar swipes at my would-be attacker's barrel-shaped belly with her massive paws, sending bright-red blood splattering across the ground and trees as she attempts to drag him away.

I flinch as the gore hits my face, the hot viscous liquid dripping onto my lips and coating my mouth with the taste of iron.

The metallic tang snaps me out of my shocked stupor, forcing me into action. I fire a single bullet into the air, advancing on the duo with my gun trained on the cougar and my opposite arm held out to the side in an attempt to appear as large as possible.

Maw stained with blood, the cougar's amber eyes—both beautifully intelligent and terrifyingly bloodthirsty—flick to mine, barely stopping her assault for a millisecond before she sinks her teeth back into the man's shoulder. He shrieks when she shakes her head, tearing loose a chunk of flesh and flooding the canyon with the nauseating squelch of muscle being ripped from bone.

My confident steps falter from the unfamiliar warmth I can only describe as calm satisfaction blooming inside my chest. *He deserves this,* the devil on my shoulder whispers. *This is the price of the choices he's made and the people he's hurt...*

I start to lower my gun... Then, just as quickly, I raise it back up, aim at the mountain lion, and shake my head. *Get it together, Willa. You're a federal agent, for fuck's sake.*

Gritting my teeth, I fire off another round, this one grazing the mountain lion's shoulder.

Still, she doesn't stop.

"Dammit," I growl. With the way she's positioned on top of him, I can't shoot her without also risking hitting the bastard beneath her.

The man attempts to scream, but with the cougar's jaw clamped down on his throat, it comes out as a gurgle. The second she lifts her head for another attack, I fire again, this time hitting my mark straight through the murderous creature's skull.

The mountain lion collapses atop the man, who claws uselessly at the bloodied shreds of his mangled chest and throat—as if he can somehow undo the damage.

Closing the distance between us, I kick away his gun and hastily verify the cougar is no longer breathing before kneeling by the man's head. Already, blood loss has stolen the color from his face and hands, his pale skin nearly gray in the blinding sun.

A spray of gore erupts from his mouth as he reaches for me with a bloody hand—

No, not me... *My gun.*

I scoot backward, just out of his pathetic grasp, and make a *tsking* sound. "You weren't going to try to shoot me, were you?" His lips pull into a tight, stubborn line, and I can't stop my smile. He knows he needs my help, otherwise he'd be spewing profanities right now.

Using the barrel of my gun, I tilt his chin up to get a better visual of the wound, grimacing as blood surges from his shredded flesh in time with his rapid pulse. *Yikes.* The cougar must've nicked an artery, which means he's got minutes at best.

I suck in a breath through my teeth and rest my forearms on my thighs so that my gun hangs between my knees. "That doesn't look good," I say, mouth scrunched to the side in mock sympathy.

Eyes wide and frantic, the man tears his attention away from my pistol to meet my gaze.

"*Help*," he whispers, and I have to bite my lower lip to keep from laughing. It's not the first time I've watched an evil man die, but it never ceases to amaze me how they all seem to think there's a way out —like they can negotiate with death itself.

I scoff. Maybe the nutjobs are right and the human race is too far gone.

Maybe we really are doomed...

I bring my free hand to my chest to cover my racing heart. "You want *my* help?"

The man nods vigorously, my vindictive sarcasm apparently failing to cut through his panicked adrenaline. I glance at the wound on his neck and then to the sky, calculating how long it would take medevac to get here and how much time he has left based on blood loss.

Best-case scenario, I could get someone here in an hour or two. There's absolutely no way he'll make it that long, but he doesn't need to know that...

I blink slowly. "I'm not sure you deserve my help."

His lips gape open and closed, a hoarse gasp escaping his throat like he's trying to speak. But whatever he's saying, it's too quiet for me to make out.

Curiosity overcoming my better judgment, I lean forward.

"*Evil bitch*," he hisses. "*Abomina—*"

I cover his mouth, rage reigniting a dormant fire in my chest as his blood and spit seep between my fingers. "None of that," I chide, bringing the barrel of my gun to the center of his forehead. "You might not deserve my help, but I'll make you an offer anyway. Confess, and I'll call a medevac."

It's a lie, *obviously*. He'll die no matter what I do, but at least he can give me some closure—let me know once and for all if it was true.

He shakes his head in refusal, alarm or maybe the movement itself robbing his face of the last of its color.

Disgusting coward.

Then again, a man like this has committed so many sins he might not even understand which one I want him to confess to.

"I want you to admit what you did to her," I clarify, fighting the urge to close my eyes as the image of a tiny, frail body in a hospital bed comes flooding back to me with a tsunami of other memories from the day I left Deadwood.

Wind howls through the canyon, hot and fierce, whipping dirt into my face and ripping strands of my hair from my bun. My lip quivers, but my eyes remain open, the violence thrumming in my veins growing each second I wait for his answer.

Still, he doesn't speak.

I grind the gun into his forehead, my hand shaking with the effort not to pull the trigger and be done with this. Blood surges from the man's throat and belly, his slippery hands falling to his sides as he loses strength.

"Tell me," I scream, my vision momentarily turning red as my opportunity for answers leaks out of his arteries like sand through an hourglass.

The man pauses, his mouth thinning as he motions for me to come closer with a weak crook of his bloodied finger. For some stupid reason, I do it, mouth souring while the rancid smell of his breath mixes with the coppery tang in the air.

Then he speaks.

Eyes wide and horrified, I listen to every word of his whispered confession, the vile truth squeezing the air from my lungs.

"Who else?" I croak once he finishes.

A volatile mixture of spit and blood splatters across my cheek with each new name he chokes out, but I don't react. I can't. I'm frozen solid, unable to think or breathe through the revulsion twisting my gut into knots.

"And the fire?" I whisper, keeping my eyes on the tree line

because I can't bring myself to fucking look at him. "Was that your idea?"

"Which one?" he whispers with a bloodied grin.

Ice slithers up my spine, but then the man gurgles and coughs, sending a spray of blood into the air as he gasps for breath. I glance down, noticing the deep-red halo blossoming on the ground around his shoulders.

"*Help me*," he pleads, weak fingers clawing at my boot.

Rocking onto my heels, I stand and slowly wipe the dirt and blood from my face with my sleeve. "No, I don't think I will."

My boots are filled with lead as I position myself by his feet. Then I aim the pistol at his chest, take a deep breath, and squeeze the trigger.

Chapter One

Willa, Age 18

7 Years Earlier

The second my boots hit the scorching pavement, dread presses down on my lungs until it's difficult to breathe.

I hate it here.

With a sigh, I lean around the tail end of the SUV, scalding my hand on the metal bumper when I check to see if my path across the parking lot is clear. It's not, so I hang back a second, frowning at my brother's back as he marches away in the opposite direction.

Maybe dividing and conquering our errands wasn't such a good idea after all...

No matter where I go in this damn town, I'm always met with hushed whispers, pitying glances, or offers of assistance—like I have a terminal disease or I'm too fragile to function on my own. At eighteen years old, fourteen of those spent living with these mangled scars on my back, shoulders, and neck, I should be used to their reactions, but it grates on my nerves every time.

There's a part of me holding on to the hope that one day I'll walk into a room and no one will notice. That one day, the only thing people will see when they look at me is Willa Dunn, not what happened all those years ago. Judging by the old man using his cane to make the sign of the cross on his chest by the cart corral, today is clearly not that day.

Taking a deep breath, I blow the hair out of my eyes and head across the black-tar parking lot toward the grocery store, bracing myself for what awaits me inside.

The second the automatic doors creak open, the sickly sweet scent of overripe fruit assaults my senses, along with a dozen other smells: rotting fish from the seafood department, dust from the health food aisle, whatever chemical astringent they used to clean the yellowing laminate floors.

My stomach roils as the odors permeate my lungs and swell inside my throat, but my cupboards are empty, so with one final reminder to breathe through my mouth, I step into the store and grab a basket.

Avoiding eye contact with my unwanted spectators, I scurry up and down the aisles, quickly collecting what I need for dinner tonight and the eclipse party tomorrow, as well as a few other staples we've been out of for a week.

"*Merciful Lord*, was that Willa Dunn?" a woman whispers from an aisle over. "Maybe I should offer to help the poor dear with her shopping?"

"You'll do no such thing," a second woman hisses, this voice twangy, high-pitched, and much older. "That girl's been milkin' her past for far too long."

The second woman, who I now recognize as Dorothy Black-thorne, clicks her tongue and continues, "I can't believe her father doesn't force her to hide those hideous white streaks in her hair. And did you see what she's wearin'? Dark colors from head to toe—like she *wants* to invite the Devil into her life."

I glance down at my outfit—a high-neck black mini dress, my favorite green suede jacket with fringe on the sleeves and back, and my signature red bandana tied around my neck. I'd finished off my look with silver-accented black leather boots and some winged eyeliner that took me twenty minutes to perfect.

There's not much I can do about the white streaks in my otherwise nutty-brown hair, and the dress might be a *little* short for what's generally deemed appropriate in small-town East Texas, but after trying to blend into the background for so long, it feels good to finally find my style. I like the way I dress, and as far as I'm concerned, anyone who doesn't can shove right off. It's not like I care what people in Deadwood think anyway. Especially not the town busybody, Dorothy Blackthorne.

Ignoring them, I readjust the basket on my forearm before rising onto my tiptoes to grab three jars of Nutella off the top shelf.

Last year, when the Deadwood rumor mill discovered that a local girl had been drugged and sexually assaulted at a party a few towns over, the first twangy question out of Dorothy's mouth was "what was the girl wearin' when it happened?" She'd promptly followed up that banger with "was she leadin' him on?"

The only thing Dorothy hadn't asked for was proof, and that's probably because she knew there was a mountain of it, including a drug tox screen from the hospital and videos taken by the friends of the asshole who drugged the girl.

My boots click on the linoleum as I stomp down the aisle to grab a box of rice pilaf.

The audacity of that woman is *unreal*. To make matters worse, the judge assigned to the case ended up being Dorothy's brother. Not only did Abbott Blackthorne throw out the whole lawsuit without letting it go to trial, but a few months later, we found out the accused was also a distant Blackthorne cousin.

Go figure.

Unfortunately, it's not just Dorothy and her corrupt brother I find disgusting, it's the entire Blackthorne bloodline. There's just something off about them. I highly suspect inbreeding, although I'd never say it aloud. But seriously, if this was Salem in the 1600s, the

Blackthornes would be the family leading the witch hunts and Dorothy would be manning the gallows.

"Maybe her mother was right and there really is something wrong with that girl," Dorothy scoffs, apparently keeping up with me on the opposite side of the aisle. "*Maybe* Annalee was trying to do us all a favor by getting rid of that abomination."

I flinch at the mention of my mother's name and blink away the unwelcome image of flames dancing in my memory.

"Oh, hush now," the first voice whispers, followed by what sounds like a fleshy smack of an arm. "Give the poor thing a break. With what she's been through, Lord knows she could use a little grace and understanding."

I roll my eyes. The only thing I need a break from is this damn town.

Deciding my cabinet restock can wait until the grocery store is a little less crowded, I grab a few more essential items, opt for the self-checkout line, and head to the parking lot where I unload my haul into the trunk of my brother's rusted-out 1985 Chevy Blazer. Noah isn't exactly known for taking good care of his belongings, but much to my surprise, he's kept this scrap of metal running since he bought her in high school.

I always look forward to the two weeks a month when Noah's home from the oil rig. Not only does he let me borrow the Chevy when he's sleeping off a hangover, but sometimes, like today, he'll occasionally tag along when I have errands to run. Having a body double for boring activities keeps me motivated, and having my brother with me usually serves as a deterrent for anyone giving me a hard time or, *God forbid*, trying to help.

When he rolled out of bed this morning still reeking of alcohol, I was sure he'd decline to join me. But he'd almost seemed eager when I'd mentioned my plans to grab groceries and a few tomato trellises for my vegetable garden from the hardware store—going so far as to offer to pick them up for me while I grocery shopped.

My brow creases when I spot the trellises in the trunk and realize there's one less than I asked for. Shielding my eyes with my hand, I peer around the parking lot for any sign of my absent-minded brother, but he's nowhere in sight. Deciding he must've gone back inside for the one he forgot, I lean against the shaded side of the bumper and wait.

Fanning out my dark-green jacket to alleviate some of the sweltering heat, I tilt my chin skyward, soaking up the late-afternoon sun and the overly warm breeze cascading across my sweat-dampened cheeks.

The air is heavy with exhaust fumes from passing cars and laced with an odd mixture of sugar from Benny's Ice Cream Parlor across the street and smoked meat from the barbecue joint a few blocks over. There's another scent riding the wind, too.

Wet earth and something staticky and sharp.

I close my eyes and breathe deeper, catching that odd plant smell you only get right before it rains. A storm must be rolling in, not that you'd know it from the bright-blue sky overhead.

A sharp peal of laughter draws my attention to a group of girls huddled together in front of Benny's, the sight of their smooth skin on proud display in tank tops and cropped tees suddenly making my light jacket feel stifling.

This close to the Texas-Louisiana border, stepping outside between the months of April and October often feels like wading through a swamp. Unlike other parts of Texas, we get some semblance of seasons here, but three out of four of them are still oppressively hot. Which means most days I cover up my scars with long sleeves and jackets knowing I'll be absolutely miserable.

I take a deep breath, choking on the fumes of a passing diesel engine before shaking my head. All I need to do is get through the summer, then I can leave Deadwood behind for good.

Pulling three sheets of folded-up paper from my jacket pocket, I quickly look left and right, making sure I'm alone before unfolding them.

The first one is an admissions letter from the University of Texas at Tyler, my dad's Alma Mater and the only school he approved of me going to because I could commute from home.

With a sigh, I shuffle that one to the back, my heart rate picking up as I stare at the letter I received this morning—the one with the beautiful burnt-orange University of Texas at Austin emblem at the top.

After months stuck on the waitlist, I'd almost given up hope. But with this acceptance letter, I'm finally so close to leaving Deadwood I can taste the freedom. Problem is, now I have to grow a pair and tell my dad I want to move to Austin and never set foot in this god-awful town again.

Which brings me to the third sheet of paper—

I laugh when I place it on top of the others and spot the new underlined additions.

I left Isabel alone for five seconds last night... When did she even have time to do this?

With an eye roll, I scan the list to see if she changed anything else.

Deadwood Bucket List

1. Buy a cheap car
2. Tell Dad and Noah you can't stay in Deadwood → (MOVE TO AUSTIN!)
3. **Punch Cooper Blackthorne**
4. Go to the solar eclipse party
5. Explore the Cartwright mansion
6. Hang out with Dad and Noah as much as possible
7. Stop hiding. Go out more. → (AND ISABEL!)
8. Be daring and live a little
9. **GET LAID !!!**

"Yeah right," I mumble, scoffing at Isabel's last addition.

Every item on this list is about setting me up for success. I don't *need* to get laid. I do, however, need a car. And I definitely *need* to find a way to tell Dad about Austin without breaking his heart. There's also no way I can leave town without punching Cooper Blackthorne in the face at least once.

Cooper was my first kiss. *And* the reason my dad yanked me out of public school.

I close my eyes, remembering the overpowering scent of Axe body spray and popcorn as Cooper pulled me under the bleachers and pressed his chapped lips against mine. The kiss was clumsy and awkward, but it was perfect. Even though he tasted like a disgusting mix of stale beer and Twizzlers, it was the first time I'd ever felt normal, like I might actually belong in this town.

A week later, he asked me out on a date and that illusion was stripped away. We were supposed to go to a drive-in movie. Instead, he took me to the abandoned mortuary on the west end of town, called me an abomination, and locked me in the incinerator room where I found a canister of gasoline, a matchbook, and a note on the loading ramp that read: Do us all a favor and finish the job.

Now that I think about it, I should have put punching that idiot as number one on my list.

A small smile curves the corner of my lips, but it's quickly wiped away when I spot my brother thundering across the parking lot with his phone plastered to his ear.

His blond mustache bristles, the muscles in his biceps contracting as he nods along to whatever's being said to him. Then he picks up his pace, pale panic slowly replaces the ruby color of his normally smiling cheeks while his eyes grow dark and worried.

Alarm bells blare inside my skull.

"What happened?" I call out when he's close enough to hear me. "Is it Dad? Is he okay?" There's a mile-long list of questions swirling around inside my mind, but as the child of a police officer, those first three are the most pressing.

My brother doesn't so much as blink in my direction, causing a ball of ice to drop into the pit of my stomach.

"Noah," I screech. "Is Dad okay?"

Without breaking his stride, he pins the phone between his ear and shoulder before dragging me over to the passenger door. Unable to break away, I stare up at him, taking in the rapid movement of his eyes while he processes whatever the muffled voice on the other end of the line is saying.

"Yeah, Willa's with me." His blue-gray eyes flash to mine. "She's not going to like that."

"I'm not going to like *what*?" I whisper-hiss, but his focus is once again on the conversation.

"Jesus fuckin' Christ. You're kidding me... *Shit*. Okay, I'm on my way." He covers the phone. "Willa, you need to stay here. I'll be back for you later."

Without thinking, I snatch the keys hanging out of his back pocket, throw myself inside the SUV, and lock the door. Noah bangs his fist against the glass, his ridiculous mustache twitching angrily before his fist freezes midair, pausing to listen to whoever's on the phone.

My brother is freaking crazy if he thinks he's leaving me behind. Whatever happened, I refuse to let him deal with this on his own.

After placing the keys in the ignition and reaching over to unlock the driver side door, I fold my arms across my chest and wait for him to come to his senses.

He tries my door one last time, flips me off and then jogs around the hood. By the time he rips open the door, my hands are pink from how hard I've been wringing them. I've also come to terms with the fact that something must've happened to Dad *and* come up with a semidecent list of what I'll need to do to get our affairs in order now that we're orphans.

I'll have to forgo college and get another job to keep up with the mortgage on the house, but Dad's life insurance will cover the first few months and the funeral. Noah will need therapy—which will be expensive, but maybe his health insurance will cover that? Either way, I have to be strong and keep it together. He's so much more sensitive than he lets on—

"You're a real piece of work, you know that?" Noah grumbles, slamming the door as he flops into the seat. The engine sputters to life a millisecond later, and then we're careening onto Main Street in a cloud of tire smoke. "Before you spiral out of control, Dad's fine."

"Thank God," I breathe out, using the center console and the dashboard to keep from being tossed around.

Noah casts a tentative glance toward me. "Aw shit, you already spiraled, didn't you?"

"It's not your fault." I try to force a smile, but with my body stuck in fight-or-flight mode, I'm having trouble relaxing all my muscles.

Imagining the worst-case scenario and coming up with a plan is basically standard operating procedure for how I deal with unexpected news. I have what my dad likes to call "a chronic case of overthinking" and what the psychiatrist I saw last spring called "ADHD with a healthy dose of hypervigilance likely related to CPTSD"— *whatever that means.*

Noah does a double take. "If you're already overthinking, I might as well tell you I'm meeting up with Dad and he specifically told me *not* to bring you."

"What? Why not?" I wrinkle my forehead. Dad's still in the middle of his shift, what could he possibly need my brother for?

"It doesn't matter." He shakes his head, refusing to meet my eye. "Just don't put up a fuss when I drop you off at home."

"Noah," I say firmly. "What's going on? What aren't you telling me?"

My brother grimaces, sneaking a barely perceptible glance in my direction. "Ryker's back in town. If I don't get there soon, Dad said he'll have no choice but to arrest him."

I blink, trying to make sense of what I just heard and failing miserably.

"Ryker Bennett?" I clarify, disbelief clinging to my tone as my brother nods. "Your best friend and the bane of my existence... The same guy who swore he'd never set foot in Deadwood again... *That* Ryker Bennett?"

Noah scoffs. "Who else?"

I slump into my seat, groaning as my peaceful summer plans slip through my fingers.

If he really is back, then Deadwood better buckle up because Ryker Bennett is trouble—always has been, always will be. Nothing will ever change my mind.

Chapter Two

The decaying remnants of Deadwood's once thriving antebellum town center flicker by the window as we fly through town. The ornate columns and gabled roofs of the ancient mansions quickly give way to manufactured homes with sagging porches and junk-filled yards, eventually leading to grassy fields and rusted monuments of failed family farms. The stark contrast between crumbling wealth and germinating poverty is only made less startling by the one thing everything in Deadwood has in common—*rot*.

I rub my temples, a monstrous headache already forming from just the mention of Ryker's name. "How long is he in town for?"

"Dunno," my brother says, blowing past a stop sign with a shrug.

I keep prodding. "Not long, though, *right?*"

Noah glances at me from the corner of his eye, his lips curling downward. "I already told you, I have no idea. What's your deal?"

My chest deflates, sour trepidation curdling my stomach. Ryker might be my brother's best friend, but growing up, he made my life a living hell.

If I was feeling down, Ryker would add to my misery by hiding crickets in my bed. Any time I had a crush, he and Noah would pick a fight with the guy, further isolating me from my peers who already had a hard time accepting me. After said crush was good and scared away, Ryker would mock me with fake-flirty jabs until my cheeks were flushed with embarrassment and Noah was threatening to beat him up.

The torture was relentless and inescapable. No matter the time of day, Ryker was always at our house, popping out from behind random objects to scare me and tugging on the white strands of hair in my bangs, temples, and near the base of my skull.

Unfortunately, his antics only intensified as we got older.

Ryker is the reason my brother almost got a DUI when they were fourteen. He's why we have security cameras in the Old Town Square, and he was solely responsible for my neighbor's insurance premiums continuously going up on their ranch every time he tried to break in a new horse only to break his arm instead. Hell, when Noah went to visit Ryker at college a few months ago, he came home with a broken wrist, alcohol poisoning, and a black eye that took forever to heal.

Ryker Bennett is impulsive and arrogant, and the cocky prick has never shied away from using his pretty face as a get-out-of-jail-free card while my brother gets stuck paying the consequences for both of them.

"Willa," Noah clips, interrupting me from my thoughts. "What's the problem?"

"It's just..." I pause, trying to decide how to word this delicately. "You know what Ryker's like. And you've got a good thing going for you on the rig. I'd hate it if—"

Noah shifts in his seat, angling his body ever so slightly away from me. *Dammit.* He does this every time he thinks someone's insinuating he's a fuckup. I need to backtrack, and I need to do it quickly before he shuts down completely and doesn't talk to me for a week.

"Your schedule already means you won't be home for most of the summer. I was hoping we'd get to hang out a little more before I start school."

Noah's expression eases, and I release a relieved breath.

"Wills, the Tyler campus is like forty minutes away and you'll be home every night. We'll literally see each other just as much as we do now." He winks, jabbing a too-rough elbow into my shoulder from across the center console—which hurts far less than the guilt constricting my throat.

I want to tell my brother that I got into UT Austin—or UT, as most of us Texans refer to it—but after everything he and Dad have done to make life tolerable for me in Deadwood, would Noah be excited? Or would he view me leaving as an insult, the same way Dad did when Noah took the job in the Gulf?

Fingernails digging into my seat, I clear my throat. "Do you know how long this is going to take? There's something I kind of wanted to talk to you about."

Noah's expression grows serious once again. "I'm not sure. When I answered Dad's call, the first thing I heard was one of the other officers threatening to bring everyone to jail if they didn't calm the fuck down."

Perfect. That sounds exactly like the sort of situation Ryker would find himself tangled up in sixty seconds after coming home. My brows knit. "Why's he back in the first place?"

Noah accelerates, the Blazer shuddering under the strain of our speed. "Sounds like now that Beau's out of prison, he wants custody of Charlotte again. I guess Ryker found out, and Dad said they were already trying to kill each other by the time he got there."

Beau Blackthorne... Another idiot member of the Blackthorne clan and Ryker's piece-of-shit stepdad. A thick, slimy feeling rolls through my insides.

"Sounds like a mess."

The corner of Noah's mouth twitches. "You can say that again."

We take a rapid turn onto the dirt road leading away from town, the tires squealing as I throw my hands out to brace myself.

"But Beau's a felon now," I say once I'm sure we're not going to crash into the ditch. "He can't actually get custody, can he?"

Charlotte, Ryker's half sister and Beau's only biological child, was five when her dad went to prison for killing his wife in a drunk driving accident. She and Ryker went into foster care while their older half brother skipped town. However difficult being separated was after the devastating loss of their mother, getting out of that house and away from Beau was probably the best thing to happen to her and her brothers.

"Hell if I know. I'm running on the same information you are." Noah's knuckles blanch as he tightens his grip on the wheel. "All Dad said was I have to get Ryker away from that house, and I still haven't figured out how to do that."

Ryker might've been a pain in my ass growing up, but no one deserves to go to jail for looking out for their sister... Sighing, I close my eyes before glancing back at my brother.

"I could try to lure Beau away with a six-pack of Lonestar while you grab Ryker?" I tap my lip thoughtfully. "Or we could grab some rope from the Crowes' Ranch and hog-tie him?"

Noah side-eyes me, like he can't tell if I'm messing with him or not.

"What?" I ask indignantly. "You thought I wouldn't help just because I don't like the guy? Don't be ridiculous. I had nothing to do this afternoon anyway."

My brother laughs. "While I'm touched by your enthusiasm...and slightly terrified by your creativity, Dad would kill me if I—"

We come to a screeching halt, the SUV fishtailing forcefully enough that the momentum throws me against the door. For a moment, the dirt billowing up around us is so thick that it blocks out the sun. The darkness is suffocating, and my breaths heave in and out so quickly I feel dizzy as I struggle to make heads or tails of what's happening. But then the dust settles, allowing little streams of dirty orange light to seep in through the windshield until I can breathe again.

Once I regain my bearings and verify that we're still in one piece,

I scowl, wrinkling my nose at the sharp tinge of dust and burnt brake pads filtering in through the vents.

"Dammit, Noah. For once in your life, can you *not* drive like a complete psychopath?"

Tongue poised to spew venom when he doesn't immediately start apologizing, I whirl on him, the scolding I'd prepared dying mid-breath when I catch sight of what he's staring at. In the distance, I can just make out the flashing red-and-blue lights of two cop cars parked below a wispy plume of black smoke rising steadily into the air.

"Get out," Noah says, leaning over to open my door. "You can walk the rest of the way home from here."

I blink. *He can't be serious...*

"Get out," he repeats. "You don't need to see whatever's going on over there."

Holy shit, he is serious.

I grab the door handle and slam it shut without bothering to respond.

Noah's mouth is tight as he throttles the air between us. "For once in *your* life, can you just listen to me? Dad will have my head if I bring you down there."

I lift a brow, unsure why he's bothering with this charade when we both already know the answer. "Not a chance."

"Dammit. I don't have time for this," he huffs, but he's already straightening out the car and speeding toward Beau's house. "You're impossible sometimes. Can you at least promise me you'll wait in the Blazer?"

"Nope." Settling back into the seat, I tuck away my satisfied smirk as Noah curses and slams on the gas.

On the left, we pass Crowe Ranch and then our little brown house, my garden barely visible between the two as we fly by. I've barely had time to think about what we're about to walk into when Noah mutters something under his breath and leans over the steering wheel to peer down the road.

"*Shit*," we say at the same time, but shit is an understatement.

Despite living a half mile away, I've never actually been inside the house Ryker grew up in. I must've passed by here a thousand times, though, and it never seems to surprise me how derelict the place is.

At some point, the house must've been white, but it's long since faded to a yellowing mixture of peeling paint and rotted wood paneling. A tattered American flag hangs behind the broken screen door in the junk filled entryway—the moth-eaten holes in the fabric visible from here. And while a few metal posts remain, the chain-link fence surrounding the property has been lost somewhere between the overgrown weeds and rusted scrap metal scattered throughout the dead grass.

Ryker's familiar rusty-brown 1970s pickup truck with an ombre red-to-yellow stripe down the side is parked in the middle of the yard. There's a smashed planter box and a crushed trash can lying in the truck's path of destruction, as well as a steady stream of black smoke rising from beneath the dented hood.

It almost looks like someone took a crowbar to the thing... I grimace when I spot blood in the driveway amid shards of what I think used to be a wooden baseball bat strewn across the grass near the two patrol cars parked at odd angles in the culvert. The truck blocks most of whatever is happening inside the house, but I can just make out the top of my father's Stetson bobbing side to side in a window.

My stomach twists. On second thought, maybe I should wait in the car...

"Fuck," Noah says, shutting off the Blazer and bounding away without bothering to close the door, which means I can hear more of what's going on inside.

Most of it is garbled, except for Dad's sharp commands in rapid succession.

"That's enough, Beau. Come on out of the room so we can discuss this like men—

"Beau, we're going to take down this door. If you still have a weapon—"

"Goddammit, Noah. I told you to find Ryker and get out of here, what are you doing?"

Great. Now I have to drag my brother back inside the car before he does something stupid to make this worse... Reluctantly, I reach for the door handle and ease myself out.

I've barely taken ten steps when Beau Blackthorne crashes out of a window, shredding the hole-marked screen to bits as he flops onto the rotted porch in a heap of ruddy flesh. Recovering quickly, he stumbles to his feet and barricades the front door using fragments of a broken lawn chair—trapping my father, brother, and the other officers inside the house.

His stained white tank top rides up over his hairy belly when he stoops down to grab something off the deck before staggering onto the grass and heading in my direction.

I freeze, unable to move as the sharp, pungent tang of musky body odor makes my stomach roll and my vision swim—which is why I almost overlook the jagged handle of a broken baseball bat clutched in his left hand.

"You!" Beau slurs, tripping over his dirt-caked bare feet as he angles his body in my direction. There's so much blood dripping from a gash on his eyebrow that he looks like a zombie straight out of a horror film.

"*Me?*" I ask, heart so high in my throat my voice sounds like a squeak.

"Yes, *you*," he sneers. "You're that harlot from Child Protective Services, aren't you? Did my asshole stepson call you?"

Backing up, I glance over my shoulder to see who he's talking to, but there's no one else around.

"*Goddammit.* Beau must've blocked the door," my father's stern voice rings out from inside the house. "Did anyone see where he went? I lost visual."

From this position in the yard, I can't see my dad or the officers over Ryker's truck, which means they can't see me either.

"Noah, find me something I can pry this open with," Dad grunts after a loud banging sound that must be his shoulder against the wood. "Everyone else, go see if that back door is still boarded up. Beau's car is blocked in, so it's not like he can get very far, but I don't feel like chasing him down the road."

Shit. Guess I'm on my own out here...

Trying to show Beau that I'm not a threat, I put my hands out to the side and slowly back away, like I do with the spooked cattle at the ranch.

"I'm not from CPS," I say as soothingly as I can, but the second I say those three initials, he charges, raising the bat like he intends to impale me with it.

On reflex, I spin away and drop to my knees, missing the swing he takes at my face by a millisecond and absorbing most of the blow with my upper shoulder. Pain rips through my arm as I hit the ground, but I ignore it, covering my head with my hands and curling forward to make myself as small as humanly possible. I suck in a sharp breath and tense, preparing myself for the next blow...

Thwack. Crack. Thunk.

The sound of knuckles pounding into flesh and bone hits my ears a second before Beau slams onto the dead grass next to me, the dirt around me shaking with the impact of his massive body.

A coppery odor slinks inside the safety of my tiny cocoon. And when I peek to my left, Beau is being pummeled by a flash of furious fists connected to a mass of muscle and a head of raven hair.

A sharp *crack* rings out through the yard, and Beau's body goes slack, his obnoxious snores shaking the ground beneath me a second later.

Heart racing, I watch my savior stand and toss his head back to get the hair out of his face, but with the bright sun directly behind him, I can't make out any of his features.

I glance lower, vaguely recognizing an old jean jacket with band patches sewn into the front and back, but not the way the fabric is pulled taut over the man's biceps and chest. A flash of silver catches my eye, and I drag my gaze south, my stomach sinking when I spot the all-too-familiar death's-head hawk moth belt buckle adorning the man's form-fitting jeans—the same belt buckle Ryker always used to wear.

Oh God, no... It can't be.

I swallow audibly when he peers down at me, blocking out the sun as he wipes away the blood dripping from his split lip with the sleeve of his jacket.

"Did he hit you?" Ryker asks, chest heaving and body all muscle and hard lines as rage radiates off him in heated waves.

Slowly, I rise onto my knees, staring at him in stunned silence.

Jesus. He really grew up, didn't he...

"Willa, I asked if Beau fucking hit you?" Ryker's brow furrows above his piercing-green eyes. The shade is different from what I remember, like moss after a heavy rain.

My throat bobs.

The Ryker I knew was a boy. But with that sharp nose, chiseled cheeks, and shoulder muscles so big they dwarf my head, the stranger standing in front of me is very clearly a *man*.

"Barely," I manage to say through the assault of adrenaline in my veins. *Jesus,* my heart is beating so fast I'd almost swear I was drunk...

"Where?" he demands.

"Where *what?*" I blink, trying to focus on anything except the horrifying realization that Ryker might be the hottest guy I've ever seen. *Gross.* Just thinking that traitorous thought makes me want to gag.

Ryker rolls his eyes, his expression softening into exasperated irritation as the corner of his lips quirk to the side. "Where did he hit you?"

"*Oh.*" Still on the ground, I raise my right hand to my opposite shoulder, wincing at the light contact.

After a quick glance behind him toward the house, Ryker steps over Beau, flooding my senses with the smell of tobacco and a light scent that reminds me of summer storms and rain dripping through the pine trees in my backyard.

"Show me," he says firmly, the command in his voice snapping me back to the moment.

I shake my head. If I take off my jacket, he'll see my scars, and that's *not* happening.

Ryker leans forward, blocking out the sun as he towers over me. "Listen, Princess, I'll admit you look pretty damn good on your knees, but why don't you stand up so I can see if you're hurt?"

My cheeks flush with a mixture of anger and embarrassment.

I'd forgotten about that damn nickname...

"Don't call me that," I snap, face pinching into a scowl as I rise unsteadily to my feet.

I've never understood why Ryker uses that stupid nickname in the first place. Princesses don't cook and clean as much as I do. Well, apart from Cinderella, but she at least had a fairy godmother who could magically transform her appearance...

Eyes narrowing, he looks me up and down. "Why not?"

I fold my arms across my chest. "Because I'm not a—"

Pounding sounds from behind the front door, the whole thing separating away from the frame with each blow as Dad bellows, "Goddammit, Noah. Is that Willa out there? I *explicitly* told you not to bring her."

"She wouldn't let me leave her behind!" Noah shouts, but Dad just keeps yelling at him.

Ryker smirks and lifts a pointed brow. "Not a princess? And yet here you are, still doing whatever the hell you want, just like when we were kids. That's some spoiled princess shit, if you ask me."

Hot anger swirls inside my gut, quelled only by a spray of splintered wood from the front door bursting open. Dad's blond-gray hair is a mess, his Stetson clutched in his hand and uniform all cattywampus as he pours out onto the porch. Then he whirls on us, eyes widening in horror the moment he spots Beau on the ground.

"Ryker Bennett and Willa Dunn, what the hell happened?" he roars, closing in fast with two officers hot on his heels.

Ryker visibly pales, and judging from how icy my blood suddenly feels as it sludges through my body, so do I. It takes a lot for Joel Dunn to lose his temper, but when he does...

I shudder.

"Mr. Dunn—" Ryker takes a step toward my dad, but I grab his arm.

Even though my touch is light, he flinches the second my fingers connect with his sleeve, like he's expecting me to dole out a major blow.

Shit. I'd forgotten about that too...

Dropping my hand, I bite back the urge to apologize because Dad will be within earshot any second and we're running out of time.

"Don't you dare tell my dad that Beau hit me," I say under my breath.

Ryker quirks a brow as he peers down at me. "What's my silence worth to you?"

God, I hate him so much.

"I'm not asking for me, I'm asking for Noah," I whisper-hiss. "*He's* the one who'll get reamed out for bringing me here, and he's already walking on thin ice with Dad." I breeze past him with a huff, only stopping to toss a final threat over my throbbing shoulder. "Keep your mouth shut."

Dad stops to check Beau's pulse and then directs the other officers to load him into one of the cruisers. I fidget with the hem of my jacket while I wait for him, scowling when Ryker brushes against my side.

"Can you not stand so close to me?" I snap, quickly jerking my arm away.

"If you want your dad to see the hole in your sleeve," he takes a step left, "then sure."

My eyes drop to the three-inch gash in the suede. *Dammit.* I lean closer to Ryker, doing my best not to touch him while praying that his large arm covers the torn fabric.

When I look up, Dad is already standing in front of me, chest heaving while the other officers handcuff and drag an unconscious Beau to the patrol car.

"Are you okay, kiddo?"

A zing of guilt zips up my spine from the worry in his tone. Taking a deep breath, I inhale the peppery scent of his aftershave and the tinge of the outdoors that always lingers on his skin after a long day of work.

"Yes, Dad. I'm fine."

With a low hum of disapproval, he inspects my face and then sighs, the fine lines near his eyes so much more pronounced than they were this morning.

"What are you doing here, Willa?" There's an irritated sharpness in his tone that I'm not used to hearing directed at me. "Did Noah ask you to come with him? I swear, sometimes I wonder if your brother has a single brain cell in that head of his. You're supposed to be helping me keep him in line."

I'm so thrown off-kilter by Dad's angry tirade, all I can do is blink until Ryker nudges me with his elbow. At first, I think he's trying to say the rip in my jacket is visible, but when he does it again after I've confirmed the tear is covered, I realize it must be something else.

Against my better judgment, I risk glancing up, finding Ryker's chin inclined toward the porch where my brother is sitting on the bottom step with his head hung low.

"This isn't Noah's fault," I blurt, finally catching on to Ryker's train of thought. "He told me to stay in the car, I just didn't listen."

Dad shakes his head. "Which is exactly why I asked him to leave you behind in the first place. He should have anticipated your stubbornness."

A tight, unpleasant feeling surges through my stomach. I'm eighteen now, more than capable of shouldering the consequences of my own decisions. So why is he blaming Noah when I'm clearly the one who messed up here?

Dad pats my cheek once before turning his attention to my left. "And *you*." Ryker stiffens as Dad wipes away the sweat beading on his brow with the back of his uniform sleeve. "*You* should be in cuffs right alongside that idiot stepfather of yours. What was your plan here?"

Ryker drops his chin, kicking a rock in the grass with his worn leather boots. "Beau is blocking Charlotte's adoption and trying to have his parental rights reinstated. I came to see if I could convince him otherwise," he says, reaching into his back pocket and shoving a stack of photos into Dad's hand. "I wanted to show Beau how good Charlie's life is with her foster parents, but he wouldn't hear it."

"Dammit, son," Dad says, flipping through the pictures with a sigh. "You know better than to try to reason with a Blackthorne. If I hadn't arrived here when I did—" Dad pinches the bridge of his nose. "When's the court hearing?"

Ryker shoves his hand into his pocket, removing something small and silver that he spins between his fingers like a nervous tick. "Sometime in the next few weeks."

"I'll make a few calls." Dad rubs his hand up the stubble on his cheeks, the sandpaper noise resonating in my teeth until I can't help but cringe. "Are you headed back to Denton?"

My entire body goes rigid.

Please don't say what I think you're about to say...

"I'm not going anywhere until I get my truck fixed." Ryker shrugs. "Figure I'll stick around for a few days. If Beau doesn't want to listen to me, maybe I can get his mom or Kane to try. Can't stay too long, though. The semester's over, but I'll lose my spot in the work-study program if I miss too many days."

Dad lets loose a slow breath. "I'm assuming you don't have a place to stay?"

Ryker shakes his head. "I haven't really thought it through yet."

Oh, please no, I silently scream while my gaze volleys between them. *Please don't—*

"Then you'll come stay with us," Dad says simply.

"I don't want to impose." Ryker takes a step backward, and I exhale a sigh of relief.

Thank God. My life is finally falling into place, the last thing I need is Ryker hanging around and ruining it.

"I insist," Dad says sternly, and then more quietly, "Besides, if you're sticking around, having you stay at the house will be the easiest way to keep you and Noah out of trouble."

Ryker's answering laugh is devious and sinful, his brilliant smile sparkling with the promise of mischief as his eyes flash to mine. "We'll see about that, sir."

Chapter Three

The driveway is empty when I glance out the kitchen window, the storm clouds brewing in the distance turning the sky a deep shade of purple that matches my lovely new bruise from Beau.

So much for being home two hours ago...

With an exasperated huff, I grab a plastic container from the cabinet, my shoulder twinging in protest as I slam the door closed and continue putting away the cold, uneaten dinner I made. No one is home, so this temper tantrum is entirely for my benefit, but it feels good to blow off a little steam.

Dad knows how I feel about Ryker, but he still invited him to stay with us. This house is *my* sanctuary, but he didn't even ask me if I was okay with a house guest.

Come to think of it, no one consulted me the last time Ryker stayed with us either. Granted, it was right around the time of my disastrous date with Cooper Blackthorne, so I barely registered him being here, but still.

I place the pitcher of sweet tea in the fridge while my thoughts drift back to how rough those first few months were after Cooper locked me in the incinerator. I'd spent weeks in a near-catatonic state, moping around my bedroom and refusing to go to school until I was too far behind to finish the semester. That was when Dad decided to enroll me in an online homeschool program. I'd been reluctant at first, but the idea of not having to face Cooper every day was enough to bring back some semblance of peace.

Having always been a bit of a pariah, I was relieved when transitioning out of public school in our unincorporated small town meant Dad could no longer force me to play soccer or participate in the drill team—because those were Deadwood High sponsored activities. Problem was, without extracurriculars I suddenly found myself isolated with significantly more downtime than I was used to.

That's when I discovered my unoccupied mind's propensity for intrusive thoughts.

For weeks, I existed in a constant state of paralysis, binge watching TV while a small voice in my head whispered that maybe Cooper was right. Maybe I was too much trouble and not worth the sacrifices my dad and brother were always making for me.

Then one day, our neighbor Mrs. Crowe barged into the house and forced me to spend the afternoon gardening with her while she talked my ear off about some nonsense or another. Not only did I get the worst sunburn and subsequent farmer's tan of my life that day, but I developed a hyperfixation for weeding and pruning tomato plants *and* landed myself a job tasking around Crowe Ranch.

Staying busy helped quiet my mind, and I threw myself into taking on more household responsibilities. I started by helping Dad manage the bills. Then—although I *hated* these tasks with the fiery passion of a thousand suns—I added grocery shopping, cooking, and cleaning, until eventually there wasn't any time for my mind to wander.

It's gotten to the point where Dad and Noah no longer offer to pitch in, and even though I still dread these tasks, I think I prefer it that way. Every time one of them tries to help with chores, they do it wrong, creating twice as much work for me in the long run. If I'm being honest, I take pride in being the glue that holds our little family together, and I like feeling needed...especially when I find myself struggling over whether or not I'm *wanted*.

I grab the salt and pepper shakers off the counter and shove them into the cabinet before slamming it closed, nearly knocking myself out when the top hinge separates from the frame.

Fantastic.

I guess I'll have to figure out how to fix that later. I shouldn't be taking out my frustrations on our poor little kitchen. Lord knows this old place is barely hanging on as it is.

Except for the electric stove and the bathroom we remodeled last summer, everything in this house is straight out of the early seventies. In the kitchen, avocado-green cabinets and Talavera-tiled countertops are accented by yellowing linoleum flooring. The rest of the floors and walls are covered in blond oak, including the open dining and living room right off the kitchen where brass fixtures line the walls and a big, chunky fireplace sits unused in the corner.

It's old and outdated, and I absolutely love our little capsule of 1970s perfection.

"Sorry," I whisper, gently patting the cabinet.

We live in the second to last house on the way out of town. With the exception of the cattle ranch next door and Beau's place down the street—which I like to pretend doesn't exist—we couldn't be more isolated if we tried. The quiet is nice, though. It brings a sense of peace that's hard to come by, especially for people like my dad with high-stress jobs.

After Grandpa Dunn died, Daniel Crowe—who we affectionately refer to as Old Man Dan—and his wife, Elanor, sort of adopted my dad, who worked on their ranch until he decided to go into law enforcement in his early twenties. After he became a single parent, the Crowes took in Noah and me, too.

I glance out the window to where their pale-white Victorian-style farmhouse is just visible in the smoky-lavender haze of early twilight, and then beyond to the set of headlights traveling down the otherwise empty dirt road.

My fists clench at my sides, and by the time the car pulls into the driveway a few seconds later, my anger is back tenfold.

The front door opens, flooding the dim house with my brother's bright laughter and the smell of his sage-and-cedarwood cologne.

"Where have you been?" I snap, cringing at my high-pitched tone.

Noah's laughter putters out. "Chill, Wills," he says, shutting the door behind Ryker, whose smile falters the second he lays eyes on me. "We've been at the Cartwright Estate, trying to talk to Kane."

My eyebrows shoot up. Kane, Ryker's half brother, spent the last few years with some doomsday church in New Mexico—Children of the Corn, or something equally stupid.

A few months ago, he waltzed back into Deadwood and bought the old Cartwright Estate. No one has seen him since. The last time Dad went out to the property for a welfare check, he'd been stopped at the gate and refused entry by a group of men he'd never seen before.

Where Kane got the money and who the creepy people he brought with him are has been a hot topic for the Deadwood rumor mill. More than once, I've found myself eavesdropping on the speculation. I listen mostly so I can avoid repeating whatever mistakes brought him home, but part of me just wants to understand. Kane was always different from the rest of us. In some ways, he was even more ostracized than me. For the life of me, I can't wrap my head around why he'd come back.

Reluctantly, my anger gives way to curiosity. "Did he tell you what he's been doing up there?"

"Never saw him," Noah snorts. "His weird friends stopped Dad at the gate again. I still don't know what he did to make Kane hate him so much, but that guy sure can hold a grudge. They wouldn't even let Ryker on the property because Dad was with us. The whole thing was actually kind of creepy."

"It wasn't *that* bad," Ryker says, plopping onto one of the couches and propping his booted feet up on the coffee table like the absolute heathen he is.

"Dude," Noah deadpans. "They were all wearing the same white button-up shirts. It was freaky as fuck." He shimmies his shoulders, as if warding off a chill. "If you ask me, your half brother's really gone off the deep end."

"You can just say brother," Ryker says with a drawn-out sigh. "And lay off. I wouldn't have had an early warning about Beau blocking Charlie's adoption if it wasn't for Kane."

"Whatever." Noah tosses himself onto the adjacent couch before throwing a tentative glance in my direction. "We did see something, though..." He exchanges a quick look with Ryker and shifts in his seat like he can't get comfortable.

"They've got a lot of construction equipment up there," my brother finally says, not quite able to meet my eye. "It was a little difficult to see, but I think Kane's rebuilding Divine Mercy."

Our living room goes eerily quiet, and the scars on my neck and back become unbearably taut. I try to speak, but the words get lodged in my windpipe.

"What?" I finally manage to squeak, voice barely a whisper. "Why would he do that?"

Noah's lips pull into a tight line, settling into an expression that's somewhere between a sympathetic smile and a grimace. "Couldn't tell you, Wills. I guess he's starting up his own church and wants to use it? Whatever the reason, I figured it was best you heard it from me."

Mouth dry, I swallow down the shards of glass in my throat and nod. He's right, it would've been so much worse if I'd found out from someone in town. Still, it takes me longer to process this information than I'm comfortable admitting—the occasional flash of candles and a wall of flame in my memory not making the situation any easier.

Misreading my silence, Noah grimaces. "I didn't fuck up by telling you, right?"

"No," I croak, pausing for a second until I'm sure my voice won't betray me. "I'm glad you told me. It's like Dad always says: Ignorance isn't a shield, it's a—"

"Blindfold that robs you of your ability to fight back," Noah finishes for me with an exaggerated eye roll.

We exchange a small smile, both of us jumping when the front door bursts open.

"I'm so hungry I could eat a damn horse," Dad announces, kicking the door closed behind him and wafting in a draft of humid air that smells like wet grass and hay with a touch of Dad's peppery aftershave.

"What's for dinner?" He tosses his Stetson onto the entry table, knocking over a picture frame that he doesn't bother picking up. "I have just enough time to eat, and then I need to head to the office to finish up some paperwork."

Noah pops up. "Guess movie night is a no go, then?"

"You guys still do that?" Ryker rises from the couch, glancing between all of us like we're an exhibit at a zoo. I expect his expression to be judgy, but he almost looks...*envious.*

Noah shrugs. "Every Thursday night." He pauses to rub the back of his neck. "Well, every Thursday night I'm home and Dad's not working."

My lungs constrict. *Doesn't he realize we haven't had a movie night in over four months?*

"Best night of the week." Dad pats my shoulder as he heads to the table. "Maybe we can all watch a movie this weekend?"

My ribs tighten along with my strained smile. "You're going to that conference in Austin, remember?"

"That's right." He swipe-snaps his fingers through the air. "Sorry, kiddo. I'm not too sure when I'll be able to make it work, then. Chief Thompson put me in charge of readying the department to go digital at the end of summer. I've got a mountain's worth of records to pull out of storage and sort through for digitization, and then I'll need to get the whole building prepped for new security cameras. My schedule's going to be a little wonky for the next few weeks."

"Don't worry about it," I say, voice cracking as I wave away his apology. I try to hide my disappointment by heading for the refrigerator while Dad and Noah take seats at opposite ends of our teak dining table, but he sees right through me.

"Willa," he says in that flat, no-nonsense tone he usually reserves for my brother or work, "I promise my schedule will settle down soon. We'll have plenty of time for family movie nights. That's the beauty of you going to college so close to home."

I swallow the tightness in my throat. While I believe he means it when he says things like that, I don't know if he realizes how much time he's spent away from home over the past six months.

For weeks, Dad's been switching back and forth between mid and night shifts. He's also been out of town at least once a month since January, attending various policing conferences to update his certifications and then working twice the hours to make up for the missed time. With the increased oddball hours, he's been spending more and more nights at the police station's crash pad. So much so that I've found myself wondering if he's lying about all the extra shifts to cover up a secret girlfriend. But he's never lied before... Why would he start now?

Maybe if he knew I got into UT, he'd realize how few of these movie nights we have left and prioritize spending time together...

"Hey, Dad?" I clasp my hands to hide the slight shake.

"Yeah, kiddo?"

"I was wondering if we could talk about UT again?" I bite my lip, the pulse in my temple picking up tenfold. "I know you said you hated the idea—"

"Not this again," Dad groans, waving his hand in the air as if warding off evil before pinching the bridge of his nose. "Thinking about you in that big city makes my skin crawl. I understand you're upset about getting wait-listed, but it was for the best. What would I do without you?"

A pit opens in my stomach.

I'd been so busy plotting my escape from Deadwood, I forgot to consider how if I'm not here, Dad won't have anyone around to make sure he's eating and sleeping enough. This week alone he's left his lunch at home twice... I also can't remember the last time he went grocery shopping, and I'd bet all my savings he doesn't remember how to work the washing machine.

"Okay. But—" I pause as Ryker's hulking form saunters toward the table in my periphery. *Shit.* He'd been so quiet I'd almost forgotten he was here. This is definitely not a conversation I want to have in front of him. Not when he's already glaring at me, likely scheming up new ways to make my life miserable.

I snap my mouth shut, and Dad dips his chin, grinning like he won the argument.

More annoyed than I should be and feeling oddly irritable, I rip open the fridge and start removing all the covered dishes I'd just finished putting away.

Once dinner is reheated, I head for the table, intentionally ignoring Ryker's cocky grin from the chair by the window—the seat he *knows* belongs to me. I have the momentary notion to *accidentally* knock the pitcher of sweet tea into his lap, but after years of seeing his eyes spark with amusement every time his idiotic games got a volatile reaction out of me, I refuse to give him the satisfaction.

Noah lets out a low whistle at the massive bowl of lemon rice pilaf I set on the center of the table. "Looks great. Perfect meal before a night out with the boys. Thanks."

My brow furrows. "You're going out?"

"Is that a problem, Princess?"

Again, I avoid looking directly at Ryker, but that doesn't stop me from smiling when Noah kicks him under the table.

"Don't antagonize her. She's asking because she's my DD." He straightens in his seat. "But yeah, if Dad's bailing on movie night, we're going out. Sorry, Wills."

Number seven on my bucket list floats through my mind: *Stop hiding. Go out more.*

42

I move to the other side of the table, slowly lowering into the vacant seat. "Where are you guys going?"

Now that school is out and most of the college students are home for the summer, there's been a party of some sort every day of the week. Ever since they started serving food and boozy shakes, Benny's Ice Cream Parlor tends to be the hangout spot during the day. But at night, the party moves to someone's house or down by Widowmaker Springs.

Beyond dropping Noah off and picking him up drunk off his ass, I've yet to participate. A prickling sensation spreads beneath my skin. Tonight's as good a night as any to start checking things off my bucket list. It would also be good practice prior to the eclipse party...

"Can I come?"

Noah's eyes widen. "To actually hang out?"

The shock in his voice makes my shoulders curve forward protectively. "Yeah."

I've barely finished saying the word when Noah shakes his head. "Not tonight. We're going to that new bar in Jonestown."

"Like hell you are," Dad snorts, not bothering to look up from the mountain of pilaf he's shoveling onto his plate. "Ryker's not twenty-one yet. If he still wants a career in law enforcement, he can't—"

I burst out laughing, the boisterous sound slowly tapering off as the entire table turns my way with a mixture of quirked and heavy brows. "I'm sorry," I say through a chuckle. "Ryker wants to be a *cop?*" The idea is so ridiculous my laughing fit starts all over again.

"Is that not your plan anymore?" Dad asks, directing his question to Ryker.

"It's still the plan, sir," Ryker replies, but his eyes are on the table, the muscles in his jaw feathering and cheeks flushing as he fiddles with something silver in his hand.

An unfamiliar sensation ripples through my chest at the sight, tightening and squeezing in a way that makes it difficult to draw in a full breath.

Dad claps his hands together. "Great, then it's settled. No bar."

"Come on, Dad. I know the bartender, it'll be fine." Noah winks at me and launches into a ridiculous speech aimed at convincing our father that it's perfectly acceptable for them to go out a few weeks before Ryker's *technically* twenty-one.

I roll my eyes. Sometimes I think he forgets what our dad does for a living.

Drowning them out, I shift my attention across from me where Ryker's eyes are downcast and moving rapidly as he reads what I assume is a text message under the table.

Here we go. Now that they can't go to the bar, I bet he's already making alternate arrangements for tonight. Maybe I should warn the Crowes their cows are about to be tipped...or call Mayor García and tell her the fountain in the Old Town Square is about to be soaped again.

Ryker sets his phone on the table, screen facing downward where it immediately starts buzzing. He silences it, but it starts up again.

And again.

And again—the vibration against the wooden tabletop growing louder with my annoyance.

"Do you want to get that?" I huff, dropping my fork onto my plate with a clatter.

Softly setting down his own utensils, he crosses his arms over his chest. "That depends, Princess. Do *you* want to drop the shitty attitude you've had since I walked through the door?"

Despite the undertone of snark in his voice, Ryker's demeanor is calm and controlled, making my outburst look childish and pathetic. Heat flushes my ears as I open my mouth to save face with a witty retort, but nothing comes out.

This is the other reason why I've never liked Ryker. He always says exactly what he's thinking.

"Well?" he prompts with a raised brow.

Still flustered, I fold my arms and lean back in my seat. "I rather like my shitty attitude. So no, I don't think I will."

44

"Go figure." He sighs, cocky expression faltering as his shoulders slump and his eyes drop to the table.

I pause, confused by the exhausted sound emanating from his too-full lips, a sound I've only ever heard from Dad after a particularly taxing shift at work.

Ryker's phone vibrates again, and I jump when he abruptly scoots away from the table and excuses himself to take the call out on the porch.

"Dad," Noah argues once the front door closes, "can you imagine if it was Willa in this situation instead of Charlotte? I'd be losing my shit. Come on, Ryker needs a fucking break. He *needs* a night out on the town."

A seed of doubt pushes through the cracks of my annoyance and twists up my insides. Maybe Ryker was right and I should adjust my attitude. God only knows what Noah or I would be like if we'd grown up the way Ryker did. Not to mention how either of us would act if we thought the other was potentially in danger...

Dammit. I need to apologize—and quickly if I want to keep the wounds between me and Ryker from festering and growing more uncomfortable than they already are.

An echo of thunder rolls in the distance, and I sigh, pushing my pride aside as I rise to my feet and follow after him.

Chapter Four

Wind whips through my hair as I step onto the porch. The air is damp and sticky, laced with the sharp tang of electricity and the earthy aroma of wet dirt, while in the distance, a single bolt of lightning streaks across the deep blue-black sky.

I close my eyes and count to ten before a rolling *clap* of thunder reaches my ears.

Good, the storm's still at least two miles off.

Zap. I flinch as the light trap Dad installed a few weeks ago claims its first victim of the night. The winged carcass of a large moth drops onto the wooden deck with a soft *thunk*.

Evenings on the rocking bench might be much more tolerable without a swarm of winged critters in my hair, but the incessant hum of the contraption feels ominous, its purple glow eerie and somehow cruel...

I shiver, rotating my body toward the heavy footsteps crunching across the gravel on the right side of the house. A second later, Ryker's exasperated sigh spills from the darkness. "God no, don't do that. Stay in Denton."

My stomach tightens. Denton? If that was his little sister calling, then I'm even more of a jerk than I thought I was. With my arms wrapped around me to ward off the guilt nibbling at my insides, I head for the far corner of the porch. In true Texas fashion, the temperature's dropped at least twenty degrees since sunset, but it's still so hot out I'm almost tempted to go back inside to wait for him in the air conditioning... Then again, the thought of apologizing in front of my brother is enough to give me hives.

My ears perk up as Ryker's voice draws closer, but with the wind howling through the trees, I can't pinpoint where it's coming from.

"Dammit, Jenny," he snaps, this time at full volume. "We agreed it was just fucking. I don't have the energy for this right now."

Okay. Definitely not talking to his sister...

"It was fun while it lasted, but no," Ryker says firmly. A few seconds go by, and then he laughs. "Driving three hours for a booty call is a bit excessive. There are apps you can download if you're really that horny."

I lean away from the railing. *Is he seriously telling someone he's been sleeping with to download a hookup app? What a dick.*

"Fuck," Ryker groans, and my brow lifts at the gravelly shift in his tone. "Don't fucking say that. I'm twenty feet from my best friend and his family."

A light flares to life in the yard about ten feet from where I'm standing, the soft-white glow illuminating Ryker's pensive brow as he glances at the screen.

"*Fucking* hell," he breathes, tilting his chin skyward before returning the phone to his ear. "Did you just take that? Are you touching yourself?"

Every muscle in my body tenses. *Oh my God.*

My first instinct is to run inside—because I do *not* need to be listening to this—but he's so close there's no way I can move without drawing attention to myself. My heart races. If he sees me now, he'll think I was spying on purpose...

With no other option, I lean against the support beam while praying the shadows and poor lighting keep me hidden.

"If I make you come," Ryker growls, gravel crunching beneath his boots when he starts walking again, "will you leave me the hell alone?"

A bolt of lightning tears through the sky, highlighting Ryker's massive shoulders as he paces back and forth across a small patch of grass.

"Fine, but this is the last time. Put me on speaker and place the phone on your stomach so I can hear." He's so close now that the tobacco clinging to his clothes tickles the inside of my nose. "Good, now slide your hand between your legs and tell me how wet you are."

Holy shit. My pulse skyrockets so quickly I feel lightheaded. At this point it doesn't matter if he sees me or not, I need to make my escape.

I've barely lifted my foot when Ryker starts talking again, his voice several octaves lower. "Yeah? Then beg me to help get you off."

My entire body freezes as the command slams into my chest, his tone so low and dangerous that I shudder... It almost sounds like he's talking to *me*.

The girl on the phone must say something because Ryker laughs, the timbre throaty and a little demeaning. Heat courses through my traitorous body, each rapid beat of my heart sending an odd sensation of fear and lust straight between my thighs.

"Tell me what you're imagining. Am I fucking you with my fingers or my cock?" Another pause. "It's my cock, isn't it? You never were patient enough to be properly finger-fucked. Such a shame."

My jaw drops and I clench my legs together. It might be my inexperience showing, but I didn't know people *actually* talked to each other like this. And I definitely didn't expect it to be so...*hot*. If it were anyone but Ryker saying these things—

Nope.

I shake my head. Absolutely not. There's no point in finishing that thought because it *is* Ryker, and something is obviously wrong with me... I place my palms over the pulse points on either side of my neck, hoping it will slow my erratic heartbeat so I can come up with a plan on how to get myself out of this situation without him realizing I'm here.

All I need to do is stay quiet. Then, the second he turns his back, I'll dart inside.

"You're close? Already?" Ryker says in a mocking lilt. "Then stop touching yourself." He pauses. "You heard me. You interrupted my night, which means you don't come until I say so. Do. Not. Touch. Yourself."

His voice is so authoritative that my hands lift from my neck without conscious thought.

"Good. Now squeeze your tits for me."

Mindlessly, my hands slide across my breasts, gently palming them over the fabric of my T-shirt as my nipples pebble into sharp points.

"*Harder*," Ryker orders, and once again, I listen, closing my eyes and kneading myself roughly enough that I have to bite my lip to keep from making a sound.

It feels incredible and so unlike any way I've ever touched myself before that I can almost imagine it's someone else. Someone with a smoky voice and calloused hands... A shiver drags up my spine, and I keep going, losing myself to the delicious sensation of my thumbs running over my hard nipples as I suppress a breathy moan.

"Is someone there?" Ryker calls out.

My eyes shoot open, hands flying away from my body.

Oh God, I didn't actually moan...did I?

"No, *Jenny*, not you." He glances around, eyes straying to the bug zapper when another moth succumbs to the light. "I swear I just heard somebody out here with me."

I hold my breath, not daring to move a single muscle as Ryker charges straight for the house. My brain screams for me to run, demanding I vault myself over the railing and hide in the yard, but my feet won't move. It's like my body already died of embarrassment and I'm frozen solid with mortification.

Normally, I'd have come up with seven different plans to deal with this by now, but for the second time today, I'm having trouble forming coherent thoughts. Even so, I can't let Ryker catch me out here, and under no circumstance can he *ever* find out I was listening to his weird phone sex. Or what I was doing while I listened...

The first porch step groans beneath Ryker's weight, and I stop breathing. He's close enough that if he looked just a little to his left, he'd see me standing in the shadows... Close enough for me to notice the crease forming on his brow when his phone lights up with a new incoming call.

Without a second's hesitation, he ends the previous conversation and swipes right.

"Hello? Mrs. Palmer?" he says in an anxious tone that couldn't be more different from the one he was just using. "Yes, ma'am, I'm stuck here until I get my truck fixed. Is Charlie okay?"

Palmer—that must be the last name of Charlotte's foster parents.

Ryker turns back toward the yard. "Okay, good. One of the cops here thinks Beau's arrest today might damage his chances at having his parental rights reinstated... Yes, ma'am, I'm fine. I'd let that bastard wail on my face every day if it kept Charlie safe and out of his house."

My chest pinches at the slight tremble in his voice—the odd mixture of fear and defeat drenching each syllable erasing all traces of whatever madness was coursing through my system a few moments ago.

"Not likely," Ryker laments. "Beau's uncle is still a local judge. I'm sure he'll be out in twenty-four hours, like every other time... No, I haven't talked to Kane yet. I'll try again tomorrow to see if he'll help us." He bobs his head. "Absolutely. Hey, I know it's close to bedtime, but do you mind putting Charlie on? I promise I won't keep her long... Yes, ma'am. Thank you."

With one hand on the back of his head, Ryker takes a deep breath and walks off the stairs onto the grass. My own breathing slowly evens out with each step he takes away from me.

"Hi, Charlie." Ryker's voice is cheery and bright, only a slight strain buried beneath it. "Oh yeah? Well, did you tell them your big brother is visiting in a few days?" He laughs, the sound deep and rumbly like the distant thunder. "Good."

A beat goes by before he says, "For you, I've got all the time in the world. Tell me everything."

Ryker moves farther and farther away from the house until the howl of the wind steals his voice and the black night once again swallows him whole.

Tension easing from my strained muscles, I head for the front door. But instead of opening it, I pause, glancing over my shoulder to stare into the darkness. In a matter of minutes, I've seen three sides of Ryker I never knew existed. He was calm and respectful with Charlie's foster mom, gentle and patient with his sister, and then there's whatever *that* was on the phone with his not-girlfriend...

What else don't I know about him, and why does that question feel oddly terrifying?

Shivering, I turn back toward the house and slip inside, softly closing the door behind me.

"I don't care how old you are," Dad says, pounding his fist on the table forcefully enough that it rattles the glassware. "You live in *my* house and you eat *my* food, that means you follow *my* rules. If you fuck up again or mess up Ryker's plans, I'll kick you out."

"That's rich," Noah spits through a bitter laugh. "Especially since *you're* the one who begged me to stay and look after Willa."

My eyes bulge. That's why Noah didn't move to the coast when he got the job on the rig? Because Dad guilted him into staying here for me?

Appetite ruined, I keep my head down and scurry across the living room to take a shower. The rain starts not long after I step out of the bathroom, the excruciating throb in my shoulder pulsing in time with the downpour pinging against the roof as I change into pajamas and collapse into bed.

With my brother's revelation still heavy on my mind, I'm about to drift off to sleep when my phone vibrates. I crack an eye open, a smile creeping over my lips when I read the name on the text.

> **ISABEL**
>
> Have you heard anything from UT? Because I just found the perfect apartment for us in Austin.

Two years ahead of me in school, Isabel technically started off as Noah's friend. But she quickly caught on that I was the superior Dunn sibling, so I don't hold it against her. She was also the one who encouraged me to apply to UT in the first place. Although, I think that has just as much to do with her struggling to declare a major and find friends as it does with my need to get out of Deadwood.

I grab my phone, two more texts coming through before I've responded to the first.

> **ISABEL**
>
> Also, are we still going to the eclipse party tomorrow? I desperately need some fun.
>
> You're thinking about bailing, I can feel it. Don't make me remind you about your bucket list.

Clutching the phone to my chest, I glance at the new black bikini draped across the faded mustard-yellow armchair in the corner. It's too dark to see, but after staring at the very small, *very* cheeky triangles of fabric for the last month, I can imagine every detail of the white lace trim around the edges and the cute little cowboy boots scattered throughout like polka dots.

It's adorable and looks amazing on me—*until I turn around.*

Dammit. I never should have told Isabel about the bucket list because, like the good friend she is, now she's going to force me to *actually* do the things on it.

So annoying.

I guess I could just wear the long-sleeve one-piece I've been sporting whenever I go fishing on the lake with Dad, but that feels like a cop-out. If I'm making changes and taking control of my life, shouldn't I go all in?

I roll onto my side, the sharp twinge of pain in my shoulder giving me an unrelated idea.

WILLA

I need to run an errand in Jonestown before we go. If you give me a ride AND swear not to ask me about what I'm doing, I'll promise not to bail on the eclipse party.

ISABEL

Deal. Yay! We're going to have fun, I promise.

A GIF of a blue-haired granny cannonballing into a river pops up in our text chain, and I set the phone down to charge with a grin.

Even if I never get in the water at the Springs tomorrow, I'll still be checking off the eclipse party from my bucket list. Technically, it also counts toward number seven: Stop hiding. No one said I have to show my scars, and I can always find other ways to be daring and check off number eight later.

Listening to the rain pelt against the roof, I can't help but feel proud. This list might seem like a stupid idea to some, but for me, it's the first step in taking control of my life and not allowing what happened to define me.

My text alert goes off again, and the smile slides straight off my lips when I see the name on the screen. Against my better judgment, I grab my phone and pull up the message, my stomach bottoming out as I read.

TROUBLE

Was that you on the porch, Princess?

Chapter Five

Isabel picked me up bright and early this morning with a pearly white smile on her face and two cups of coffee clutched in her fists. As promised, she didn't ask me what I was doing on my secret errand *or* why I was upset afterward, but she did spend the whole ride back to my house pestering me for more details about what I overheard Ryker saying on the phone last night.

"Hold up," Isabel shrieks, her silky black hair fanning out around her golden-brown shoulders as she throws herself onto my rust-brown linen bedspread. "Start from the beginning and this time tell me with *excruciating* detail."

I toss my purse onto the floor and kick off my boots before belly flopping onto the bed beside her. "Please don't make me repeat it," I whine through an exaggerated sigh. "It's already bad enough that Ryker suspects it was me on the porch. Forcing me to relive the embarrassment is just cruel."

Ears burning, I bury my face in the comforter.

"Fine, but I still can't get over the fact that he was having phone sex in your front yard," she says, flicking my forehead and flooding my senses with her jasmine perfume. "I guess it makes sense, though."

I rise onto my elbows. "What do you mean?"

"Ryker and my cousin go to the same university..." Isabel hums thoughtfully. "Let's just say I've heard a few things about him."

I don't want to be interested, but I find myself leaning in. "Like what?"

"Well," she wiggles her perfectly shaped eyebrows, "apparently Ryker is *quite* the sought-after commodity on campus."

"Why? He's so..." I recoil, struggling to find the right word. "*Aggravating.*"

Isabel laughs. "Magic fingers. Massive co—"

"Shut up," I barely manage to cough out, too busy choking on my own spit. "How could you possibly know that?"

"My cousin and Ryker used to mess around. I got the whole rundown a few months ago." Isabel sits up, nodding her head rapidly as if to reiterate her earnestness. "When she found out he was from Deadwood, she called to ask me a few questions."

"What did you say?"

"That he was already gone by the time I moved here and I really didn't know anything about the guy." She shrugs. "After that phone call, though, I know *too* much." She grabs my hand and lowers her voice conspiratorially. "The first time they had sex, he blindfolded her, tied her hands behind her back, and made her explode like a pleasure piñata for *several* hours. One orgasm after another."

Isabel pantomimes an explosion with her hand.

"*Hours?*" I swallow audibly and rise to a seated position. "Do people really like that?"

"Everyone likes coming, Willa," she replies with an eye roll.

Considering how, despite my best efforts, I've had exactly *one* orgasm that I accidentally gave myself when I woke up humping one of my decorative pillows after a particularly vivid dream about a Henry Cavill look-alike ranch hand next door... I'll have to take her word for it.

"I *meant* being tied up," I clarify, cheeks and ears ablaze. "I thought that was just a porn thing."

"Oh, right. I'm not into it, but everyone has their kinks. If you'd put yourself out there a little more, we'd know what yours were..." She winks, but something in my chest deflates at the subtle dig.

Isabel is barely two years older than me, but sometimes those two years feel like a decade. Lately, I've found myself wondering if she really wants me to move to Austin or if there's a part of her that's worried I'll hold her back there the same way I do here. Then the small voice in my head whispers that we're only friends because she feels sorry for the poor little broken girl in town...

"Anyway," Isabel says after a drawn out pause, "how long is Ryker staying?"

Grateful for the change of subject, I clear the tightness in my throat and lean against the forest-green wall. "I don't know. A few days, maybe?"

I'd gotten up early to make Dad breakfast and a sandwich for work, only to find him having coffee with Ryker in the kitchen. After slinking back into the hallway unseen, I'd spent the rest of the morning hiding in my bedroom until Isabel came to get me.

Dropping my eyes to the comforter, I smooth my palm across the soft fabric. "I never should have tried to apologize. I'll probably just lock myself inside my room until he's gone."

"There's no way I'm letting you miss the eclipse party because of some stupid boy," Isabel says, tucking a loose strand of onyx hair behind her ear. "If he and Noah are going to be gallivanting all over town for a few days, that just means I don't have to share you. Come on, is there anything we can knock out on that list of yours before we head to the Springs?"

I pinch my lips to the side. "You could hold Cooper Blackthorne down while I smack him across the mouth?"

"Ooo, kinky." She wiggles her eyebrows. "Let's do it."

I let loose my first genuine laugh of the day, leaning forward and clutching my belly to quell the hardy ache.

Isabel's face pales, and I sober, glancing down at my now-bared shoulder and the raised pinkish-white flesh exposed there. By some miracle, my sweater sleeve only slipped enough to flash the very top of the bruise from Beau and she doesn't seem to notice the contusion —which means maybe I didn't waste twenty minutes hiding it beneath two pounds of makeup after all.

Isabel clears her throat. "Are you going to wear your new bikini to the party?" she asks in a feeble attempt to regain some normalcy after being caught staring.

I sit up, sliding my sweater into place before responding. "I think so."

She still can't seem to tear her eyes away from my now-covered shoulder, which does nothing to ease the jittery feeling bouncing around in my stomach. While I'm well aware of my body dysmorphia issues, I can also admit being friends with someone as beautiful as Isabel doesn't make things any easier.

My eyes drop to the light-blue bikini popping out of her pale-pink summer dress, both colors perfectly complementing the golden-brown hue of her flawless skin. Everything about her—from her silky black hair to her perky boobs, pert little nose, and perfectly mani-cured toes—is lively and vibrant.

Me, on the other hand... Well, my nose is small and a bit too pointy, my boobs too big for my frame, and the dark clothes I wear tend to make me look even paler than I already am. It also doesn't help that the same scars on my back travel out onto my shoulders and creep up into my scalp. The scars on my head aren't nearly as severe as the others, but they still turned sections of what should be brown hair in my bangs and the nape of my neck stark white...like I'm the freaking Bride of Frankenstein.

I rise from the bed and head for the armchair, trying with all my might to ignore the hot feeling of Isabel's gaze glued to my back. She's only seen the full extent of my scars once during a sleepover, but it was enough. A year later and I still catch her staring like she can see the gnarled flesh beneath my clothes.

I grab the bikini, stomach souring as I slide the silky material through my fingers. If my only friend looks at me like that, how am I going to have the nerve to be in my swimwear in front of a third of the town? Especially after this morning's errand already shook my confidence.

Maybe the eclipse party was a bad idea...

After a long stretch of silence, Isabel shifts on the comforter. "Do they still hurt?"

I close my eyes for the briefest second before answering. "Sometimes."

The doctors say the sporadic jolts of pain I occasionally experience while falling asleep are caused by nerve damage, but my back also hurts anytime it's particularly cold and with any overly taxing upper-body workout. I keep that to myself, though, because I'm grateful she's asking at all. No one ever asks. Most people take one look at my scars and assume they already know everything about me. Not Isabel.

Her family moved here during her junior year, after I'd already started homeschooling. So when she found me hiding out in the garden during Noah's seventeenth birthday party, she had no idea who I was or what had happened to me.

Instead of making new friends and sneaking beers inside with everyone else, Isabel spent the next few hours giving me omegaverse book recommendations and reminding me what it felt like to laugh by describing fictional characters' schlongs in *explicit* detail while I yanked out weeds. We've been friends ever since.

Isabel stands from the bed abruptly. "I don't think you should cover up anymore," she says firmly. "Fuck what people think. If anyone says anything, I'll stab them."

I laugh, but it comes out awkward and forced. I know she didn't mean any harm by it, but her initial unfiltered reaction to seeing just a hint of my scars was a good reminder of what I'll be in for at the Springs, and I suddenly find myself doubling down on the idea that I shouldn't go.

"Let's take this one step at a time. I need to get through today first."

She nods like she understands—which of course she doesn't, but I appreciate the sentiment.

An hour later, I've finally worked up the courage to slip on the cowboy boot–dotted bikini. It only takes one twirl in the mirror for me to immediately cover it with an old pair of jean shorts and one of Noah's long-sleeve fishing shirts with UV protectant woven into the fabric. It's not exactly the most breathable shirt for such a warm day, but I'm hoping that motivates me to take it off.

Once Isabel finishes touching up my hair, we load a cooler with plenty of water and a few beers she stole from her older brother before shoving the oversized icebox into the tiny trunk of her pale-yellow Volkswagen Bug. Then, much to Isabel's protest, I head back inside to use the restroom.

I don't actually need to pee, the same way I didn't need Isabel to fix my hair earlier, I just panicked when I couldn't think of another excuse to keep us here... But now that I'm inside—wringing my hands as I watch Isabel through the window while she patiently taps her sandaled foot and tries not to look annoyed—it's all too apparent that I'm being a shitty friend.

With a sigh, I step out onto the porch and lock the front door, freezing mid key-turn when a car door slams and my brother's unmistakable laugh rings out like a bell behind me, followed by Ryker's smoky chuckle.

Panicked, I clutch Isabel's arm with a death grip as I teeter between fumbling with the keys and vaulting myself over the side railing.

"Isabel," I plead, my nails digging into her flesh, "get me out of here."

Eyes wide and locked in the direction of the driveway, she

shakes her head. "Holy shit. *That's* the infamous Ryker? I think you and my cousin might've left out a major detail in your stories..."

"Keep your voice down," I hiss. "I didn't leave anything out."

"Uh, *yes*, you did." I turn as she gestures to Ryker, whose black hair and sharp cheekbones are highlighted in silver and gold from the early afternoon sun. "He's freaking *gorgeous*." Isabel sighs. "I totally get it now. I'd be an eavesdropping perv too if—"

"*Isabel!*" I clamp my hand over her mouth, but it's too late.

"Well, well, if it isn't Isabel Castillo." Noah bounds up the steps, taking her hand and spinning her once. "Look at you, darlin'. Where do you think you're goin' dressed like that?"

I roll my eyes. Noah flirts with everyone—and I mean *everyone*. Doesn't matter if he's not interested or doesn't have a shot in hell, he just can't help himself.

Isabel rips her arm away and takes a step toward me. "I'll go wherever I damn well please, and I'd appreciate it if you kept your hands to yourself."

Stumbling backward, my brother clutches his heart. "You wound me."

The two of them continue bickering, but the only thing I can concentrate on is the tightening of my chest as Ryker draws closer.

Oh God. He's going to call me out in front of my brother for spying on him...

My stomach churns. I'm dreading his first dig of the day so much that each of his booted footsteps feel like they're shaking the deck beneath my feet.

Ryker saunters over and leans against the railing with a smirk, like he enjoys watching me squirm. I can practically taste his amusement in the air—citrusy and bright, like the orange juice he and Noah polished off this morning without leaving any for me.

"Is that Isabel?" he asks after a moment of tortuous anticipation.

My shoulders slump in relief at the same time something bitter and green snakes around my rib cage. I push the second feeling away, instead clinging to the hope that maybe he doesn't know I overheard him after all.

"Yep, that's Isabel," I say, popping the *p*. "Why?"

He makes an amused humming noise that instantly puts me on high alert. "I go to school with her cousin, Jenny. That's who I was on the phone with last night."

My stomach drops, but I even out my expression and respond as dryly as humanly possible. "How interesting."

I can't tell if Ryker's baiting me or not, but I decide to try to steer him toward a safer topic of conversation. "Listen, I want to thank you for saving me from Beau and not ratting me out to my dad. I also want to apologize for how I acted last night. After the day you had, you didn't need—"

"Save it."

I take a step backward, the force of his dismissal sucking the air right out of my lungs.

"*Save it?*" I repeat. My fists ball at my side, my previous shock bleeding into annoyance. "You're seriously refusing my apology?"

He shrugs. "Words are cheap."

I catch a flash of silver as he fishes something out of his pocket, and my entire body stiffens a moment later at the distinct *click* of a lighter flicking to life. I close my eyes, turning my head slightly to avoid the glow of the flame from Ryker's silver boot-shaped lighter while praying he didn't notice my reaction.

Oblivious to my plight, he strikes the spark wheel again, causing my muscles to lock up tighter and tighter until I'm rigid as a board.

Relax. It's just a tiny flame, I remind myself, but there's a wall of fire dancing behind my closed eyelids, the heat of which licks across my back, singeing my hair and lungs.

My keys fall from my hand, clattering onto the deck.

Heartbeat thrashing against my temples, I force my eyes open and suck in a breath. The sudden influx of rich tobacco burns as it slides down my throat, but it also smothers the thoughts of fire in a way that would almost be a relief if it wasn't making my head swim.

Out of habit, I inhale again, like the psychiatrist suggested I do whenever I feel disoriented or overwhelmed, but the potent aroma of smoke is so suffocating it amplifies the hazy feeling in my brain.

I sway when the porch shifts beneath my feet, but it's not until a rough hand clamps around my bicep that I realize it's not the deck teetering, *it's me.*

"Willa?" Ryker's deep voice sounds through the fog.

"Oh no," Isabel shrieks, stomping over and snatching the cigarette straight out of Ryker's mouth. "What's wrong with you, asshole?" Her furious face blurs while she tosses the confiscated item into the yard, coming back into focus again as she fans my cheeks, slowly replacing the smoke smell with hints of jasmine. "Do you need to sit?"

I shake my head, but Noah is already pushing over the wooden rocking bench from the opposite corner. "Come on, Wills, we've talked about this. Bend your fucking knees or you'll pass out."

"I'm fine." I attempt to wave him off, but the motion causes me to stumble.

Ryker's grip on my arm tightens while Isabel's frown deepens.

"Willa, just sit for a minute," she begs.

"I said I'm fine."

At my second refusal, Isabel and Noah begin arguing over how to get me onto the bench. I expect Ryker to join them, or at the very least shove me onto the seat, but he doesn't. He just stands there, silently making sure I don't fall.

Part of my brain screams for me to push him away, but there's another part that appreciates how he isn't babying me or trying to force me into the chair like Isabel and my brother.

When I tilt my chin to look up at him, he's staring at me with a heavy brow. "Was it the lighter or the smoke?"

"Both, I think." I don't mean to give him an honest answer, but I'm still feeling a bit woozy and it just sort of slips out. I also can't stop watching the rapid movement of his moss-green eyes roaming over my face or the way the muscles in his jaw keep pulsing.

With his gaze still locked on mine, I clear my throat. "You can let go now."

Ryker's attention drops to my arm, his eyebrows lifting like he's surprised to find he's still holding on to me. One by one, his fingers unfurl. And when he finally lets go, I have to rub the spot where his hand was to get my circulation going again.

Isabel swipes my keys off the deck and swoops in, her mouth pinching to the side as she links her arm through mine. "Maybe the Springs was a bad idea. We could watch the eclipse from here instead? I still have to work later, so it's not like I could stay the whole time anyway."

"Wait, what? Willa's not going to the eclipse party," Noah says with a laugh.

"Yes, I am," I snap, ripping my arm away from Isabel. I was about to take her up on her offer, but my brother's response just changed my mind. "The next eclipse isn't for another twenty years. You guys can stay if you want to, but I'm not missing this."

"Willa." Noah's blond mustache puffs as he exhales and lowers his voice. "There will be barbecues and lots of drinking. A third of the town is going to be there—"

"*Noah*," I say in the same patronizing tone, "I'm going. End of discussion."

A smile creeps back over Isabel's beautiful lips as she grabs my arm. "Well then, let's get out of here before either of these boys tries to stop us."

Noah curses under his breath while Isabel leads me to the car.

"Listen, man," he grumbles a few seconds later, "I know you're pissed that Kane refused to see you again, but would you mind if we headed to Widowmaker Springs for a few hours? I don't want Willa there without backup."

Palm on the handle of Isabel's Volkswagen, I wait for Ryker's answer. When none comes, I risk the tiniest peek over my shoulder.

The corner of his mouth kicks up into a mischievous grin when our eyes meet. "Sure, let's see what kind of trouble we can get into."

Chapter Six

This was a massive mistake.

There are at least forty cars in the patchy grass and dirt clearing with more filing in by the minute, each one packed to the brim with people.

I tug my sleeves down to my knuckles and fold my arms over my stomach, which currently feels like I ate a pound of Pop Rocks and washed it down with a gallon of soda. Adjusting my position in the tiny passenger seat of the Bug, I turn toward Isabel. "How long did you say you can stay before you have to leave for work?"

"A few hours. I'll probably end up missing most of the eclipse, but I don't want to risk being late during my first week on the job." Her tone is easy and patient, but the way she's bouncing her leg and longingly glancing toward the path leading down to the water tells me she's eager to get out there.

"Why don't you go on ahead, then?" I offer, plastering on my softest smile. "I'll catch up with you in a second. I need to wait for Noah so I can put a few things in his car."

It's a blatant lie, but there's no need to cut her day any shorter than I already have by making her wait for me to find my courage.

She reaches for the handle and hesitates. "You're sure? I just can't stay very long and—"

"*Go*," I insist, pantomiming a little *git goin'* motion with my hands. Her face immediately lights up, the joy radiating from her brilliant smile making my throat clog with sticky shame.

After an excited little shimmy-dance, Isabel grabs her bag from the back seat and jogs over to catch up with some of her and Noah's friends meandering down the path. Not a single one of the girls is wearing a shirt over their bathing suits, which means I'm going to stand out like a sore thumb.

Noah's beat-up Blazer pulls into the clearing a few minutes later, kicking up a plume of dust as he parks under a large oak tree. The engine idles for a second before shutting off, and then he spills out of the driver's side door in a fit of laughter.

I slump down in my seat, low enough that he won't see me or the burn of jealousy creeping up my neck. There's something different about my brother when he's around Ryker—a playful radiance and a lightness to his step that I rarely see anymore. He looks happy...and so much less burdened than when I'm around.

Noah's head whips toward the low rumble of an approaching diesel engine. His shoulders stiffen, and the smile drops from his mouth the second a bright-red Dodge Ram turns the corner and cuts through the tall grass next to the clearing, completely disregarding the established path the rest of us used.

What an asshat.

I swear Cooper Blackthorne thinks the Deadwood Fire Department sticker on his back windshield means he can drive like a maniac and park wherever he wants. In reality, it only makes me question how safe this town is with idiots like him on staff. I shake my head. No matter how hard I try, I can't imagine the guy who locked me in an incinerator running into a burning building to save anyone.

Ryker balls his fists like he's gearing up for a fight, and I roll my eyes. *Perfect.* As if breaking up brawls between Noah and Cooper wasn't bad enough, now I'll have to account for my brother's hotheaded best friend as well.

With a sigh, I push the door open, my foot barely touching the ground before Noah elbows Ryker and leans over to say something I can't hear. Ryker shakes his head, stopping me dead in my tracks when instead of charging across the lot to fight Cooper like he used to when we were kids, he and Noah head in the opposite direction—toward the water. A second goes by and then he says something to my brother, who once again doubles over, chortling and grasping his stomach like he can't breathe.

With Noah fully distracted, Ryker pauses just long enough to slowly peer over his shoulder, giving Cooper a look filled with so much violence I feel the heat of it from thirty feet away.

I shiver. *Jesus.* If looks could kill, I'd be calling in the coroner. Considering how Cooper is technically Ryker's step-cousin, there must be some history there I'm not aware of.

Sighing, I grab the cooler from Isabel's car and lock up. I wait for Cooper and his friends to disappear down the path before heading out myself, where I'm immediately accosted by the obnoxious trill of cicadas and the oppressive early July humidity, both of which only seem to intensify as I travel farther away from the clearing.

The cooler, although small, is significantly heavier than I'd anticipated and requires two hands to carry. Trekking down the rocky, uneven path is a feat in and of itself, but carrying the icebox with my bruised shoulder makes the journey twice as challenging. Before I'm even halfway down, so much of the icy water has sloshed out the sides that my hands are numb and my shins and feet are soaked.

The shoreline is about a quarter mile from here, but already the booming bass of several competing stereos and the low hum of drunken conversations thud inside my chest. Shade canopies in various colors are just visible through the brush—most of them some variation of the Texas flag or the bright-red and white emblem of H-E-B, our state's favorite grocery store.

I slow my steps as I near the edge of the tree line, mentally preparing myself for the onslaught of aromas awaiting me, and the moment everyone stops talking and turns to stare at me—*like they always do*—but when I emerge from the path, that's not what happens.

Sure, the pungent odor of smoky charcoal and various charred meats is nauseating, as is the musty, damp scent of the spring itself, but what nearly knocks me off my feet is that, for the first time in my life, not a single head turns my way.

I set the cooler down and wipe off the sweat beading on my brow with my sleeve.

So this is what anonymity feels like...

Jutting my hip to the side, I glance around, taking in the blue-green water cutting a path through a mix of muddy shoreline and yellowing Texas limestone. To the left, a natural spring bubbles up from the depths of the earth before spilling over a waterfall to join up with the only other water source for at least a hundred miles, a trickling creek that's dry so often no one ever bothered naming it.

Towering live oaks and loblolly pines create shady patches along the shore, which is why Widowmaker Springs draws quite the local crowd during the summer. Thankfully, it's too far out in the middle of nowhere to attract many tourists. I've only been here once, and there were way fewer people that time, but it's just as beautiful as I remember.

I'm bringing my hand up to shield my eyes and search for Isabel when I spot Ryker in the middle of a forming crowd. His posture is rigid and his smile forced, but there he is, looking like a rock star cowboy in boots and tight jeans while everyone around him wears swim gear.

How they miss his subtle flinch every time one of them claps him on the back or how they ignore the way he pinches his eyes closed each time a girl pulls him in for a hug is beyond me. But judging by the increasing chatter rippling through the Springs as more people spot him, I guess everyone is too excited about his return to Deadwood to notice his discomfort.

My ribs squeeze uncomfortably.

"Hey, Ryker," I call out, loud enough for him to hear over the nearby speakers.

His sharp, moss-green eyes snap to mine before I finish saying his name. Several other curious partygoers in the immediate vicinity follow suit, and it only takes a second after spotting me for their heads to lean together and the whispers to start.

I clench my teeth and bear it. *So much for anonymity.*

With one hand on my hip, I gesture to the cooler with the other. "Do you mind helping me with this?"

Without bothering to excuse himself, Ryker pushes through the crowd and strides straight for me. The tension in his shoulders and spine melts away so quickly that if I hadn't seen his unease only a moment ago, I'd never have known anything was amiss.

"Was the icebox too heavy for you, Princess?" he mocks, bending down and effortlessly lifting the cooler with a cocky smirk.

"Not at all." I bat my eyelashes and pointedly glance in the direction of the dissipating group of his old classmates. "You said actions speak louder than words."

Technically, he said words are cheap, but same difference, right?

Ryker looks over his shoulder and then back at me, eyes widening. I expect him to stomp off toward where Noah and his friends are hanging out upstream, but he just continues glaring at me—his thick brow kinked at odd angles, like he's both curious and confused.

Feeling exposed under his heavy scrutiny, I fight the urge to cross my arms by reaching for the cooler. "I can take that back now."

"I've got it." He rotates away from me, the movement highlighting his muscular biceps and a flash of a moth tattoo on his inner forearm that I didn't notice earlier. "Just tell me where it needs to go."

Tearing my eyes away from his way-too-buff arms, I glance toward the water. "Looks like Isabel and Noah are at the very last canopy. Anywhere in the shade should be fine. Thanks," I tack on as an afterthought.

Being civil to each other is weird. *I kind of hate it.*

After another few seconds of awkward staring, we set off on the short walk upstream in total silence. I keep my eyes on the rocky ground as we pass whispering partygoers, sighing in relief when we reach the last canopy. Ryker sets the cooler down next to the ones belonging to Noah's friends. And without another word, we go our separate ways—him stripping down to a borrowed pair of gym shorts while leaving his shirt on to grab a beer, and me collapsing into an unoccupied chair away from prying eyes with all my clothes on.

Ignoring the warm greetings Ryker receives and the musical peal of Isabel's laughter as she jokes with friends, I squint and peer at my surroundings. At the farthest point upstream where you can swim without having to climb down a slight drop to get to the water, I couldn't have picked a better spot myself. Especially since the only people who can really see me over here are Noah's friends.

The actual spring is still about three hundred feet north of here, near the top of an outcropping of weathered limestone. There's a crystal-clear pool where the aquifer surfaces before plunging over the cliff to form a thirty-foot waterfall, but the basin itself is small and no one swims up there. According to Noah, the current is strong, and if you've been drinking all day, the slippery rocks make it all too easy to accidentally plummet to the shallow, rocky water below.

It happened once, about ten years ago. A guy from out of town went over the edge and broke his neck. He drowned before his friends could rush down to save him.

I shudder.

What a horrible way to go, fully aware but unable to move or save yourself with only your friends' panicked screams and the sound of rushing water for company.

"Earth to Willa!" Isabel's melodic voice sounds over the babbling water and music. "We've still got thirty minutes before the eclipse starts. I'm going to float around for a bit, you comin'?"

She's trying to sound casual, but several girls within earshot stop what they're doing to look our way. Pretending I don't feel their eyes on me, I remove my shoes and then my shorts.

This is it, Willa. Moment of truth.

Pop Rocks making a resurgence in my gut, I grab the hem of my shirt—

Only to immediately release it, the fabric ten times heavier than it was a moment before. "I think I'm going to hang out here for a bit. You go on ahead."

Isabel's smile slips, but she nods and heads into the water with Noah and a few others while I sag into one of the chairs and watch them like a stalker. Sweat pools between my breasts as the sun beats down on the surrounding rocks, and it takes less than a minute before I'm already considering going home.

An hour slips by, and while I'm still seated under the shade of the canopy, everyone else has moved their chairs and coolers into the shallow water to avoid the sweltering heat. The eclipse technically started thirty minutes ago, but I didn't realize it would take a full two hours for the sun to be completely covered...

Noah and Isabel have checked on me twice, but now they're both back in the water. I could go sit with them and just keep my shirt on, the way Ryker did, but somehow that feels like more of a defeat than sitting here alone. Besides, aided by the copious amount of beer Ryker keeps handing out left and right, everyone is already good and drunk. The last thing I need is to subject myself to a careless comment.

I'm pretending to take a nap when a sharp scream rips through the air.

My eyes shoot open just in time to see Cooper toss Mandy Cromwell over his shoulder, her perfect butt on proud display in her Texas flag thong bikini bottoms. Her smooth sun-bronzed skin glistens with whatever sparkly suntan lotion she and all the other girls seem to be wearing, and once again, I find myself with the strong urge to pack up my shit and leave.

Ice-cold water drips onto my legs, and I startle, jumping in my seat as Ryker's brooding form steps in front of me, the bottom of his shirt and the entirety of his gym shorts soaked through.

"Take your shirt off," he growls.

"Excuse me?" I rise to my feet and draw myself up to full height, making sure to keep my focus on his face and not the way the wet fabric clings to the ridges of his stomach.

Ryker's mouth pulls into a thin, tight line as he works his jaw and narrows his eyes. "It's over a hundred fucking degrees," he spits. "Moping around like a self-absorbed little brat is stressing your brother out. And watching how you've stared at these girls all afternoon is really starting to piss me off. What's the point of hiding when you don't give a shit about these people? Just take it off and get in the damn water."

"If Noah's so stressed out, why don't you get him another beer?" I cross my arms. "And you have no idea what you're talking about. I give a shit."

He quirks a brow. "Really?"

"Yes, *really*." Hands flying to my hips, I stare defiantly right back at his stupid face.

The corner of his mouth ticks up, the movement so quick and subtle I almost think I imagined it. "No one out here is looking at you, *Princess*." He gestures around to the different groups of people peering up at the slowly darkening sky, all of them with their eclipse glasses on. "You're drawing more attention to yourself by being the last one fully clothed and not in the water with us."

"*Ha*," I snort. "That's rich coming from the only other person with his shirt still on."

Ryker's gaze drops briefly to his chest before he grits his teeth. "You're right." In one easy move, he grabs the hem and tugs it up over his head.

My jaw drops.

Holy... Wow.

He has abs. Like, eight of them.

Hungrily, my eyes rake over every inch of his exposed skin, pausing on a cluster of little scars. And then another...and another. My insides twist and sour. Ryker is covered in marks of every shape and size imaginable—too many to count. The majority of the circular scars seem to be clustered around his shoulders and collarbone, but there's a grouping of them on his lower abdomen. Some even dipping beneath the low-slung waistband of his borrowed shorts.

I close my eyes, trying not to think too hard about what that might mean.

"Are those—"

"Cigarette burns," he says with forced nonchalance. "Kane started off as Beau's favorite ashtray. Then me. You might hate that I'm back in town," he turns sideways, pointing to a raised burn mark in the shape of the letter B on his rib cage, "but I won't let this shit happen to Charlie. Not ever."

Beau fucking Blackthorne. My stomach roils.

The worst thing I could possibly do right now is reach out and touch him, and yet my hand lifts to do just that. Curling my fingers, I push aside my urge to offer comfort.

"I didn't know. I mean, I knew Beau was awful, but I didn't realize—"

"You're not the only one with scars, Princess." He shakes his head. "Do you honestly care what any of these assholes think?"

"No." The admission feels like a giant weight off my shoulders. "I don't."

"Then why are you still letting them dictate the way you live your life?" His lips curve into a snarl...like my weakness disgusts him.

"I'm not." My voice quivers slightly with my answer, and even though part of me wants to run and hide, I can't seem to look away from Ryker's piercing gaze.

"Then take off your damn shirt. Don't make me say it again."

His heady, authoritative tone sends a shiver dancing up my spine. Even though I don't mean to listen, the next thing I know, my hands are on my shirt and I'm pulling it up over my head. A rush of cedar-and-barbecue-scented air fills my lungs as I inhale a deep breath.

Now that I'm free of the stifling long sleeves, wind whips across my sweat-dampened back and relief floods my system in tiny, trembling waves of pleasure. I let go of a drawn-out sigh and close my eyes.

This is the first time I've ever felt the sun directly on my back and it's...magical.

"*Fucking* hell," Ryker says hoarsely.

My eyes shoot open to find him staring at my chest and stomach.

He diverts his gaze skyward with a disbelieving shake of his head. "You're ten times hotter than any of these fucking girls," he growls, eyes still on the clouds. "Why the hell would you hide any of that?"

Grateful he can't see my flushed face, I force a half-scoffing, half-embarrassed laugh. "You have to say that because you're my brother's best friend."

Biting his inner cheek, he shakes his head and slowly drops his eyes to mine. "You don't get it, do you?" he says lowly.

Unable to stop myself, I lean forward. "Get what?"

"First off, I don't have to say *shit*." He glances over his shoulder toward the water before returning his gaze to me. "Second, I shouldn't have said anything *because* I'm your brother's best friend."

My stomach flutters.

Before I can come up with a response, he's shoving his hands into his pockets and softly cursing to himself. "Don't let me catch you moping again."

"Yeah, okay." Cheeks ablaze and needing anywhere else to look, I crouch down, rifling through Isabel's bag to hide the blush I know must be visible on my face. While I absolutely *loathe* that it's Ryker's words giving me such a confidence boost, the fact that he probably hated saying them almost makes it mean more.

"What are you doing?" He takes a step closer, the scent of rain-soaked pine dancing around my head as he peers into the bag.

"I need sunscreen." I stand, placing the bottle and my hands on either side of my mouth to call out for Isabel. "Hey, Isa—"

"I'll do it." He grabs the bottle. "Turn around."

I hesitate, floundering for a second in the hollow pit opening up in my stomach.

He won't want to touch me, not when he sees—

"I said. Turn. Around." Ryker's tone is gruff and firm, leaving no room for negotiation.

Reluctantly, I obey, fortifying myself for the moment he sucks in a harsh breath and calls Isabel over because he's repulsed by the sight of my mangled flesh. But he does neither. Instead, the slightly chemical scent of coconut sunblock blossoms in the air around us a moment before he uses his calloused hand to apply the cool lotion to my mid-back.

I shiver, goose bumps pebbling over every surface of my skin.

Ryker doesn't hesitate when covering each inch of my burn scars with sunscreen, and he doesn't trace the raised, cross-shaped scar that was carved into my back all those years ago. In fact, his application is so straightforward I'd almost think there was nothing wrong with my back at all. Which is crazy because even medical staff and my dad have never seen the damage without shuddering or murmuring something about how sorry they were for me.

"Hold your hair up," he orders, adding a second hand to spread the lotion across my shoulders before gently kneading my neck to work it in.

Fighting the urge to melt into him, I close my eyes. No one has ever touched me like this, and I can't help but sigh contentedly when his hand slides under the strap of my bikini top.

Ryker's breath hitches. "You did a shitty job of covering that bruise."

I roll my eyes. "Thanks."

"If your shoulder hurts, I can do your lower back, too." His voice is a full two octaves lower than it was a second ago, like he's speaking through clenched teeth.

74

"You don't have to," I murmur. "It's sore, but I can still reach."

My response comes out so breathy it almost sounds like I'm begging him to do it for me. Which is probably why he spreads the sunscreen lower and lower, until he eventually grips my waist with one hand and dips the other ever so slightly beneath the waistband of my swimsuit bottoms.

I shiver and sigh again, ignoring the pounding pulse at the apex of my thighs. *Jesus. What's wrong with me? This is my brother's best friend—my childhood nemesis.*

"Don't fucking do that," he growls.

"Do what?" I bite my lower lip to keep from sighing again, but that just makes it come out as a whimper instead. Ryker's grip on my waist tightens, and then he turns me so quickly I have to brace myself against his biceps to keep from falling over.

Chest heaving against mine, he works his jaw and stares down at me. "Don't make that fucking sound unless you want me to—"

"Hey, asshole," Noah shouts from the shoreline, slapping the water with an open palm to get our attention. His words are slightly slurred, but at least he's not stumbling over the slippery rocks. *Yet.*

"Yeah?" Ryker calls back, never taking his eyes off mine.

My pulse races as a swarm of conflicting emotions pound through my bloodstream, but he doesn't let me go. In fact, I'd almost swear he tugs me closer. Rain-soaked pine and a hint of tobacco wrap around me like an embrace, along with a bone-deep desire to throw something at my brother's face.

The idea catches me off guard. Why am I mad at Noah? For interrupting Ryker? That's ridiculous... I don't even like the guy, and I definitely don't care what he has to say.

Noah slaps the water again, clearly pissed. "What the fuck are you doing?"

Ryker grumbles under his breath, but my heart is hammering too violently for me to hear what he says.

"Dude, seriously," Noah calls out again. "Get your hands off my sister."

With a sigh and one final squeeze of my waist, Ryker lets go. I stumble forward, realizing too late how much I was leaning into him.

"If you're not in the water in the next sixty seconds," he warns, handing me the bottle of sunscreen, "I'm coming right back up here and throwing you in myself."

He takes five steps toward the water before I finally find my voice.

"Hey, Ryker?"

"Yeah?" He stops, but doesn't turn around.

"Thank you," I say, quiet enough that Noah can't hear, and then add, "This doesn't mean I like you."

Ryker's head tilts to the side, giving me just a glimpse of a tiny grin as the sun gleams off his golden skin. "I know, Princess."

Chapter Seven

I'm not sure if it's the looming darkness or the eclipse-viewing glasses making it impossible to see anything except the sun, but Ryker was right. Not a single person has looked my way since I removed my shirt.

It probably helped that seconds after leaving the shore, Ryker bet my brother he couldn't climb an oak tree and cannonball into the deepest part of the water without breaking a leg. Never one to back down from a challenge, Noah sprinted for the tree while their friends cheered him on. He drunkenly snapped almost every single branch on his way up and belly flopped with a loud *slap* when he hit the rushing creek below, but the dangerous distraction at least allowed me to swim with Isabel unbothered.

Now that we're nearing the peak of the eclipse, almost everyone's face is tilted upward, except for a few stragglers still playing cornhole on the shore or throwing a ball around in the water. I slipped my shirt back on when a pouty Isabel left for work about twenty minutes ago, but I no longer feel guilty about wearing it. And since I moved a borrowed chair into the creek, I'm also no longer overheated.

The water comes up to my belly, ice cold and refreshing as classic rock plays from the speakers someone finally managed to sync together. Overall, I'm feeling pretty damn good about today. I can't believe I spent so many summers hiding—

A football lands in the water next to me, the impact sending a shock of icy droplets onto my arms and cheek.

"My bad," an all-too-familiar voice barks out.

A sinking feeling fills my stomach when I'm hit by a potent whiff of Axe body spray, and my dread only amplifies as sloshing footsteps head my way.

"Oh. It's you," Cooper Blackthorne says with dark amusement. "I didn't think your kind were allowed out in the sun."

"That's funny, I didn't think you had enough brain cells to form a full sentence."

I don't bother turning to look at him, not when I already know what I'd find. Nutmeg-brown hair that's been cropped way too short on the sides, cruel hazel eyes, a slightly crooked nose, and the tanned body of a narcissistic god.

Cooper leans into my line of sight, flexing like the pretentious asshole he is as he tucks the football under his arm. Lowering his voice so only I can hear, he says, "Thanks for putting your shirt back on. Some of us were trying to enjoy the day and it was a little difficult to keep our booze down with you making us all sick."

Balling my fists, I stand so abruptly I knock my chair over in the process.

Maybe I should get the whole punching-him-in-the-mouth thing over with now. Checking off two bucket list items in one day *would* be pretty spectacular. The eclipse is also about to reach the point of totality. I could use the darkness to make a quick escape...

"You know what, Cooper—"

Heavy footsteps splash through the water behind me a moment before a hard, smoky voice says, "Is there a problem?" Ryker's arm brushes my elbow as he steps to my side, the sky steadily darkening around us.

My brother arrives half a second later, strategically positioning himself between Cooper and the shore. Judging by his telltale squint, he's three sheets to the wind and rearing for a fight.

"Wills, go wait for us by the car," Noah says, taking a wobbly step closer.

"Noah, I've got this. *Please*, just let it go," I plead, eyeing Cooper's equally drunk friends down the creek who are slowly inching their way over.

"What's the problem, Blackthorne?" Noah taunts, swaying slightly and completely ignoring my request.

Cooper doesn't respond. He just stands there, staring at something behind me until his twisted sneer slowly flattens into a pronounced frown.

"What?" Noah laughs. "Nothing to say now that she has backup? Come on, Coop, we both know what this is really about. Get the fuck outta here."

"Just shut up for a minute and turn around," Cooper snaps, eyes wide and head tilted to the side as he takes a tentative step backward. "Who the hell is that?"

The sky darkens further, and an eerie stillness falls over the party as people stop what they're doing to point behind me.

"Dude, that's creepy as shit," one of Cooper's friends shouts from a few feet away.

"What the fuck is that guy doing?" another says.

Turning, I follow their gazes to the top of the cliff, goose bumps erupting over my flesh at the sight of a hooded figure skulking near the ledge.

A fierce wind rips through the Springs, making the fabric of the figure's billowing black robe undulate like a sea of maggots on roadkill. And when they crouch down, the gnarled branches behind them suddenly look like twisted antlers or horns.

My blood chills.

"Oh my God, I think he's poisoning the water!" a feminine voice shrieks.

My head whips to Mandy Cromwell for that ridiculous declaration, but when I glance back at the top of the waterfall, the hunched figure is indeed pouring some sort of liquid into the Springs.

Stomach shrinking in on itself, I step backward as dark-red streaks spill over the cliff's edge into the churning water below, filling the air with the metallic scent of iron and decay.

The figure soars upright, splaying their arms out wide at the exact moment the eclipse reaches the point of totality and the world is plunged into darkness.

People scream, splashing and falling over themselves to flee, but all I can do is stare into the darkness above the falls. It might've been a trick of the low light, but it almost looked like an animal skull was peeking out from under the hood where a face should've been...

Someone grabs my arm, and my brother's familiar sage-and-cedarwood scent hits my nostrils a second before he starts dragging me through the water.

"What the hell, Noah. Let go," I squeal, struggling against his hold while everyone around us continues to panic. It's dark enough that it almost feels like night, except, of course, for the black orb in the sky surrounded by a bright fiery ring of white light.

"We need to go. *Now*," my brother hisses. "Ryker, grab the cooler and the bags."

"On it."

Noah slips on a wet rock, giving me just enough time to glance over my shoulder to the spring as another robed figure joins the first. I do a double take.

"Who are those people?" I whisper, struggling to free myself from Noah's grip while simultaneously trying to keep him from falling again.

"People? What do you mean *people*? It was one guy." He drags me out of the water and down the path toward the Blazer, not stopping for anything. Which is why he never sees the flickering flame appear at the top of the falls...

Or the shadows that crawl out from the woods.

The sky is slowly returning to normal, but the three of us haven't said a word since we got in the Blazer—the combination of Ryker's silent brooding and my brother's agitated fidgeting leaving my brain wide open to tussle over a million things at once while I drive us home.

Who the hell was that hooded person at the falls? And why did they look like a creature right out of one of Mrs. Crowe's stories...

Turning onto our road, I glance to the passenger seat where Noah is leaning his sunburnt forehead against the window. He's definitely buzzed, which is expected after a day of guzzling Shiner Bock in the sun, but he's never *this* quiet. Maybe the robed figure unsettled him as much as it did me?

I nudge him with my elbow. "You good?"

His gaze briefly darts to the rearview mirror. "I'm fine."

Keeping my face forward and my hands on the wheel, I check the mirror for myself.

Ryker's eyes meet mine for a fraction of a second before he looks away and clears his throat to say, "What was that shit back there?"

"Who knows," Noah sighs. "But it ruined a once-in-a-lifetime party."

I scoff. He wasn't even going to the Springs until Isabel mentioned our plans.

"Who said the party had to end?" Ryker chirps from behind me. "I'll be heading back to Denton as soon as my truck's fixed and I've talked to Kane. We should round up the rest of the old crew tonight while I'm still in town."

Noah sits up abruptly, barely catching himself on the dashboard as I pull into our driveway and slam on the brakes. "Fuck yeah, we should," he says excitedly after a snarky scowl in my direction. "Everybody is off work for the holiday tomorrow. We could drink here, or Willa can drop us off and pick us up if we go out. She never has plans."

Ouch.

I cut the engine, frowning when Noah rips the keys from my hand. "Don't you think you guys have had enough to drink today?"

"Don't *you* think you should loosen up a bit and let your brother live his life?" Ryker scoffs from the back seat.

There's the Ryker I know and despise. I knew the sunscreen thing had to be a fluke.

Noah opens his door with a goofy grin. "Yeah, Wills. Let me *live*," he says, slamming it closed and chuckling to himself as he stumbles up the porch steps.

The second he disappears inside the house, I turn in my seat. "Seriously?"

"Relax, Princess. I won't let anything happen to him. Your brother deserves to blow off a little steam every now and then."

My chest tightens, anger roiling through my veins. "You have a record of returning him in worse condition than he left in. Noah's still in the probationary period on the rig. Don't you dare get him into trouble, or I'll make sure you regret it."

Ryker's brow quirks. "Is that a promise?"

Slightly flushed from the sudden dark shift in his tone, I scrunch my nose up and turn away without bothering to respond. What's the point when he'll only find a way to throw whatever I say back in my face?

Locking eyes with me in the rearview mirror, Ryker leans over the center console. My entire body shudders when his breath ghosts across the shell of my ear.

"Come on, don't back down now, Princess. Not when we're just starting to have a little fun." He makes a *tsking* sound of disapproval that drops my attention to his mouth. "You know, it really is a shame you're Noah's baby sister."

Every surface of my skin tingles from the heat in his voice and the pouty curve of his lower lip. No matter how badly I want to look away, I force myself to meet his gaze. "And why's that?"

The corner of his mouth kicks up into a smirk. "Because I think you might enjoy a lesson on letting loose just as much as I'd enjoy giving you one."

Chapter Eight

Noah and Ryker invited what sounded like the entire starting lineup of their old football team to the house last night. They drank and laughed and exchanged crude jokes until somewhere near dawn when Dad finally came home and kicked them all out.

I, on the other hand, spent the night locked in my room with noise-canceling headphones, trying not to think about the robed figure at the Springs *or* the last thing Ryker said to me in the Blazer about needing to let loose.

Once the sun came up, I groggily transitioned to setting up my new tomato trellises and anger-gardened all morning. Hours later, I'm still out here, aggressively trimming damaged pepper plants and haphazardly ripping up weeds by their roots. Only now, instead of sleep-deprived images of the eclipse floating through my mind, I keep seeing shadows move in the forest—specifically around the path I've refused to acknowledge for the past fourteen years.

Readjusting the bandana around my neck, I yank out some more weeds and toss them into my compost pile before driving my gloved hands back into the dirt.

The most annoying part about this whole thing is that when I *do*

84

manage to shift my thoughts away from the shadows, it's once again Ryker's stupid face that pops into my head. Then it only takes a second for me to start thinking about the way his rough hands felt on my bare back. How his fingers dug into me when he gripped my waist...

Sweat drips down my spine, and I close my eyes, imagining it's Ryker's touch trailing across my skin—

My eyes shoot open. *Nope.*

Thank God he's leaving soon. He makes me feel...*off balance.* Like I'm constantly walking on a tightrope and one wrong move will send me plummeting into the abyss.

Okay, that might be a bit dramatic, but still, Ryker needs to go.

I let loose a frustrated sigh and swipe my sleeve across my sweaty forehead, flinching when something hard smacks me on the mouth. I glance at the dirt-covered object in my hand, cursing as I realize I pulled out more than half my carrots. *Dammit.* They weren't even fully grown yet...

With a growl rumbling low in my chest, I rise to my feet and kick over the metal pail holding my gardening tools. Leaving them scattered on the grass, I fill up the newly emptied container with the carrots and other discarded remnants of my gardening massacre.

Looks like the Crowes' goats are getting an extra special treat today.

The sweltering breeze picks up, and a rustling sound draws my attention to the ground where a piece of crumbled, yellowing paper is trapped under one of my small shovels. Crouching, I pick it up, my brow furrowing as I read the two handwritten sentences.

Anything that can withstand the fire must be put through the fire.

Only then will it be cleansed.

A shudder racks through my body, the scarred skin on my back pulling taut as I stand and look for any sign of where this came from. My logical brain knows this note isn't for me. It's just a random piece of trash the wind blew in, but that doesn't stop the uneasy feeling weighing on my shoulders from spreading.

Over the fence, the horses whinny, kicking at the dirt until a brown plume of dust lingers in the air. The hairs on my neck rise as a shadow moves in my periphery.

What the hell—

An ear-splitting scream tears from my throat when a heavy hand lands on my shoulder.

"Whoa there, easy now." Old Man Dan chuckles, backing up a step with his weathered hands raised in surrender.

I clutch my chest and exhale a sigh of relief. "Sorry about that."

"No problem, darlin'," he says, giving me a quick side hug. "I should've known better."

I hug him back, breathing in the deep woodsy scent of his cologne. Wait, that's not right. Mr. Crowe always smells like a mixture of hay, horse, and sunbaked leather after long hours in the saddle under the Texas sun.

Pulling away, I scan his outfit, my eyebrow quirking at the opalescent buttons of his pale-blue western-style dress shirt and the clean brim of his pinched-front Stetson.

"You're looking mighty dapper, Old Man. What's the occasion?"

His gray beard twitches, the visible portions of his ebony cheeks flushing with a ruddy smile at my compliment. "Me and the missus were plannin' on headin' over to Rib Cage for supper before fireworks in the square, but Elanor isn't feeling too well."

My brow creases. "What fireworks—" *Damn.* I forgot today is the Fourth of July...

Well into their late seventies, the Crowes have steadily slowed down over the past few years, but they've never missed the celebration in the Old Town Square. If Elanor's opting out this year, she must really be feeling under the weather.

"I'm sorry to hear she's not feeling well. Is there anything I can do for you guys?"

"That's what I came here to talk to you about." He takes off his hat, spinning it in his slightly shaky hands. "We've had a few *incidents* around the ranch lately."

My hackles rise. I've never known Old Man Dan to mince words or beat around the bush before, but the way his eyes dart back and forth across the landscape, lingering a second too long on the forest, is making me nervous. "What do you mean *incidents?*"

"Disturbances with what's left of the herd—some of the cattle and a few of Mrs. Crowe's goats wandering off. That sort of thing." He looks left and then right before lowering his voice. "We found a few animals with missin' parts..."

"*Missing parts?*" I lean away, all at once horrified and confused. "Have you told my dad or filed a police report?"

"I have, but that's not why I'm here." He spins his hat again. "You remember how I said we didn't have the budget to hire you for more hours this summer?"

I frown, the sting still too fresh. "Yes, sir. I understand, though."

"Well, about that. I was wonderin' if maybe you'd mind taskin' 'round the ranch with the missus? It'd be three to four days a week instead of the two you've been doin', and quite a bit more hours."

Wide-eyed, I nod enthusiastically. "Absolutely."

Without consistent access to transportation, I've been shit out of luck finding another job, making saving up for a car near impossible. This is exactly the sort of opportunity I need to check off number one on my bucket list.

"Hold on now, I haven't told you the rest of it," Old Man Dan says with a nervous smile. "Instead of feedin' the animals and muckin' out the stalls, you'd be escortin' Mrs. Crowe while she checks on the hands and the fences, that sort of thing. I hate the idea of her out on her own with that hip of hers, and that stubborn woman of mine refuses to take a ranch hand with her."

I bounce on my toes. "I'll do it."

"Excellent." Old Man Dan beams, popping his hat back onto his head. "That was easier than I thought. Let's have you start a little earlier, too. Six sharp at the big house work for you?"

"I'll be there." I dip my chin, fighting off a massive grin.

"Great. Before I forget..." His smile disappears again. "Do you still have that pistol your pa gave you for your birthday last year?"

My left brow rises at the note of worry in his tone. "I do..."

"Good. Go on and bring it with you. Until we find out what's happening to the animals, I wouldn't want you caught out there unprotected."

A chill skitters up my spine. *I wonder if whatever's been hunting the Crowes' livestock is what I kept seeing in the shadows today...*

"I can do that."

"Excellent, see you tomorrow, then."

Not one for a drawn-out goodbye, Old Man Dan is already walking back toward the break in the fence when I remember the carrots and other garden scraps I'm carrying.

"Wait!" I shove the weird note in with the vegetables—it's not like it was intended for me anyway—and jog over to hand Old Man Dan the bucket. "This is for the goats."

He smiles. "We sure are lucky you're not leaving us in the fall, darlin'. I don't know what your pa or Mrs. Crowe would've done if you'd decided to go away for school."

I try to force a smile, but guilt weighs down the corners of my mouth.

With one last wave, I walk to my house, trying not to let my guilty conscience overshadow my excitement. It's not like I've actually filled out the acceptance paperwork for UT or withdrawn from Tyler. And I'd need a car even if I was planning on staying local. This job is perfect for me, especially since Noah heads back to work next week and Isabel will be busy at the bar. At least now I'll have someone to spend my days with.

The front door *clicks* closed behind me, a blast of icy air conditioning sending a wave of goose bumps cascading across my arms as I bend over to remove my boots. I'm so sweaty I can feel the dried salt on my tight skin, and if I don't get to the toilet soon, there's a good chance I might pee my pants.

I rush toward our only bathroom, but when I try the handle, it won't budge.

What the hell? No one ever locks this door...

I put my ear to the wood, fists clenching at the faint hum of the shower on the other side.

Dammit.

Split into three compartments with two separate interior doors, the bathroom is set up in a way that allows for all three of us to get ready at the same time *and* retain our privacy. Noah can be brushing his teeth while I shower and Dad takes one of his hour-long toilet breaks. The only reason we've been able to make having one bathroom work as long as we have is because of our rule that the outer door *always* stays unlocked.

I pound my fist against the frame, but there's no answer.

"Noah," I bark in the direction of my brother's room. "Your dickhead friend locked the bathroom and I have to pee!"

89

With the shower still running, the door swings open, sending a hot blast of honeysuckle-scented steam billowing into my face.

"What did you say about my dick, Princess?"

My eyes go wide.

Jesus. Christ. He's so...*wet.*

After witnessing a shirtless Ryker at the Springs, you'd think I'd be immune to his physique, but there's something infinitely more intimate about seeing him with just a tiny towel draped around his waist...especially when I know he's not wearing anything beneath.

I swallow the lump in my throat.

"Can I help you? I'm sort of in the middle of something here," he says, water dripping over every surface of his chiseled body.

Thankfully, the snark in his tone is enough for me to remember my anger. Cheeks flushed, I push past him, inhaling another whiff of honeysuckle.

I stop in my tracks. "Are you using *my* body wash?"

Ryker shrugs, nearly losing his grip on the towel in the process. He grins like the Cheshire Cat when he catches me staring. "Like what you see?"

After peeling my gaze away from the additional inch of skin around his waist—and away from all the veins and muscles leading south—my throat constricts.

"Of course not," I say, voice hoarse and somehow slightly squeaky. "I'm just curious why you're using *my* stuff when Noah and Dad have plenty of—"

Ryker takes a step forward, pressing me into the wall with his wet chest mere inches from my face.

"Maybe I enjoy smelling you on me." His voice drops dangerously low. "Maybe I used your body wash because I wanted to pretend it was *your* slender fingers wrapped around my cock instead of my fist."

My breath catches in my throat. He's fucking with me, right? He has to be, but that doesn't stop me from imagining the scene he described: me in the shower with him, his hand covering mine as he shows me exactly how he likes to be touched...

My heart pounds so violently against my ribs it makes me dizzy.

Ryker smiles, like he can see the obscene image my brain conjured and can hear my racing pulse.

"Or..." he leans closer, the water from his raven hair dripping onto my cheek while I struggle to draw in a full breath, "maybe I just grabbed the wrong fucking bottle of soap." He straightens his posture with a sardonic laugh. "Don't flatter yourself, Princess. It was an accident."

"*Asshole,*" I seethe. Pushing off the wall, I stomp toward the toilet and slam the door behind me to hide my rapidly heating ears.

God, he's infuriating.

After quickly using the restroom and waiting a few extra seconds to make sure I don't run into Ryker again, I march over to the sink and wash up as fast as possible—which is why I don't notice the door to the shower was left partially open until I start drying my hands.

I grip the towel tighter. That little shit is using my body wash again, I can *smell* it.

Ready to tear him a new one, I turn toward the door and catch a flash of skin through the fogged-up glass that might be his wrist or maybe even his—

My stomach tightens. *Oh my God...*

Ryker wipes away a window of steam so I can see the devilish smirk plastered across his stupid mouth. "If you're not coming in, do me a favor and shut the door on your way out."

———

Hours later, I find myself curled up on the couch in my pajamas, struggling to get into the book Isabel lent me. It's not a bad story, I just can't relate to these cookie-cutter characters, and I can't seem to get on board with the light and fluffy atmosphere. Where's the angst and the tension? Where's the touch of alluring darkness threatening to pull you under with every page flip?

The porch creaks, and my head snaps to the entryway.

"Ryker?" Noah calls out, shutting the door and pocketing his phone. "Marco just got off work at the hardware store. Are you still trying to get a hold of Kane or are you ready to go?"

Bootsteps sound from the hallway, followed by a deep, smoky voice and a hint of honeysuckle that makes my blood boil. "Good to go."

I peek up from my book as Ryker rounds the corner, wearing the same form-fitting jeans and hawk moth belt buckle he had on the day he arrived. He at least had the decency to borrow one of Noah's clean white T-shirts, but the one-size-too-small fabric hugs his biceps in a way that's almost sinful.

Swallowing the tightness in my throat, I force myself to look away, catching the slightest flash of another one of Ryker's arrogant grins, like he thinks I was checking him out instead of plotting my revenge for the body wash.

"You coming to Rib Cage with us, Princess?"

More than ready to say no, I've just scrunched my face up into a mocking smile when number seven on my bucket list pops into my mind: *Stop hiding. Go out more.*

My exaggerated smile falters. What am I going to do, say no every time someone invites me out next semester? If I end up going to UT, how many times can I opt to stay in for the night before Isabel finally gives up on me?

Ryker's invite definitely wasn't genuine, but Rib Cage *is* technically a barbecue joint that just so happens to be attached to the oldest bar in the region. I normally spend the Fourth of July on my porch, watching the fireworks from a distance, but I *could* go with them...if I wanted to.

I chew my lower lip. Isabel is working tonight... If I went, I could hang out with her *and* make sure Noah doesn't get himself into too much trouble.

I release my lip, ignoring the way Ryker's gaze zeroes in on my mouth.

Face twisting into a scowl, my brother takes the slightest step away from Ryker. "Dude, give it a rest already. She doesn't want to—"

"I'll go." I rise to my feet, setting my book down on the coffee table. "I need a few minutes to get ready, but I'll drive if you wait."

Noah lifts a brow, his expression hovering between surprise and skepticism. "You sure? There'll be a lot of people there, and I can't take you home early if I'm drinking."

My stomach squirms as I try to decide if he's worried about me or just doesn't want me to go... "I'm sure."

Ten minutes later, I've changed into a sleeveless black denim romper; a pair of black leather cowboy boots with silver embellishments on the toes, heels, and pull straps; and of course, my favorite green fringe jacket—which still has a hole in the sleeve from Beau. I probably should've worn red, white, and blue, but once again, I'd forgotten it was the Fourth of July until I was already dressed.

After spending the day gardening in the sun, I opt for light makeup that not only makes my brownish-hazel eyes pop, but will also play to my benefit under the unforgiving neon-orange lights inside the bar. All in all, I'm ready in twenty minutes. I would've been done sooner, but letting my hair air dry after my shower meant my curtain bangs were in need of a good flat-ironing. It's still a little messy, but at least the light hints of red that only come out in summer are *finally* starting to peek through again.

"Ready," I announce, my boots clicking on the worn hardwood floors as I tie the red bandana I laced with lemon-scented essential oil around my neck.

Noah stands abruptly from the kitchen table and shakes his head. "Absolutely not. Your entire ass is hanging out of that thing. Go change. *Now.*"

It's my first time wearing this thrifted romper, so for a second I'm nervous, but when my hands fly to the crease of my butt to check for coverage, I find the length more than appropriate.

Rolling my eyes, I snatch the Blazer's keys off the entryway table and glance over my shoulder. "You two comin' or what?"

Noah looks at my romper one more time, groaning as he heads for the pile of shoes by the door. "Whatever. Just walk behind me so I don't have to see that shit."

I bite back a laugh. "Deal."

Ryker ambles up to Noah's side, head cocked in my direction as he leans against the doorframe. His eyes drop to my boots before he slowly works his gaze up the length of my legs, sliding over the curve of my hip like an intimate caress.

Blinking slowly, he shakes his head. "Goddamn shame."

"What is?" Noah grunts, hopping on one foot while aggressively shoving the other into his boot. Once both his feet are on the ground, he follows the direction of Ryker's stare.

Red-faced, he thrusts two fingers into his best friend's chest. "Not funny, dude." Ryker bats him away, but Noah shoves his fingers right back where they were. "I'm serious. Keep your eyes, hands, and jokes to your goddamn self."

"Fine," Ryker grumbles.

Noah whirls on me. "I told you that outfit was too short. Go get in the damn car."

I scurry past them, leaving the front door open behind me as I dash across the driveway.

"I mean it, man," Noah whisper-yells after they step out onto the porch. "Willa has a hard enough time with the assholes in this fucking town as it is. She's not a toy for you to taunt or fuck with."

When I glance over my shoulder, Ryker's eyes flash to mine for the briefest second. "She's not a kid anymore. She can fight her own battles—"

I flinch as Noah slams the door.

"No, she fucking can't," he shouts, the air vibrating with his ire. "You haven't been here. You have no idea what it's been like for her—or for me."

Ryker puts his hands up, and then tentatively reaches out to

94

squeeze my brother's shoulder. "Alright, I get it. I was just having a little fun. I'll back off."

Having heard enough, I throw myself inside the Blazer, a boiling pressure between my ribs making my chest rise and fall in rapid succession. My hands shake as I turn over the engine and grip the steering wheel.

Noah's wrong. Not only can I fight my own battles, but I'm more than capable of going head to head with Ryker fucking Bennett.

Chapter Nine

"Do y'all mind *not* staring at us like a bunch of fucking assholes?" Noah shouts into the dimly lit, overly crowded bar of Rib Cage Tavern.

I drop my eyes to the concrete floor, blood rushing to my overheated ears as every face that wasn't already looking at us turns our way. *Dammit.* I knew my presence would draw attention, but I'd forgotten to account for Noah's uncanny ability to make everything ten times worse.

After drawing in a sharp breath, I pick my eyes up off the floor, realizing too late what a mistake that was when the room starts spinning. The overpowering mix of perfume, stale beer, wet wood from a leak in the roof, and something sickly sweet—from what I assume is a cocktail mixer or barbecue sauce—is possibly the worst combination of odors ever.

I take a deep inhale from my lemon infused bandana and pull my next breaths through my mouth, which isn't quite so bad.

Dad and I have been here a few times for lunch, but we always sit on the patio where the air smells like brisket and smoked turkey with small traces of the cedar trees lining the property. I thought more of that delicious aroma would permeate in here, but I guess the thick Country Rubble walls adorned with various metal street signs and neon beer logos create two distinct biospheres—one appetizing and the other reeking of bad decisions.

In the 1920s, this place was called The Devil's Rib Cage, derived from the curved wood-plank ceiling that's now covered in hundreds of dollar bills. But somewhere along the way, I guess they forced the Devil out of Deadwood.

Even so, with the haunting red-orange glow of the beer signs and how humid it is in here with all these bodies packed tightly together, I can't help but wonder if the original name might've been more fitting.

Someone fires up George Strait's "All My Ex's Live in Texas" on the jukebox, and the room erupts into dismayed groans from the younger crowd and hoots and hollers from the elder patrons—both reactions thankfully taking the attention off of us, allowing Noah and Ryker to abandon me for their friends on the opposite side of the room and me to finally relax my shoulders.

The floor clears, and a few couples pair off to start two-stepping as I hover by the door.

Among them, I spot Isabel's older brother, Marco, dragging a reluctant Luciana García, Deadwood's mayor and Rib Cage's owner, out onto the floor. The woman is in her mid-forties and absolutely gorgeous. She's also smart as hell and has a tongue sharper than a blade.

Damn. Marco's braver than I give him credit for. Isabel's brother might be Deadwood's most eligible bachelor, but he's also the nicest guy in town. Last week, I saw him literally help a little old lady cross the street. And even though he'd received a full-ride scholarship for football to the University of North Texas and probably could have gone pro, he still came home after graduating to help run his family's hardware store and take care of his grandparents.

I'm not sure who was happier to see him, Isabel or my brother—which is a little weird since Noah and Marco barely hung out in high school.

Marco gives me a wink, his dark hair falling forward, making him look like one of the stars in the telenovela their grandma is always watching as he maneuvers poor Luciana into a low dip.

He spins her, and from the corner of the bar, Noah claps and shouts encouragements. A reluctant smile spreads across my cheeks at the sight of my brother's infectious grin, but it's quickly wiped away when a scowling Ryker hands Noah a beer and leans over to whisper something in his ear.

Draining the bottle, Noah scans the room, his carefree expression falling the second he sees a group of cowboys from Crowe Ranch. The same group that usually hangs out with Cooper Blackthorne. Thankfully, Cooper is nowhere in sight, but as if a rain cloud appeared over his head, Noah's entire demeanor changes. He chugs his beer in one go and plucks another bottle out of the bucket on the table.

Perfect. If he keeps going at this rate, I'll be carrying him home in a few hours. What the hell did Ryker say to make him react like that?

"Willa?"

I've barely turned around when I'm ripped into a warm, jasmine-scented embrace and dragged through the crowd to the overly shel-lacked bar.

"Sit," Isabel shouts above the music before shoving me onto the vacant stool beneath a string of red, white, and blue bunting connected between two pillars on opposite ends of the bar.

For a split second, I wonder how I lucked out with the only open seat in the room, but then I scoot back a little and the whole damn stool wobbles so violently I nearly topple over. It happens two more times while Isabel makes her way behind the bar, but eventually I find a good position.

Leaning across the ancient countertop, she wiggles her perfectly manicured brows conspiratorially. "Quick, tell me what you want to drink before Luciana comes back."

A smile creeps over my lips. This is exactly why no one under the age of twenty-one should be allowed to bartend, but Texas laws don't make sense, so who am I to argue?

I scan the wall behind her, unfamiliar with any of the labels except a few of the beers I've seen at the house. "I don't care. Give me whatever I'm least likely to get caught with. Go easy, though, I'm driving."

"Done." Isabel dumps at least two shots' worth of vodka into a clear pint glass and fills the rest up with soda water before sliding it across the bar.

"*Isabel*," I chastise, "that's *not* going easy. Are you trying to kill me?"

"You'll be fine." She pushes the drink closer and lifts a brow in challenge. "You said you wanted to live a little. Here's your chance."

"I never should have shown you my bucket list," I grumble, eyeing the fizzing concoction. She's right, though. Knowing Noah, we'll be here for hours... Plenty of time to sober up before I need to drive home. *Ah, to hell with it.*

Clutching the glass, I take one massive gulp and immediately start choking. "Holy shit," I sputter, trying not to gag. "That tastes like nail polish remover." Mouth puckered, I push the glass back across the bar. "I can't drink that."

"*Shh.* Keep your voice down!" Isabel hisses, reaching for a lime that she squirts in the general vicinity of my glass, like that will somehow make it taste better. "I don't care how gross it is, you better act like it's candy because we have incoming and I can't afford to go to jail." She grabs a rag and starts wiping down the bar.

"What do you mean—"

"Willa Dunn." My spine stiffens at the abrasive tone of Mayor García's voice. "You're way too young to be sitting at my bar. Get the hell up and move to a table."

I turn on the stool, hunching my shoulders as I give her denim on denim and turquoise jewelry a quick once-over. I've always loved her sense of fashion, but obviously now's not the time to tell her. Instead, I drop my eyes to the floor.

"My brother needed a sober driver," I offer, doing my best to sound repentant. "I was sort of hoping I could hang out here with Isabel and keep an eye on him instead of sitting alone in my empty house." I lift my gaze to hers, pushing out my lower lip in a ridiculous pout.

As if on cue, Noah lets out an obnoxiously loud and very drunk-sounding laugh from across the bar.

"Oh." Luciana's frown falters, the crinkle near her eyes softening as she shuffles from one foot to the other. She reaches for me, her delicate hand hovering a few inches from my forearm before dropping. "I forgot Joel was working tonight... Fine. You can stay. Just don't distract my bartender and *don't* let me catch you drinking."

I flash her a brilliant smile. "Yes, ma'am."

She continues staring at me, her expression *too* thoughtful, like she's already second guessing her choice.

"I promise I'll behave," I say quickly. "All these work trips the chief has Dad going on have made him more irritable than ever. I'm not going to risk my hide by doing something stupid in the mayor's bar."

Eyes narrowing, Luciana tilts her head. "Joel's been traveling for work?"

"*Mm-hmm.*" I bob my chin. "To Austin, mostly."

Her eyes widen for a fraction of a second, and then her lips pinch together. "Right, of course. How could I have forgotten?"

You'd think she'd know how her departments are spending their funds, but I suppose that'd be a lot for anyone to keep track of. We stare at one another for a tense moment, and I'm convinced she can smell the vodka in my drink, but then she gives me an awkward smile.

"Okay, well..." The front door swings open, and Luciana glances over her shoulder, cursing under her breath as she takes a backward step. "Excuse me, I need to talk to Dominic Cromwell about that fucking fence he put up on Main Street." She gives me one last stilted smile and disappears into the crowd.

"*Holy shit.* She didn't even look at my drink." I spin around to face Isabel, who's blinking at me with her jaw practically on the floor.

"You dirty rat," she says through an incredulous laugh. "I've *never* seen you play the sympathy card on purpose before! Do you think that would work at the liquor store?"

I shake my head vigorously, the motion sending a potent wave of lemon into the air. "There's absolutely no chance I'm going to try that somewhere with security cameras. My dad would literally kill me if he found out."

I cringe at my poor choice of words, but thankfully Isabel doesn't seem to catch it.

"Fine." She throws a wicked grin in my direction. "But if people want to treat you like you're made of glass, it's about time you start using it to your advantage."

The corners of my mouth tug downward. I've never thought about it in those terms before, but it's as good a description as any. Isabel, Noah, Dad, and even the Crowes are all guilty of treating me like they're afraid I might shatter at any moment. Honestly, I'm not sure which one is worse: being teased or coddled.

The realization that those have been my only two experiences with the fine citizens of Deadwood makes it painfully obvious that if I stay, I'll never escape the past.

My mind wanders to the acceptance letter burning a hole in my pocket and then to Dad's reaction when I tried to talk to him at dinner the other day. How am I ever going to break free of this place if every time I bring up Austin, he immediately shuts down the conversation?

"Why are you making that face?" Isabel prompts, placing a beer in front of the guy sitting next to me.

"It's stupid," I say, glancing at the man for the first time and realizing I've never seen him around town before. *Why does it look like he spilled ink on his inner wrist? And who wears a suit to a dive bar?*

Isabel reaches for my hand. "Lay it on me."

"Promise you won't tell anyone?"

She releases me to draw a *T* for trust over her heart, and I roll my eyes.

"What?" she gasps, pretending to be affronted. "You cross your fingers if you're lying. Why wouldn't crossing your heart mean the same thing? Go on now, spill."

After another glance at the suited guy next to me to make sure I don't know him, I lower my voice. "I got into UT."

Isabel squeals loudly enough that half the bar glances our way. "Sorry," she murmurs once they return their attention to their drinks. "I'm just so freaking excited."

I take an enormous sip from my glass, enjoying the burn of lime and vodka sliding down my throat. "Don't get *too* excited. I haven't told my dad or accepted the offer of admission yet."

Isabel bobs her head, as if processing. Then her eyes brighten. "Give me your phone. I'll do it for you." Again, I roll my eyes, but she holds out her hand forcefully. "I'm serious. It takes less than a minute to enroll. You can complete all the financial forms at home and worry about telling your family later."

When I make no move to reach for my phone, she frowns and brings her hands to her hips. "Willa Dunn, you've been plotting your escape from this town for as long as I've known you. Are you seriously going to chicken out now that you have your chance?"

Okay, damn.

"I'm not chickening out, I just haven't decided if I should go yet." My eyes drop to the sticky bar top. "And you know my dad *hates* the idea of me living in the city. Every time I bring it up, he just reminds me how much he and Noah need me at home..."

"They're grown-ass men," Isabel insists before glancing at Noah, who's attempting a *very* sloppy cartwheel by the jukebox. "Well, at least your dad is."

She grabs my arm. "It's a big change, but I'll be there with you. Don't let your family hold you back from going after what you want. More importantly, don't use them as an excuse because you're scared."

Her words hit me so hard I nearly tumble off my wobbly stool.

She's right. That's *exactly* what I'm doing...

Before I can overthink it, I rip my phone from my pocket. It takes less than two minutes to fill out all the forms, including my credit card information for the rather pricey deposit. But when it comes time to hit Submit, my thumb hovers above the screen.

Sweat pools at the base of my spine while the obscenely loud chatter of the bar rises up around me, battering against my senses like a physical assault. I try to drown it out, but that only makes the individual lines of conversation clearer.

"*No, the Old Town Square is always too crowded on the Fourth. I'll be watchin' the fireworks from home this year,*" a bored-sounding man says behind me.

"*Have they figured out who that weirdo at the eclipse party was yet?*" comes a woman's voice from my right.

Then someone on the dance floor says, "*Is that Willa Dunn sitting alone at the bar? Poor thing, I can't imagine not having any friends. I think I'd die if—*"

My thumb slams down on the Submit button.

Throat dry and neck stiff, I turn my phone to show Isabel the 'Congratulations on your Enrollment' message stamped across my screen.

She squeals, a sparkling grin pulling at the corners of her glossed lips. "Holy shit, you did it? We're officially going to school together next year?"

I bite my lip and nod. "Yep. I'm moving to Austin."

My heart thumps wildly against my rib cage. But for once in my life, it's not fear or anxiety making my pulse race...it's excitement. It's the promise of freedom. A weight lifting off my shoulders—

The ear-splitting shriek of a record scratching tears through the bar, and I clamp my hands over my ears to shield them from the godawful clamor. The entirety of the tavern erupts into *boos* and shouts of disapproval as the twangy guitar intro of "All My Ex's Live in Texas" starts over again on the jukebox.

Isabel frowns. "Damn thing's been on the fritz for days. I'm going to go find Luciana and see if she can fix it. Hang tight, I'll be right back so we can talk about apartments, okay?"

Slightly overwhelmed, I bob my head.

It's official, I'm finally getting out of Deadwood...

The jukebox makes another scratching noise, and then the same George Strait song starts over. This time, though, it only plays the first few seconds before starting over again.

And again.

And again.

Despite the hot, stale air inside the bar, a chill runs up my spine, the hairs on my neck rising. Slowly and in unison, the entire room stops what they're doing to stare at the jukebox.

Earlier the song seemed playful, nostalgic even, but there's something about those same four twangy notes repeating over and over again that's a little haunting—the warbly tune suddenly sounding like the soundtrack from a horror movie.

I look around, making brief eye contact with Ryker, who's leaning against the wall in the far corner with his hands in his pockets, a good five feet away from the table of his and Noah's friends.

The dim overhead lights flicker, and several women shriek when we're cast into darkness for a split second.

"Alright, everyone, calm down," my brother shouts, rising unsteadily to his feet and crossing the room in a few long strides. "No need to get your panties in a twist, Noah Dunn will fix it."

Once he's standing in front of the jukebox, he raises his fist and— despite the loud protests around him—brings it down like a hammer. The machine squeals, the pitch becoming progressively higher and higher until I'm sure it's seconds away from exploding... Then, as if nothing was ever wrong, it goes quiet and moves on to the next song in the queue.

I let loose a long breath. *Maybe we're just all on edge from the hooded figure at the Springs yesterday...*

Several of the old-timers meander up to my brother's side,

surrounding him with congratulatory claps on the back and handing him a beer and a shot full of amber liquid that he promptly guzzles. When he sets the glasses down, his cheeks are pink and his smile is bright beneath his mustache. Even though I'll be the one stuck taking care of his drunk ass later, he looks so pleased I can't find it in myself to be upset.

Noah and I are so different that sometimes it's hard to believe we're related. Not only are his blue-gray eyes and fair hair the opposite of my brown locks and hazel ones, but where I tend to find social interactions draining, my brother feeds off of them. He's always making sure everyone around him is having a good time, and people love him for it.

Sometimes when I see him like this, all relaxed and carefree, I find myself wondering what kind of life he could've had without the burden of me as a sister...

If I'd died in that fire, would my memory drag him down the same way my survival did?

I grab my drink, wobbling on my unsteady stool as I drain the cup. The warmth from the bubbling liquid spreads through my chest, leaving my body feeling light and my head clear.

But the relief of a quiet mind is fleeting, interrupted by the potent scent of leather and whiskey as a broad shadow approaches from my left.

Chapter Ten

"What's a sweet little thing like you doin' in a bar like this?" a deep, drawling voice asks. An unfamiliar man in his early twenties steps closer, his wide chest taking up my entire field of view as he leans against the counter, whiskey in hand.

Beneath the leather and liquor, he smells like a mix of Copenhagen and amber-and-pepper aftershave that makes my nose itch. I crane my neck to glance up at him, noting the desert-camouflage ball cap and the slightly blurry texture of his face.

Damn, the vodka might be hitting me harder than I thought...

"Same thing as you, I expect," I quip, squinting to see if the blurriness goes away.

A slightly off-white smile spreads across the lower half of his face. "Saw you at the Springs yesterday, figured I'd come introduce myself." He grabs my empty cup and places it on the counter before taking my hand in his.

"Wait," I say, brow furrowing as his thumb caresses the top of my hand. "Are you hitting on me?"

Oh, Jesus. I can't believe I just asked him that out loud...

"I sure am, sweetheart." He laughs, but it sounds flat, like he's laughing *at* me. "Name's Houston Blackthorne. I'm the new herder at Crowe Ranch."

A Blackthorne? That's a hard no for me.

I'm about to tell him to shove off when Isabel's sing-song voice interrupts my train of thought. "Can I get you two a refill?" She walks back around the bar, grabbing my cup off the counter and gesturing to the liquor shelf behind her.

Houston makes a contemplative humming noise, and I can't help but notice the shift in his expression—or the slight predatory gleam in his eyes as his gaze bounces between Isabel and me. Like he's not sure if he picked the right one of us to hit on.

My stomach sours.

"Are you ladies free tonight?" The corner of his mouth twitches. "I heard the fireworks start around nine-thirty."

Isabel gives him a quizzical look. "Let me know when you want another drink." She makes pointed eye contact with me before moving away to pour beer from a tap on the opposite end of the bar.

"Looks like it's just you and me, sweetheart," Houston says, wrapping a sweaty hand around my waist. "Should we get out of here?"

If I wasn't so skeeved out, I would laugh. He can't honestly think that pathetic display was enough to sweep me off my feet, can he?

Some upbeat pop song blasts from the jukebox, and I temporarily forget all about the creep with his arm around me as Noah belts out the first few lines at the top of his lungs and starts dancing like a maniac, using anyone in his immediate vicinity as a stripper pole.

I let loose a small giggle. Will I likely be carrying him home later? One hundred percent. But I think I'll take Ryker's advice and let my brother live his life and enjoy the moment.

"Goddamn queer," Houston mumbles.

As if slapped, my head whips so hard in Houston's direction that my neck cracks. "Excuse me?" I hiss, already leaning away to stare at him in disbelief, my slight buzz quickly replaced by roiling revulsion as his angular face comes into sharp focus.

I can't have heard him right. The Crowes would never have hired a bigoted asshole...

Houston takes a sip from his glass, tightening his grip on my waist as he juts his chin toward my brother. "I've heard rumors about that guy from some of the ranch hands. It's fucking unnatural."

Half in shock that he's doubling down on his repugnant statement, I track his gaze across the bar to where my brother is dancing next to the mayor in a highly suggestive manner, his entire group of friends laughing their asses off at the blatant way she ignores him.

"What the hell is wrong with you?" I snap at Houston. "Noah's just having fun, and there's nothing unnatural about someone's sexual orientation in the first place."

My skin crawls as I slide off the rickety stool and attempt to remove his arm from around my waist. But Houston takes advantage of the lack of a seat between us and pulls me closer, his fingers digging painfully into my hip while he smirks and drains his whiskey.

"Relax, sweetheart. I'm not lookin' for a fight or anything. I'm just sayin', if that abomination comes within five feet of me, I'll lay him out. *Bop-bop.*" He laughs, jostling me as he mimics a double punch with his now-empty glass.

Blood boiling, I push against his ribs to free myself, wincing when his grip becomes bruising. "That's my brother you're talking about, *asshole*," I grunt, jabbing my elbow into his side to create some space between us.

"Wait." His smirk slips into a pronounced look of disappointment, and he finally loosens his hold. "*You're* Willa Dunn? Dammit. The boys warned me not to waste my time with you."

I should walk away, but morbid curiosity killed the cat. "What the hell does that mean?"

Houston's grin turns razor sharp. "They told me your daddy's a cop who'd do anything to protect his *perfect* virgin angel." Eyebrow quirked, he reaches down and squeezes my backside. "Something tells me this tight little ass might be worth the trouble, though."

Every nerve in my body vibrating with rage, I shove him off of me. "I'm way more *trouble* than you can handle, and I wouldn't let you touch me if you were the last man on Earth."

"You've got some fight in you. I like that." He laughs, eating up the distance I worked so hard to create between us in a single step. "I could teach you a thing or two, and I'll be gentle the first time, promise."

What. The. Actual. Fuck?

"Hard pass," I spit, shaking out my hands to rid myself of his vile touch.

This is exactly why I don't leave the house...

I turn to leave, but Houston grabs my wrist, the bruise on my shoulder screaming in protest as he drags me backward.

"Come on, sweetheart," he coos, choking my senses with his peppery aftershave. "Let me show you what a night with a real man's like. I'll take care of—"

His words die off abruptly at the sound of approaching footsteps.

"Get your *fuckin'* hands off my sister."

Chapter Eleven

Once again, every face in the bar turns in our direction. My eyes dart between my brother's heaving chest and Houston's malevolent grin, both their bodies angled forward in preparation for a fight.

Icy dread coats the lining of my stomach. "Noah, *please*. I'm handling it."

"Wait outside, Willa," he growls, swaying slightly until he steadies himself.

Houston's smile stretches into a sneer. "Yeah, *Willa*," he taunts, somehow managing to make my name sound like an insult. "Why don't you go wait outside? I'm gonna have a quick chat with your brother, and then you and I can—"

Crunch. I flinch as Noah's fist connects with Houston's jaw.

The entire bar quiets and then fills with the high-pitched squeal of moving chairs as people rise to their feet. After a second, low murmurs flare to life in pockets around the room—like the patrons are trying to decide if this is a fight they need to get involved in or not. A few of the old-timers take their seats once they realize who the argument is between, but Noah's friends and some of the newer cowboys from Crowe Ranch roll up their sleeves and inch their way over, crowding around us in a silent standoff with one another.

"Is that all you've got?" Houston says through a laugh, taking a step closer so he and Noah are chest to chest. "You'll have to hit a lot harder than that if you want me to feel it."

I grab onto my brother's arm. "Noah, *don't*. He's not worth it."

Too lost in a cloud of rage to even look in my direction, he shrugs me off and gets right back up in Houston's face.

My lungs pinch and my pulse quickens when Noah's friends start arguing with Houston's ranch buddies in earnest, the air around us thickening like a pressure cooker about to explode. *Dammit.* If I don't act quickly, Noah's going to get himself hurt—or worse, arrested and kicked out of the house.

An ear-splitting whistle rings out through the bar, and I turn just in time to see Luciana pulling two fingers away from her lips.

"That's enough! I'm callin' the cops on whoever throws the next fucking punch," she hollers. "Unless you want to watch the fireworks from a jail cell tonight, I strongly recommend goin' back to your drinks."

Seizing the momentary distraction, I shove myself into the minuscule amount of space between the men, placing two hands on my brother's heaving chest and pushing him toward the door. "Noah, let's just go."

His eyes meet mine, glassy and a little bloodshot. "That asshole touched you, Wills," he whispers through a hiccup. "I saw from across the bar. He fuckin' *touched* you."

Houston laughs. "I was going to do a lot more than that. If you think your twink ass—"

Gritting my teeth, I jab my elbow backward into Houston's gut as hard as I can.

A *whoosh* of air escapes his lips as he doubles over. "What the fuck?" he grunts, clearly caught off guard by the assault. "*Crazy bitch. Fuck you and your fa—*"

I spin around, fist poised to land another blow, when a hand appears out of nowhere, grabbing Houston by the throat and slamming him against the poster-lined pillar. The whole ceiling shakes with the impact, several of the ancient dollar bills falling to the floor around us.

"Think *very* hard before you finish that sentence," Ryker growls, his jaw tight and cheeks stained with fury. Houston's mouth gapes open and closed like a fish, but Ryker keeps up the pressure on his windpipe, cutting off his air supply along with whatever vile filth he was going to spew.

"Are you okay?" Ryker asks out of the side of his mouth while a commotion of some sort erupts behind us.

"Yeah, I'm fine," I croak, earning me a curt nod.

"Marco," Ryker calls over his shoulder, biceps straining against the tight white fabric of his T-shirt, "take Noah outside. I'll meet you there in a sec."

Out of the corner of my eye, I see one of the guys Houston came with break a beer bottle over someone's head and turn towards us, but he's on the ground a second later with three of Noah's friends piled on top of him. The brawl only escalates from there, threats and fists exchanged like oxygen as more drunk patrons join the fray. The mayor's sharp command for them to "knock it the hell off" rises above the music a second later, but no one stops fighting.

Marco hoisting Noah's arm over his shoulder draws my attention back to the problem at hand. "Alright, let's get you out of here," he says, tone void of his normal patience.

Leaving a trail of citrusy cologne in his wake, Marco flashes me a small smile before leading my less-than-cooperative brother through the brawling crowd toward the door. Noah fights him every step of the way, making vague threats about breaking Houston's face while repeatedly trying to join the fight with his friends.

"Willa." I jump a little at the rough way Ryker says my name, his voice full of gravel and rage. "You have approximately five seconds to hit this guy in the face or I'm doing it for you."

Shocked, I just stare. Noah would never let me—

"Three seconds, Princess. Two..."

I ball my fist and throw the hardest punch I can right into Houston's ugly mug. Molten pain streaks up my arm at the same time something in the asshole's nose *pops*, sending a spray of blood pouring down his lips and onto his shirt.

God, that felt good. Hurt like hell, but otherwise really good.

I take a step away, running my thumb across my throbbing knuckles to soothe the ache.

"I said that's enough! Take it outside," the mayor bellows over the chaotic chorus of cursing and cheering patrons, but no one is listening to her.

The second Ryker releases Houston, his hands fly to his bloodied face. "You little *bitch*," he growls at me, blood-tinged spittle spraying from his mouth.

Still fuming, I ball my hand and line up my next punch, only to watch Houston's head snap back when Ryker's fist connects with his jaw.

"*Goddammit*," Houston cries out, voice high-pitched and nasally as he struggles to remain upright. "She's the one who broke *my* nose, you fucking prick!"

"Yeah, well, you hurt her hand," Ryker says simply. Then, in one swift move, he swoops me up and tosses me over his shoulder like a sack of feed. My stomach slams into his shoulder, knocking the wind right out of my lungs.

"Put me down," I screech as soon as I can breathe again, flailing against his hold and kicking my feet.

"No fucking way." Ryker makes a muffled grunting sound, and then I'm momentarily airborne as he readjusts my position and wraps a single arm around both my legs, securing them firmly to his chest before heading for the door.

With my ass in the air and zero ability to cover myself, my face flushes with heat. "Ryker Bennett, put me down this instant!" I squawk as he weaves us through the fight.

113

"Not happening." He kicks the door open, and fresh evening air and a chorus of cicadas erupts around us. "What the hell was that back there?" he seethes. "Didn't Noah teach you how to throw a punch?"

"You're joking, right?" I grunt, trying to free myself—to no avail.

"*Fuck*." He rakes his free hand roughly through his hair, the tips of his fingers grazing my ribs. "If I'd known you were just going to try to break your hand, I never would've let you hit that guy. Your dad's going to kill me."

"You didn't *let me* do shit. I didn't need your permission to break that idiot's nose," I say indignantly, my voice so squeaky I sound hysterical.

It might be the vodka making me bold or maybe the adrenaline from punching Houston, but I'm tired of everyone thinking they need to protect me.

"Put me down." I kick my feet.

"Stop it, Willa," Ryker warns, voice low and dangerous, but I'm rearing for a good fight.

I aim the tip of my boot at his gut. "Or wha—"

Smack.

Ryker's palm connects with my ass, the sharp slap ringing out through the night air...

Heart hammering rapidly against my rib cage, I go entirely still.

Did he just...spank me?

Warmth seeps into my stomach, pulsing lower and lower until I feel it in my toes. Confused and slightly embarrassed, I squirm to get free. "Ryk—"

Smack.

He spanks me again, and I must be drunk or out of my damn mind because my body floods with a new sensation that's concentrated entirely at the apex of my thighs. Slowly, the feeling fans out until my skin is tingling and my brain feels all fuzzy.

What the hell is wrong with me? Why did that feel so...*good*?

With the sting still reverberating across my backside, all the other noise in my head goes quiet. My dad is probably already on his way to arrest me and my brother for punching Houston, but the only thing I can think about is the searing handprint-shaped sensation on my butt and the deep feeling of calm each time I inhale the rain-soaked pine and faint honeysuckle scent of Ryker's back.

Worse yet, I've clearly lost my mind because I want him to do it again. My pulse picks up, my breaths becoming shallower with each forced inhale.

"Behave," he warns, delivering another sharp *smack* across my ass when I start to squirm and accidentally kick him in the ribs. This time when his hand connects, I arch into it, letting loose a whimper at the delicious sting.

"Jesus. Knock that off," Ryker mumbles under his breath, the fingers of his opposite hand contracting against the back of my thigh.

My mouth drops open, my skin thrumming as every nerve ending in my body comes to life. "Ryker, I—" I don't even know what I'm asking for, but I need *something. "Please."*

"Please *what?"* His voice is low, his breaths uneven. "Put you down? Are you going to behave now?"

My body pulses like a live wire. "No," I say, biting my lip as I shake my head.

Ryker hums, like he's pleased with that answer, the vibration of his rumbling back against my stomach sending another wave of heat through my body. He pauses for a millisecond before removing his hand, then—

Crack.

He spanks me again, this time *much* harder. I cry out at the impact, the pulse between my thighs going wild and my head flooding with a warm glow. *Jesus Christ.*

"What about now, Princess?" I can hear the smile on his lips and feel the light electric buzz of his amusement in the air. There's something else there, too. Something dark and heady. "Are you going to keep fighting me, or do you think you've learned your lesson?"

A slight bubble of panic seeps into my consciousness. If I say no again, he'll realize I'm enjoying this. But if I tell him I'll calm down, he'll stop... I close my eyes, biting the inside of my cheek to ward off a swarm of emotions I'd rather not analyze too carefully.

To hell with it. He's leaving town soon anyway.

"I haven't learned anything," I say breathily, slowly inching my legs apart.

"*Fuck.*" Ryker's hand contracts again, fingers digging roughly into my leg for the briefest second before starting their painstakingly slow ascent up the back of my thigh—

"Uh, guys?"

Ryker's hand stops, and my head turns so fast to look behind me I think I give myself whiplash.

"Marco," I gasp, spotting Isabel's brother a few feet away. He lifts a brow at my squeaky tone, but I pretend like I don't notice. With Ryker's shoulder still digging into my abdomen, I glance to his left and right, but my brother is nowhere in sight. "Where's Noah?"

"He just finished puking in the bushes." Marco's eyes dart to Ryker then back to me, suspicion casting shadows across his handsome features. "I didn't have the keys to the Blazer or else I would have put him inside with the AC."

I exhale. "Thanks. I owe you one."

Eyes still narrowed, he shoves his hands into his pockets. "No problem. Y'all might want to hit the road. The mayor was calling the cops on my way out."

"Shit. Thanks for the heads up," Ryker mumbles, already striding toward the Chevy and making absolutely no move to put me down.

I wave to Marco as I'm carried away, the blood draining from my face when he waves back with his car keys in his hand.

Oh no. I can't drive after the drink Isabel made me...

"Ry-ker?" I say, but his quick pace is bouncing me so much it comes out stilted.

"We're almost to the car. I'll put you down in a sec." His grip on my legs tightens.

"No, that's n-not it... I can't drive us home." Shame coats my cheeks. What was I thinking? I was supposed to be the DD. I've never done *anything* this irresponsible before.

"I can drive," he says, sliding me down the length of his body to place my feet on the pavement.

Sirens sound in the distance, and I do my very best to concentrate on the problem at hand—and *not* think about the way his hard body feels against mine, or the way his warm palm is still lingering on my hip.

Heart racing, I shake my head. "You've been drinking, you can't drive us anywhere."

Unfazed, Ryker lifts an eyebrow. "Have you seen me drink a single thing tonight?"

I think back. "No, but—"

The hand he has on my hip slips into my pocket, followed by the sound of jingling keys. "Help me get your brother in the Blazer so we can get the hell out of here."

I nod and follow him over to the curb where Noah is sitting with his head in his hands.

"Time to go, bud," Ryker says, grabbing my brother's arm and yanking him to his feet. "Your dad's on the way and we've got to get you home."

"We can't go home 'til I sober up," Noah drawls, swaying unsteadily as he shakes his head. "Shit. I threw the first punch, didn't I? He's going to kick me out this time..."

Ryker looks at me as if seeking confirmation.

I bob my chin, holding his stare as the sirens draw closer. "Dad's going to find out either way, but it'll help if Noah's at least sober enough to defend himself. Wouldn't hurt if we found a way to wash the barf off his shirt either."

I move to my brother's side, draping his arm over my shoulder and helping him to the back seat so he can lie down. Once he's situated, I shut the door and turn toward Ryker.

"There's a water pump at the gas station on FM 31 that still works. We could clean him up there?" I play the driving route out in my head and curse. "Never mind, the cops are coming from that direction. We'd have to go right by Dad."

Ryker claps the back of his neck, pausing for a second before his eyes snap to mine. "Get in," he says, reaching for the passenger door handle and ushering me through the opening. "I think I know a place."

Chapter Twelve

Spine arched, I crane my neck, tracing the path of the rickety ladder leading up the side of Deadwood's very first water tower.

"You're kidding, right?" I say with an incredulous laugh. "Even if Noah was sober enough to climb that deathtrap without breaking his neck, he'd need a tetanus shot or a thousand stitches after slicing his hands open on the rusty metal. And that's *if* the whole thing doesn't collapse on us first."

As if emphasizing my point, the rusted structure groans in the light summer breeze, the sound not unlike an ancient monster rising from a long slumber. I shiver as the disconcerting clangor echoes through the surrounding hillside and swaying branches.

"The top of the tower has the best view of the fireworks in all of Deadwood." Ryker's eyes drop to mine with a devious smirk. "The danger just makes it more fun."

It's the first time he's acknowledged my existence after the awkward car ride over, and for some ungodly reason, his crooked grin has tiny wings taking flight inside my belly. I quickly stamp them out with a literal stomp of my boot.

"This isn't funny. Noah's in no state to climb that thing."

"You sure about that, Princess?" He inclines his head in the direction of the crumbling tower. "From where I'm standing, it looks like he's already halfway to the top."

My head whips toward the structure, but with nothing but the pale moon for light, I have to squint before I spot the human-shaped blur scampering up the ladder. Heart lodged in my throat, I take one step to follow his drunk ass, only to be yanked backward by my wrist.

"You do know you're not his mother, right?" Ryker says against the crest of my ear.

I whirl around, my well-practiced death glare firmly in place. "I like to think I'm a hell of a lot better than our mother, but thanks for the lovely comparison." I give him a sarcastic, squinty-eyed smile for good measure.

What an asshole. How dare he compare me to *her*.

Mouth pinched to the side, Ryker sucks in a breath through his teeth. "Sorry. Bad choice of words."

"Whatever." I yank my wrist out of his grip. "And just so we're clear, it's not wrong to look after the people you care about. You don't see me giving you shit for protecting Charlotte."

"Charlie's *nine*. And even she knows to keep her thumb on the outside of her goddamn fist when she throws a punch." He brushes past me, leaving a trail of rain-soaked pine and a hint of my honeysuckle body wash in his wake.

I sigh heavily and stomp after him. "I'm pretty sure Houston's broken nose would disagree with your bleak assessment of my fighting skills. I know how to—"

"Trust me, you don't." He grabs the base of the ladder, gesturing for me to go first with a jut of his chin.

Rolling my eyes, I slam into him on my way past and immediately wince. *Perfect.* With my shoulder still bruised from Beau and my hand sore from punching Houston, climbing this beast should be real fun. Face aimed skyward, I swallow audibly.

Should I even be doing this? Putting my life in danger definitely isn't on my bucket list—

"Your shoulder is fine." Ryker pushes me forward, like he can read my mind. "Your legs should be doing most of the work on the way up, anyway. Oh, and one more thing." He waits until I glance back at him before continuing. "Try not to look down. Noah will kill me if you freak out halfway up and fall to your death."

Too annoyed by his cocky grin to come up with a witty response, I scrunch my face into another mocking smile and grab the railing, trying not to think about how slippery the soles of my boots are on the metal rungs *or* the view I'm about to give Ryker of his lovely *handi-work* from earlier.

My ears heat. I'm more than happy to add that little lapse of judgment to my list of things I pretend never happened.

Annoyingly, it only takes a few steps up the ladder for me to realize Ryker might've known what he was talking about. Reaching over my head for the next rung is uncomfortable, but with my legs doing the majority of the heavy lifting, the bruise doesn't hurt too bad, nor does it encumber my movements.

I hate that he was right, but I also hate that we're here in the first place. Dad would lose his shit if he found out we were climbing this should-be-condemned monstrosity.

"I can't believe *this* is where you brought us," I mumble under my breath. "Should've just made Noah stay home with me."

"Do you even hear yourself?" Ryker scoffs, breath ghosting across my calves as he cages in my legs. "*This* is why I give you shit. You and Noah are so busy trying to protect one another that neither of you see how much you're holding each other back."

"That's not true. Noah is—"

A breeze rips through the hillside, the ladder swaying right along-side my rebuttal as I realize I was about to prove his point. My first instinct was to defend my brother, but shouldn't I defend myself?

"Holy shit, Wills!" Noah calls down from overhead. "You've gotta see the view. Hurry up, this is insane!"

A smile creeps over my lips, and I shake my head, the humid air whipping my hair across my face as I climb higher.

"You don't get it," I say over my shoulder. "Noah and I didn't grow up like other siblings—"

"Because you had a shitty parent and almost died when you were a kid?" Ryker snorts. "Who the hell hasn't? Trauma doesn't make you special, Princess. It builds character and gives you a good sense of humor."

My jaw drops. Jesus, that's dark. It also might be the funniest thing I've ever heard.

An unexpected laugh bubbles out of me and, momentarily distracted, I miss my next step. My boot slips off the ladder and my stomach lurches as I go weightless... But before I get the chance to panic, Ryker catches my heel, narrowly avoiding a blow to the face as he places my foot back on the rung. Even once I have my footing, he runs his rough palm up the back of my thigh, holding me in place a second longer than necessary, like he needs to reassure himself I'm not going to fall.

There's nothing overtly intimate about the touch, but I shiver all the same.

"I think I'm good now. Thanks."

Ryker's hand twitches before he removes it, finally freeing me to draw a full breath.

"You know," I clear my throat, continuing the climb and trying to ignore the tingling sensation where his hand was, "what you said about trauma was pretty funny. I think you might be the first person to acknowledge what my mom did to me without batting an eye. Dad and Noah avoid the subject at all costs, like they think talking about it will break me into a million pieces."

Ryker scoffs. "Yeah, well, closing your eyes won't protect you from the monsters hiding under your bed. And pretending something didn't happen just makes the wound fester, rotting you from the inside out. Kane's a prime example of that."

There's a slight edge to his voice that wasn't there a moment before, but what really gives me pause is how eerily similar his words are to Dad's motto. *Ignorance isn't a shield, it's a blindfold.*

We're almost to the top now, but instead of being excited, I find my pace slowing. Ryker and I have talked more in the past two days than the entire fourteen years we lived a stone's throw away from one another. He's different from what I remember, and while he still annoys me to high hell, I also find myself wanting to know more.

"What's Kane doing back in town anyway?"

"Who the hell knows." He pauses to guide my foot placement when he notices me struggling on a rusted out rung. "A few months ago, Kane had a falling out with that new-age bullshit church he was involved with in New Mexico," he says once we're past the unstable section of the ladder. "I hadn't heard a single word from him until he called to warn me about Beau trying to get custody of Charlie. I thought if he was back in Deadwood, it meant he'd come to his senses, but—"

A chill tiptoes up my spine. "But what?"

Before Ryker can answer, bootsteps pound on the metal grate above us.

"Will you guys hurry up?" Noah shouts. "The fireworks are starting!"

Reluctantly, I climb up the last few rungs and hoist myself over the railing, ignoring the burn of Ryker's hand on my bare leg as he once again steadies me. As soon as I dust myself off, Noah slides an arm over my shoulder and turns me toward the rainbow of explosions lighting up the night sky in four different clusters.

"Holy shit. That's incredible," I breathe, awestruck by the sight before me.

Everything in Deadwood is in some stage of decay, but up here, seeing her lit up in bright pops of color, you can almost pretend she's beautiful.

Ryker positions himself on Noah's other side, his face cast in alternating bursts of red and yellow light as he leans forward to rest his elbows on the railing. "On a really clear night, you can see the fireworks three counties away."

"This is legit, man. Fuckin' magical." Noah squeezes my shoulder. "Way better than sitting at home on the porch, right, Wills?"

"Way better." I laugh, still mesmerized by the white and gold flower-shaped explosions and the flash of green sparkles crackling like fairy dust in the night sky.

How can I ever watch fireworks any other way after this?

The display picks up in intensity, more fireworks going off all at once, both in our town and in the distance. The sound is deafening, and we're so high up I feel the blasts of light in my stomach and lungs.

Out of the corner of my eye, Ryker's head tilts in my direction, but I'm too in awe of the grand finale to risk missing a single second to figure out why. I want this view to be one of the last images I have of my town. For this to be how I remember Deadwood, not any of the other bullshit that's haunted my steps for so long.

Chapter Thirteen

The firework display is over all too quickly, the night sky once again cast into inky darkness as sulfur and smoke ride the light breeze, wrapping around me like a death shroud. It feels momentous, like the start of my final chapter in Deadwood.

I'm really doing it. I'm finally leaving this place...

"That was definitely worth the ass-chewing I'm going to get from Dad later," Noah says, mussing my hair to snap me from my thoughts of Austin.

I nod and push my long bangs out of my face. "Agreed."

With his opposite hand, Noah claps Ryker on the shoulder. "There's a spigot up here, right? I need to wash this beer-vomit off my shirt."

Ryker flinches, his reaction to being touched so subtle I don't think my brother even notices, but I do. Our eyes meet for the briefest second, and I'd swear his cheeks darken before he looks away.

"The valve is at the base of the tower," Ryker replies coolly. "I'll go with you."

"Not you too," Noah says through an exaggerated groan. "I've already got one babysitter, and I'm comin' right fuckin' back." He gives his best friend's shoulder a final squeeze and disappears down the walkway.

Sighing, I start to follow but stop when Ryker laughs.

"What?" I snap.

"You can't help yourself, can you?" he says with a snort and disapproving shake of his head. "He's fine, let him go."

My eyes trail Noah's descent for another beat before I reluctantly force myself to look away. Dammit, he's right—I was trying to take care of my brother. *Again.*

"I don't know what you're talking about," I respond with feigned innocence and a hair flip. "I was just going to check out the rest of the water tower."

Ryker lifts a brow.

"Oh, shut up." I push his shoulder playfully, like I would Isabel's or Noah's, and he winces, shying away with a small shudder...*as if I'd struck him.*

My chest pinches as I drop my hand and curl my fingers. "How does it work?"

Jaw hard, Ryker turns toward the railing. "How does *what* work?"

"You had me over your shoulder earlier and you were fine." I flush at the memory of his hand on my ass. "But now I barely touch you and you..."

"Flinched like a little bitch? Yeah, I know." He laughs humorlessly. "I don't have a problem with being touched. I just like to be the one to initiate it."

That's interesting. I wonder...

Stepping closer, I lean forward and rest my elbow on the railing next to his, close enough for the hairs on his arm to brush my jacket, but not so close that our arms actually touch. I know I shouldn't push him, but if he can call me on my bullshit, why can't I do the same?

"So, you like to be in control. Is that it?" I brush my arm ever so slightly against his.

"No, I—" Ryker starts to pull away, then stills, glancing down and then back at my face. "Clever." His eyebrows lift, his expression a mix between surprised and impressed. "Yeah, I guess I do like to be in control."

"Me too," I sigh.

"Could have fooled me," Ryker says through a moonlit smirk.

"Fine, I'll bite," I drawl, tone heavy with exasperation. "What's that supposed to mean?"

I follow the movement of his corded arm as he reaches into his pocket and extracts a pack of Marlboro Reds and his silver boot-shaped lighter. He tucks a cigarette between his lips but doesn't light it.

"It means I think you've been waiting for someone to step up and take the reins, or at least share the burden and give you a goddamn break every now and then, but no one ever does."

I laugh, but my tight throat makes it sound strained. "Do you have a degree in psychology I'm not aware of?"

Ryker shrugs, the cigarette now stuck to his lower lip bobbing with his response. "I don't need a degree to point out the glaringly obvious. Noah's trapped in an endless cycle of beating himself up over what happened to you. Your dad works himself to the bone so he won't have to face his guilt over letting it happen in the first place. And you... Well, you've been running around for years trying to make up for something that was never your fault to begin with. All of you need a fucking break. That's too much for one person."

A humorless laugh slides from his downturned lips as he gestures vaguely in my direction. "I mean, look at you. You're so fucking sick of having to take care of everything you're probably planning on leaving it all behind and running away from this place the first chance you get. So yeah, I'd say you hate having to be in control."

Stripped bare by his psychological scrutiny, I cross my arms over my chest, my jaw hanging open for a few solid seconds until I regain the ability to form words. "You don't know anything about me," I say with a less-than-ladylike snort—because how else do you respond to an accusation that presumptuous? Especially since he's wrong. I'm running away from Deadwood because it's the shittiest place on earth. Not because of my family.

Leaning on his elbow, Ryker angles his body toward mine. "Princess, I know more about you than you do about yourself."

This time, I laugh in his face. "Oh yeah? How do you figure that?"

"Because I *am* you." He shakes his head, like he's disappointed I didn't make the connection myself.

Affronted, I take a small step backward. Besides our affection for our siblings, Ryker and I are nothing alike. I'm a rule follower, he's a menace to society. I rarely take risks, he thrives off them. I am neat and orderly, he is a chaotic storm.

Then again, I was the one sneaking drinks while Ryker stayed sober tonight. It was also me who essentially started the bar fight, and he was the one who got us out of there...

Ryker squints. "You really don't see it, do you?" he asks, tone low, almost hurt. "You don't see how I've spent my entire life paying for the actions of others—spent every waking second trying to protect my brother and sister..."

He drops his head and scoffs. "You know what, forget it. It's not like any of us are going to change anyway. Your dad and brother will never stop feeling guilty. You and I will never go after anything we fucking want in life because we're too busy making sure everyone else is okay. I don't know why I'm wasting my breath."

Cupping the air around his unlit cigarette, he brings the lighter to his mouth but pauses, his eyes glinting in the moonlight as he lifts an inquisitive brow in my direction.

I'm so hung up on how much he and I actually do have in common and so distracted by the heavy feeling weighing on my chest, it takes me longer than it should to realize he's asking me for permission to smoke.

"Go ahead," I say, thrown a little by how quickly he went from basically telling me off to checking in—or that he would check in at all.

"You sure?" He waits, scanning my face.

"Yeah, the wind will carry most of it off. I need to get used to this sort of thing for school anyway." I nod my confirmation and lower my brow. "Can't let a little cigarette smoke stop me from *going after the things I fucking want in life,*" I tack on, sarcastically wobbling my head as I do a terrible impression of his deep voice.

Ryker's lips crack into a smile. "In that case, do you want to light it?"

Unfurling his fingers, he holds the lighter in his outstretched palm, the silver boot gleaming in the pale moonlight. For the briefest moment, my mind is filled with the image of a hundred flickering candles and a wall of flame. The scars on my back tighten and my stomach twists. But then I blink, and the image is gone.

There is absolutely zero part of me that wants to light Ryker's stupid cigarette, but I *do* want to prove him wrong—prove I *can* change—so I snatch the damn lighter out of his hand and stare at him defiantly.

"How do I work this thing?"

I wait for him to make a joke at my expense, or at least say something snarky about not knowing how to do something as simple as use a lighter, but he does neither. Instead, he takes the cigarette from his mouth and places it behind his ear.

"It's easy, you just use your thumb to press down on the spark wheel." He grabs the silver boot, pressing his thumb in a downward motion over the circular mechanism on the side until a tiny flame flicks to life before winking out of existence just as quickly. It happens so fast I barely flinch, although my pulse does kick up a notch.

"It's a little finicky, but once you get a flame, hold down the button to keep it going." He must sense my unease because he leans forward, the loose strands of his wind-blown raven hair falling into his eyes. "It won't hurt you. See?" He strikes the lighter again, this time bringing it up to his mouth and letting the fire flick back and forth across his outstretched tongue.

I should be afraid, but like a moth to a flame, I inch forward, my low belly clenching as the urge to rise up on my tiptoes and capture his mouth with mine becomes overwhelming.

The wind picks up, and the lighter sputters out. Ryker tries to restart it but only gets sparks. "Come here," he orders, snaking his arms around my waist and spinning me so that my back is pressed against his chest to create a shield from the wind.

It happens so fast I don't have time to overthink it, which is kind of thrilling. Everyone is always so gentle and cautious with me, but not Ryker.

"Your turn." He leans down, tilting my chin so I'm looking up at him as he lifts the lighter toward my mouth. I nod, but my limbs tremble with nervous anticipation.

Eyes locked on mine and with a softness in his expression I didn't think him capable of, he strokes my cheek with his thumb. "I won't let anything happen to you."

I nod again, this time more confidently because for some crazy reason, I believe him.

"Good girl," he says with a satisfied smirk that has my belly erupting with the phantom flutter of a thousand butterfly wings. "Open your mouth and stick out your tongue for me."

With my back still pressed against his chest and his thick arms barricaded around me, I slowly extend my tongue, never letting my gaze stray from his—not even when he brings the lighter to my chin and strikes the start.

I jump, every muscle in my body contracting as the lighter sparks to life, but there is no pain. In fact, I can barely feel the warmth dancing across the tip of my tongue.

My gaze drifts from the fire up to Ryker, the exhilaration blossoming low in my stomach making me feel feverish. He only keeps the flame going for a second, but by the time he pulls the lighter away, I'm already bouncing on my toes.

I feel invincible. *Alive.*

"I did it!" I squeal, cheeks straining under the stretch of my massive smile as I turn to face him.

"Fuck yeah, you did." Ryker's grin sets off an explosion of fireworks inside my chest. The approval and genuine excitement in his tone is so tangible that it sends a pulse of warmth radiating beneath my skin. I sigh in contentment—although I can barely hear it over the blood *whooshing* through my ears.

Adrenaline making me bold, I lean into him, my belly gently pressing against his groin as I stare into his eyes. "Do it again," I breathe, desperate to chase more of this feeling. "*Please.*"

Ryker sucks in a sharp breath, his chest hitching beneath my palm when I grab onto his shirt. Then his hands slide to my waist, his fingers digging into my flesh to grip me tighter.

My lips part in a silent gasp, and when his attention drops to my mouth, I forget how to breathe.

Releasing my hip, he trails a hand up the side of my neck and cups my jaw. We're so close now his chest presses into mine each time he inhales.

Heart in my throat, I rise onto my toes—

"Are you drunk?" he asks abruptly.

Dazed, I blink and draw my head back. "What? No. Of course not."

Ryker just stares at me, brows scrunching together like he's suddenly in pain.

Cocking my head to the side, I step out of his arms. I might've been buzzed earlier, and I definitely didn't feel comfortable driving, but all of that has long since faded. Why is he asking me this now?

A muscle feathers in his jaw and then he roughly removes the cigarette from behind his ear, shoves it between his lips, and lights it himself—a cloud of smoke temporarily shrouding his features.

My stomach sinks. *I thought he was going to let me do that...*

Ryker's cheeks hollow as he draws deeply from the cigarette, an orange glow tinting the opaque veil of tobacco rapidly filling the space between us. "You were drinking at Rib Cage," he says with a bitter laugh. "That's why you couldn't drive earlier. That's why you let me— *Fucking hell.*" Shaking his head, he takes another long drag.

"It was *one* drink." I cross my arms, unsure why I'm even explaining myself...*or* why he's acting like this.

Turning away from me, he leans on the railing and exhales a puff of smoke through his nostrils. "Doesn't matter, I'm not interested."

I throw my hands in the air. "Not interested in *what?*"

"Don't play coy, Princess." He dips his chin in my direction. "Your brother would kill me if I touched you. And like I already said, I'm not interested."

It takes my brain a second to reboot after short-circuiting. *He can't actually think I wanted him to— What, kiss me? No possible way. I was just caught up in the excitement of not freaking out about the lighter.*

"You're delusional," I say with a snort, my ears growing ridiculously hot.

Ryker glances at me out of the corner of his eye and quirks a brow.

I stomp my foot like a child. "Listen, asshole, I wasn't—"

Ryker lunges forward, his massive body crowding my space until I can barely think, let alone breathe. "Stop talking," he hisses, eyes wide and expression drawn as he backs me up against the rusty metal tank.

Head spinning, I swallow the lump in my throat, trying to ignore the physical and mental whiplash of his mood swings. "I don't know what game you're playing, but I'm—"

"Fucking *look*," he whispers, pointing at the grassy field directly below us.

The wind picks up, howling through creaking branches while the ancient water tower sways ever so slightly. I can't bring myself to follow his gaze, not when my muscles are already locking up at the sight of the growing orange glow reflected in his eyes...

I try to turn away, but Ryker grabs my chin, roughly pointing me toward the blaze burning in an almost perfect circle in the tall grass.

My knees wobble and sweat drips down my lower back. The fire isn't large, but it's bright enough to illuminate the surrounding forest...and the six shadowed figures gathering amid its smoky tendrils.

I tell myself not to look, but I can't tear my eyes away. Not when beyond the fire, barely visible against the distant black silhouette of the tree line, lies the Cartwright mansion. And beyond that, the ruins of Divine Mercy Bible Church where my mother tried to burn me alive.

Dread washes over me, extinguishing all traces of the elation from moments ago.

"*Fucking hell*, I think they're using some sort of accelerant to light the field on fire," Ryker growls, cigarette dropping from his mouth as he leans so far over the railing his boots lift from the metal grate. "That's the Crowes' land, right?"

I hear him speaking, but I'm too busy trying to blink away the wall of flames rising up in my memory to respond. My body locks up and I stop breathing, my blood pounding into such a dizzying crescendo my knees give out and I stumble into Ryker's back.

He flinches, but I grab onto his shirt anyway, burying my face before he can shrug me off. It's selfish of me to hold on to him like this, but I can't help it. All I can do right now is force myself to breathe so I don't pass out and topple over the railing.

"*Shit*," Ryker says, finally realizing I'm freaking the hell out. "It's just like the lighter, Willa. I'm not going to let that fire hurt you." He wraps his thick arm around my waist and presses me into his side.

"I want to leave," I whimper, voice muffled against his shirt and the hard wall of muscle beneath. "*Please*, can we find Noah and leave?"

"Yeah, okay. Promise me you won't look at the field until we're on the ground."

I nod, concentrating on the honeysuckle and rain-soaked pine scent of his skin instead of the smoke already threatening to suffocate me.

Letting me use his body as a shield, Ryker leads me to the ladder where he pauses to tie my lemon-scented bandana around my nose and mouth. "You'll tell me if you get dizzy on the way down?" he asks, gently making sure the knot is secure.

I think I nod, but I'm not really sure.

Eyes watering, I climb on the ladder after he does, focusing all my attention on the feel of his chest cocooned around my lower half during our slow descent. By some miracle, I manage to make it through the growing cloud of burnt foliage and the bitter tang of gasoline without falling to my death. When we reach the bottom, I can just make out the six shadows scurrying around the field through the white smoke billowing up around them like a bubbling cauldron.

My pulse picks up, my breath coming so quickly my head swims. "What are they doing?"

"I think they're putting it out," Ryker says, voice a mixture of concern and curiosity.

Holy shit, he's right. I can't see a single flame anymore... And here I am, still shaking in my boots like I'm about to die.

The sweat coating my skin turns sticky and oppressive. After the high of conquering the lighter on my tongue, I thought I was finally making some progress with my fear, but one glimpse of fire and it's like I've taken ten steps backward.

I glance over to the Blazer where Noah is passed out on the hood, using the windshield as a backrest. He slept through the whole thing. God, why is that even more embarrassing?

"Let's wake him up and get out of here," I say with a downcast shake of my head.

"Shouldn't we call the fire department?"

I wrap my arms around my middle, heart thudding against my forearms. "So Cooper Blackthorne and my dad can come yell at us? No, thank you. The fire's already out, anyway."

I sigh, still furious I let myself get so worked up. "That part of the Crowe Ranch butts right up to the Cartwright Estate. Idiot kids from all over come out here to vandalize the church and party in the surrounding woods. They probably ran out of beer and fireworks and are just messing around. I'll tell the Crowes about it in the morning."

"What if they're not kids?" he asks through a grimace.

The little hairs on my neck stand on end. "Who the hell else would they be?"

Just then, low voices begin chanting, growing louder with each second, like the low roll of thunder from an approaching storm.

Every hair on my body stands at attention as my head snaps toward the sound, but there's so much thick smoke lingering in the air, I can only tell that the shadows are fanning out, two of them moving in our direction. The breeze picks up, shifting some of the smoke...

My blood runs cold.

"Ryker, tell me you're seeing this," I whisper, already backstepping toward the car while I struggle to understand what I'm looking at. "Why are they wearing hooded robes?"

He doesn't get a chance to answer before a woman's voice slices through the night.

"Brothers and Sisters," she calls out, gliding over the charred grass to the center of their newly formed circle. "We've come so far, but our work has just begun."

A torch flickers to life in her hand, the flame licking skyward. Muscles tense, I take another quivering step toward the Blazer as she spreads the fire to the others in the group. One by one, their torches bloom in the darkness, smoldering bright orange and yellow against the black sky.

"This land is a blessing," the woman bellows, voice scratchy with strain and face obscured by the shadow of her massive hood as she extends her hands and lights the last torch.

"The fire is a cleansing," the others call back, raising their own flames in the air.

Ryker and I take one look at each other and sprint for the car.

Chapter Fourteen

The next morning, I wake to the scent of dark roast coffee and the savory aroma of hickory bacon.

It's dark out, which means Noah must still be under the influence and trying to teach himself how to cook again. *Perfect.* I force myself to sit up, groggily attempting to blink awake and failing miserably. As if I didn't already lose enough sleep from nightmares full of fiery fields and hooded monsters, now I have to go stop him from melting the stove—*again.*

Shrugging on a sweatshirt, I head into the hallway where I'm greeted by Dad's soft laughter. My shoulders instantly relax with the knowledge that the house is no longer in peril from Noah's drunk cooking adventures, but they stiffen right back up when I remember what happened at Rib Cage.

With a sigh, I glance over my shoulder at my door. I'd love to crawl back into bed, but Dad leaves for Austin today and this might be my only opportunity to explain the bar fight last night. Even though all three of us punched Houston, I have a strong suspicion Noah is the one who's going to get into trouble for it.

Rounding the corner, I spot Dad at the kitchen table with a cup of coffee in one hand and a piece of toast in the other. There are dark-gray smudges on his cheeks, nose, and forearm, and a big smile on his face as he talks to a sweat-drenched Ryker, who is currently removing sizzling bacon from the electric griddle in a pair of very sweaty running clothes that, judging by the cutoff sleeves, look like they belong to my dad.

It can't be sanitary to cook like that, but there's something so wholesome about the scene I can't find it in myself to interrupt.

"I mean it, son," Dad says through a bite of toast. "With the way this town is growing, I'll need people on the force whose judgment I can trust. And as long as you're twenty-one, you don't need a degree. The next academy is over six months away, but I might be able to work something out if you're interested."

"Thank you, sir," Ryker says, pulling the last of the bacon off the griddle and loading it onto a plate. "But I'm not staying in Deadwood unless Beau has custody of Charlie. And I refuse to let that happen."

He walks the bacon to the table, chewing on his inner cheek as he sets it in front of Dad. "But let's just say I *did* come back... Do you really think the chief would go for it? I did sort of torment him when I was a kid..."

I suppress a scoff. *Torment* is an understatement. To this day, Chief Thompson still claims Ryker and Noah are the reason he went prematurely bald.

Dad's answering smile lights up the whole room. "Doesn't matter what he thinks." He gestures for Ryker to take a seat. "Between you and me, Chief Thompson is retiring soon and I'll be taking over the department. Which means I'm in charge of filling the two vacant positions."

My fingernails dig into the wall. *That's* why Dad's been working so hard and acting all cagey about it?

I loosen my grip on the drywall. This is significantly less fun than a secret girlfriend. Not to mention how weird it is that he's keeping it a secret from me—especially since I sort of love the idea of him primarily stationed behind the safety of a desk.

"That's incredible, sir. Congrats. But did you say *two* positions?" Ryker leans back in his chair, running his palm over the rough stubble on his cheek, as if mulling something over. "Have you thought about asking Noah?"

Dad barks out a laugh, then clears his throat awkwardly when Ryker doesn't join him. "You're a good friend, but no. My son's got a whole lot of growing up to do. If Willa was old enough, I think she'd make a great cop. But she's got some time yet."

Dad glances in the direction of my bedroom, and I dart back into the hallway, stubbing my toe so hard on the back of my opposite heel I have to clamp my hand over my mouth to keep from screaming a slew of profanities.

I must've missed part of the conversation while I was wallowing in pain because when I peek around the corner again, Dad is shaking his head. "No, I haven't had a chance to tell her yet. I don't want her fussin' over me when she's got school to worry about."

"You don't think she's going to figure it out when she sees the badge on your shirt every morning?" Ryker asks with a laugh before sobering. "Seriously, you should tell her. I bet she'll be happy for you. But if you keep this a secret, she'll be hurt."

I swallow, unsure if I'm more annoyed that Ryker once again thinks he knows me well enough to make statements like that *or* by the fact he's one hundred percent correct.

"You're right," Dad says, extending his hand like he's going to pat Ryker on the shoulder but redirecting at the last second to grab a piece of bacon. "See what I mean? You're good at reading people. Just promise me you'll think about it."

"I will. Thank you, sir."

A comfortable silence falls between the two while they eat, and after a minute of stewing over why Dad wouldn't want to tell me about his promotion, I decide it's safe for me to announce my presence.

I force a yawn as I round the corner, heading straight for the coffee. "Morning."

"Mornin', sweetheart," Dad chimes. "You're up early."

Ryker doesn't say anything, but I catch his eyes running up the length of my legs from behind the rim of his mug—*and* the way he immediately averts his gaze, like he's disgusted by what he sees.

My ears heat as his words from last night come back to me. *I'm not interested.*

After pulling down the hem of my shorts to better cover my butt, I fill a cup of coffee for myself and open the dishwasher to unload the dishes, my head cocking to the side when I find it already empty. I glance around from one clean kitchen surface to the next. Not only is the coffee made and the toaster already put away, but everything besides the griddle is spotless.

It looks like it was done correctly, too. No streaks on the counters, no fingerprints on the fridge... I flounder for a minute, unsure what to do with myself without my list of dreaded cleaning tasks to accomplish.

"Dad, you didn't have to do all this."

"I didn't," he says into his cup. "I came home and found Ryker cooking and tidying the place up. He fixed the cabinet, too. Come sit."

My brow furrows as I eye the perfectly level cabinet hinge.

Inexplicably annoyed that Ryker fixed it so quickly when it would've taken Dad and Noah weeks to even look at it, I grab my coffee and head for the table, catching the subtlest hint of wood smoke and peppery aftershave as I ease into the chair next to Dad.

"Does that mean you just got in?"

"It does," he says with a long exhale before wiping at the gray smudge on the back of his hand. "We had five different fires pop up across town last night. It was a nightmare."

Uneasiness streaks up my spine.

"Did you find who set them?" Clutching my mug, I catch Ryker's eye across the table, trying to tell him without words not to mention what we saw or where we were. Noah's in enough shit without adding that he let me climb the water tower to the mix.

139

"Not yet, but don't worry yourself." Dad reaches over and musses my hair. "Everyone gets a little rowdy on the Fourth. It was probably just some bored teenagers. Now that the old Cartwright place is occupied, they're finding other ways to waste their time."

Ryker lifts a brow, eyes boring into mine like he's waiting for me to tell my dad it wasn't kids in that field…

I shake my head ever so slightly, again trying to convey my subtle plea for him not to say a word. Once I'm satisfied he's going to keep his mouth shut, I reach for the bacon, surprised to find that it's perfectly crispy without being overcooked—which again is a little annoying.

After quickly devouring the first two pieces, I grab another, catching the hint of a smile on Ryker's lips out of the corner of my eye.

Yep, definitely annoying.

Dad lets loose an exaggerated yawn, snapping me from my glowering. "I'm tapping out. I need a few hours of shut-eye before hittin' the road. Ryker, thank you for breakfast. You might be a better cook than Willa here, and you for sure make a better pot of joe."

"I wouldn't recommend biting the hand that feeds you, sir," Ryker replies with a chuckle. "But I'll take the compliment."

"Joel, son. I keep telling you to call me Joel." Dad winks at me and then reaches out to pull a feather from my hair. "Get into a fight with your pillow, kiddo?" His smile slips into a pronounced frown as he zeroes in on a lock of my hair before looking away.

I glance down to see if I have food or something else on me, but find nothing.

"Oh, Dad, before I forget," I start, pushing the odd look from my mind with a large gulp of coffee, "Old Man Dan asked if I could help out around the ranch a few more hours a week. He wants me to bring my pistol until they figure out what's been taking their livestock."

Dad rises to his feet with an exhausted sigh, his back cracking loudly as he stretches his arms over his head. "When did you clean it last?"

I roll my eyes. "Tuesday. When you *forced* me to go to the range with you...*again*."

Every once in a while, Dad decides I spend too much time on my own and plans a day of activities for us. We spend the morning fishing, the afternoon at the range, then grab dinner. Dad's not an overly emotional man or a big sharer, but he always has new smile lines near his eyes when we get home, and I always feel three inches taller.

Honestly, those days spent out in the sun are the only times I don't feel like I should be doing something else. Something *more*. Even the whispers and stares I get in town are less obvious when Dad's around.

A warmth spreads from the center of my chest out to my limbs as I stare at my father's soot-stained face. I don't tell him often enough how much I enjoy our little outings, but I should.

Last Tuesday, however, was an entirely different story. Dad insisted my brother tag along with us. A very hungover Noah slept through fishing, threw up the second we got to the range, and then proceeded to argue with our father for the rest of the day.

"Ah, that's right. You can grab it from the safe while I'm in the shower, then," Dad says before turning his attention to Ryker. "What are your plans today? If you still need to talk to Kane about Charlotte, feel free to take the Blazer. If the reports from Rib Cage were accurate, I don't imagine Noah will be awake or needing it anytime soon."

"He'll be up. We're going to track down Kane around ten." Ryker shifts in his seat, jaw hardening as he meets my dad's gaze. "For the record, Noah was defending Willa. That Blackthorne asshole deserved way worse."

Dad pinches the bridge of his nose, and I tense. Smoothing over the bar fight was the whole reason I came out here in the first place. How could I have let myself get so distracted?

"Oh, I'm aware. That's the only reason I didn't drag him out of bed the second I walked in the door. Well, that and the bacon." Dad lifts a brow. "Good trick, by the way."

My eyes bounce between the two of them and then to the empty plates and the spotless kitchen... That can't be what this whole break-fast charade was about?

Ryker shrugs, the picture of nonchalance as he relaxes into his seat.

Holy crap, that *is* what all this was about.

"I couldn't sleep," he replies with a smirk, eyes bright and full of mischief. "I went for a run and didn't know what to do with myself after. Breakfast seemed as good a task as any."

Dad laughs. "Like I said, you're a good friend with an excellent head on your shoulders. Think about my offer." He leans down to kiss my temple. "I'll be gone by the time you get back, kiddo. Look after these boys for me, will you?"

"Sure thing, Dad."

He smiles before trudging down the hallway toward the bathroom, shaking his head slightly as he mumbles to himself. "Thinks he can bribe me with bacon, *the nerve*."

Ryker drops his chin, his dark hair falling forward and a smile ghosting his lips. Then, just as quickly as it appeared, the look is gone and he puts two hands on the table, his biceps and chest flexing as he stands.

Throat dry and at a loss for words, I stare, dumbfounded, as he clears the table and starts loading the dishwasher. When he places the first coffee cup at an angle, I rise to my feet.

"The cups will fall over if you load it like that."

"No, they won't," he says, continuing to load dishes in a manner that makes my eye twitch. "This way, water won't collect on the top and everything comes out dry."

"But that's not how—"

"Not how you do it? Too bad, Princess."

I blow out a frustrated huff of air and attempt to move around him, but he steps in front of me, blocking my way to the dishwasher. I shift left, and he does it again, this time causing me to smack into his chest.

"You're working the ranch later?" he asks, popping my chin up with a knuckle and forcing me to meet his gaze.

I narrow my brows, but he just smiles. "I am..."

"There's no way a few pieces of bacon will get you through the morning, let alone the entire day." He points to the kitchen table. "Sit down and I'll cook you up some pancakes."

I blink at him, struggling to recall the last time someone actually made breakfast for me. Not that it matters. Even if I wanted to take him up on the offer, I never restocked our pantry.

"We don't have pancake mix," I say a bit too sharply before softening my tone. "I was trying to avoid good ol' Dorothy Blackthorne at the grocery store and didn't get to finish my shopping."

He rolls his eyes. "First off, you already have all the ingredients. I checked. Second, fuck Dorothy Blackthorne and the rest of those Blackthorne assholes. Except Charlie, of course."

A smile creeps over my lips. "Of course."

He grins back at me, and we just sort of stand there, staring at one another, my heart beating faster and faster until the sound of Dad dropping something in the shower breaks the moment.

Ryker clears his throat but doesn't move away. "Go sit."

"I can make breakfast for myself," I reply with a shake of my head. "Let me Google the recipe and—"

I squeal when he grabs my hips, hoists me into the air, and unceremoniously dumps me onto the counter.

"Fucking hell. You really don't know how to take it easy for a single second, do you?"

He crowds my space, his skin flooding my senses with a mixture of salt, pine, and hickory bacon as he plants his hands on either side of my ass to box me in. I swallow audibly, which only seems to encourage him because he leans closer, inching my knees apart with his hips until his nose is centimeters from mine.

"Offer still stands, Princess. I'd love to give you a lesson on how to relax. All you need to do is say the word."

Heat courses through my body, a pounding warmth settling in my center at the memory of the *lesson* he tried to teach me yesterday

—the way his rough palm slid up the back of my thigh and the sharp sting when he spanked me.

My breath quickens before abruptly stalling out when Ryker's declaration that he's *not interested* once again snaps me back to reality—because apparently the thought of me as anything other than Noah's little sister is laughable. He's clearly trying to mess with me, which makes my body's ridiculous reaction to him that much more embarrassing.

Just like that, the heat is overshadowed by the hollow pit forming in my belly. Ryker implied that I was safe with him up on that water tower yesterday. But this sure as hell doesn't feel safe. It feels... confusing and a little demeaning to have my defensive walls slipping while his remain so firmly in place.

"Why do men do that?" I whisper, not really expecting an answer.

He leans closer, trailing his nose along my jaw like a predator scenting prey. "Do *what*, Princess?"

"Pretend to flirt with a girl just to mess with her head? Cooper did it in high school." I push against his chest so I can gesture to his body between my legs. "You're doing it right now. I don't get it. We're not kids anymore. Playing with someone's emotions for your own amusement isn't funny or cute. It's cruel."

A weighty silence blankets the small kitchen. He opens his mouth, closes it, and then tries again. "Willa, I—"

The shower shuts off down the hall.

After a quick glance over his shoulder, Ryker pulls away, and my heart gives a painful thud as cool air rushes into the space between us.

Brow heavy, he backs up toward the other side of the kitchen— like he can't get away from me fast enough. Without a word, he takes out flour, sugar, and baking soda from the pantry. After removing a few more items from the fridge, he nods as if deciding something and then turns to face me.

My eyes drop to the floor, bracing myself for an insult. When it doesn't come, I glance up to find Ryker still staring at me with his hands on his hips.

"I'll play nice," he says thoughtfully. "But I need something from you in return."

Of course he does. I let go of an exhausted breath. "What do you want?"

"Let me make breakfast for you."

Blinking, I stare back at him, taking in the slightly hunched set of his shoulders and the way he's fidgeting with the hem of his shirt.

"Fine. Anything else?"

Ryker's answering grin is pure mischief. "Try not to let your ego get *too* bruised when my earth-shattering cooking abilities put yours to shame. Think you can do that?"

Eyebrow arched, I fight the grin tugging at the corner of my mouth.

"Always so arrogant," I chide, hopping off the counter and heading for the cabinet where I grab one of the Nutella jars and toss it to him. "Seeing how you already forgot the most important ingredient, I don't think my ego has anything to worry about."

Chapter Fifteen

With only the locusts for company, I traipse through the yard toward Crowe Ranch. At ten 'til six, the sun is just now peeking over the horizon, giving the eastern clouds an almost ethereal glow while the deep blue of night clings to its futile claim of the heavens to the west.

It's humid as hell, and while my Stetson, jeans, and lightweight flannel aren't exactly helping me stay cool, I'll be grateful for the protection from the sun later. What I'm *not* grateful for is how tight my pants are after eating *three* stacks of pancakes. I should've stopped after one, but with Ryker softly humming to himself while he cooked, I couldn't bring myself to say no each time he resupplied my plate.

I'm sure I'll have a massive mess to clean up when I get home tonight, but it was a nice change of pace having someone cook for me for once. It somehow made the drab avocado kitchen feel brighter and my morning way less lonely. The pancakes were also surprisingly delicious, and my reluctant enjoyment of them seemed to please Ryker, who said he'd be making French toast tomorrow.

I'm not gonna lie, I'm looking forward to being fed again.

Despite how tired I am, I cross over the property line of the ranch with the ghost of a smile plastered on my lips and a lightness in my step.

I glance toward the light streaming out from the half-round windows of the big house, then to the other structures dotting the property. The windows and doorways of the barn and the bunkhouse glow a warm-yellow while soft music plays from somewhere in one of the paddocks. Crickets chirp from their perches atop tall blades of grass, and cows bellow in the distant fields. A goat bleats, and a cowboy curses while the rich aroma of hay and coffee ride the thick morning air. Crowe Ranch is *alive*, and there's something about this place that's always given me a sense of nostalgic longing, although for what, I can't say.

I glance over my shoulder toward my house, where a single light remains on in the kitchen. Maybe I should've asked Ryker if he wanted to come along. He used to do odd jobs around the ranch before he moved, and Mrs. Crowe would've loved to see him. Hell, she probably would've put him to work for a few hours—at least until Noah woke up.

I shake my head. *No.* That's crazy. Ryker might've made breakfast and said he'd play nice, but that doesn't mean we're friends. I mean, he literally threw me over his shoulder and spanked me yesterday, for God's sake. If that's not an indication that I should steer clear of him, I don't know what is.

"Willa!"

I jump at the sound of Elanor Crowe's shrill voice and the steady click of her cane against the wooden wraparound deck. It's way too early to be using that volume, but judging by the gleam in her eye, she's likely been up for hours.

"You ready to track down some missin' livestock, darlin'?"

"Yes, ma'am." I bound up the steps, giving her a tight hug and breathing in her familiar almond-oil-and-clean-laundry scent that always reminds me of warm evenings spent on the wraparound porch watching fireflies.

Both sets of my grandparents passed away before I was born, so

Elanor stepped up to not only fill the role of surrogate mother but their vacant roles as well. When I was younger, she watched Noah and me when Dad was at work—usually bringing us to the ranch where we got ourselves into more trouble tramping around and over-feeding the animals than we would've if we'd been left home alone.

As I grew, Elanor became a confidant, helping me navigate the emotional turmoil that is early womanhood, including picking out period products when Dad was rendered mute on the subject and taking me to get a birth control implant in my arm last summer to help with my painful, irregular periods when Dad was too squeamish.

I adore Elanor and don't know where I'd be without her.

She squeezes me tighter and then releases me, snagging her sleeve on my hip holster when she pulls away.

"Oh good, you're armed and dangerous," she says with a wink, her tawny skin crinkling near her smile lines when she flicks the brim of my Stetson. "A gun won't be much use against skinwalkers, but it'll help against everything else."

"Do I even want to know?" I ask with an exaggerated eye roll. "Or is this going to be like when you told me about the Chupacabra and I couldn't sleep for a week?"

"I'm afraid skinwalkers are much worse," she says solemnly.

I look away, biting my lip to keep from barking out a laugh.

Mrs. Crowe has a habit of collecting cryptid legends from her transient ranch hands. When I was younger, her tales were full of harmless half-rabbit, half-deer jackalopes and fairy rings, but as I've aged, the legends have gotten progressively darker.

Any time the ranch gets a new hand, I brace myself for the day she shows up with an excited glint in her eye, knowing without fail that my nightmares will soon be plagued by various monsters—like the blood-drinking coyote-esque Chupacabra; the unholy half-wyvern, half-demon Leeds Devil; or the shape-shifting werewolf-like Rougarou.

If she's got a new creature to torment me with, I'd prefer not to hear about it, but I'd also never dream of robbing her of the joy of telling me.

Steeling my spine, I fill my lungs with a big gulp of fresh oxygen and make a mental note to invite Isabel for a sleepover this week. "Alright then, tell me about these skinwalkers."

Mrs. Crowe leans on her cane. "Let's hold off on that story until we grab the side-by-side. We've got a lot of miles to cover today and I don't want to scare you off just yet."

I breathe out a small sigh of relief but then cock my head.

"Side-by-side? We're taking a UTV instead of horses?" I try to keep the excitement from my tone, but it leaks through anyway. I'm of the firm belief that some body frames just aren't made for horse-back, mine being one of them. No matter how many lessons the Crowes gave me, I've never quite gotten the motion down, and no matter how hard I try, I always end up so sore I can barely walk the next day.

The Crowes, on the other hand, are old-school ranchers through and through. And while I've seen a few of the hands using four-wheel-drive UTVs, I never thought I'd see the day Elanor chose a vehicle over a horse.

"I'm afraid my days in the saddle are done." She pats her hip with a tight smile, the drawn set of her mouth and the deep sadness in her eyes sending a ripple of pain straight through my heart.

"Don't you dare make that face at me, Willa Dunn," she scolds playfully. "Age is a fate none of us can outrun, and I won't have your pity. Not when I've loved harder and lived better than most."

I force a weak smile, the weight on my chest heavier than it was moments before.

On the walk to the barn, I match Elanor's slow, steady pace, nodding along as she points out the birds emerging to greet the dawn. Above us, the sky fades from orange to pink, while the deep-purple horizon finally gives way to soft-morning blue.

Unfortunately, the exquisitely painted sky isn't enough to drown out the nauseating smell of manure as we pass the horse stalls.

Holding my breath, I untie the bandana from around my throat, unroll it, then retie it around my nose and mouth. Thankfully, I came prepared, the sharp tang of lemon essential oil giving immediate relief to my overwhelmed nose.

"We'll run the perimeter of the north fence to check for any holes or gaps a predator might be using to slip inside." Elanor grabs onto my arm when the path becomes uneven where rain washed away the crushed granite last month. "I've got lunches and water all packed up in the barn fridge. Be a dear and load them up for us when we get there."

"Sure thing."

Mrs. Crowe waves to a ranch hand I don't recognize. When he's out of earshot, she taps my shin with her cane. "By the way, I heard about what happened with Houston."

I grimace. Of course she did.

She tuts in displeasure. "We should've known better than to hire a Blackthorne. Daniel fired him as soon as we heard he was harassing you last night. Didn't even let the moron through the gate when he came rollin' in, drunk as a skunk, at damn near three in the mornin'. I won't have a man who can't respect boundaries workin' my land."

I grab the barn door, holding it open for Elanor as she wobbles through, her limp already more pronounced than it was when we set out from the house.

"You didn't have to do that."

Truthfully, I wish they hadn't... It makes my own actions feel ineffective. Like I couldn't defend my brother or myself and needed someone to step in for me. It's also frustrating that what started off as calling out an idiot's problematic bigotry somehow morphed into being solely about his unwanted advances on me...

"That's what family does, hon. We look out for each other." She points to the ancient yellowing fridge near a neat line of rusty red fuel cans. "Don't forget the lunches."

"On it," I say with a half-hearted smile.

"You ready for that skinwalker story?" she asks, shuffling feet kicking up a cloud of dust and hay as she heads for the side-by-side.

"*Ready as I'll ever be,*" I mutter under my breath, followed by a dip of my chin and a much more audible, "Hit me with it."

Elanor beams. "You've seen the man riding with Daniel?" She waits for me to bob my head before continuing. "Well, he and his family own a horse ranch out in Colorado."

"Why is he working here, then?" I grab the mini cooler and water from the fridge, wincing at the sharp twinge of pain in my bruised shoulder when I load them into the side-by-side.

Elanor frowns, a strained grunt escaping her thin lips as she plops into the passenger seat. "Chayton doesn't exactly work here. He's been shadowing Daniel to learn the business before we sell the rest of the herd to his family."

I stop dead in my tracks, clutching the roof of the UTV to steady myself. It'd been quite the shock when the Crowes cut their cattle operation by half last year, but this is damn near unfathomable. "What do you mean the *rest* of it?"

"*Ah*, well, I've been meaning to tell you, honey... Daniel and I are finally retiring."

"You're not moving away from Deadwood, though, right?" A jolt of panic zips up my spine. Austin is five hours away and Noah works in the Gulf half the month... If the Crowes leave, who's going to take care of Dad? More importantly, when will I see them again?

My pulse batters against my temples as I scramble into the seat next to hers.

"Hush now, sweet pea," Elanor comforts, extending a hand for me to take. "I can see that busy mind of yours going a mile a minute. We're not going anywhere. Not yet, anyway."

The tension in my shoulders eases as I place my hand in hers, but the crease in my brow remains. It feels like she's only giving me partial information. "What do you mean *not yet?*"

A soft smile stretches across her lightly freckled cheeks, one that doesn't quite touch her eyes. "After the herd is carted off, our plan is to sell off the majority of the land but keep the big house," she says, rubbing soothing circles over the back of my hand when my frown deepens.

"This is the natural order of things, sweet pea. People get old, children leave the nest. You and that brother of yours will leave one day, too. Although, I suppose Noah will insist on goin' wherever you go so he can look after you... Who knows, maybe once you two are out of the house, Joel will go out on a date every now and then."

There it is again, the reminder of how I hold everyone back.

I retract my hand, but Elanor just keeps smiling.

"You're stuck with me for a few years yet, darlin'. So unwrinkle that pretty forehead of yours and let's get to work."

Six hours later, we've found no sign of the missing livestock, but Mrs. Crowe *has* relayed every single horrifying fact she's learned about skinwalkers in excruciating detail.

I don't think of myself as someone who spooks easily, but the idea of malevolent shape-shifting beings that can take the form of any animal will haunt me for the rest of my life.

Each time a twig snaps, I almost break my neck trying to find the source of the sound. Even now, as we sit under the shade of a massive oak tree near some crumbling stone ruins on the ranch's northeastern fence line, I can't help but eye every hawk and rabbit with narrow-browed suspicion.

"Oh dear, I've terrified you, haven't I?" Elanor laughs, popping a dried apricot into her mouth. "One day on the job and I've already managed to scare you off. Daniel will be furious."

"You didn't scare me," I say indignantly, forcing myself to stop eyeballing the falcon soaring overhead. "And even if you had, I'd do just about anything for a car, including fighting a skinwalker."

"Is that so?" she says thoughtfully, like she's speaking more to herself than to me. "In that case, I might have a way to entice you back a few more times. Remind me when we get back to the house or I'll forget."

"Sure," I reply, although there's a high probability I'll also forget. Without a list to keep me on track, things tend to go in one ear and out the other. On the off chance I do actually remember, it's at two in the morning three weeks too late.

Something slithers in the grass next to me, and I scoot farther to my left, stopping when Elanor reaches for me.

"Not that way, dear," she says hesitantly. "You see those weed-lookin' flowers behind you—the ones with the thin stems and clusters of small white flowers on the top?"

I barely have to tilt my chin to see what she's talking about. "Yes, ma'am."

"That right there's hemlock. It usually needs to be ingested to be poisonous, but if you touch too much of it, you might find yourself hallucinating or on the wrong end of a seizure. You're gonna want to steer clear of it either way," she says, retying the bandana she used as a napkin around her neck. "We lost thirty head of cattle a few years back from just a few bales of hay tainted with that little devil plant."

Cautiously, I scoot away.

Skinwalkers, poisonous plants... I can't catch a break. It's bad enough that we decided to have lunch so close to the water tower and the burn patch from last night. What's Elanor going to tell me next, the stone ruins behind us are haunted by one of the Cartwrights who originally settled this land?

I am curious, though, what she meant by *usually* needs to be ingested... Is there a chance I could get sick from being close to it?

Something rustles in the bushes just beyond the fence.

Something *big*...

I scramble to my feet, fear constricting my chest with an icy grip as my toxic brain conjures up images of skinwalkers and the rabid Chupacabra. Attention on the tree line, I bring my shaking right hand to my gun, slowly sliding it out of my holster when a hunched shadow emerges from the thick cedar.

My blood screams, terror freezing my fingers in place at the sight of the unnatural shape before us. I squint, trying to understand what the hell I'm looking at, but with the sun blinding me, I still can't make sense of it.

What the hell is that thing... Where is its head?

"Kane?" Elanor calls. Rising unsteadily to her feet, she hobbles her way over to the rickety fence. "What are you doing out here?"

Reholstering my pistol, I bring my arm up to shield my eyes as Ryker's half brother lumbers out of the brush. His half-up, half-down raven man bun glints in the sun as he dusts off his pale-blue western-style shirt and tweed sport coat.

"Elanor Crowe," Kane drawls, sliding his wire-rimmed Jeffrey Dahmer-esque glasses up his nose before adjusting his silver bolo tie that looks like it's been molded into the shape of some kind of bug. "It's a pleasure seeing you out and about on this beautiful day."

At twenty-three, every item of clothing he's got on has to be thirty years older than he is...but it works for him—even if he is crazily over-dressed for this heat. The thing I can't get over is how different he looks from Ryker.

The Bennett brothers both have broad shoulders as well as their mother's black hair, defined cheekbones, and maiden name, but that's where the similarities stop. While Ryker is all hard lines and defined muscles, Kane is lean and slightly gangly. Ryker's style is a little 1950s and *a lot* of rock 'n' roll cowboy, while his brother's fashion sense is straight out of a 1970s western. Kane's not an unattractive man by any means, quite the opposite, but the way his oversized clothes droop off his shoulders definitely isn't doing him any favors.

"And who might—" Kane pauses, dark eyes twinkling in the after-noon sunlight before his mouth twitches up on one side. "Well, if it isn't Willa Dunn. Deadwood's very own phoenix. You sure grew up right, didn't you?"

He holds his hand out over the fence, palm facing upward and angled in my direction, beckoning me to him.

The hackles on my neck rise, but not wanting to be rude, I step forward, hesitantly placing my palm on his. The moment our flesh touches, a shiver ripples across my skin—the feeling so unsettling I almost rip my hand away.

Kane just smiles, as if my disquiet gives him satisfaction.

"Let go of the girl and answer me," Elanor says with significantly less courtesy than I'm used to hearing from her. "I asked what you're doing all the way out here. Our attorney already told you we'd consider your offer, but we're still thinking it over."

Kane releases me, albeit a bit slowly, and opens his arms—the same way someone does when showing a cop they're unarmed. That's when I notice the faded black leather book he's carrying. There's something red etched onto the cover, but I can't quite see what it is.

"You take all the time you need, Elanor. Selling the land is a big decision," he says with a solemn nod. "As to why I'm out here, I heard there were a few fires set around town last night. I needed to make sure my property wasn't affected." His eyes flash to mine, something unreadable in their depths.

Elanor's head snaps in my direction, brow knitted, as if she expects just mentioning fire around me will leave me shattered in a million pieces—which is exactly why I haven't told her what Ryker and I saw on her land yesterday.

"Well then, we'll leave you to it." Her tone is clipped and cordial, but her brow remains creased. "Come along now, Willa." She grabs my arm as if to pull me back toward the side-by-side, but I plant my feet, digging my boot heels into the dry dirt.

"Ryker's been trying to get a hold of you," I toss at Kane, hoping he feels the bite in my tone. "Are you seriously going to lay the entire burden of your sister's safety on your *younger* brother's shoulders?"

His expression hardens, a deep shadow flashing across his eyes that almost makes me regret saying anything. "My brother and I spoke a few hours ago and sorted things out." He tilts his chin up to watch the buzzard circling above us. "You should stop by the estate sometime. I'm working on some changes to the property I think you'd be interested in seeing."

What the hell? Why would he think I'd care about him rebuilding that godforsaken church?

I clench my fists. First the lighter, now Divine Mercy? It's almost like these Bennett boys have a sick obsession with wanting me to face my fears...

Kane's eye twitches when I don't answer. "Think it over," he says with a smile, but there's something about his toothy grin that makes my stomach crawl. "You can stop by any time, day or night. They have your name at the gate."

"Sure," I say offhandedly, already stepping away.

Kane inclines his head, his brow bone casting deep shadows beneath his eyes. "I'll be expecting you."

Chapter Sixteen

Mrs. Crowe and I searched the property line for ten excruciating hours and came up with absolutely nothing. No missing cattle. No wayward goats. Not even a mysterious hoof or bootprint.

I'm exhausted, I smell like dirt, and the heat of the day is radiating off my body like a furnace... And that's not even mentioning the appetite I've worked up.

My boots drag as I trudge my way across the yard and up my front porch steps, mentally going over what I have in the freezer while trying to decide what meal requires the least amount of effort to make. I've barely opened the front door when I'm met with the delicious, savory smell of beef, rosemary, and thyme. I think there's some garlic and onions in there too...but it might just be my sweaty pits.

Gag.

"Are you hungry?" Noah hollers from the kitchen while I kick off my boots.

My stomach grumbles loud enough for him to hear, but I answer anyway. "Freakin' starved. Where'd you pick up food from?"

"Didn't order," Noah says through a mouthful, already shoving a plate into my hands the second I finish hanging up my hat. "Ryker made it."

There's a momentary hitch in my breathing as Noah takes a seat at the table. *Ryker cooked this?* Grabbing the fork, I push around the mouthwatering mounds of roasted meat, potatoes, and carrots piled on top of fluffy white rice. Ryker must've also grocery shopped because while I might've had a few carrots left in the garden, I know for a fact none of the other ingredients were in the house when I left this morning.

Scanning the kitchen for evidence of a mess or an errant grocery bag, I find that besides the Crock-Pot and a bowl of rice on the counter, the kitchen is once again spotless.

The corner of my lip twitches up as I walk to the table.

Plopping into my seat by the window, I take a massive bite, groaning at how tender the roast is when it practically melts on my tongue. *Jesus.* Either Ryker really is a fantastic cook or having a meal made for you just makes it taste better.

"Where is he?" I ask, already loading up my next bite.

"Who? Ryker?" Noah mumbles, barely coming up for air from his own dish. "His truck was ready early, so he headed back to Denton."

"Oh." A heaviness drapes across my shoulders while a twisting feeling ravages through my middle. *I guess he got whatever information he needed from Kane...*

Noah laughs, chunks of rice flying from his mouth onto the table. "You don't have to pretend to be disappointed. I know how you feel about him."

My brow furrows. Is that what this is... *Disappointment?*

I shake my head. That can't be it. I'm just freaking exhausted after a long day.

Taking another bite, I chew slowly and search for a different topic of conversation. "I saw Kane today. Did he let both of you onto the property when he met with Ryker?"

Noah scrapes up the rest of his meal with a fork, swallows the overflowing mouthful in one bite, then leans back in his chair. "Hell no. We finally got a hold of him this morning, but it was near impossible to convince him to meet us at the gate. He's a fucking weird dude. Kept droning on and on about his vision for Deadwood and how the estate isn't ready yet."

That's odd... Why would Kane invite me to stop by?

Noah drops his gaze to the table and shifts awkwardly in his seat. "He asked a few questions about you and then called Dad a *deceiver*... The whole thing was unsettling as fuck."

I stop chewing, rethinking my own encounter with Kane. Unsettling is actually a pretty good way to put it. "Did you know he's trying to buy the Crowes' land? Elanor seemed less than pleased to see him."

Noah rolls his eyes. "No, I didn't, but can you blame her? Motherfucker looks creepy as shit. He's got to be robbing graves for those clothes."

"I kinda liked his outfit." I shrug before remembering the uneasy shiver that rippled across my skin when our hands touched. "But there's definitely something off about him."

"He was probably strung out," Noah says simply, reaching over to steal a carrot off my plate. "Ryker said that the religious group Kane was with—Children of Salvation, or whatever—were into heavy psychedelics use."

"Maybe that was it." It was more than that, but I highly doubt I could verbalize my feelings about Kane in a way that would change my brother's mind. I shift my food around on the plate and then glance around the quiet house. "Do you want to watch a movie tonight?"

Noah's entire body tenses the same way it used to when Dad would catch him sneaking cookies before dinner. "I don't think so." The table shifts, wooden legs squealing against the floor when he abruptly rises to his feet. "I'm going to bed early tonight—right now, actually."

Pausing my fork mid-route to my mouth, I glance at the clock on the microwave. "It's not even five o'clock. Are you hungover or getting sick?"

Pink splotches blossoming across his cheeks, he collects his plate, giving me his back as he heads for the sink. "Jesus, Wills, neither. One of the guys on the rig got fired and they need someone to fill in. I'm going to take a nap so I can hit the road in a few hours and catch the first boat out in the morning." Still not turning to look at me, he drops his plate into the sink...*without* bothering to rinse it first.

My brows scrunch together. Noah is the least experienced roustabout on his oil platform. Why would they call him? "Is this a seniority thing? They can't make you go in a whole week early, can they?"

"They're not forcing me, I volunteered. If I can get in the boss's good graces, he'll be more likely to give me the 28/28 hitch instead of the 14/14. You know how badly I want that month on, month off schedule." Noah's voice cracks, and after a quick cough, he suddenly becomes *very* interested in an invisible speck of dust on his shirt.

My eyes narrow. "You volunteered?"

"Yeah."

"For more work..."

"*Yes*," he insists, cheeks a deep shade of red as he angles his body away from mine.

My head cocks to the side. Noah *has* been vying for the twenty-eight days on, twenty-eight days off shift since he got hired, but I could've sworn he said he's not eligible to apply for another year.

I can't shake the feeling he's hiding something from me...

It's probably something stupid—like he got in trouble and needs the additional hours to keep his job—but what's the use in lying about it? Why is everyone in my life so hellbent on sheltering me from the truth? Dad doesn't want me to know he's taking over as chief of police, the Crowes kept their retirement plans a secret until the last possible minute... And now Noah.

"Is there any way you can get out of it?" I ask softly, making sure to keep my growing frustration in check. "With Dad gone, I was hoping we could hang out."

I shove another bite of pot roast into my mouth while Noah rocks back and forth on his feet, continuing to look anywhere but my face. Then his shoulders slump and he sighs, like he's resigning himself to an unpleasant task.

"Willa, I *want* to go in. With Ryker gone, it's not like there's much to do around here anyway. You understand, right?"

The food in my mouth dries out mid-chew. Noah might be lying about the reason he's volunteering for more hours, but whether he meant to or not, he just let a sliver of the truth slip through.

He's bored.

I shake my head and snort. "Sure, I get it. Why spend any more time in Deadwood or with me than absolutely necessary? It's not like Dad *specifically* planned his trip to Austin when he knew you'd be home so that I wouldn't be stranded without a car. It's not like you live here rent free and have all your meals made for you. Or like you—"

"For fuck's sake, Wills." Face twisting, he throws his hands in the air.

"Don't *for fuck's sake* me. I heard you the other day." No longer hungry, I push my plate away. "You shouldn't let Dad guilt you into staying in Deadwood on my account. If you want to go, then go. If you want to move, then *move*. Just don't lie to me about it."

"Willa, I was mad at Dad. I didn't—"

"Save it." I rise to my feet and brush past him, dumping my mostly full plate in the sink before stomping off to lock up my gun and wash off the grime of the day.

A few minutes of drowning my temper with a cold shower does wonders for my shitty attitude. Unfortunately, it also helps me see the hypocrisy of my anger.

Yes, my ego was bruised, but I can't blame Noah for not wanting to stay in Deadwood when I'm also actively trying to get out. Especially since I *still* haven't told him or Dad I'm going to school in Austin...

Leaning back under the spray, I fill my mouth up with water before spitting it out like a fountain and turning up the heat.

Muscles slowly unwinding in the steam, I glance around at all the details Noah, Dad, and I installed when we remodeled the bathroom last summer. Onyx river rocks on the floor, long black subway tile all the way up to the ceiling except for the massive window near the top that we put in for ventilation, and an entire wall of glass for the shower door.

It's the only room in the house that's not straight out of the seventies, and all I had to do was mention one time that I might want to study interior design before Dad encouraged me to find out if I liked it. He and Noah had the old shower demoed that same night, and we were at the hardware store first thing in the morning.

The bathroom took four weeks to finish, and by the end of it, I knew with absolute certainty I had zero interest in designing home interiors or remodeling.

Or in trekking over to the ranch for a shower ever again...

But it's always been like that for us. Preparing for job interviews with Noah. Covering household duties so Dad can get some rest after working long hours. No matter how big or small the need and despite all the shit the three of us have been through, we've always been there to support one another.

Until lately.

Now it feels like there's a growing river of secrets standing between me and the people I love most.

If I just told Noah about UT, maybe he'd want to stick around. It might even help him understand why I overreacted. Either way, we need to put this stupid tiff behind us.

Rinsing the last of the soap from my body, I sigh and shut off the faucet, pausing at the sound of heavy footsteps and a door slamming so loud it rattles the glass. Wrapping a towel around my torso, I step out of the shower, my wet feet padding against the cool tile as water drips onto the floor.

"Noah?"

No response.

I shake my head. He might be mad, but ignoring me is childish.

Unless that wasn't him, a small voice whispers in my head.

Skin sprouting goose bumps, I crack open the door to the main part of the bathroom, the steam that billows out momentarily making it difficult to see. For one horrifying second, I think the shadow in the mirror is another person in here with me, but quickly realize it's my own reflection.

"Noah?" I call again, pulse galloping as I peek into the hallway.

Still no response.

Adjusting my towel, I glance at my brother's vacant room before tiptoeing into the main living area...which is also empty. My nose wrinkles. Earlier the pot roast smelled delicious, now the scent is unbearably potent...and slightly different? There's an underlying note of sweetness to it that leaves a sticky feeling on my tongue, the same way overly aromatic perfume does.

Did Noah get a new cologne?

I glance toward the window, hoping to see his Blazer in the driveway, but that's empty, too.

A pit opens in my stomach. *He left...*

Intent on putting this stupid argument behind us, I turn toward the hallway to go grab my phone, but my steps falter when I spot a large egg carton perched precariously on the edge of the coffee table.

My head cocks to the side.

Closing the distance, I ignore the note taped on top and lift the lid, my nose scrunching when I find dirt and little green sprouts in each compartment.

What is this? Was Noah high?

I unfold the note quickly and scan the black handwriting scrawled across the yellowing paper.

There is no escape from the fire that devours in front of him.
No running from the blaze behind him.
Ask him where he goes. Ask him what he hides.

—N

The truth never stays buried.

Something is written above the last line, a signature maybe? But dirt and moisture have smudged whatever it is beyond legibility.

A chill runs up my damp skin, my head snapping left and right as my spine prickles with unease.

This isn't Noah's handwriting...

Which means someone else was inside my house.

I suck in a sharp breath, the potent smell of pot roast suddenly so overwhelming I feel dizzy. "Hello?" I call out, gripping the towel more firmly around me.

No one answers and nothing stirs.

I grab the carton again to look for another clue as to who might've left it, only to scream and hurl it to the floor when something cold and slimy slides across my thumb.

Breath ragged, I glance down, the tightness in my chest uncoiling as an earthworm slithers out of the spilled dirt. With one hand on my towel to keep it in place, I quickly scoop up most of the mess, leaving the note and clumps of dirt on the floor as I rush out onto the porch and toss the egg carton into the yard.

Darting inside, I quickly bolt the lock behind me before checking the back door and then the windows, verifying with trembling hands that everything is sealed up nice and tight.

When I've finally caught my breath again, I head straight for Dad's room to grab my pistol, suddenly very aware of just how alone I am.

Chapter Seventeen

The next morning, I drag my tired feet into the kitchen in search of a lifesaving pot of coffee.

After a sleepless night of tossing and turning with my gun tucked under my pillow, it took every ounce of my willpower to force myself out of bed, which makes the sight of my brother's dirty dishes still in the sink an unwelcome one.

Can't be bothered to respond to any of my texts or clean up after himself. What a winner.

The coffee pot sputters and bubbles, the louder-than-normal sounds making me jump each time a new waft of steam pops the lid. I tell myself to relax, only to startle again when my phone vibrates on the counter.

Too groggy and high-strung to care who it is, I ignore the text.

I'm really hoping the caffeine helps calm my nerves. Right now, it's taking all of my motivation to stand here and wait for the magic bean juice to finish brewing.

With Dad always working and Noah gone for two weeks at a time, it's not like I'm a stranger to being on my own, but last night was different. The unease of knowing someone had been in my house made me hyperaware of each tiny bump in the night. Every creak of the house settling felt sinister. Even the howl of the wind through the branches outside my window sounded like whispering voices. At one point, I thought I smelled cigarettes. Logically, I know it must've been some lingering trace of Ryker in the house, but I managed to convince myself someone was watching me outside.

Sighing, I rest my elbows on the cool tile counter and place my head in my hands. I need to relax and stop overthinking this. The note was probably Cooper Blackthorne's idea of a sick joke. It could just as easily be from someone pissed at my dad for a speeding ticket or an arrest. Either way, invading my home when I was alone and in the shower is a whole new level of messed up, even for Deadwood.

It's also the second note I've found—

I jump when my phone vibrates again, reminding me that I still haven't checked the text.

After pouring myself a massive cup of coffee, I lean against the sink and click on the message.

ISABEL

Did you make it through the night?

If you don't respond in the next sixty seconds I'm going to assume you're dead and I'll be PISSED.

I roll my eyes. In a moment of weakness, I'd texted to see if she'd come over last night only for her to tell me she was working.

WILLA

I'm alive, no thanks to you. How was Rib Cage?

ISABEL

Fine. That Houston asshole decided to stick around. He and Cooper got into a bar fight with some out-of-towners.

Great, another resident Blackthorne to deal with. I swear more of them show up every year. Pretty soon, they'll be an army.

ISABEL

Still want to hang out later?

WILLA

Yeah, do you mind picking me up?

ISABEL

No problem. I'll come get you around three.

I slide my phone across the counter and take a tiny sip of my piping hot coffee before heading to the fridge. Opening the door, I reach for the creamer on the top shelf, instead finding an oversized Tupperware container blocking my way. I shift it aside, but not before I catch a glimpse of its contents.

"No freaking way..." Grabbing the container, I wrench open the lid, my eyes fluttering closed as chocolaty, hazelnutty, French-toasty goodness fills the air.

My jaw gapes.

Ryker had to have been eager to get out of Deadwood, but he still followed through on cooking breakfast. *He even remembered the Nutella...*

I squeal and do a little happy dance on my way to the microwave. Throwing the whole container inside, I watch it spin around and around while my cheeks burn with a massive grin.

After binge eating a ginormous breakfast and forcing myself to clean up the dirt on the living room floor, I started obsessing over the note taped to the egg carton.

Ask him where he goes. Ask him what he hides.

I'd tried distracting myself in the garden, but the list of questions bouncing around inside my skull made that impossible. Why would someone break into my house to deliver barely sprouted seedlings and a cryptic message? Was the note about my dad or my brother?

Considering Noah's abrupt departure yesterday, it could be either.

When Isabel's VW Bug pulls into the driveway at exactly three, I'm already waiting for her on the sunbaked gravel. I don't even let her put the car in park before I rip open the door and throw myself inside.

"Well, hello to you, too," she says, brows pinching together as she points to the tear in my jacket sleeve. "I saw that the other night and forgot to ask what happened. Do you need my mom to sew it?"

Shit. True to her word, Isabel never asked any questions about my secret errand, which means I never actually told her that Beau hit me...

"*Nope*, I'm fine. I must've snagged it on something while cleaning," I offer a bit too casually.

She points to the dirt under my fingernails. "And what happened there?"

"I spent a few hours gardening this morning."

"And over there, in the yard by the porch?"

"Hot damn, woman. What's with the third degree?" I follow her gaze to the tipped-over egg carton in the grass. "Oh. That." I hesitate, biting my lower lip. "That's sort of why I wanted you to come over last night."

I explain what happened—the footsteps I heard from the shower, what I discovered in the living room—and then pull out the yellowing sheet of paper from my pocket.

"This is actually the second note I've found," I admit, holding it up between us. "I didn't keep the first one, but I'm almost *positive* it was on this same type of paper."

She lifts a single brow, like she can't decide how serious to take this. "Why the hell didn't you keep it? Do you at least remember what is said?"

My ears burn from the slight chastisement in her tone, and I shrug. "Something about fire and a cleansing? It was creepy, but I thought it was trash. Now, I'm not so sure."

"*Hmm.* Well, that's not very helpful, is it... Let me see this one." She snatches the paper from my hand and proceeds to type the contents into her phone.

That's smart...why the hell didn't I think of that?

Isabel's eyes slide back and forth across the screen, her frown deepening with each passing second while sweat continues to pool on my lower back.

"I think the note might be a weird paraphrasing of a Bible verse," she finally announces, brow set into a perplexed squiggle. "Listen to this."

Tilting her phone so I can see, she clears her throat and reads aloud.

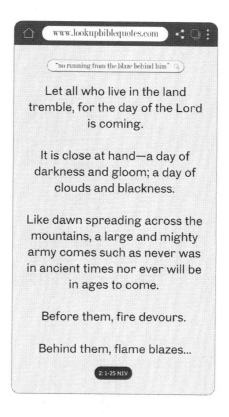

www.lookupbiblequotes.com

"no running from the blaze behind him"

Let all who live in the land tremble, for the day of the Lord is coming.

It is close at hand—a day of darkness and gloom; a day of clouds and blackness.

Like dawn spreading across the mountains, a large and mighty army comes such as never was in ancient times nor ever will be in ages to come.

Before them, fire devours.

Behind them, flame blazes...

2:1-25 NIV

Her voice trails off, and a shiver crawls up my spine.

"It's talking about the end of the world," she whispers with a new spark in her eye. "But that first part kind of sounded like the eclipse, didn't it? I overheard some people at Rib Cage saying the eclipse was the beginning of Judgment Day, or whatever the proper term is."

I blink, the scars on my back growing tight and itchy. "I wouldn't know," I say flatly. "My mom was always the religious one."

Awkwardness floods into the space between us, hot and sticky as the gleam in her expression dims. "Sorry." She clears her throat. "Do you mind if I keep this? I can ask around the bar to see if anyone's found something similar or knows where it came from?"

"It's fine, and go for it." I stare at the crumpled paper in her outstretched hand before chewing on my bottom lip.

Ask him where he goes. Ask him what he hides.

"The verse you read only covers the first section of the note. What do you think that last part means?" I tap my lip thoughtfully. "It says *him*, so it has to be talking about my dad or Noah, right?"

She hesitates, avoiding my gaze as she clutches the phone to her chest.

"What is it?" My voice cracks, but instead of responding, she glances at her screen again. "*Isabel*," I say, a little louder than necessary. "Spit it out."

In slow motion, she turns her head and locks eyes with me. "The passage I read was from the New International Version of the Bible... specifically from the book of Joel."

Swallowing the lump in my throat, I lean back in my seat.

She places a comforting hand on my shoulder, the pungent odor of her fresh nail polish stinging the inside of my nose. "Maybe you should show your dad when he gets back from Austin and file a police report?"

"Right," I say with an exaggerated eye roll, "because Joel Dunn has *never* overreacted when it comes to my safety."

Which, coincidentally, is *exactly* why I didn't call him last night.

Isabel grimaces. "Good point. If the note really is about your dad,

I guess he wouldn't be a good person to ask anyway. Maybe see what Noah thinks?"

"Yeah, I guess." My brother still hasn't called or texted me back, but I keep that thought to myself and opt for changing the subject instead. "What should we do today?"

She scrunches her mouth to the side, giving me some serious side-eye.

"Come on. I was up all night thinking about that stupid note," I groan and throw my head back. "*Please*, can we talk about literally anything else?"

"Fine," Isabel sighs. "Marco took a last-minute trip to Corpus Christi with some friends. We could hang out at his new place, eat all his food? Steal all his liquor?"

Still overly full from the French toast I ate a second serving of at lunch, I place a hand on my stomach. "I'm not really hungry and if I put a single ounce of liquid into my body, I think I might explode."

"Fair enough. I have to work tonight, so I shouldn't be drinking anyway." She hums. "We could drive by the old Cartwright estate and see what that freak Kane is up to? Exploring the mansion is on your list, right?"

"He's not a freak." I think back to what Ryker said about their stepdad using them as ashtrays. "Kane is just..."

"Creepy as fuck?" Isabel supplies flatly, a light waft of jasmine flooding my senses as she flips her hair.

"Well, yeah," I snort, momentarily forgetting that I'm trying to behave myself. "But seriously, the Bennett brothers had it rough growing up. We should give them a break."

Even if Kane does make my skin feel a little crawly...

"*Them*, huh?" She wiggles her brows. "I thought you and Ryker hated each other? Sounds like somebody might have used his magic fingers to change your mind..."

"Jesus Christ. He absolutely did not," I sputter, neck sinking into my shoulders. "I just realized we have more in common than I thought... He's different from what I remember."

My phone vibrates in my pocket. It's probably Noah finally calling me back, but I don't really feel like talking to him after the way he bailed on me, so I ignore it. As soon as the vibrating stops, it starts up again. I grind my teeth. He better not be expecting me to apologize. That opportunity disappeared the second he walked out of the house yesterday.

I whip my phone out, my muscles tensing when I see the name on the screen.

Incoming Call: Trouble

Wide-eyed, I tilt the screen to show Isabel. She mouths Ryker's name, and when I nod, she makes a *go on* motion with her hands.

I take a deep breath. "Hello?"

"*Fucking hell*, does no one answer their goddamn phones anymore?" He lets loose an exasperated sigh that sounds both frantic and relieved, but it comes out so forcefully I have to pull the phone away from my ear.

"What's wrong?"

"I can't fucking get a hold of your dad or your brother. Can you put one of them on, preferably your dad?"

I eye Isabel, who's leaning so far over the center console she's practically on my lap. Pushing her away, I put him on speaker. "Dad's in Austin and Noah left last night to pick up an extra shift on the rig."

"*Fuck!*" Sharp pounding pulses through the phone, like he's slamming his fist against something.

Alarm bells go off in my head. "What's wrong?" I ask again.

"Charlie is in Deadwood." Ryker's tone is grated yet even, like he's forcing himself to stay calm. I, on the other hand, feel like I'm about to lose the contents of my stomach.

"How is that possible?"

"I have no fucking idea," he says with a sigh. "I guess CPS did a home inspection last week and a visitation is the next step? All I know is that she'll be there overnight. I was hoping your dad could go over and make sure everything is okay. I'm still two goddamn hours away."

There's a long pause and then he says, "She's going to be alone... with *Beau*. I don't know what to fucking do."

Pain and desperation leak through the phone, wrapping around my lungs so tightly my eyes water. I force myself to take a breath and mull over possible solutions.

"I'll watch the house until you get here," I announce, verbalizing the idea as it comes to me. I glance over to Isabel to make sure she's okay with that plan, but she's already backing out of the driveway.

"*Too hot to walk*," she mouths.

My chest tightens further. She really is the best.

Ryker still hasn't accepted my offer, but there are faint traffic noises coming from his end of the line, so he hasn't hung up either.

"I could page my dad on his work phone? But I'm not sure what he can do from Austin," I say quietly, trying to elicit some sort of response.

With every second that ticks by, my heart rate kicks up a notch—right along with my anxiety. Did I overstep? Was I too pushy?

Just when my head is about to burst from the weight of his silence, Ryker clears his throat. "Don't page him," he grits out, and then a little softer, "Are you sure you don't mind waiting at the house?"

I nod before remembering he can't see me. "This is Charlotte we're talking about. Of course I'm sure."

"Okay." He breathes out a long sigh. "This could work. Don't let Beau see you, though."

"I won't."

"And if you see Charlie, tell her I sent you. If she asks you for a code..." The line goes quiet for a second. "Jesus. Just tell her it's Dildo Baggins."

"Dildo Baggins..." I stammer, undecided on whether I should laugh or not. "Does she actually know what that means?"

"I fucking hope not, but she has four foster brothers and says all sorts of crazy shit she doesn't fully understand yet." He laughs, the sound lifting some of the pressure off my chest. "Took me over an hour to talk her out of 'pterodactyl weenus' when I first brought this up, so I consider it a win."

I bite my lip to keep from smiling. "Dildo Baggins. Got it."

Silence leaks back into the line.

"Willa?"

"Yeah?"

"Thank you."

He ends the call before I can respond, and when I glance up from the phone, Isabel is already backing her car into a copse of trees across from Beau Blackthorne's house.

"What now?" she asks, putting the car into park and angling her body toward me.

I shrug. "I guess we wait."

Chapter Eighteen

It's so freaking hot I think the scorching boulder I've been sitting on has permanently fused my shorts to my flesh.

Over three hours have passed since Ryker's call and he's still nowhere to be found. Worse yet, Isabel left for work forty minutes ago and, as of thirty seconds ago, my cell phone is officially at three percent battery.

Where the hell is Ryker?

I'm tempted to call and ask, but with so little battery left, I need to make sure I can call for help if Beau does anything shady. I glance down the road to my house... It's so close and I'm *so* thirsty, but I can't leave. Not when Charlotte's still inside.

The caseworker pulled into the driveway about ten minutes after Isabel parked in the trees, then left about an hour after that. Thankfully, it didn't seem like she or Beau noticed us over here, but I'm pretty sure Charlotte saw me when she got out of the van.

As someone who hasn't been around kids often, I guess I thought a nine-year-old would be...bigger. She's just a kid—a baby, really—complete with dinosaur toys that she's been playing with on the windowsill since she got here. It breaks my heart to know she's been through so much at such a young age.

That any of us have.

Childhood should be sacred.

As if sensing my thoughts, Charlotte looks directly at me from across the street. I thought I wasn't noticeable, perched on my rock beneath the slender pines and thick cedar. Apparently, I was wrong.

I wave, and she waves back before disappearing from the window altogether.

Shit. How can I tell what's going on in there if I can't see her?

To hell with it. If Ryker's going to be delayed, I want the kid to at least know she has someone looking out for her.

Jogging across the street, I creep through the yard and crouch below one of the windows. I'm just about to peek inside when the front door cracks open and out walks Charlotte.

"Hi," I whisper, realizing I must look like an absolute weirdo. "My name's Willa, I'm Ryker's...*friend.*"

"I know you," she says, a little too loudly for my comfort. I glance toward the screen door and take a few steps backward, but Beau doesn't appear.

I wait a few extra seconds, and once I'm sure we're not in the line of sight of any windows, I take a seat in the dirt. "Yeah? How do you know me?"

"Well, I don't *know you* know you," Charlotte says, inching closer, "but you're the girl with two-toned hair. My brother told me about you."

"Really?" I ask, hoping whatever Ryker said wasn't too mean or this kid is never going to trust me. Just in case, I lean back against the house to make myself less intimidating. "What did he say? Did he tell you how smart and funny I am? Or how good I am with animals, or that I can say my ABCs backward?"

"No," she says matter-of-factly. "He said if you could walk through fire and survive your evil parent, so could we."

Jesus. I fight the urge to clutch my chest. That's a sentiment no kid should understand. Especially not one who still smells like crayons, for God's sake.

Charlotte glances around the yard, her lower lip trembling almost imperceptibly as the sun bounces off her nutmeg-brown ponytail.

"Where's my brother? I thought he'd be here."

I pat the ground next to me. "Ryker's on his way. He asked me to come hang out with you until he gets here."

She lifts a skeptical brow. "Hang out?"

Poor kid, she has no reason to trust anyone after what she's been through. "Oh, that's right," I say, smacking my forehead with my palm. "He told me to tell you..." *I can't believe I'm about to say this to a kid...* "Dildo Baggins."

Jesus Christ. They're going to put me on the registry for that one.

Charlotte's high-pitched giggle pulls me from my mortification spiral, and in the blink of an eye, her entire demeanor changes as she grabs her belly and chuckles like a little old lady.

"Oh my gosh. We've never had to use the code word before. That was so worth it. Your face—" She doubles over, plopping onto the ground next to me. "That was awesome. You can call me Charlie, by the way."

I stick out my hand, and she shakes it, her delicate green-and-pink dinosaur bracelet jingling with the action. "It's nice to meet you, Charlie."

She sighs and sags against the house.

"Rough day, huh?" I ask, forcing a note of positivity into my tone while leaning over to bump her with my elbow. "You'll be home with your foster brothers before you know it."

After meeting my gaze for a fraction of a second, she wraps her arms around her shins, her tiny shoulders slumping forward to rest her cheek on her knees. "If it goes well today, the CPS lady said I'll move in with Beau next month."

My stomach drops. *Next month? Ryker's going to lose his shit.*

"I'm so sorry, Charlie. Your brother's been doing everything he can to stop that from happening." Unsure how to ask my next question, I chew on my lip. "Has your dad been nice to you since you got here? He hasn't yelled or—"

The eye roll she gives me could rival my own. "Beau fell asleep the second the lady left. I think pretending to be nice tired him out."

Now it's my turn to laugh, although my heart is heavy as I do. "You're pretty observant." I give her another soft elbow to the shoulder, and she dips her chin, the hint of a smile peeking through her Blackthorne-brown bangs that have just a touch of red in them when the light hits.

"My brother says the same thing." She sounds so proud when she says it, like his opinion of her is the highest compliment.

"What else does he say? Any words of wisdom you think I might benefit from?"

"*Umm*. Our actions are more important than the things we say? Somethin' like that..."

"Words are cheap," I whisper more to myself than to Charlie, but she nods anyway.

"Exactly!" She looks left and then right before raising her eyebrows conspiratorially. "He also tells me to stand up for myself and not to take shit from anyone. But I'm not supposed to say that word at home."

"That's solid advice, and don't worry, I won't tell." I laugh, but there are so many emotions clogging up my throat it comes out strained. "Ryker's a good brother, isn't he?"

Charlie beams at me. "He's the best."

***

Hours later, the sky is a deep shade of orangey-pink and Charlie and I have talked about everything under the sun. I know her favorite movie—*Jurassic Park*. I've learned the names of all of her foster brothers and their dog—Chewbarka—and that she wants to be a paleontologist when she grows up. She also made it a point to tell me that her brother is her best friend and if I'm not nice to him, I'll have to answer to her. Since she didn't mention Kane's name once, neither of us needed to clarify which of her half brothers she meant.

A grumbling noise interrupts our conversation, and I grab my stomach before realizing the sound came from the tiny tummy next to me. "You hungry?"

She puffs her cheeks and blows the hair out of her eyes. "Yeah, but Grandma Dorothy is coming by with dinner. Beau said I can't eat 'til she gets here or I'll spoil my appetite."

I frown. *It's almost eight. Isn't that a little late for kids to be eating dinner?*

The grumbling grows louder, and my head snaps toward the road in search of Dorothy's van. The tension in my chest eases when I spot the rusty-brown silhouette of Ryker's pickup in the distance.

Jumping to her feet, Charlie sprints toward the road before I can even stand, leaving behind the scent of crayons and green-apple shampoo in her wake. For one second, I get nervous Ryker won't see her, but he slams on the brakes, coming to a screeching halt before throwing open the door and meeting her halfway.

Charlie launches herself into his open arms, and they hug each other fiercely, her face nestled into the crook of his neck and his eyes shut tightly. The low murmurs of their hushed conversation reaches my ears a moment later, but I'm too far away to hear what they're saying.

Ryker lowers her to the ground and takes a knee, brushing the hair away from her face and running his palms down her arms like he needs to reassure himself she's unharmed. I drag my boots against the dirt road, kicking up little plumes of dust as I walk with deliberate slowness to give them space, but they're still talking by the time I make my way over.

"I promise I'll never leave you on your own again," Ryker rasps, gently taking her chin into one of his massive hands. "Do you hear me?"

"I wasn't alone," Charlie says with another one of those killer eye rolls. "Willa told me that you sent her. She gave me the code word and everything." Charlie chortles, bouncing on her toes until Ryker is forced to release her face. "You should've seen how awkward she was when she said it. It was so much funnier than I thought it would be."

His moss-green eyes flick to me for the briefest second, a thousand emotions flashing through them at once. "Willa was here the whole time?"

"Yeah, she was outside when I first got here. And when her friend left, she hid in the bushes like a weirdo." Charlie looks over her shoulder at me and lowers her voice in that childish way that's not actually any quieter. "She's really pretty. You never mentioned that before."

Ryker rises to his feet with an exasperated groan and ruffles her hair. "Of course I didn't. A person's value isn't based on looks. And Willa was kind of a jerk to me when we were kids."

Charlie shoves her hands into her pockets, taking a tiny glance at me with a sly grin before returning her attention to her brother. "So you have a picture of her on your home screen because you *don't* think she's pretty?"

My cheeks flush with heat at the same time a deep voice rings out. "Girl? Where the hell are you?"

Ryker drops to his knee. "Go," he says, placing a hand on each of her shoulders. "I'll be outside all night if you need anything. If Beau makes you feel scared for any reason, *leave*. I'll be parked next to those trees across the street."

"He told me to call him *Papa*," Charlie says, face scrunching together in obstinate disgust, but there's a new hesitancy in her tone and a wobble in her lower lip that makes the pressure on my chest unbearable.

Ryker grabs her face and brings his nose so close to hers that their foreheads touch. "I'm right across the street. I'm not going anywhere. I promise."

Charlie nods, her lower lip quivering.

"Hey, it's okay," Ryker whispers, wiping away a tear with his thumb. "You still have the iPad I gave you?" Charlie gives him a little nod. "Good. Use it to message me when he falls asleep and when you wake up. Okay?"

"Girl!" Beau calls, this time from the junk-riddled backyard.

"*Hurry*," Ryker urges.

Charlie takes off, ponytail bouncing behind her as she reaches into her pocket and removes a little dinosaur figurine that she fidgets with along the way. Something cracks inside my chest, and I find myself fighting back the waterworks threatening to spill from my eyes. She's so little...far too young to have been exposed to any of this. And her poor brother...

When I turn around, Ryker's in the same spot, leaning forward with his head in his hands.

"If he so much as looks at her the wrong way," he growls at the pavement, "I'll fucking kill him."

Without being fully aware of what I'm doing, I close the distance and crouch next to him. I don't say anything. Not when we both know words won't change what's happening or make him feel any better, but I want him to know I'm here. That I see his pain, even if no one else does.

"There was a fucking car accident on the highway," he grits out after a second or two. "Then my phone fucking died while I was talking to my attorney about filing for guardianship of Charlie. I didn't mean to be so late. Thank you for being here."

"Anytime. She's a good kid."

Ryker glances at me, jaw hard and eyes unreadable. "I mean it," he says. "Not many people would have stuck around for over four hours... You really came through for me. Thank you."

"Y-you're welcome," I stammer, thrown off-balance by the sincerity in his tone.

Ryker stands, grabbing my bicep and dragging me up with him. Instead of releasing me or stepping back to create space between us, he draws me closer, a heady mix of tobacco and pine swirling around me. It's not quite a hug, but our chests are pressed up against one another, his nose and mouth so close to mine I can taste his last cigarette and the caramel candy he must've eaten after.

"I—" His voice cracks, and he clears his throat. "I should move my truck before Beau sees it," he all but whispers, making no move to step away or let me go.

"Okay," I say breathlessly, searching for some explanation as to why the air swirling around us feels charged, like a storm is on the way and we only have seconds to get ourselves free of its path.

As the humid wind whips my long bangs into my eyes, Ryker reaches up and pushes the hair out of my face, tucking one of the unruly white strands behind my ear. Instead of dropping his hand, he lets it linger there, fingertips barely skimming the crest of my ear.

My heart hammers against my rib cage at the ghost of a touch while my muddled brain struggles to find a reason not to lean in... He's so close it's difficult to breathe.

Ryker's throat bobs as he swallows and slides his hand down my hair to the rapid pulse point on my neck. He pauses for a single second before trailing lower to trace my collarbone with the pad of his finger, never once shying away from the burn scars obstructing his path.

I shiver, my breaths coming quicker as his gaze drops to the swell of my breasts, and when he licks that pouty lower lip of his...my knees all but buckle.

Jesus. No one's ever looked at me like that before—so feral and hungry.

Molten heat spreads from my chest to my low belly as I struggle to make sense of what's happening and why there's a thrill of exhilaration thrumming through my blood. Just like there was after he held the lighter to my tongue.

Ryker's head drops an inch closer to mine. "I'm going to go move my truck," he says again, a muscle feathering in his jaw, like he's trying to force himself to do exactly that but can't.

A smile tugs at the corner of my lips. "You said that already."

Ryker blinks and, like a bubble bursting at the slightest hint of provocation, the moment is gone—the shrill song of the cicadas in the nearby pines and muggy summer air enveloping me as he releases my bicep and takes a step back. "Wipe that smile off your face, Princess."

Already missing the closeness, it's on the tip of my tongue to tell him to *make* me, but without the heat of his body fogging up my brain, I just nod.

"Move your truck. I'll go grab the spare charging packs for our phones and be back in a bit."

Shoving his hands into his pockets, Ryker drops his head. "You don't have to—"

"I know," I say, already backstepping on the road. "Hurry up and hide your truck. Dorothy's on her way over, and she'll rat you out to Beau."

"Right," he agrees with a startled shake of his head, like he's just now remembering why he's here in the first place.

Knowing I should go but struggling to actually walk away, I scuff the dirt road with the toe of my boot and blurt out the first question that comes to my mind. "Do you really have a picture of me on your phone?"

Ryker throws his head back and laughs. "It's not what you think," he says, reaching into his pocket for his cell before unlocking it and flipping it around so I can see the screen. "Charlie's just a little shit stirrer."

I glance down at the old picture of me, Noah, and Ryker in our fishing gear lighting up his phone. He used to invite himself on so many of our family fishing outings that I can't remember when or where this was taken, but it's a good picture. The sun is bright and the leaves on either side of the river are bursting with variations of vibrant red and burnt orange, the three of us centered perfectly between them.

"Your dad emailed me some pictures a few years ago," Ryker says, dragging a hand through his hair. "This was the only one where all three of us were smiling."

I lean closer, noticing how my head is dropped down mid-laugh while Noah stares straight at the camera with the mischievous smirk he saves exclusively for the punch line of dirty jokes. Then there's Ryker, who's standing slightly off to the side with his gaze locked on me. Instead of the scowl I always remember him sporting, there's an uncharacteristically soft smile gracing his full lips and a longing gleam in his eye that cracks my chest wide open—leaving me exposed and vulnerable.

Swallowing the lump in my throat, I glance up at him, nearly stumbling over my own two feet when I'm greeted with the same soft expression he's sporting in the photo.

"Ryker—" I don't know what I was going to say, but the sound of a distant car engine saves me from having to figure it out. "Go move your truck and I'll see you later, okay?"

With a tight-lipped nod, he shoves a hand into his pocket and heads across the street.

For several beats, I just stand there and watch him go, wondering why he'd want a picture of all three of us in the first place. When I finally tear my eyes away and set off for home, my thoughts are still entirely consumed by that damn smile.

Chapter Nineteen

Sometime later, I trek down the half-mile stretch of road to Beau Blackthorne's house with a packed-to-the-brim Yeti cooler slung over my still-bruised shoulder.

I brought chips, sandwiches, fresh veggies from the garden, a few bottles of water, four separate thermoses of coffee, and a portable charging bank for Ryker's phone.

Unsure whether or not he actually *wanted* my company, I took my time showering and changing into a pair of leggings and an over-sized Fleetwood Mac T-shirt before finally working up the courage to make my way back over.

The last remnants of my gravel driveway crunch beneath my feet as I step onto the dirt road, the echoing sound punctuated by the synchronized song of crickets and cicadas under the star speckled sky. The air is laced with the scent of dried grass and the dirt I'm kicking up, but it's surprisingly temperate—which isn't saying much since anything under ninety degrees feels like heaven this time of year.

My stomach vibrates with nervous energy and my hands tremor slightly with each step I draw closer. Readjusting the cooler strap, I try to tell myself that this is fine, *it's just Ryker*, but that makes the jittery feeling worse.

Something rustles in the tall grass, and my head snaps left, horrid images of the snarling Chupacabra and all the other cryptids Elanor tortures me with flashing through my mind with terrifying clarity.

Quickening my steps, I squint and peer into the inky blackness. But it's useless. It's so damn dark out here a creature could be five feet away and I wouldn't see it until after it'd already taken me down.

Darkness is something I never really appreciated before my visit to the University of Texas at Austin campus last year. I hadn't realized that the city never gets dark—not really. Not like *this*. Not so dark you can barely see your nose in front of your face. Out here, something is always watching you, and nine times out of ten, you're never the wiser.

A chill skitters up my spine, but it's swiftly erased by the pungent scent of tobacco tickling my nostrils. My lips twitch up on one side, and the tension in my shoulders instantly softens as I step into the spindly grass.

The burning ember of Ryker's cigarette flares to life when he steps out from the tree line, an ocher glow briefly showcasing the deep hollows of his cheeks and heavy set of his brow.

"You came back," he says, voice low and rough.

"I said I would." Needing something to do with my hands, I fuss with the cooler strap.

"People don't usually follow through with their promises when it's inconvenient." He inhales another deep drag and closes the distance, leaving the cigarette perched precariously between his lips as he takes the cooler from my shoulder. "Come on, we can sit in the truck for a bit."

I glance across the street, zeroing in on the well-lit living room window where Beau looks like he's passed out on the couch. I shift my gaze, spotting Dorothy bustling in and out of the kitchen. "Where's Charlie? Shouldn't we be closer to the house?"

Ryker takes one last drag before dropping the cigarette and

grinding it into the dirt with his boot. "She just went to bed. I was saying goodnight at her window when I overheard Dorothy arguing with Beau about staying the night and making breakfast. Charlie won't be alone, so as long as we know where Beau is, we're fine over here."

Exhaustion radiating off his body in palpable waves, he lets loose a long, tobacco-scented exhale, his unkempt hair falling forward as he dips his head.

My fingers twitch with the need to reach out and brush the dark strands away from his face. Instead, I quietly follow him to the truck hidden in the trees, pausing in mild surprise when he not only opens my door for me but waits until I'm situated before softly closing it.

Still debating whether I should have come back or not, I rub my sweaty palms on the rough pattern of the striped wool Serape blanket covering the worn bench seat. It's too dark to see much detail, but from what I can tell, the interior of the truck is well kept and clean, especially for something that's almost fifty years old.

My nostrils flare. It smells like Ryker in here, but there are other scents, too—the unique hay-like odor of the wool blanket, the comforting smell of old leather seats, and something else that reminds me of dusty back roads and cool evening breezes.

The rusty hinges of Ryker's door creak when he climbs in, the truck swaying gently as he settles his massive form onto the seat and closes the door. After he places the cooler on the floor near the shifter, a tense silence creeps into the cabin, settling into the space between us and coiling around my throat until I can't breathe.

I shouldn't have come. This is too awkward. What the hell are we going to talk about? Noah would kill me if—

"Why did you hesitate when I opened the door?" Ryker blurts, his gruff voice cutting through my spiraling thoughts.

I clasp my hands together, struggling not to wring them. "I didn't."

"Don't play coy. Are you afraid to be alone with me?"

Terrified, I think to myself.

188

"Of course not. It's just…" I exhale sharply, cursing myself for what I'm about to admit. "I'm not used to you being so nice. It caught me off guard, that's all. People don't usually open doors for me," I add as an afterthought, not wanting to disrupt the tentative truce between us by dredging up old wounds.

Ryker manually cranks down his window before leaning into his seat with a scoff. "None of the morons you've dated open doors for you?"

Thankful for the darkness hiding my heated ears, I roll down my window and breathe in the warm summer air. "This is Deadwood," I say with a humorless laugh, making sure to keep my head angled away to avoid seeing his reaction. "The *morons* in this town are too scared of my scars to ask me out, and Noah and Dad are pretty good deterrents for anyone who isn't."

Muscles tightening, I wait for the teasing, but it never comes.

Ryker sighs after a long stretch of silence. "I fucking hate this place."

"Me too," I admit. Then, comforted and emboldened by our shared animosity for the town we grew up in, I add one more thought. "Sometimes it feels like the ghosts in Deadwood have more power than the living. I can't even remember my mother *or* what happened to me, yet here I am, haunted every single day by what she did."

"You really don't remember any of it?" His voice is thick with an emotion I can't quite pin down—curious and somehow probing.

"Not really. I was four and only know what I've been told, which is that Dad was at work and Mom ordered Noah to go to his room and not come out for any reason. I guess she and I walked up to Divine Mercy using the path behind our house—like we had a hundred times before—but when we got there…" My voice trails off.

"You don't have to keep going."

I shake my head. "I've just never said this out loud before. No one's asked…"

Ryker leans back in his seat, patiently giving me the time to figure out how to continue.

189

A wall of candle flame flashes through my memory, but I swallow down the lump in my throat and blink them away. "My mom was really sick during her pregnancy, and my birth was even worse. According to Noah, it didn't get any easier for her when they brought me home either—I had colic as a baby and frequent ear infections as a toddler that made me cry through the night," I clarify at his confused expression.

"I guess my mom got it into her head that all those complications meant I was possessed. Once we were at Divine Mercy, she tried to perform an exorcism by carving a cross into my back and anointing me with holy oil as I bled on the church floor." I touch my back and then the white streaks at the top of my forehead to show him where.

"No one really knows what happened after that, but it's safe to assume she realized the exorcism didn't work when I continued wailing like a banshee. After that, she must've decided the only solution was to burn the whole place down with us in it." I allow myself one shuddering breath before continuing. "I get flashes of the fire and a wall of candles every now and then, but otherwise, I don't remember any of it."

"I guess that's for the best," he says with a slow shake of his head. "A memory like that would leave scars time could never heal."

"Really, Ryker?" I deadpan, trying to lighten the mood by gesturing to my hair and shoulder. "You had to use *that* phrase?"

A small smile curves his lips, but then a light shutting off across the street has our heads whipping toward Beau's house.

"It's just Dorothy locking up," he says with a sigh of relief when the kitchen light goes dark next. Thankfully, the flickering blue and white of the television allows us to see Beau snoozing on the sofa.

"Hey, there's something I've been meaning to ask you," I say as Dorothy settles into a recliner next to her son.

"Shoot."

"If Beau's a felon now, how can he file for custody of Charlie?"

Ryker scoffs. "Beau's Uncle Abbott has been using every connection he has as a judge to smooth over Beau's history with the law. On paper, the accident that killed my mom looks like a momentary lapse in judgment on his part. Not that the courts care. They just see it as one more kid reunited with their family."

My stomach roils with indignation. "But aren't there records of what happened to you and Kane? Why would they consider placing your sister in an abusive household in the first place?"

"There are no official records. It's one of those things everyone knows about but turns a blind eye to. Everyone except your dad." He glances over at me, but it's too dark to see his expression.

"He tried for years to get my mom to file a report. She refused and guilted me into staying quiet by claiming that she wanted to keep our family together. She said the state would take us away from her or some bullshit like that. Now that I'm older, I realize she was just as scared as we were." There's so much bitterness dripping from his voice that I'm drowning in it.

"What about Kane? He was older, he should've—"

Ryker holds up his hand. "You don't understand. What Beau did to my brother was... It was worse than what he did to me. More frequent, too. He—"

Bile rises in my throat as Ryker struggles with his words.

"The day Kane turned eighteen, he finally agreed to let your dad help us. He took my brother to the hospital and—" He shakes his head. "I guess they wanted to do an assault examination or collect evidence? Whatever it was, the second Kane saw the rape kit and the camera, he recanted his statement and accused your dad of making the whole thing up."

A heavy weight settles on my lungs, but before I can fully process that gut-wrenching information, he's speaking again.

"A Blackthorne in the room across the hall overheard the commotion and immediately called Beau to warn him what was going on." Ryker goes rigid. "I tried to keep Beau and Mom at home...but he was so fucking drunk. And Mom was so fucking pissed when she realized not only was Kane going to the cops and breaking up our *happy* family, but I knew about it. She wouldn't let me explain..."

He drops his head and lets go of a bitter laugh. "Beau crashed on the way to the hospital to confront your dad, and none of it mattered in the end because my mom was dead and we were all separated anyway. I should have just filed the report myself while I still had the fresh marks to prove it. But Beau was gone. I thought we were all safe..."

Jesus. "Couldn't you do it now?"

"I tried the first time he was up for a parole hearing, but Abbott Blackthorne shut that shit down before the ink dried on the paperwork. Kane might have a solid case, if he ever decided to pursue charges, but I can't ask him to go through that. He's not ready to."

A raging storm of emotions battle for dominance inside my chest. My heart aches for Kane and Ryker, but the murderous rage pumping through my veins demands I march across the street and smother Beau in his sleep. On top of it all, there's also guilt and confusion for not knowing any of this was happening.

I have vague memories of the night Ryker showed up at our house with Charlotte on his hip and a duffle bag on his shoulder after his mom died. But at the time, I'd been such a mess over the whole Cooper Blackthorne incinerator fiasco, I barely acknowledged his existence.

Further back, I have fuzzy memories of Ryker sitting at the dinner table with bruises on his arms and cheeks, but he was always picking fights with the older kids at school and constantly finding new trouble to get into on the ranch. That's not an excuse, though. Maybe I just didn't want to see that someone was struggling more than I was...

I shift in my seat, reaching for the hem of the blanket to fidget with and ignoring the slicing pain down my middle when Ryker flinches—like he thought I was reaching for *him*. "I should have done more to help you."

"Don't worry about it," he says, gripping the wheel with both hands. "You were dealing with your own shit."

"More like not dealing with it at all," I snort, once again grateful for the darkness hiding my embarrassed flush.

"It's fine, Princess."

Ouch. Even without malice behind it, the nickname stings more than it usually does.

Ryker and I have both experienced unexpected bumps in our lives, but when things got difficult for him, he stepped up and took care of his sister. What did I do? Let half the town baby me while tolerating the other half's bullying. I never even tried standing up for myself. How could Dad and Noah *not* think I'm fragile?

Even so, at least I had them *and* the Crowes to lean on. Ryker only had my family. Well, part of it. I never extended a hand. Not once.

That realization weighs so heavy on my chest I'm having trouble drawing in a full breath. "I was jealous when you left," I confess in a rush, a single crazed snort bubbling up from my throat. "I guess you were right. I really am a spoiled little princess."

Ryker tilts his head in my direction, his expression unreadable in the shadows. Then he slowly reaches over and takes my chin between his thumb and forefinger. "You'll get out, too. Whenever you're ready, you'll leave this place in the dust."

My lower lip quivers when I nod.

Ryker swipes his thumb back and forth across my chin, the tip of it grazing against my bottom lip until the trembling stills. When he lets go, silence floods in through the open windows, taking the heaviness of the moment with it.

After a minute, he angles his body toward me. "If you could live anywhere, where would it be?"

Grateful for the change of subject, I drum my fingers across my thigh, thinking over my answer. "I've never been anywhere outside of Texas," I admit. "But I think I'd be happy anywhere with trees and water. Bonus points if it's not humid and I can watch the leaves change color in the fall." I turn, pulling my knees up to my chest and

193

resting my back against the door. "What about you? Do you like Denton?"

"Not particularly. I—" He stops speaking abruptly and leans over the steering wheel to stare intently at Beau changing positions on the couch. "What was I saying? Yeah, Denton is fine, but I only went to UNT to be close to Charlie. I want to work in law enforcement so I can help kids the same way your dad tried to help me. After that, I'll retire young and buy some land. A ranch or a farm, maybe." He holds an arm out, moving it from left to right with an outstretched palm. "I want lots of open space—far enough away from town that I don't have to worry about neighbors. You don't get that in a big city."

"Something like Crowe Ranch, then?"

He nods. "Exactly. Just not in Deadwood."

"Of course not. *Never* in Deadwood." I grin to myself, remembering how often Ryker walked past our house to see if Old Man Dan had any odd jobs for him when we were kids. When there wasn't any work, he'd challenge ranch hands twice his age to a race on horseback. He'd win occasionally, too. Usually wearing the same jean jacket he has on now, the fabric billowing in the wind behind him and a smile plastered on his wind-chapped cheeks.

There's a sudden pressure on my lungs as I realize those were some of the only times I saw him smile. Then again, after seeing the picture on his phone, maybe I wasn't looking...

"You should do it—run a farm," I clarify. "I think you'd be good at it."

"Yeah?"

"Mm-hmm." I bite my lower lip to keep from laughing at how pleased he sounds with my assessment. Exactly like Charlie did when I mentioned how observant she was.

"Maybe that's what I'll do, then." Ryker's teeth flash pearly white in the darkness, and something tight uncoils from around my chest at the sight.

Chapter Twenty

A car door *clicks* closed, and my eyes flutter open to take in my surroundings.

It's so bright out I have to squint, but I'm still in Ryker's truck, my cheek squished against the open window frame while my hair is gently tousled by the light breeze.

I shoot up. "What time is it? Where's Charlie?"

"Mornin', Princess," Ryker says, a small grin crinkling the corners of his eyes as he turns the key in the ignition and the engine roars to life. "It's a little after eight-thirty, and Charlie just left with the case-worker. She's fine, not a scratch on her."

I grab the oh-shit bar as Ryker pulls the truck onto the road, the abrupt motion causing the cloth draped over my body to slide to the floor. Brows knitting together, I grab the familiar jean jacket and rub the worn denim between my fingers. Did he cover me with this when I nodded off?

That's...unexpectedly thoughtful.

Pinching the bridge of my nose, I try to think back to the last thing I remember. After binge eating the snacks, we'd taken a lap around the house to make sure Beau was still asleep. Ryker was telling me about his major... Criminal Justice, I think? Then I have a vague recollection of him pointing to the east when the sky started to turn pink...

"How long was I asleep?" I yawn, wincing as I catch sight of my ghastly reflection in the windshield.

Good lord, did I get run over by a tractor?

"Two-ish hours," Ryker says, the current of air from the open window whipping his hair around his face and threatening to dislodge the cigarette perched behind his ear.

I blink. We spent the whole night talking. Not that you'd know it by the sight of him. Besides the dark circles under his eyes, his clothes are unwrinkled and his raven hair is still styled in that messy way that seems purposeful but isn't.

What the hell? How is he this put together when I look like a discarded Troll doll with my two-toned hair sticking out every which way?

We take a sharp right turn into my driveway before Ryker promptly shuts off the engine and climbs out. I'm about to reach for my handle when I notice he's still holding his door open, waiting for me. After scrambling awkwardly across the seat, I seize the opportunity to frantically smooth down my hair and rub the dried drool off the corner of my mouth while Ryker grabs the cooler.

It doesn't help my appearance one bit, and I swear I catch the faintest whisper of a chuckle when Ryker brushes past my shoulder to retrieve two large duffle bags from the truck bed. His shirt rides up as he leans over the edge, and my stomach coils tightly at the sight of his muscular lower back.

"Are you planning on staying for a while?" I mean for the question to sound sarcastic and annoyed, but it comes out a little breathy and excited. Probably because it's taking all of my concentration to pretend like I wasn't just ogling the shit out of him.

Hoisting the bags and cooler more securely onto his shoulder, he turns to face me. "As long as it takes to make sure Charlie doesn't wind up with Beau."

"Don't you have a job back in Denton?" I reach for the cooler, but he brushes me away.

"Not anymore," he says bitterly, averting his gaze to the distant horizon. "I was canned and evicted within thirty minutes of getting back on campus. Fucking bullshit."

My face scrunches up with confusion. Ryker spent a good hour telling me about his work-study program as a teacher's aide last night, but he never hinted that he'd been fired...

"What happened?"

"I was here instead of at work." He juts his chin toward Beau's house with a pointed look that has my mouth falling open.

"You're kidding. They fired you and kicked you out of your dorm because you had a family emergency? They wouldn't make an exception once you told them what was going on with your sister?"

A muscle in his jaw ticks. "As far as my boss was concerned, there was no excuse for missing three days of work." He rubs his hand roughly across the stubble on his chin. "The thing that really gets me is that I've been his TA for two years. I've literally been to the man's house for dinner. I attended his daughter's christening, for fuck's sake... But the very first time I slip up, none of that seemed to matter. He wouldn't even give me a chance to explain. The motherfucker told me to *stop causing a scene* and walked away."

Judging by the heated disdain drenching his voice, there's a good chance he *was* causing a scene...but after learning that Ryker's mom didn't allow him to explain what was going on with Kane the day she died, it makes sense he'd be defensive about not being given the chance to explain himself.

My fingers twitch as I struggle not to reach out and comfort him. "I'm sorry that happened," I say instead. "Thinking you know and trust someone just makes it that much more of a betrayal when they finally show their true colors."

Ryker glances at me out of the corner of his eye, his brows pinched like he's mulling over my assessment. "Yeah, I guess it does." He clears his throat and once again readjusts the bags on his shoulder, even though they haven't moved. "Anyway, I texted your dad this morning, and he said I could stay with you guys until the Charlie situation is cleared up. If you're not okay with it, I can start looking for another place this afternoon. I'm dead on my feet, though. Would you mind if I crash here for a few hours first?"

Is he asking me for permission? Even though Dad already said it was fine?

I shake my head. "You stayed here a few days ago without consulting me, why are you asking now?"

"A night or two is one thing, a month or more is a lot to handle." He quirks a bushy brow. "This is your house. I won't invade your sanctuary any more than I already have if you don't want me here."

Well, I'll be damned. Someone's actually consulting me on something that affects me...

I'd have been fine with him staying here anyway, especially since he's back in town for his sister. But I like being asked more than I'm willing to admit, not to mention it creates the perfect opportunity for me to set a few ground rules.

"If I let you stay," I say, tapping my lip thoughtfully, "will you clean up after yourself *and* leave the main bathroom door unlocked so the rest of us can pee and brush our teeth?"

His green eyes twinkle with a hint of amusement in the bright morning sun. "Sure, I can do that. Anything else?"

Fighting my own smile, I push further. "Actually, there is. Can you cook breakfast and dinner once a week *and* do the dishes after?"

The corner of his mouth twitches. "How about three times a week? I'll even let you show me how you like things cleaned so I don't fuck it up."

"Sounds great." My heart thuds inside my chest. He's almost being *too* agreeable... I wonder how far I can take this. "I also want you to stop calling me Princess."

"Not a chance."

A smile breaks free of my lips. "Okay, fine. But everything else stands." I hold out my hand. "Roommates?"

"Roommates." He takes my palm in his, and the gentle way his thumb caresses my skin sends a thrill of excitement straight up my arm. "But," he says a moment later, voice so low the air between us vibrates, "I have a condition of my own."

"What is it?"

Ryker tugs me closer, and I think I stop breathing when he bends forward to whisper against my ear. "Let me teach you how to throw a punch so you don't break your goddamn hand."

My ears flush with heat. That is *not* where I thought he was going with that...

Yanking my hand free of his, I march toward the door. "Absolutely not," I toss over my shoulder. "I'm more than capable of knocking a man out. Don't make me prove it."

He snorts. "Whatever you say, *Princess*."

Even with my back turned, I can hear his smirk as he tries not to laugh. Desperate to keep this newfound peace between us, I decide to let it slide. "Do you have a preference for Noah or Dad's room tonight?" I ask while unlocking the door. "I can change the sheets in either."

"The couch is fine." He bounds up the steps after me, mumbling something I can't quite hear but sounds an awful lot like "*Fucking Noah.*"

Confused, I lead him inside the well air-conditioned house, glancing around for any sign someone might've been in here while I was away.

As far as I can tell, there are no new notes or creepy egg cartons full of dirt. I wait for the unease to settle back on my shoulders, but with Ryker grumbling to himself a few feet away, the house once again feels safe.

He bends over to set his bags on one of the couches, and I bite my lower lip, definitely not checking out his butt and how incredible it looks in those tight Wranglers. I mean, *damn...* You could bounce a quarter off that thing.

Ryker stands, the grin sliding right off his mouth the second he turns to face me. "Don't *fucking* look at me like that," he says through gritted teeth.

"Like what?" I reply a bit too quickly for someone feigning innocence.

"Like you want me to throw away fifteen years of friendship with your brother for a single taste when I've already told you I'm not interested," he growls, eyes trailing a path from my mouth to the crest of my thighs.

My knees tremble from the heat of that single look.

Jesus. Why is his mouth always saying one thing while his feral gaze says the exact opposite... And what does it say about me that my first instinct is to ask him:

What if it's worth it?

Chapter Twenty-One

I FaceTimed Dad out on the porch while Ryker settled in.

I'm not particularly fond of burdening him with the details of what's going on at home when he's training, so we kept the conversation light and short. I didn't mention that someone broke into our house and left an ominous note, or that Noah went back to work a week early. Dad doesn't need the extra stress, and I was nervous that if he thinks I'm unsafe here in Deadwood, I'll never convince him I'm ready to be on my own in Austin.

After showering, I changed into little pajama shorts and an oversized T-shirt, forgoing a bra since I was going straight to bed to take a nap anyway.

At least, that was the plan.

Now that I'm clean and refreshed, the sheets are too scratchy, the sun is too bright, and my brain is buzzing too loudly to sleep. I also can't stop replaying the conversation I had in the living room with Ryker when he caught me checking him out.

For a second, my attention-starved brain thought he was saying he was tempted to throw it all away for a single taste of *me*. But if that was the case, why would he double down on reminding me he's not interested?

Ears burning and feeling a little pathetic for thinking anyone would *actually* be interested in me, I throw off my comforter and hop out of bed. Since I'll never get to sleep like this—and I can't exactly watch television when the only TV is in the living room—I might as well go grab the book Isabel lent me so I can hide out in here for the rest of the day.

Hoping Ryker's already zonked out, I cautiously slink out of my room, wincing each time the aging oak floor creaks beneath my feet. Other than my obnoxiously loud footsteps, the house remains quiet.

"Can't sleep?" Ryker calls out.

I curse under my breath, then square my shoulders and round the corner where I find Ryker slouched on the couch, still fully dressed with the blankets and sheets I set out for him folded neatly on the coffee table.

"Yeah," I choke out. "I'm kind of wired after being up all night."

"Same." Removing his hand from its resting place atop his death's-head hawk moth belt buckle, he sits up a little straighter. "Should we put on a movie to make up for the missed movie night?"

My chest pinches.

"Don't let Dad and Noah fool you, we haven't had a movie night in months," I say with a slightly bitter-sounding laugh. But even I can admit his plan sounds way better than lying in my bed, staring up at the ceiling while I pretend to read a book. "Could we watch one of my shows?"

"Sure." He laughs when I shimmy with excitement, bouncing from one foot to the other before plopping down next to him.

I lean forward, my butt hovering off the couch as I reach for the remote on the coffee table. "Do you need me to get you up to speed?"

"Give me a quick run down," he croaks, voice strained, like he's got something stuck in his throat. When I settle back into the couch and glance over, his eyes are closed.

Ignoring the sudden shift in the air, I mull over how to summarize the plot. "It's a vampire show. The only thing you need to know is that the main female character is part fairy and can read minds. Oh, and we like the tall blond love interest, not the brunette. Vampire Bill can suck a big one. No pun intended."

Ryker's eyes crack open. "Got a thing for blonds, Princess?"

Appalled, I tuck my chin into my neck. "*Ew*, no. But I do have a thing for morally gray." I cross my legs and flip on the TV. "Do you have any questions, or should I just start it?"

"I'm sure I can figure it out." His gaze drops to where my bare leg is pressing against his jean-clad thigh. *Good Lord*, any closer and I'd be sitting on his lap.

I lift my knee, attempting to fold in on myself and give him space without making a big deal or drawing attention to his discomfort, but before I can, his rough palm lands on my inner thigh, pushing my knee firmly against his leg, as if to prove he's fine.

"Start the show," he grits out, voice so low I feel it in my stomach. Jittery, I press Play, but when the show starts, the only thing I can concentrate on is the heat of his hand still resting on my thigh.

Ryker says something, but it's drowned out by a chorus of breathy moans emanating from the television where an orgy unfolds on the screen. Panic sizzles in my blood, my throat all but closing at the sight of the naked, sweating bodies undulating in the glowing light of tiki torches.

Oh God. When did it get so hot in here, and why is this so much worse than when a sex scene pops up while Dad and Noah are in the room? Can Ryker feel how much I'm sweating?

"Willa, did you hear me?"

"Huh? Sorry, what?" My voice is high-pitched and squeaky, and I have the sudden urge to bury my face in my hands and dart from the room.

"Is it the tiki torches in the show?" He grabs the remote, fast-forwarding to a scene without flames before relaxing back into the cushions like nothing happened.

"What? Oh, right. Maybe?" I breathe out, not wanting to admit it was the on-screen sex that got me all hot and bothered. "Fire in movies and on TV doesn't usually bother me, though."

"How does it work, then?"

"How does *what* work?" I clip, echoing his response from when I asked that same question up on the water tower.

"When you see fire." His green eyes meet mine. "What does it feel like?"

For a few seconds, all I can do is blink. Then I shake my head. "You keep doing that."

"Doing what?"

"Asking me things no one's ever asked before." I bite my lip, trying to think of a good way to explain it. "You know when you hydroplane in the rain and there's that one second when you lose control and you're convinced you're about to crash and die?"

He nods.

"Well, my body reacts exactly like that when I see fire. All my muscles lock up, my heart rate goes through the roof, and everything freezes. Even when the logical part of my brain recognizes that I'm fine, the rest of me just doesn't get the memo."

Ryker's eyes are still locked on mine, but he doesn't say a word.

"Is that what being touched feels like for you?" I ask, taking in the hard set of his jaw and the rapid movement of the pulse in his neck.

His hand flexes on my thigh, his Adam's apple bobbing as he swallows and dips his chin. "Pretty much."

"Is it okay that I'm this close?" My voice is so low it's almost a whisper. "I can move to the other couch if you want me to."

Teeth clenched, he briefly closes his eyes—as if battling with himself. "If you can hold a lighter to your tongue, I can sit next to my best friend's little sister and watch TV."

Ouch.

That's not the simple yes or no response I would've preferred, but the pointed reminder that I'm his best friend's sister does reiterate his disinterest. Which again has me feeling like a moron for the way my body reacts when he's close. "Can I ask you another question?"

"Go for it."

"When we were up on the water tower, you said touch was fine as long as you were the one initiating. In the future, how do I avoid making you uncomfortable by accident, like I did by sitting too close? What can I do to make things easier between us?"

Ryker shakes his head, mumbling something under his breath before saying, "I already fucking told you, I'm *not* uncomfortable."

Annoyed by his shitty tone when I was so candid with him, I fold my arms across my chest. "No need to get snippy. It was a legitimate question, and it's not like I asked what I can do to make being *intimate* with you easier."

"Fucking hell," Ryker chokes out, breaking into a small coughing fit before glancing over at my wide-eyed and probably stunned expression.

I can't believe I said that out loud, but it's too late to take it back now. I might as well keep going. "Vulnerability is a two-way street. You can't ask me personal questions and not answer any yourself," I quip, once again surprising myself. "You might get away with using that pretty face of yours as a deflection tactic with everyone else, but it won't work on me."

Ryker's face lights up. "You think I'm pretty?"

"You know you are," I say with an eye roll. "And from what I hear, everybody at your school knows it, too."

"Have you been asking around about me, Princess?" His mouth twitches up on one side.

"Isabel," I supply simply, angling my knees away from him in the hope it might make breathing a little easier.

"I see." He follows the movement of my legs with a frown.

After a long stretch of silence, he roughly drags a hand through his hair. "There's nothing you need to do differently around me. You're already trying harder than most people do, and I promise you I don't mind." He sighs. "As for your other ridiculous fucking question, *intimacy* has never been an issue for me."

Not wanting to scare him off but needing to show him I appreciate the reciprocated honesty, I slowly turn my body toward him. "Why not?"

"The girls I've been with have a very clear understanding of what our time together means. They aren't looking for a relationship and neither am I. They also never touch me unless I *let* them." I must look confused because he sighs again—this one slightly growly and annoyed—before he keeps going. "I'm more of a giver."

"Oh..." My eyebrows furrow as I try to process, but then I remember Isabel's story about Ryker and her cousin.

The first time they had sex, he blindfolded her, tied her hands behind her back, and made her explode like a pleasure piñata for several hours.

Although inexperienced with actual orgasms, I've enjoyed playing around with the lead-up. I also read spicy books and occasionally, when I have the house to myself, diddle around on Pornhub or other adult sites, exploring what turns me on in search of the elusive Big O... Or at least I used to before the Texas State Legislator started regulating adult entertainment websites and blocked access. But that's neither here nor there.

I have more than enough material to run wild with all the possibilities of what being "a giver" means, as evidenced by the mental montage flashing through my brain: *women on their knees, head control blow jobs, restraints, begging to be allowed to come...*

Although, I suppose in those situations the woman is the one giving?

More mental images float to the surface of my fucked-up brain: *women being eaten out with their legs spread wide, getting fingered while bent over someone's knee...*

Spankings.

Suddenly overheated, I swallow audibly and return my attention to the TV, which Ryker seems to appreciate because he sinks back into the cushions.

"You shouldn't have asked," he says after a few tortuously long seconds.

I really shouldn't have, but not for the reasons he thinks.

One episode ends and then another, neither of us speaking and a solid four inches separating us on the couch. Despite my best effort to keep my eyes open, I begin to drift somewhere into that peaceful space between dreams and wakefulness.

I'm vaguely aware of some sort of battle happening on the television, but I'm too warm and comfortable to open my eyes. Or at least I *was* until the sound of slapping flesh and moaning once again echoes through my living room, bringing me back to full awareness.

Not again. Why didn't I put on a different show?

My eyes pop open to take in my surroundings, but I immediately regret it. Not only is there an insanely hot vampire-on-human fuck-fest unfolding on the TV, but Ryker and I are now horizontal on the couch with his arm wrapped around me and my body draped halfway on top of his.

My torso is firmly sandwiched between him and the back cushions, and judging by the drool on his shirt, I've been using his incredibly toned chest as a freaking *pillow*. Worse yet, I've somehow managed to toss my leg over his waist and there's a *very* hard mass digging into my inner thigh...

I should get up, but I can't seem to move as the vampire on screen continues to fuck a girl who's been suspended from the ceiling by her wrists. She moans in ecstasy, her breasts bouncing with each hard thrust, which of course only spurs the blond vampire to fuck her harder.

My heart rate picks up, and my clit pulses.

"I can see why you like this show," Ryker says gruffly, his fingers digging into my upper waist while he, too, watches the girl on screen get absolutely wrecked.

Shit, now he knows I'm awake.

Cheeks aflame, I reach for the remote on the coffee table, but I'm too deep in the couch and my arm doesn't even come close. Frantic as the sound of fucking intensifies, I rock my body and then try again, stretching with all my might.

Ryker tenses beneath me, and I launch myself over him, barely touching the power button before I topple off his chest and careen headfirst toward the floor. At the last possible second, his hands fly to my hips, saving me from smashing my nose. With barely a grunt, he lifts me up and effortlessly sits me atop his lap.

"Thanks," I say breathlessly, bracing myself with two hands planted precariously low on his abdomen. When I glance down, Ryker's brows are pinched, his attention locked on something between my legs.

"What the fuck happened there?" he demands, abruptly spreading my knees apart with one hand, while using the other to trace the sensitive skin of my inner thigh.

Unable to form words, I close my eyes and shiver from his touch.

"It's a fucking moth," he says, continuing to trace some sort of pattern dangerously close to my pussy.

My eyes fly open and my muscles go rigid—

Did he just say a *moth?*

Panicked, I lean forward and squirm to see what he's talking about before sighing in relief. It's not a real bug, *thank God,* but he's right, there *is* a pink indentation of a moth surrounded by delicate little flowers right below the inseam of my thin cotton shorts.

My head cocks to the side, and I'm about to ask where the hell it came from when it dawns on me. "It's the impression of your belt buckle."

"I branded you," he whispers, voice low and husky as he drags his thumb over the indentation. Every cell in my body hums to life at once. I think I even scoot forward, subconsciously yearning for him to move a few inches north.

When he swipes his thumb just a fraction of an inch higher, jolts of electricity dance across my skin, shooting straight to the now-throbbing bundle of nerves at the apex of my thighs. I let loose a breathy sigh, drawing my lip between my teeth to stop myself from doing it again.

"Do you like it when I touch you like this, Princess?" he says, the heat in his smoky voice seeping into the deep recesses of my rapidly clouding brain.

Too nervous to speak, I bob my head.

"Tell me what you like about it and I'll keep going." It's a command this time—one with a *very* enticing payoff that has arousal flooding to my center with renewed force.

Everything about this feels dangerous, but I need him to keep touching me, and somehow that drive is overriding the nervous flutter in my belly and silencing the self-doubt in my head.

"I like—" His thumb slides a fraction of an inch higher, making the heartbeat in my clit go wild. "I like the way I feel when you look at me, but when your hands are on my skin—"

I shudder, remembering the way he spanked me. "It's like all the noise in my head shuts off. All I can think about is how I want more. How much I need you to..." My voice trails off, unable to verbalize what I'm feeling, but Ryker nods like he understands.

A second later, his hand leaves my thigh, moving to my mouth where he uses his thumb to tug down my lower lip. "Has anyone touched you here before?"

I suck in a sharp breath. "Once."

Ryker's chest rumbles in what sounds like a displeased growl, but he doesn't say a word as he runs his palm down the length of my neck to rest over my racing heart. Eyes locked on mine, his palm shifts to the left, gently cupping my heavy breast over my shirt. When his thumb grazes across my peaked nipple, my core clenches with a heady mixture of heat and desire.

"What about here?" His voice is so low I feel it vibrating *every-where*. "Has anyone touched you *here* before?"

"*Never*," I breathe out on a sigh, clenching my thighs around his waist to stop myself from grinding against him like my aching body begs me to as he massages my breast.

This time, the answering sound he makes is low and pleased. "Is this what you wanted from me, Princess?"

Brow furrowing, I slowly shake my head from left to right.

"Because you want more?" he prompts.

I nod, and he rewards me by kneading my nipple between his fingers.

"Show me where you want me to touch you," he whispers.

Body trembling, I wait for him to dip his chin before placing my hands over his and guiding them down the length of my torso and up under the hem of my shirt. Terrified and elated all at once, I guide him to my breasts and then shiver—the feel of his rough palms on my bare skin ten thousand times better than my own when I was listening to his phone call on the porch.

Ryker's movements are deliberate and glacially slow as he takes control, cupping both breasts and lightly flicking my nipples.

"I've been thinking about these perfect fucking tits since the eclipse," he growls, pushing them together under my shirt and lightly rolling my peaked flesh between his fingers until my clit is throbbing so furiously I'm sure I'll explode.

I lean into his touch, and I think I moan or maybe gasp. Whichever it is, Ryker responds by grabbing my waist and thrusting upward, forcing my aching core onto the hardening bulge in his jeans.

"Princess," he groans, sliding his hands up and down my torso before settling on my hips and bucking up again. "If you keep grinding against me like that, we're going to cross a line we can't come back from."

I hadn't realized I *was* grinding on him, just that the growing heat in my belly had spread into my chest while little bursts of ecstasy streaked up my spine. Now that I know, I still can't seem to stop myself from slowly moving back and forth across his rigid length. Especially when each roll of my pelvis is aided by the gentle pressure of his thumbs on my hip bones and fingers on my ass.

"What if I want to cross that line?" I pant, rocking against him with increased urgency.

"*Fucking* hell." Ryker's eyes are desperate, his movements frenzied as he thrusts against my center and groans again. "Fuck it, keep going. Make yourself come like this." His voice is low and guttural when he issues the command, sending a cascade of chills across every surface of my skin.

Gaze locked on his, I bite my lip and grind my hips again, and again, each heated wave of pleasure winding my body tighter and tighter until it feels as though I might snap. When I lose my rhythm, Ryker takes control.

"Fuck, that's hot," he grunts, the muscles in his forearms straining and flexing as he zealously guides me back and forth atop his hard length. The added friction of his coarse jeans through my thin shorts only heightening the sensation. My eyes flutter closed. His movements are so much rougher and quicker than mine that tiny panting moans spill from my lips unbidden. It barely takes a minute before my spine starts tingling and I'm about to burst.

"Ryker— Oh God. Please don't stop," I whimper.

His pupils flare, and his cock grows even harder beneath me while a devilish grin spreads across his full lips. "Fuck, that's it, Princess. Keep going—"

Someone pounds on the front door, and Ryker bolts upright, holding me against his chest as my approaching crescendo devastatingly slips beyond my reach.

Disoriented, I follow the direction of his gaze to the window where an off-white 1980s Cadillac Eldorado is barely visible in the gravel driveway.

"*Dammit*," he bites out. "What the hell is Kane doing here?"

With my brain less clouded with lust, there's just enough room for reality to slip in. Was I seriously just dry humping Ryker Bennett in the middle of my living room...with all the curtains open in broad freaking daylight?

Dread pools in my stomach. *Noah is going to kill me...*

"Did he see us through the window?" I whisper-shriek, heart racing in my throat.

I attempt to climb off Ryker's lap, but with my arms pinned between us and the death grip he has on my waist, I can't move.

"Kane didn't see anything," he says reassuringly, the dark edge in his tone softening as he grabs the white strand of hair draped over my eye and tucks it behind my ear. "Even if he did, that's his problem, not ours."

I laugh awkwardly, shivering when his hand trails to the back of my neck. "But Kane wouldn't say something to Dad or Noah if he *did* see anything, right?"

Ryker's face falls, his full lips pulling into an impossibly tight line. "*Fuck.*"

Still clutching me to his chest, he rises to his feet and slides me down the length of his body, making sure I have my footing before stepping back to adjust himself. It doesn't help. *Like, at all.* Even when he shoves his whole hand into his jeans to try again, the denim is still so tented it's almost comical.

I bite my lower lip, a self-satisfied hum buzzing through my blood with the knowledge that *I* did that to him. It was my body, scars and all, that made him hard.

"*Fucking hell,*" he grumbles following the direction of my gaze to his dick.

Kane pounds on the door again, and Ryker scowls as he calls out, "I need a fucking second." Then his attention snaps back to my face, his jaw firm and eyes blazing.

"Don't even think about finishing yourself off without—" His mouth clamps shut, and after one more angry shake of his head, he stomps across the room, leaving me with my heart in my throat and a ghost of a smile on my lips.

Chapter Twenty-Two

Flies swarm around the half-desiccated carcass of what was once a goat... At least I *think* this thing was a goat. The head, horns, and feet are all missing, so it's a little difficult to tell.

I swat the flies away from my face, fighting off rolling waves of nausea from the god-awful stench of decay that doesn't seem to have any effect on Mrs. Crowe.

She hands me her bandana, even though I'm already wearing my lemon-oil infused red one around my nose and mouth. "Are any of the organs left inside, sweet pea?"

Holding the additional handkerchief over the lower half of my face, I sink into a crouch and use my pocketknife to lift up a section of rib. "I don't think so, but with this many critters around, we wouldn't expect there to be, right?"

"Very good."

Buzzing at her praise, I prop up what's left of the neck section of the skeleton, inspecting the spine and then the severed legs, exactly the way Elanor taught me.

I frown. "Looks like these were cut, not torn or gnawed off." A maggot crawls onto the tip of my blade, and I shake it off, wiping my knife in the dirt to clean it before rising to my feet. "I don't think one of your creepy legends did this," I admit, scanning the shin-high straw-colored grass for any clue as to who could be responsible.

"No," she says after a drawn-out moment. "I don't think so either, darlin'."

Shoulders heavy with thoughtful silence, we head for the side-by-side, draining a water bottle each before taking our seats. This is the fourth dead animal we've found over the past few days, each one missing more and more parts.

"Another ranch hand quit today," Elanor laments, taking the bandana from my outstretched hand and tying it around her aging neck. "That makes three this month. They keep seeing shadows in the woods at night."

Sweat drips down the small of my back as the cicadas in the surrounding trees grow ten times louder. "Have you reported it to my dad?"

"Daniel spoke to 'im a few days ago. Joel suspects someone is trying to speed up the process of the land sale. Maybe even drive down the price."

"That's beyond messed up." My head cocks to the side. Dad's been broody and irritable since he got back from Austin. I'd assumed he was annoyed with Noah for leaving early, but maybe this is what he's been preoccupied with?

"Who do you think is behind it?" I ask. "One of the Black-thornes?"

"Could be." Elanor turns her head to the east where the pitched roof and single octagonal tower of the Cartwright mansion is barely visible on the hill above the tree line. "Or it might be Kane Bennett."

I scowl, thinking of the other Bennett brother...the one I haven't seen since he left three days ago. "As far as I'm concerned, the Black-thornes *and* the Bennetts can all shove off." A muscle in my jaw flexes as I kick on the engine and set out for our next destination

Elanor frowns and reaches over to pat my forearm.

"Joel mentioned Ryker hasn't come back yet." She squeaks,

bracing herself with a palm on the dashboard when I swerve to avoid a log. "You haven't seen or heard from him at all?"

"Nope." I shake my head, annoyed I wasn't able to keep the bitterness from my tone.

After Kane interrupted our heavy petting session on the couch, he and Ryker had a heated conversation on the porch before hopping in the Cadillac and leaving a trail of dust and a deep divot in my driveway.

Three days later and I haven't heard hide nor hair from Ryker.

His truck is still at my house and his duffle bags and wallet are lying on the coffee table where he left them, so he hasn't skipped town, but that makes the whole thing worse.

After he left, I spent hours obsessing over the vexed expression he'd made before stomping out the door. Had I been too aggressive when I guided his hands under my shirt? Or when I was on top of him? Was it because I mentioned my dad and brother?

Then the text message had come.

TROUBLE

> I will be at my Brother's house for a few
> days. -R

The worst part is the text was sent to a group chat with Noah and Dad. I'm not sure what I was expecting after our little...whatever you want to call it on the couch, but I guess I thought touching someone's boobs and ordering them to come while grinding on your dick would at least warrant a personalized text.

I snort humorlessly and veer left as we approach Old Man Dan moving a small group of cattle into a nearby paddock. Elanor waves at her husband and then turns to me. "Daniel really shouldn't be doing that by himself," she says with a worried curve of her brow. "Would you mind texting Ryker for us, sweet pea? See if he's interested in picking up some hours?"

That's literally the last thing I want to do right now, but Elanor so rarely asks me for anything... I bring the side-by-side to a stop and shut off the engine so the noise won't spook the cows.

"Yeah. I can do that." Reluctantly, I grab my phone and type out a message, paying special mind to keep it as cordial as possible. If Ryker can be standoffish and detached in his texts, then so can I.

WILLA

> The Crowes need a tasker and want to know if you're available?

I hit Send. "Done."

Elanor lights up. "Thank you, dear."

While we wait for a reply, I watch Old Man Dan effortlessly use his horse to steer the cattle through the gate. He might be pushing eighty, but he rides like the massive animal is an extension of his body.

"Do you ever worry about him on that thing?"

"Who? Daniel?" Elanor asks, following my gaze. "Never. That man's been riding since he was five and he's never been thrown. I worry more 'bout the fence mendin' and the hands than I do about my Daniel ridin'." She looks at me meaningfully. "But that doesn't mean I like him out here on his own. Sure would be nice to have some more help."

Taking the hint, I glance at my phone.

That's odd...

I have full bars on my cell, but for some reason, the message wasn't delivered. I try resending it, but the same thing happens.

"What's wrong, dear?"

I stare in the direction of the Cartwright mansion, an uneasiness churning in my gut. "The message won't go through. I think his phone's off."

Elanor hums thoughtfully. "That doesn't sound right. You'd think he'd want to be reachable at all times, considering what's going on with Beau and Charlotte."

She's right. Ryker wouldn't have his phone off while the custody

216

battle was still so up in the air. Not when he *swore* to Charlie that he'd never leave her on her own...

"Maybe we should ask Joel to go out there and check on him?" Elanor suggests uneasily.

With the last of the cattle safely in the paddock, I restart the engine. "Kane won't let Dad past the gate. I could go up there and see what's going on, if you'd be willing to let me borrow one of the four wheelers."

"*Hmm.* It might be best to let your father handle this one. But that reminds me..." She slaps her knee. "Take us to the garages, would ya?"

"Sure thing." I force a smile, trying not to worry about why Ryker's phone is off as I turn us back toward the big house.

Elanor has always been a "fly by the seat of your pants" type of boss, which means side-questing in the middle of a workday is a fairly common occurrence. That being said, I'm not exactly mechanically inclined, so I'm a little nervous to see what she has in store for us.

During the drive, I sift through about twenty different scenarios of what she might need help with. I consider everything from clearing out rat traps to soaking up oil stains, but it's not until we're inside the garage and Elanor drops a ring of keys into my hand that I realize exactly how far off track I was.

Slack-jawed, I let my gaze volley between Elanor and the dust-covered 1953 Chevy pickup truck before us. "You can't be serious."

"As a heart attack." She smiles, albeit a bit sadly, while the scent of rust, dust, and damp garage swirls around us. "The truth of the matter is without power steering, I just can't drive her anymore. You need a car and she needs a good home. I was gonna sell her to a collector, but with a new engine and a hodgepodge of random parts, she's not worth as much as she could be. Besides, I'd much rather sell her to you."

Awestruck, I run my palm over the paneling of the truck's rusted body. I've seen faded pictures of her original soft-teal paint job, but years of use have chipped away the top coating, leaving behind a beautifully sun-weathered patina.

"She's perfect." My grin slips away, and I shake my head. "But there's no way I can afford her."

Even with the rough shape of the exterior, this is a classic car—one I'm sure a number of rat rod enthusiasts would pay a pretty penny for. I won't rob the Crowes of that cash, especially not this close to their retirement.

Elanor wipes a light layer of dust off the hood with her sleeve. "Can you do four grand?"

My heart sinks. "I've only got $2,500."

She hums, like she's deep in thought. I'm about to offer her the eight hundred dollars I put aside for textbooks, but she cuts me off before I can. "Let's do three, then. If you pay two now, I'll let you take the truck and work off the rest." I open my mouth to refuse, but she silences me with a look. "You're family. If you make me sell her to a stranger, I'll never forgive you. Go on, do us both a favor and get some use out of her."

Overwhelmed, I wrap my arms tightly around Elanor's middle, breathing in her comforting almond scent. "I don't deserve you. Thank you."

She squeezes me back, patting my hip before pushing me away. "You deserve the world and more, my love. Now go, take her for a spin. I need to tell Daniel about the goat we found and then take a nap."

Elanor leaves me in the garage, keys in hand and mouth open wide enough to catch flies.

I can't believe I own a car. Squealing, I jump up and down with a little victory dance. I'm tempted to run home and scratch number one off my bucket list, but there's one thing I have to do first:

Find Ryker fucking Bennett.

Chapter Twenty-Three

Sweat-slickened palms clutching the wheel, I ease my foot off the gas pedal and approach the dirt road turnoff to the Cartwright Estate at a crawl.

The loblolly pines are so thick here, they make the air stagnant; so tall, it feels as though the walls are closing in on me. On my left, a crumbling rock wall separates me from the graying tombstones of an ancient cemetery. But I don't dare glance over, because the moment I do, I'll be confronted by the charred ruins of what was once Divine Mercy Bible Church.

Stomach twisted in knots, I let the engine idle and peel my thighs off the worn leather seat of my new-to-me truck. I'd rather be anywhere else right now, but I need to make sure Ryker is okay...and tear him a new one if he is.

Here goes nothing.

Puffing out my cheeks with a long exhale, I pass through a wide-open, rickety wooden gate and begin the slow climb up the hill. I'm tempted to keep my eyes forward and ignore Divine Mercy altogether, but then I remember what Ryker said about how closing your eyes won't protect you from the monsters hiding under your bed.

That pretending something didn't happen will only rot you from the inside out.

Swallowing the bile in my throat, I force myself to look at the soot-stained skeleton tucked beneath the shadows of the forest.

It's a quick glance, barely long enough for me to spot a towering timber steeple and an excavation tractor parked in the adjacent overgrown field, but my skin is instantly hot and tight, like the scars on my back still remember the kiss of the flames.

My vision blurs and I want to throw up... No, I'm *going* to throw up—

Keeping my eyes on the road ahead, I force myself to swallow down my nausea and take a deep breath through my nose.

This is the reason the Cartwright mansion is on my bucket list. Because for fourteen years, I've been too chickenshit to pass by the church where my mom tried to kill me.

My shoulders droop and I shake my head. I'm not even looking at the damn thing right now, but I *feel* it. The blade against my back. Fire melting my flesh and smoke tearing the oxygen from my lungs... A shadow haunting my every breath.

My sweat-drenched body screams for me to run, to flee this place before it's too late, but I'm here to check on Ryker. The sooner I do that, the sooner I can leave.

Gritting my teeth, I focus on the mansion up ahead instead.

Locked behind an expanse of brick walls and a vine-covered wrought iron gate, the old Cartwright house is a monstrosity, dominating the hill it sits on and dwarfing all of the surrounding buildings on the property. Everything is overgrown, a good portion of the trees, grass, and shrubs mangled together and half dead as they choke the life out of each other in their futile competition for sunlight.

I park behind another tractor near the gate, this one with some sort of hydraulic drill attached to the arm, and stare up at the chipped brick and peeling paint of the old mansion looming above the neglected hedge. It looks more like a castle than a home. And with bits of the roof entirely missing and good portions of the exterior crumbling, I can't begin to imagine how much it would cost to fix up a building like this.

Movement in one of the stained glass windows catches my eye, but when I lean over the steering wheel for a better look, there's nothing there. Taking a deep breath, I cut the engine and climb out.

It's eerily silent. No birds, no insects. No cars. Just the scuff of my boots against the dusty road and the rustling of the wind through the trees.

"Hello?" I call out, searching for a way to open the ridiculously tall metal gate while the sun beats down on my forehead. Maybe there's some sort of intercom system I can use.

I lift a section of crawling vine, taking two steps backward and clutching my heart when a slender man dressed in all white appears on the other side of the wrought iron. Tall and lean with a face dotted with scars, he scowls and crosses his arms over his chest—the gun holstered at his side only adding to his intimidation factor.

"How did you get past the first gate?" he growls.

"*Uh...*" I fumble my words, trying to regain my composure. "The gate down by the cemetery? It was open."

The breeze picks up, and I sneeze. *God, what is that smell?* It's so sickly sweet and floral I'm nearly choking on it. There's something else, too, like rotten eggs, but it's faint enough I almost think I imagined it.

I clear my throat, doing my best to breathe through my mouth. "I'm here to see Ryker...and Kane," I add as an afterthought. "Kane said I could stop by. That y'all would have me on a list or something?"

The man purses his lips. "What's your name?"

"Willa Dunn."

Eyes widening, his gaze slithers across the white streaks in my hair before zeroing in on my neck and shoulders. Unease ripples up my spine. I've never seen this man in my life, but it feels like he's looking for my scars. Fidgeting under the weight of his gawking, I take another step backward, thankful that at least my dirty ranch clothes cover as much of me as possible.

"My apologies," he says after a beat too long. He inclines his head. "One moment, please." Then he backs away, bringing a radio to his mouth once he's out of earshot, never once taking his eyes off me.

What a welcome wagon...

The humid breeze picks up, the sweat on my neck making my hair stick to my damp flesh in the oppressive heat. Again, something moves past one of the broken stained glass windows in the mansion, and even though I can't see anyone, the prickling sensation across my scalp makes me feel like I'm being watched...

When I turn to ask the man how long this is going to take, he's gone.

"Hello?" I call out, but no one answers.

A powerful gust of wind rips up the road, and I bring my arm up to shield my eyes from the spray of dust and dead leaves pelting my face and shins.

"Willa?" I drop my arm and spot Kane heading up the small hill from the burnt church.

He's wearing the same bolo tie he had on the last time I saw him, the pendant of which I now see is molded in the shape of a cicada, and the same wire-rimmed glasses—but now he's dressed in an all-white suit, the black piping on his western shirt the only hint of color in his entire outfit. Well, that and the brownish-gray dirt covering his sleeves and hands. "I'm glad to see you took me up on my offer." He dusts his palms off as he approaches. "Unfortunately, today isn't a good—"

"Where's Ryker?" I march over, meeting him in the middle of the road and stationing myself so that his broad shoulders block my view of Divine Mercy. While not quite as tall as his brother, Kane still has at least five inches on me.

"You came for Ryker?" His tone is off, and when I peer up at him to read his expression, the position of the sun behind his head gives him a fiery halo that casts his entire face in shadow.

I step to the left, and his narrowed expression comes into sharp focus while he looks from me to my new truck. "Did that deceiving father of yours come with you? Is he hiding somewhere around the property? Where did he go?" Kane's tone is knife-edged, his speech pattern lofty and more like a play actor than a guy who grew up down the street.

"I came alone. My dad has no idea I'm here." I shift from one foot to the other while a niggling feeling, almost like I'm on the verge of remembering something, tugs at the back of my brain. But I can't quite grasp hold of it, not when I'm too busy silently cursing myself for admitting that no one knows I'm here.

Dad would be furious with me for that slip up.

I lift my chin. "I came to see if your brother's okay, then I'll be on my way."

Unblinking, he stares at me. "Let me make sure I'm understanding this correctly," he says after a heavy moment of silence. "You came all this way to check on someone who felt you up and hasn't bothered to talk to you since?" He makes a *tsking* sound. "I have to say, that's a little disappointing. You're worth so much more than that."

Neck burning with mortification, I step backward. Ryker wouldn't have told him...would he?

Kane steps closer, a new gleam in his eye that has nothing to do with the fading sunlight. "Every single person in your life has tried to snuff out your inner light, Willa. My brother included. Mark my words, he's exactly like the rest of them. He'll treat you like you're small, someone to be used and discarded when something better comes along."

Much like the time I almost got bucked from a horse and took a saddle horn to the chest, his words slam into me, robbing me of my ability to breathe.

Kane's right. My mother tried to snuff me out. My family treats me like I'm small and fragile. And then there's Ryker, who's doing exactly what he said he wouldn't, drawing me close just to push me away again...

I shake my head. Ryker's phone isn't off, he probably just blocked my number...

I never should've come.

"You see it now, don't you?" Kane asks, taking another step forward. "They say they want to protect you, but it only makes you weak and beholden to them."

Tilting his head, he sucks his teeth and draws himself up to his full height. "You know, on second thought, maybe you should stay. I'd like the opportunity to show you around and let you see some of the work we're doing to prepare."

While it's taking everything in me not to retreat to my house and bury my head in the sand, I *am* curious. I'd also love to show Ryker that I really do know how to throw a punch...

I raise a skeptical brow, still trying to regain my mental footing after this roller coaster of a conversation. Kane juts his chin toward the burnt-out church. "Come, let me show you."

I glance at my truck and then the mansion. Someone is standing in the tower window, their face and body almost entirely obscured by the dirty glass. For all I know, it could be Ryker laughing at me for thinking our tryst on the couch meant anything...

Jaw clenched, I fall into step behind Kane, wiping my sweaty palms on my shorts as we make our way down the hill. "What are you preparing for?" I ask.

Kane grins over his shoulder, his glasses glinting in the dying sunlight. "The world's on fire, Willa. I'm carving out a place to weather the storm and await the new dawn."

Chapter Twenty-Four

"What do you know about the founding of our town?" Kane asks, voice barely audible over my thundering heartbeat as we shuffle down the hill toward the skeletal remains of Divine Mercy Bible Church.

"Not much," I squeak, keeping my eyes planted on the dead grass. "Just that the Cartwrights were given a land grant to settle this area in the late 1820s."

Kane clicks his tongue. "That's all you know because that's all you were *taught*. History books are written to fuel a specific narrative. Which means the version of the past we're spoon-fed is not only biased, it's often grossly exaggerated or flat-out false."

I roll my eyes. Kane is barely five years older than me, but he's speaking as if I'm a child or a student in need of mentoring. I'm tempted to tell him to get over himself, but there's a part of me that's curious where he's going with this.

"Anyway," he continues, half-up man bun bobbing on top of his head with every step. "John Cartwright died on the trip out west, leaving the landright to his eldest son who opted to share the inheritance with his younger brother. They split everything right down the middle, equal in all things except for one."

He glances back at me over his wire-rimmed glasses. "Neither of the brothers knew it at the time, but the aquifer that runs beneath this region was almost entirely located on the younger brother's portion of the property while the water beneath the west section is unusable." He points to the copse of trees barely visible through the dense pines. "The tainted water is what killed those trees and gave the town its namesake."

Hushed voices sound from up ahead, but Kane ignores them and keeps on talking. "Over the years, the younger brother's crops and livestock flourished while every potable well the older brother dug ran dry and every crop he planted withered. One night, finally fed up with years of losses, the eldest snuck into the mansion behind us and slayed his brother and nephews in their beds—taking the younger brother's wife and the land as his own."

Despite the little hairs on my neck rising, I roll my eyes. "That sounds like an urban legend."

"Every word of it is true. Abel Cartwright and his four boys are buried in the family mausoleum near the woods. If you don't believe me, you can go see for yourself."

"He killed his own brother?" My mouth gapes open as I stop mid-step. "Why wouldn't he ask if they could share the water?"

A dark cloud passes overhead, making the deep shadows under Kane's eyes appear almost sinister. "Why would he ask permission for what was rightfully his all along?"

Someone claps their hands, and I nearly jump out of my skin.

"Alright, break's over. Masks back on, everyone," a delicate voice says.

I peer around Kane while a group of twelve or so people slink out from the shade of a gnarled tree, donning dust masks and respirators before spreading out to pick up various construction equipment and filing into the church.

Noah was right. Kane's friends all wearing the same thing is pretty damn creepy. There's just something about matching outfits that screams Heaven's Gate and cultish mischief.

I scan the group, noting how each of them is dressed head to toe in white garments caked in dirt and soot, except for one, who's dressed in a black jumpsuit that's a shade darker than her tight-coil pixie cut hair. Her deep-brown skin is dotted with freckles and beauty marks, the most prominent one heart-shaped and located right below her left eye.

She claps her hands again, and the last straggler—a petite woman whose face I can't quite see—scurries into the decaying church.

Nausea eats at my stomach, along with a renewed desire to get the hell out of here. But the scaffolding and plastic sheeting covering up the most severely burned sections of the church make the fear slightly less crippling than when I first drove in.

I blink, raise my chin, and finally take in the monstrosity before me.

First, my gaze skims up the worn stone steps leading to two metal doors with thick crosses carved out of their centers. I hover there, bracing myself for the assault of a long-forgotten memory... When none comes, I follow the rotted support pillars up to the partially collapsed roof and then higher, to the soot-stained steeple where a neon-red cross is strung up in one of the busted-out windows.

Sweat drips down my spine, and a low electric hum vibrates through the air, the red cross flickering on and off like its power source is seconds away from calling it quits.

With the hairs on my arms standing on end, I look away, uneasy for reasons I can't quite explain... It might be the creaking skeletal trees of the dead forest or the unnerving quiet of the graveyard, or maybe even the field of off-white flowers I'm almost positive Elanor told me were poisonous, but everything about this place has me on edge.

"It's beautiful, isn't it?" Kane says, placing his hand on the small of my back.

I shrug out of his touch, throwing him an incredulous, brow-heavy glance that earns me a tight-lipped half grin.

"Look again," he insists.

Silence falls between us while the shrill cry of the cicadas in the nearby branches increases tenfold. Sweat beads on my brow and my pulse pounds against my temples, but I force myself to take another look.

Even then, I have no idea what Kane thinks is beautiful. It's definitely not the three large dumpsters and what looks to be some sort of burn pit near the rock wall of the cemetery. It can't be the charred chairs, the broken desks and bookshelves, or the bits of heavily graffitied doors and church pews littering the ground.

I take another pass, finally noticing the curious, unsettling glances from Kane's creepy friends while they scurry about and diligently work on Divine Mercy.

"These people and I have spent the last few years dedicating our lives to false promises. *Here* we're finally free." Kane places a hand on my shoulder, and a shiver crawls up my spine when his pinkie brushes the bare flesh of my neck. "This church was always a monument to your survival. Now, it's also a sign of hope for the future."

My lips tug downward. If you ask me, it would have been easier to bulldoze the entire thing and put all the money and man hours into renovating the mansion, but at least he's gutting it—destroying every trace of what my mother did here.

A wall of flames dances across my memory, and I quickly avert my gaze from the ruins, pausing when I spot someone sitting under the shade of a large oak tree. I almost look away, but then I spot broad shoulders and a flash of raven hair.

"Ryker?" I call out.

Dressed all in white with his back against a tree trunk, he sways, struggling to keep himself upright. A sick feeling opens up in the pit of my stomach, and I call his name again.

He doesn't so much as turn his head in my direction.

"What the hell is wrong with him? Why isn't he answering?"

Kane just shakes his head. "My brother is helping us clear the way for the future." He slides his hands into his pockets and shrugs. "The work can be—"

"Ryker!" I shout, my patience with the eldest Bennett brother's vague answers wearing thin. I scream Ryker's name again. And this time, the sound of my voice seems to increase the odd movements of his wobbly head.

Something's not right... Leaving Kane in the dust, I quicken my pace and jog across the field.

Out of breath, I drop to my knees and take Ryker's face between my palms. His eyes are glassy, skin pale and clammy. And he doesn't so much as blink or flinch at my touch.

Panic tears through my gut, hot and sticky as it climbs into my throat.

"What did you take? Did Kane give you something?" I pat him down, ripping a cutting of white flowers from his shirt pocket like I might find whatever drugs he's on tucked beneath it. But all his pockets are empty. No cigarettes, no lighter, no cellphone—which I should have anticipated because he's wearing the same all-white ensemble as the others. Even his hair has been combed to the side in a way that makes him look nothing like the Ryker I know.

To my knowledge, he's never done drugs...and there's no way he'd start now when he wants to file for guardianship of his sister. Ryker also wouldn't be caught dead without his cigarettes and lighter...

What in the actual hell is going on here?

I run my fingers through his hair, combing it backward until he looks more like himself. He blinks, slowly bringing his gaze to mine. "*Willa,*" he whispers, cracking the tiniest smile, his face so childlike that for a moment all his hard edges are erased.

Then he frowns, swaying like he might fall over. "How can you stand to look at me?"

"Why would I have a problem looking at you?" I murmur, voice breaking as I try to keep my tone light and figure out how to get him out of here. "You're the one with the pretty face. I'm the one with the scars, remember?"

"Your scars might be more visible, but mine are worse," he whispers, clutching at his chest like he can't breathe. "You don't remember any of it, Princess. You're still whole. I remember every second. I see it every time I close my eyes."

When he peers up at me, the whites of his eyes are bloodshot and weary. My heart gives a painful thump. How can one person walk around with that much hurt on their shoulders? Not knowing what else to do and unsure of what to say, I press my forehead to his.

"Come on," I whisper, rising to my feet. "I'm taking you home."

Kane steps behind me and places himself directly in my path, like he actually thinks he can stop me. I whirl on him, shoving my finger into his chest, breathing so hard I can barely think straight. "Did you drug your brother and take his stuff?"

Kane's eyes narrow to slits. "Of course not."

"Then what is this?" I gesture to Ryker, but once again Kane just shrugs.

"Heat exhaustion is always a risk in these conditions." He turns slightly and waves over the woman in the black outfit. "I'll have one of my healers have a look at him."

I laugh out loud. "Absolutely not. You've done more than enough. We're leaving." My attention briefly shifts to the crowd of people walking our way, the one in black now carrying a leather medical bag. "Listen, Kane, I've been trying to give you the benefit of the doubt, but whatever the hell you're up to up here, leave your brother out of it."

I drop into a squat, draping Ryker's arm over my shoulder and grunting as I help him to his feet. "If you tell me what you gave him," I say to his half brother, "I'll consider not telling my father about this."

Kane's jaw hardens and his posture goes rigid, but after a quick glance over his shoulder, he relaxes his expression and laughs. "She's not ready," he calls out to the dozen faces slowly making their way across the field.

"*I'm ready to get the hell out of here,*" I mumble to myself, already dragging Ryker up the hill while Kane addresses his weird-ass friends.

"There are still preparations to be made," he continues, voice growing smaller as I put more distance between us. "Only once we—"

Tuning him out, I make it about thirty feet before the woman with the medical bag catches up, the heart-shaped beauty mark below her eye even more prominent than I'd initially thought.

"Ryker was working in the fields all morning," she says, hurrying to keep step with me as I pick up the pace. "Give him lots of water and he should be good as new in an hour or two." She smiles, her dark-brown eyes kind and almost sad.

"We don't need your help," I hiss, giving her the rudest smile I can muster to drive home my point. After a few more steps and another woeful smile, she finally takes the hint and drops back.

By the time Ryker and I stumble our way to my truck, I'm sweating and out of breath. So when he stops to stare at the derelict Cartwright mansion—that's even more foreboding now that the sun is starting to set and the storm clouds are moving in—I can't help but let out a frustrated growl. "Come on. Just a few more steps."

"Kane and I used to ride our bikes up here as kids," he says, green eyes fixed on the crumbling ornamental gables. "The property is riddled with tunnels and there's a way to get in through the basement. We found all sorts of stuff in there. Photos, town records..." He says something else, but his words trail off and I don't quite catch it. Then he shakes his head. "Kane was obsessed."

After dragging Ryker the last few steps to the truck, I wrench open the door and ease him onto the seat while making sure he doesn't hit his head.

"Yeah," I say with a grunt, lifting his booted foot into the truck, "Kane gave me a little history lesson earlier. I got to hear all about the Cartwrights' lurid past, fratricide and all. Your brother's a real fun guy." I lean over Ryker's lap to buckle his seat belt before realizing there isn't one.

Shit. Dad's going to hate that...

I startle when Ryker places his calloused palm gently on my lower back where my shirt must've ridden up, shivering as his thumb slides over the patch of scars.

"Kane always leaves out the best part," he says so quietly I almost don't hear it.

"Oh yeah?" I ask, voice trembling. "And what's that?"

"After losing her husband and children, the youngest Cartwright's widow went looking for revenge," he mumbles, hand falling into his lap. "She stabbed the eldest Cartwright in the chest and burned that bastard alive in the family mausoleum before he could bleed out. Did it right next to her husband's crypt."

"Jesus," I murmur, eyes locked on the half-dead trees near where Kane said the Cartwrights were buried. "Why would Kane leave out that part of the story?"

Ryker chuckles. "Because my brother's never been able to tell the difference between the hero of the story and the villain."

Chapter Twenty-Five

During the drive home, Ryker sobers up enough to convince me he doesn't need to go to the hospital. I regret that stupid-ass decision the second it comes time to get him out of the truck and he won't budge, even when I march around to the passenger side door and open it for him.

"Ryker, we're here." I wave my hand in front of his bloodshot eyes. No response. He does flinch when I grab his arm, which is a little more like the Ryker I'm used to, but I'm still freaked out. "Alright, that's it. If you don't walk yourself inside in the next thirty seconds, I'm taking you to the ER."

"No," he says, blinking a few times. "I've almost got it. My head is just all..." He sways in his seat, closing his eyes tightly.

My chest pinches and I fight the urge to reach out and steady him. "Fine, but I'm going to go grab a bottle of water. Maybe we can flush whatever this is out of your system."

I make it one step before Ryker grabs my arm and drags me closer until my hip is pressed against his thigh. "Don't go. *Please*. Every time I blink, I'm back inside that church."

Nodding, I swallow. "Okay. I won't go anywhere."

"Thank you." His hand slides down my wrist, and when he links his fingers through mine and pulls me a little closer, I just about melt.

"Is that what Kane had you doing for three days? Cleaning out the church?"

"Three days?" Ryker's hair falls forward as he closes his eyes and shakes his head. "What are you talking about? We were on the couch together this morning... *Fuck.*" He rakes his free hand roughly through his hair. "Noah's gonna kill me."

My heart skips a beat. But considering how his memory has several days' worth of gaps in it from whatever Kane gave him, now is *clearly* not the time for me to be relieved that maybe he didn't ghost me after all. "Come on. Let's get you inside and put you to bed."

"Trying to get me into bed already, Princess? It's almost like you *want* your brother to kill me." He cracks open his right eye, a sly grin tugging at the corner of his mouth as he looks me up and down. "Worth it."

I roll my eyes. *He's obviously feeling better.* "Come on, Casanova. Up you go."

I'm not really sure what the protocol is for this situation, but I'm going to treat it like when Noah comes home drunk off his ass. Which means water, food, and sleep—in exactly that order.

After struggling up the steps, we make a quick pit stop in the kitchen where Ryker chugs three bottles of water and scarfs down two peanut butter and jelly sandwiches. The color slowly returns to his skin as he eats, his eyes clearing not long after. Even his gait and posture are more stable.

Satisfied, I lead him to my bedroom. The mattress squeaks when he sits, still dressed in borrowed clothes, which are thankfully not covered in dirt like the others' were.

I should make him shower and change, but I settle on helping him remove his button-down shirt, leaving him in the linen trousers, a plain cotton tee, and his shoes. I check his arms and hands for needle tracks. Except for a small scratch running through one of the wings of the moth tattoo on his forearm, he doesn't have a mark on him.

My mouth pinches to the side. "What's the moth for?" I ask, dropping to my knees to start in on his bootlaces.

"Tattoos don't have to have meanings, Princess." He pauses to yawn. "Sometimes they just look nice."

Tilting my head, I lean forward and inspect the ink. I'm not the biggest fan of the flying critters. I'm always nervous they're going to get caught up in my hair, and the dust their tiny wings leaves behind gives me the heebie-jeebies, but even I can admit the tattoo is beautiful.

Unlike the moth on his belt buckle, this one doesn't have a skull in the center of its body. Instead, it has furry little antennae and gorgeous open wings with big dots on them that remind me of eyes.

"They don't have to have meanings, but this one does," I say confidently.

Ryker sighs, the sound somewhere between fatigue and annoyance. "You're a brat sometimes, you know that?"

"Sucks when someone calls you on your shit, doesn't it?" I smile up at him, grunting as I struggle to remove his boot until he lays back on the bed and holds his leg up for me. "Thank you. And you don't have to tell me about the tattoo if you don't want to."

"When Kane and I were kids," Ryker starts after a long, shaky exhale, "Beau used to burn trash in the yard. Sometimes the flames would go late into the night and we would sneak outside to watch. We'd sit there for hours, and I'd stare in horror as, one by one, moths and other insects flew right into the fire."

After finally freeing his foot from the first boot, I tap the toe of the next one. "Why would they do that?"

"Moths use the light of the moon for navigation and figuring out which way is up and down," he explains, lifting his opposite leg for me. "But they're easily confused by other light sources." He closes his eyes again, but they move beneath his lids.

"I can still see it all these years later—here one second, gone the next. Their wings incinerated in an instant. At the time, I didn't understand how anything could confuse certain death for safety.

Then one day, after my mom just sat back and watched Beau beat the shit out of me, I finally understood."

Ryker sits up and leans forward, reaching out to twist an errant strand of my white hair around his index finger. "Saltwater for a castaway. Sleep to the freezing. A moth to the flame. It's all the same. A starving man will devour poison to ease the ache for a single moment, even when he knows it'll kill him."

I sit with the bleakness of his words for a second before responding. "Why would you want to think of that every time you glance down?"

Ryker laughs, but the sound is bitter. "I took a psychology course last semester, and the professor explained how the human brain clings to false beliefs if it thinks it will protect us from pain. I can't afford false beliefs. And I can't lose focus trying to make life hurt less, not when Charlie is depending on me. I refuse to lead her into the fire—the way my mom did with me and Kane."

Overwhelmed by the intensity of his stare, I try to look away, but he drops my hair and grabs my chin to stop me. "This tattoo reminds me not to be distracted by something that looks pretty but will only end up destroying me."

Ignoring the dangerous octave of his voice, I inch forward, shivering when he does the same and his nose brushes against mine.

"Is that what you're doing, Princess?" His deep whisper is rough and smoky. "Trying to distract me? Trying to *destroy* me?"

Heart in my throat, I shake my head. "I would never—"

"Then why are you the only thing I think about when I should be concentrating on Charlie and getting Kane help? Every damn day, it's only you. I'm burning from the inside out."

My world tilts so violently I grip onto his thighs to keep from falling. "Ryker, I—"

Gravel crunches in the driveway, and he briefly looks to the window, blinking like he can't quite focus on what he's seeing and reminding me that he's still under the influence of whatever drugs his brother gave him.

My stomach churns. *He probably doesn't even know what he's saying...*

"Kiddo?" Dad calls out from somewhere outside, likely assuming I'm in the garden.

Ryker's grip on my chin tightens, guiding my face to his until our lips almost touch. "Will one taste quench the thirst, Princess? Will it douse the flame or burn me alive?"

Bootsteps pound on the porch, thudding in time with the erratic cadence of my heart. Every fiber of my being wants to press my lips against Ryker's—to climb on top of him and figure out for the both of us how to ease this burning need...but I can't. Not like this. Not when I can't be sure if this is really how he feels.

The front door opens and closes. "Willa?"

"We're in here," I say breathlessly, never breaking eye contact.

Ryker blinks, the hard look in his eye easing as he releases me a second before my dad appears in the doorway, phone clutched to his ear and his brow scrunched.

Dad zeroes in on the shirt I threw on the floor, slowly trailing his gaze over to the boot, and then to my precarious position between Ryker's knees. "I'm going to have to call you back," he says into the phone, jaw hard and lips tight. "It'll have to wait, Noah. I just walked in on your sister taking your best friend's clothes off."

"Jesus, Dad," I sputter, realizing too late how this must look to him. "Kane drugged Ryker. I was putting him to bed so he could sleep it off."

"*Narc,*" Ryker mumbles under his breath, but I'm too embarrassed to care.

Dad's jaw works as his attention volleys between us, finally landing on me. "Why didn't you call me?" Then to Ryker he says, "Do you know what you were dosed with?"

"I don't." Ryker scoots back on the mattress and away from my hand, highlighting just how far up his thigh my palm had traveled.

I slowly slide my hand off his knee and into my lap while Ryker pinches the bridge of his nose. "Mr. Dunn, if I really was drugged...

then you can't report this. Beau will find a way to use it against me for getting guardianship."

I can almost see the cogs turning in Dad's cop-brain. "Willa, I need to speak with Ryker and you need to talk to your brother before his head explodes." He holds out the phone, swiping to answer the incoming call, and I cringe when Noah's angry yammering fills the room.

Sighing, I rise to my feet and take the cell from my dad's outstretched hand, not allowing myself to look back at Ryker as I trudge into the living room.

This should be fun.

Considering how Noah nearly killed Cooper Blackthorne after finding out we'd kissed under the bleachers, I can only imagine what he's planning to do to his best friend after Dad's ridiculous comment.

The phone vibrates, and I glance at the screen to make sure the call didn't drop, frowning at the email banner that flashes across the top. I didn't think Dad got work emails on his personal phone, but this one is clearly labeled *Texas Correctional Health Care Services*, which means I definitely shouldn't be reading it.

Huffing out a breath, I bring the phone to my ear and brace myself. "Alright, let's get this over with."

"What the actual *fuck*, Willa?" my brother shrieks through the line. "My best fucking friend? Are you kidding me?"

Okay, damn. I'd assumed most of his anger would be aimed at Ryker, but I guess I deserve that. There are about a thousand snarky ways I want to respond, but instead, I bite my tongue and spend the next few minutes explaining the events of the past three days.

When I'm finished, Noah releases a sigh. "So nothing happened between you and Ryker?"

I pull the phone away and frown at the screen like that will magically help his response make sense. "Seriously, Noah? Your best friend was drugged by his creepy-ass brother and *that's* the first thing you ask me?"

"*Fuck.*" My brother's voice is so soft and fragile that if I didn't know better, I'd say he almost sounded hurt. "Something did happen, didn't it..."

I'm tempted to hang up and be done with this conversation. I barely understand my chaotic, ever-changing feelings for Ryker. The last thing I want to do is discuss them with my brother. Then again, Ryker *is* Noah's best friend. Maybe I should consider his feelings before deciding on my own... My stomach tangles into knots.

"*Wills?*" Noah says softly. For some reason, I picture him hunched over and clutching the phone with both hands. "I've never asked you for anything, but I'm asking you for this. Please, *anyone* but him."

I turn back toward the hallway where Ryker is barely visible through the crack between my door and the frame. I can only see a few inches of his downcast face, but it's enough to make the knots in my stomach unfurl and erupt into a flurry of heat.

It's like I'm burning from the inside out.

"Willa, did you hear me?"

I choke down the lump in my throat. "Yeah, I heard you. Anyone but him."

Chapter Twenty-Six

After a restless night on the couch so Ryker could have my room, I was beyond relieved when the light of a new day finally crept through the windows to chase away my cumbersome thoughts.

It might have been the shock of seeing Divine Mercy for the first time since the fire, the odd emptiness that followed my brother's solemn request of "anyone but him," or maybe even my idiotic imagination deciding that whoever broke into my house was watching me through the window while a storm raged outside, but I don't think I slept more than thirty minutes.

At least I was able to spend several of those sleepless hours researching the basics of old truck maintenance—which means I'm basically a certified mechanic now. After that, I dedicated another good chunk of time to Googling the perfect breakfast spot for Dad and me to eat at this morning—a cute little cafe a few towns over that serves German pancakes.

The floor creaks in my father's bedroom and a churning nervousness takes over my stomach. Today is the day I finally tell him about Austin. I'm really hoping his favorite breakfast food helps soften the blow, but if not, there's a gun range a half mile from the cafe with an obstacle course he can work me through until he feels better.

The second his door groans open, I pop up from the couch, my smile inverting as he steps into the living room wearing his pressed uniform. "I thought we were going out to eat?"

"Sorry, kiddo." He meets my eye for a single second before averting his gaze, leaving a heavy blanket of disappointment sitting on my shoulders.

"But we—" I cough to cover up how childish and whiny my voice sounds and try again in a calmer tone. "We haven't seen each other for more than five minutes in weeks. I *really* need to talk to you."

"My hands are tied, kid. Chief texted to say we picked up a drifter last night he thinks might be connected to those fires on the Fourth of July."

With all the other insanity, I'd nearly forgotten about the hooded figure from the eclipse party and their counterparts from the water tower.

"*Doubt it*," I mumble under my breath.

"What was that?" Dad's confused tone snaps me back to the moment.

"Nothing," I answer quickly. "I was just saying that today is your only day off. Can't someone else take care of it?"

Still not looking at me, he shrugs. "You don't say no when the boss asks you to come in. Besides, it's all hands on deck for the next few weeks until we get these records organized. You should see the basement right now. Boxes from floor to ceiling. The whole department's a damn fire hazard."

He winces at his slip of tongue, then he's scurrying across the living room to grab his keys off the table. Dad angles his body away from me to readjust the tactical backpack slung over his shoulder, almost like he's trying to hide it.

Ask him where he goes. Ask him what he hides.

For a second, I consider confronting him about the contents of the creepy note. But to do that, I'd need to tell him about the break-in, and I'm still convinced he'll use it against me when I tell him I'm moving to Austin.

It's not safe for a young woman to be by herself in a new place.

If someone can get into our home here in Deadwood, what makes you think it won't happen when you're on your own in a new city?

Yeah, no. Hard pass. I open my mouth to ask if we can do dinner instead, but he's already halfway out the door.

"Things will settle down in a few weeks, kiddo. I promise. Love you."

"Love you, too," I say, but the door is already clicking shut.

Dad's cruiser rumbles to life at the same time a floorboard groans behind me and my hair shifts in a light breeze. Lungs seizing, I spin around to face the intruder head on and scream in terror at the large figure before me.

"Jesus, *fuck*," Ryker squawks, jumping a foot into the air as he covers his ears.

Hand clutching my chest, I try to draw in a full breath and apologize, but with my pulse hammering like a battle drum, my lungs refuse to cooperate. Wide-eyed, I try to gulp down air again, but my throat is so dry and scratchy from the scream only a wheeze comes out.

"Hey now." Ryker crouches so we're eye level and takes my face in his hands. "I've got you. You're alright. I thought you heard me walk into the room. My bad, Princess."

Leaning into his touch, I inhale rain-soaked pine and let the warmth of his rough palms seep into my cheeks before forcing myself to concentrate on the rise and fall of his broad chest. Slowly, my inhales start to match his, and after a second or two, I'm finally able to draw in a full breath.

My mind quiets, the last of my adrenaline slipping away like leaves on the wind.

"There she is." Ryker smiles at me, his moss-green eyes sparkling in the delicate rays of morning light seeping in through the window. My pulse goes crazy all over again. With his raven hair all mussed from sleep, he's so beautiful it actually hurts to look at him.

Anyone but him.

Guilt slithers into the space between us, cooling my cheeks and constricting around my rib cage. Whatever this thing is with Ryker, it can't be worth upsetting my brother. Not when I'm leaving in less than a month...

Chest full of lead, I shrug out of his touch, my new position blocking the light from the window and casting a deep shadow across his handsome features. Ryker's chin dips, the grin slipping from his lips as he stares at the space I created.

"Dad went to Kane's last night," I say abruptly, trying to steer my thoughts to safer waters. "They wouldn't let him onto the property again, but at least he came home with your stuff. Your clothes are washed and in the dryer, and your cell is charging in the kitchen."

"Thank you." Ryker takes a step toward me, his bushy brows knitting together when I take an even bigger step away.

"Do you remember anything yet?" I ask breathlessly.

"Not really. Just Kane and I walking around the estate for a bit. Then you were there under the oak tree with me. I'm still not convinced he drugged me." Ryker brings a hand to the back of his neck and shakes his head. "But it did feel like I was only gone for a few hours. Are you sure—"

"It was *three days.*" My tone is harsh, but it's more from fear than anger. Ryker's memory is literally gone. I don't understand why he's not pissed off or freaking the hell out. "Do you even remember why you went to the estate in the first place? You said you were just going to talk to Kane on the porch for a minute. The next thing I knew, you guys were driving away..."

"No, I don't." He sighs. "I know my brother's fucked up, but there has to be an explanation for what happened. I'm his only ally, he wouldn't drug me—"

"Well, *something* happened," I say firmly and then soften my tone. "You were completely strung out and no one would even acknowledge anything was wrong. I get that you probably won't press charges, but at least consider going no contact with Kane."

Ryker pinches the bridge of his nose and lets loose an exhausted sigh. "Fine, I'll think about it. But there's something more important we need to discuss," he says, voice rising an octave above his usual low baritone. "About what happened on the couch—"

I hold up two hands to stop him. Whatever he's about to say will either hurt my feelings or make staying away from him harder. Either way, nothing good can come of it. "I talked to Noah after I brought you home yesterday."

"You talked to your brother?" Ryker's face is stoic and unreadable, his voice so flat and inflectionless I almost don't recognize it.

"Yeah... He's glad you're okay and warned me not to scare you off before he comes home," I lie, forcing a weak smile that makes my cheeks feel like they weigh a hundred pounds. "I don't think he's too thrilled about the idea of you and me being friends."

Anyone but him.

I take another step backward.

Shoulders stiffening, Ryker drops his gaze to the floor again, glaring at the worn oak planks between us with a heavy brow, as if the growing distance offends him. After a tortuously drawn-out moment with only the rasp of my shallow breathing and the rattle of the AC filling the room, he draws in a breath, cracks his neck, and rolls his shoulders.

Hard green eyes connecting with mine, Ryker crooks a finger, his voice low and dangerously seductive as he beckons me forward. "Come here."

My knees nearly buckle, and even though I try to ignore the way his gravelly tone resonates in my center, I can't stop the heat that spreads into my low belly and thighs.

"Ryker, don't. My brother, he—" I bite my lip because what am I going to say? That Noah's never asked me for anything except to stay away from his best friend?

"*Willa*," Ryker warns. "Don't make me tell you again..."

Knees trembling, I take one step closer but then stop and shake my head. I can't do this. I can't betray Noah's trust.

"You should call Charlie and check in with her foster parents," I choke out. "They called five times while you were sleeping."

Some of the fire fades from his expression, but he's still simmering when he rakes a rough hand through his hair. "*Fuck.*"

My fingers twitch at my sides, the vulnerability laced into that single word threatening to destroy my already flimsy resolve.

Chest aching, I back up another few inches.

"Go call Charlie," I say, voice clipped. "I'm headed out, so the house will be nice and quiet for you."

A muscle feathers in his jaw. "Where are you going?"

I smile at him sadly. *Anywhere but here.*

Chapter Twenty-Seven

Almost two weeks go by in the blink of an eye.

I filled out all of my loan paperwork for UT and applied to the work-study program on campus. I didn't find any more weird notes, no more livestock have gone missing at Crowe Ranch, and Elanor and I haven't found any more dead animals—which makes me think the drifter Dad arrested really might've had something to do with it all.

Even if he wasn't responsible for the fires...

I shake off a shiver.

The rest of my life seems to be falling into place as well. Kane and his weird-ass friends have been radio silent since Ryker came back. Isabel and I decided to live in the dorms instead of trying to find an affordable apartment in Austin. And when I took my truck in for an inspection, the engine only needed about three hundred dollars' worth of work.

As an apology for all the hours spent away from home, Dad surprised me with a Bluetooth radio, a beautiful set of whitewall tires, and of course, seat belts.

All in all, things are good and the grains of sand in the hourglass counting down my time in Deadwood are finally starting to look favorable. I just need to hold on a little bit longer and then I can leave this place behind for good.

Setting my plate in the kitchen sink, I fish out my bucket list from my back pocket and grab a pen from the junk drawer, crossing out anything I've already accomplished and adding one more item I want to tackle.

Deadwood Bucket List

1. ~~Buy a cheap car~~
2. Tell Dad and Noah you can't stay in Deadwood ⟶ **(MOVE TO AUSTIN!)**
3. **Punch Cooper Blackthorne**
4. ~~Go to the solar eclipse party~~
5. ~~Explore the Cartwright mansion~~
6. Hang out with Dad and Noah as much as possible
7. Stop hiding. Go out more. ⟶ **(AND ISABEL!)**
8. Be daring and live a little
9. **GET LAID !!!**
10. Stop Beau from getting custody of Charlie

I set the pen down and frown.

Most of these are pretty fluid, but I still thought I'd made better progress... Technically, I shouldn't have even crossed out number five, but after my little field trip to retrieve Ryker, I no longer have any desire to see the inside of the mansion.

Sighing, I tuck the note back into my pocket and take a deep breath, psyching myself up to start in on my chores. But when I open the dishwasher, someone's already beat me to it. Since the only appliance Dad has ever unloaded is the fridge and Noah is still on the rig, I know exactly who that someone is.

I slam it closed.

Ryker has been the perfect houseguest. Almost annoyingly so. Not only does he clean up after himself like I asked him to, but he's gone above and beyond the conditions we agreed on by brewing coffee *every* morning, cooking breakfast Monday through Friday, *and* making dinner nearly every night. He also grocery shops, folds his blankets before I wake up so the living room doesn't look messy, and he even mowed the damn lawn yesterday.

Ryker's done so much since he came back that for the first time in my life, I've found myself acutely aware—*and a bit resentful*—of just how little my dad and brother actually do around here.

Spending less time cooking and cleaning was already going to make it difficult to avoid being alone with Ryker, but then he was hired to task around Crowe Ranch with Old Man Dan. Which means every morning, after feeding and caffeinating me, he walks me over to the big house to collect Elanor.

Through all of this, neither of us ever says more than a few polite words to one another—which is as infuriating as it is necessary for me to continue to keep my distance. Often, I've caught him staring at me from across the field at the ranch or through the window when I'm tinkering on my truck, his gaze a heavy chain threatening to drag me back into his orbit.

The worst part is, I wake up every morning looking forward to what Ryker's going to feed me for breakfast and I fall asleep every night dreaming about the way he guided my hips across his lap that morning on the couch, wondering how much better it would've felt without all the layers of clothes between us.

Anytime I'm excited about something for school or terrified about one of Elanor's new creature stories, Ryker is the first person I think of going to. I want to ask him about Charlie and tell him about the stupid book I'm reading, but I can't...

It's driving me batshit crazy.

When I finally worked up the courage to talk to Isabel about the unhealthy amount of time I've been spending thinking about my brother's best friend, she suggested it might be the whole "forbidden fruit" thing. That I'm only lusting after Ryker because Noah said I couldn't have him. I hope she's freaking right because right now, my skin feels so tight I can barely breathe.

Laughter sounds in the yard, and I shift the curtain over and spot Ryker and Old Man Dan stealing strawberries from my garden, apparently taking a break from mending our adjoining fence. I want to smile at the pretty picture they paint in the fading orange light, but then Ryker uses the hem of his shirt to wipe his brow... Now all I can think about is the sun glinting off his sweat-drenched abs.

Heat blossoms up my spine, settling heavily behind my ears and in my low belly.

Thank God Noah is coming home soon. With Dad working an ungodly amount of hours and continuing to find any excuse not to be at home, I've been counting down the days until there's a buffer between Ryker and me again.

Gravel crunches in the driveway as a navy-blue BMW pulls up. A woman steps out, her long black hair and golden-brown skin shimmering in the last rays of the setting sun while her thin, floral sundress billows in the light breeze.

She's absolutely stunning and obviously not from around here in those expensive-ass heels. I glance at my bare feet, ratty old jean shorts, and long-sleeve T-shirt with a frown. *Jesus*, even my knees are bruised from when I tripped over Elanor's cane in the barn this morning. I glance back out the window as the out-of-towner lifts a delicate hand to shield her eyes, clearly lost.

With a sigh, I run my fingers through my hair, bringing a handful forward on each side to cover my collarbone, and head outside to offer my help.

"Hi there," I chirp, realizing that there's something vaguely familiar about her, although I can't say what. "Do you need directions?"

A cloud of cotton candy perfume nearly knocks me off my feet as she flashes me a radiant smile. "This is where Ryker's staying, right?"

My lips slip into a frown. "It is..."

"Jenny?" Ryker calls out, jogging over like she just rang the damn dinner bell.

Jenny waves enthusiastically, popping her hip to the side in a way that makes her shapely legs look even more toned before giving him a playful wink. "The one and only."

I cross my arms over my chest, fighting the sudden urge to test her balance in those ridiculous heels.

When Ryker's close enough, she extends an arm and steps toward him, like she's going in for a hug. Every muscle in my body tightens, waiting to see how he'll respond to her touch.

He takes a massive step out of her reach. "Why are you here?" he asks, tone clipped and a little breathless.

I drop my chin to hide my satisfied smirk.

"Didn't you get my text?" Jenny smiles sweetly, clearly unfazed by his abruptness. "I brought the box of stuff you left in the dorm and the textbook you let me borrow."

"I'm not glued to my phone," Ryker says dismissively.

I can't help but snort at the blatant lie, especially when we both know he keeps that thing on him day and night, checking every single alert in case it's something to do with Charlie.

Ryker briefly catches my eye, his face scrunching in what could either be confusion or surprise, before turning back toward Jenny. "I'm grateful you brought it over, but that's a three-hour drive. You didn't have to do that."

She waves him off. "It's no trouble. I'm in town to visit my cousin."

My stomach sinks at the same time something hot and sticky wraps around my throat. This must be Isabel's cousin—the girl Ryker tied up and made explode with orgasms.

"Are you free tonight?" Jenny asks Ryker.

"He's on dinner duty," I blurt, eyes widening with a mixture of horror and shock at my outburst. I quickly try to backtrack. "It's part of our deal for letting him stay here. Sorry."

"Maybe some other time, then? I'll be in town for a bit. Just let me know." She doesn't push the issue further, but the crestfallen set of her mouth almost makes me feel guilty.

Almost.

"Yeah, maybe," Ryker replies noncommittally, but he's not even looking at her when he says it. He's too busy raising an eyebrow at me and pressing his lips together like he's trying not to laugh.

"What?" I snap, blood simmering as he gives up on trying to hide that smug smirk of his.

"Nothing. I was starting to think you forgot I existed for a second there. Glad to see you know I'm still around." He winks and then opens the door of the BMW with a small laugh. "I'm going to bring these inside."

Before Jenny and I can offer to help, he's already grabbed a box and bounded up the porch steps, chuckling to himself.

Just like that, Ryker Bennett is back on my shit list.

An uncomfortably long silence follows his departure until I realize it's up to me to be the hospitable one, especially since this is my only friend's family.

"Do you want to come inside for tea or lemonade?" I finally ask, albeit a bit reluctantly.

Jenny glances wistfully toward the house, and that sticky feeling crawls back up my throat as I follow her gaze to where Ryker's broad shoulders are barely visible in the window. "No, I better not. It'd just freak him out."

"You guys aren't..." I pause, unsure of what I'm asking. Are they dating? Are they still hooking up?

"We're not together," she supplies, letting out a small laugh that's both bright and a little mournful. "I think he might be too broken for that kind of commitment. God forbid a man be good in bed *and* relationship material, am I right?"

"Ryker's not broken," I snap, a little too aggressively, before glancing back at the window. A thousand different attributes filter through my head, and even though none of them do him justice, I still have to try. "Ryker is loyal, and strong, and selfless. When the people he trusted most in life let him down, he didn't wallow in self-pity or hide away from the world. He stepped up and took care of his sister. That's not broken, that's—"

Jenny raises two perfectly manicured brows, her expression a mix of shock and sympathy.

"What?" I ask, again a bit too defensively.

"Can I give you a word of advice?" She doesn't wait for my response before continuing. "This might come off a little harsh, but I wish someone had said this to me when I was younger. If a man tells you he just wants sex, that's exactly what he means. If he says he's not the relationship type, he's not. Never let an orgasm cloud your judgment or fool you into thinking you can change someone. A moment of bliss is fleeting, emotional damage is forever."

I cough, eyes bugging out of my head as I choke on my spit. "Ryker hasn't... We're not..." I frown, realizing Ryker apparently set very clear boundaries with Jenny, but with me...

I unfurl my arms. "What if he hasn't said anything at all?"

She grimaces. "In my experience, silence always speaks the loudest."

Bootsteps crunch on the gravel behind me, and I straighten my spine, tamping down the cold feeling seeping into my limbs.

"Right, well, thank you for the advice," I say through a forced smile. "It was nice to finally meet you, Jenny. I'm sure we'll see each other around."

She gives me a sad wave. "It was nice to meet you, too. And I hope so."

Brushing past Ryker, I storm back into the house and slam the door, frustration clawing at my insides so violently I want to scream. I've been torturing myself over whether or not I'm a horrible person for being attracted to my brother's best friend while Ryker hasn't been struggling one bit. I all but stopped talking to the man and he hasn't even asked *why*.

I bury my face in my hands, renewed mortification burning holes through my ears.

Steps sound on the porch a second before the door swings open. Not wanting Ryker to see how upset I am, I pick my chin up and head for my room, but he drops the box he's carrying and beelines for me, cutting off my escape.

"What's wrong?" he says, stepping left when I step right to go around him.

"Nothing. I'm fine." I weave around the couch, but he vaults over it, once again blocking my path. I throw my hands up. "Dammit, Ryker. Can't you just go make Jenny explode like a pleasure piñata and leave me alone?"

"Like a *what?*" He laughs, eyes sparkling with amusement.

Perfect. Of all the times for me to use one of Isabel's oddball expressions... "Never mind. It's not important."

He crosses his arms over his chest, drawing my attention to his stupid bulging muscles as he leans against the back of the couch with another smart-ass grin plastered on his beautiful mouth.

"I like when you're all fired up like this. Jealousy looks good on you, Princess."

"I am *not* jealous." I stomp my foot, immediately regretting the childish move.

Ryker's smile only grows. "You are. And I fucking love it."

I tilt my head to the side, confused and wary from the shift in his tone. "You love it?"

"Of course I do." He laughs darkly. "I thought I pushed too hard and you regretted letting me touch you. But if that was it, you wouldn't have gone all territorial on poor Jenny."

"*Poor Jenny,* my ass," I grumble under my breath, and then much lower, "Of course I don't regret it."

"What was that? I couldn't quite hear you." Ryker's grin is so big and bright, his cheeks nearly cover his eyes.

I smile sarcastically but don't repeat myself.

"God, it's like you're just begging for another spanking," he says through a laugh, wiping the smile clean off my face.

My jaw goes slack. "Wh-what?"

"Come here," he says, voice low and dangerous, exactly like it was the last time he gave me that command in almost the same exact spot. Only this time, I can't stop myself from obeying.

Chapter Twenty-Eight

One tiny step forward is all Ryker needs to snatch my belt loop and tug me to his chest.

"You've been ignoring me," he says, arm snaking around my waist, preventing me from escaping. "I fucking *hate* it."

"No," I whisper, voice low and breathy. "I haven't been."

I try to step out of his grip, but that only makes him hold me more firmly. Eyes locked on mine, his thumb caresses my hip bone while his free hand moves to my lower back, sliding farther and farther south. I clench my thighs, struggling not to close my eyes and moan.

"Lie to me again, *Princess*," Ryker warns, slowly trailing his nose along my jaw. "I fucking dare you."

Heart pounding against my rib cage, I lean back just far enough to meet his stare. "I haven't been ignoring you. I just—"

Smack.

He spanks my ass, and I gasp, nearly losing my footing when all the blood in my body rushes to the throbbing pulse between my legs. Trying to steady myself, I drop my hand to his bicep, my fingers catching on something plasticky and smooth, but I forget about it the second he speaks.

"I need you to stop ignoring me," he growls against my temple.

My eyes flutter closed as he slides his palm across my ass to soothe the sting, but then he rears back and spanks me again, this time much harder.

Crack.

I cry out, but his lips are already moving again. "And you need to stop wearing such tiny fucking shorts around the house. Every time I see you, I want to bend you over my knee and remind you that I'm still fucking here."

Crack.

The impact pitches me forward, bringing my chest flush against Ryker's as something hard digs into my stomach. Brain fuzzy, I drop my eyes to his waist and realize it's definitely *not* his belt buckle this time...

"You said I was distracting you from Charlie," I whisper, cheeks an absolute inferno. "You said you were thinking about me when you should be thinking about her..."

The hand on my ass stops and squeezes. "Apparently I was fucking high. And I happen to like you distracting me—so much more than I should, Princess."

A thousand wings take flight inside my chest as I stare up at him.

"I *need* you to start talking to me again," he continues, eyes soft and vulnerable. "Everything with Charlie's custody is going to shit because I can't find a job that pays enough to support the both of us. Beau's petitioning the court for a hearing date, which means he's one step closer to having his parental rights reinstated. And on top of all that, I can't take another goddamned second of your silence and polite bullshit small talk."

He drops his forehead to mine, and the hand he has on my ass kneads the tender skin beneath my shorts with so much urgency I can't tell whether he's trying to soothe the ache of his latest slap or soothe himself.

Every nerve ending in my body fires off at once, and my brain struggles to remember why I'm supposed to be staying away in the first place while my limbs twitch with the need to wrap around him. Then Ryker brings a hand to my cheek, the sweet fragrance of stolen strawberries and a heady scent that's so uniquely him obliterating all rational thought as he trails his thumb across my lower lip.

Unsure where it's okay to touch him but needing to be closer, I grab his shirt and tilt my chin up. "Ryker—"

His lips slam into mine, rough and all-consuming. A flood of shocked delight washes over my body, and even though I have absolutely no idea how to properly kiss him back, his mouth and hard muscles feel so incredible pressed up against me that I sigh and melt into him.

Whatever sound I make seems to snap Ryker out of his momentary madness because he abruptly pulls away.

My lungs tighten when his moss-green eyes lock onto mine, scanning my face with such intensity I forget to breathe. Half in a daze, all I can do is stare when he brings his fingers to his lips, brows lifting in surprise, like he can't believe he kissed me.

I brace myself for the moment he shoves me away and retreats. But he just stands there, hand on my hip as he draws in one ragged breath after another.

The air around us turns thick and heavy, vibrating with the tension of the storm brewing between us. Too afraid to speak or move, I cling to his shirt like a lifeline, silently pleading for him to stay and kiss me again.

Ryker's jaw hardens, and the hairs on my arms rise the same way they do moments before the first clap of rolling thunder.

"Fuck it," he growls, and then his hand is in my hair and his lips are crashing into mine again, fierce and claiming as he hauls my body against his. I sigh, my heart beating so fast it might burst when I lift onto my tiptoes to meet him.

At first, I fumble to keep up, trying too hard to match the tempo of his lips and overthinking every movement of my mouth. But then his fingers dig into my scalp, sending shivers dancing across my skin, and my muscles slowly uncoil. When he captures my lower lip with his teeth a second later, it's like a switch flips in my head and suddenly my busy mind is quiet.

I kiss him back without restraint, until I'm unsure where he begins and I end. There's only him and me, our mouths and bodies perfectly synced. I'm so caught up in the feel of his lips and his sweet strawberry taste I barely notice when he picks me up, seamlessly maneuvering us onto the sofa so that I'm straddling his lap.

Gripping the couch cushion behind him for balance, I deepen the kiss, reveling in the little noise of appreciation Ryker makes when I open for him. I moan into his mouth, and his powerful muscles tense, the urgency of his touches becoming more frantic as he explores and devours me. His hands and lips are everywhere, each sweep of his tongue over mine eliciting a soft groan from low in my chest and stirring a desperate need in my core.

I shiver when his fingers roam beneath my shirt, trailing across the damaged flesh of my hips and back without an ounce of hesitation. It's not enough. I want more. I want to be closer.

Ryker growls when I pull just far enough away to grab the hem of my shirt. With shaking hands, I slide the fabric up and over my head, leaving me in only my cotton bralette and shorts.

"Look at you," he says huskily, palms sliding up the length of my scarred back as he takes in the sight of my breasts spilling over my bra.

The heat in his gaze steals my breath away.

"You're so goddamn beautiful." His voice is a raspy whisper, but the enraptured glint in his eyes and the reverent way he runs his hands across my skin makes me feel like he's shouting it from the rooftops.

I stop shaking, and a delicate warmth spreads out from the center of my chest into my limbs. I bring my hands up, intending to wrap them around his shoulders and kiss him again, but Ryker stops me, roughly capturing my wrists and pinning them to my sides.

Eyes wide with panic and cheeks flushed pink, he tries to look away, but I lean forward and place my forehead against his. Once his breathing evens out, I let my arms go limp so he can see I won't touch him unbidden.

"Show me where you want my hands," I whisper.

Ryker inhales deeply, and the next thing I know, my wrists are pinned behind my back. The arch he's forcing into my spine shoves my now heaving breasts into his face, barely an inch away from his mouth. I make a sound that's halfway between a gasp and a moan, the pulse at the apex of my thighs throbbing as my clit grazes against the tented fabric of his jeans.

Gaze locked on mine, he tightens his grip on my wrists and tugs down, like he's trying to gauge my reaction now that I can't move. A thrill shoots up my spine, and my nipples pebble into sharp points as the ghost of his breath penetrates the thin cotton of my bra. Still staring into his eyes, I relax my shoulders in surrender. If he needs control to feel comfortable, I'm more than happy to give it to him.

The corner of his mouth kicks up.

"You're fucking perfect, you know that?" Shifting my wrists so he's holding them with only one hand, he threads his fingers into my hair and licks my bottom lip before diving in to recapture my mouth. He's much rougher this time, dragging my hips across his lap and massaging my breasts over my bra until I'm putty in his hands. Before long, we're grinding against each other as we make out, a small moan escaping my lips every time his belt buckle grazes my clit.

Chest heaving, Ryker pulls away and gives my ass a quick pat. "Up."

Wrists still secured behind me, I rise to my knees so he can adjust himself, my eyes widening at the massive imprint of his dick beneath his jeans. Before I can fully process what I'm looking at, Ryker slams me back onto his lap and starts kissing my neck while guiding my hips up and down his thigh.

Holy fuck. My eyes flutter open and closed, his hard length pressed against my center sending me into a frenzy. It only takes a second before my hips move of their own accord.

Ryker hums approvingly. "You like grinding against my cock, don't you, Princess?"

"*Mm-hmm.*"

"Is this how you make yourself come when you're alone? By rubbing that sweet pussy on whatever hard surface you can find and wishing it was me?"

Jesus Christ. It will be now…

"Show me," he growls. "Get rid of these shorts so I can watch how you get yourself off." He releases my hands, and although my clit is still pounding, the feeling slowly slips away as reality comes crashing back in…

I'd rather die than confess to my accidental pillow-humping orgasm, so instead of verbalizing that I've never been able to come on purpose, I just sorta lock up.

Ryker's mouth pulls into a tight line. "You've made yourself come before, right?"

I drop my chin and look away, then I'm squealing and flying through the air as Ryker flips me onto my back, pinning one of my legs to the sofa with his bodyweight as I dig my fingers into the couch beneath me.

Placing a rough palm on my bare stomach, he slides his opposite hand to my neck and tilts my head forward until I have no choice but to look him in the eye.

"Were you waiting for my help?" he whispers, slowly bringing his face to mine. "Because if you wanted me to make you come, all you had to do was ask." He kisses my jaw. "I'd have been here in a heart-beat. I'd have helped you through those lonely nights." Chills prickle across my skin as he trails his lips down the column of my throat. "I'd have had you convulsing around my fingers while you begged for more." He nips at my neck, and then starts making his way back toward my mouth. "Were you really just waiting for me this whole time, Princess?"

Mortified, I almost shove the cocky prick off me, but then I notice the playful glint in his eye and the smirk he's desperately trying to hide, and I can't help but belt out a laugh—my chest feeling ten times lighter as my body shakes with relief.

"You caught me," I reply with an exaggerated bob of my head. "Every time you put crickets in my bed and pulled my hair, all I could think was '*Gee, I sure hope this is the boy who gives me my first real orgasm.*'"

"The crickets were funny," Ryker growls, nipping at my chin before brushing the hair out of my face and hovering his lips over mine. "And I'm fucking glad it's going to be me."

My breath hitches when he drops his mouth back to my neck, my stomach clenching as he swirls his tongue around my pulse point. "It was *always* going to be me," he says against my damp skin, slowly guiding the hand on my belly beneath the waistband of my shorts and lower until his fingers are lightly resting on the mound above my pussy.

Clutching onto the couch cushion, I moan and arch into his touch, trying to bring his hand farther south, but he doesn't budge. Instead, he barks out a husky, pleased-sounding laugh.

"Tell me what you want, Princess," he says, lips grazing the shell of my ear. "*Beg* me for it or this stops right now."

I tilt my chin up toward Ryker's beautiful face. He's breathing so fast it's making *me* dizzy, but my heart flutters just the same. By commanding me to beg for what I want, he's giving me a voice and the power to make the decision. For the first time in my life, it feels like someone sees me as an equal, not some fragile, broken little girl who needs coddling.

There are a million different ways I could ask Ryker to ease the growing ache, but there's one thing I want even more than that.

I remind myself to be daring. *To live a little.*

Heart pounding, I swallow down my nervousness. "I want to touch you."

The heat in his expression fades, but when he doesn't pull away, I slide my hands out from beneath me and bring them toward his face, hovering my palms a few inches away from his jaw to wait for permission. "I want to touch you, and then I want you to kiss me again."

I feel more vulnerable asking him for this than I would asking him to bend me over the couch and have his way with me...but this is what I want—what we both *need*. No holding back.

Breaths shallow and mouth drawn into a thin, tight line, Ryker shakes his head. "It's not you. I just don't like being touched when I'm..." He closes his eyes. "I have to be able to move my head."

Something inside my heart cracks, a pool of warmth spilling out that I wish I could wrap around Ryker like a protective bubble. Wanting to show him that I can respect his boundaries, I lower my hands.

"I don't like lighters, or fire, or rickety water towers. But I like you. I *trust* you." I take a deep breath. "You can trust me, too."

Ryker gets a faraway look in his eye, jaw clenching and unclenching like he's mulling something over.

A beat goes by.

And then another.

My stomach sinks when he starts to lean away. But then he shifts his weight, grabs my hand, and brings it to his cheek, kissing the soft skin of my inner wrist before pushing his face against my open palm.

My chest swells in time with my rapidly beating heart as I graze my thumb across his rough stubble. "I promise I'll never hurt you," I whisper.

Eyes hard and smoldering with heat, Ryker brings his nose to mine. "Don't make promises you can't keep." Then he's kissing me, and I'm sliding my hands into his raven hair and lightly dragging my nails across his scalp as he moans into my mouth.

The kiss is different this time—slower and deeper, tugging at something inside my chest while slickening my core with each subtle rotation of his hips between my thighs.

At first, I'm delicate with my touch, but after a minute or two of him rocking his body against my aching center, I'm so riled up I can't think of anything but my singular desire for *more* of him. I have to use all my restraint not to claw at his shoulders and draw him closer.

Ryker's hands are everywhere—at the nape of my neck, between the valley of my breasts, gliding up and down my sides like he can't memorize the curves of my body fast enough. When he places his palm back on my stomach, stopping just shy of where I need his touch most, I can't stop myself from using the arm wrapped around his shoulder as leverage to buck my hips. It's not nearly enough, as evidenced by the absolutely pathetic whimper that escapes my lips.

"You said you wanted me to kiss you," Ryker whispers, nibbling at my jaw. "Did you change your mind? Does that needy pussy of yours want some attention, too?"

Heat pulses through my core. "Yes," I moan. "*Please.*"

"I love it when you beg," he groans, the rumbling sound of his voice making me shudder as his knuckles slide across my belly to unclasp the button of my shorts. Heart rate pounding violently, I lift my hips so he can slide them off, and he makes a satisfied huffing noise against my mouth. "Are you going to behave yourself and let me play as long as I want to?"

Jesus, yes.

I nod a little too enthusiastically.

Chuckling darkly, like he can hear my frenzied thoughts, he slides his hand up the inside of my thigh, brushing his thumb painfully close to my pussy as he spreads my legs apart. My entire body quakes when he drags a knuckle over the thin fabric of my underwear, my stomach coiling tightly enough that I might come apart.

"Look at you," he breathes. "Already drenched. Is all this for me?"

Chest buzzing with warm delight at how pleased he sounds, I bite my lip and nod.

Ryker smiles. And with eyes so dark they're almost black, he leans forward, trailing his lips down my throat while grinding his thigh against my center. I arch into him and moan.

Between kisses, he shifts to the side, trapping one of my legs beneath his while the hand on my hip slides my underwear off. I shiver as cool air brushes across my pussy, my eyes fluttering open and closed with a mixture of desperate want and a jittery sensation in my stomach that feels like there's an electric current beneath my skin.

"Keep those legs spread for me, Princess." He kisses me again, and at the first tease of his fingers dragging over my wet center, I groan, the feel of his rough skin against my most intimate flesh making me feral. My hips rise up to beg for more, and he rewards me by circling my clit.

My nails dig into his shoulders, eyes rolling into the back of my head when Ryker grunts his approval. He's barely touched me and already my inner walls are clenching, like that will somehow draw him inside me faster.

"So fucking needy," Ryker pants. Kissing me, he increases the pressure and speed, groaning against my jaw each time my mouth falls open to whimper or catch my breath. Then his fingers dip lower, teasing my opening before returning to my clit. My muscles contract and little jolts of pleasure shoot up my spine as a steady pressure builds in my low belly.

"Ryker," I gasp, pinching my eyes closed as my body coils and begins to quake.

"Keep those pretty eyes on me," he orders, his voice a raspy growl full of the same frantic desperation taking root inside my core.

My eyes open and I nod before intertwining my fingers at the nape of his neck.

He brings his forehead to mine. "Good girl. Just like that," he hums. "I want to see your face when I—" He slides a finger inside me, his mouth dropping open with a moan in response to the absolutely pathetic mewl of pleasure that escapes my throat.

I arch my back, moisture pooling between my legs as he begins to pump. His movements are slow and exquisite, the sensation so overwhelming, it feels like each stroke is drawing out my pleasure the same way the tide is drawn out before a tsunami.

"Please don't stop," I manage to gasp, keeping my gaze locked on his while I struggle to breathe.

"Fuck," he hisses, kissing me deeply before adding another finger.

I cry out, all at once surprised by how easily it slid in and shocked by the intrusion. I've barely registered the fullness when he begins to move again, the heel of his hand brushing my clit once, twice, three times—each thrust slightly harder than the one before.

My stomach contracts and the pressure builds, the heat coursing through my veins threatening to consume me as I rock into his hand. My pussy flutters around his fingers.

"Ryker—"

"That's it, Princess," he grunts, rutting against my thigh as he finger-fucks me. "Come for me."

My mouth drops open, and when he grinds his heel into my clit again, I shatter, convulsing as wave after wave of ecstasy crashes over me. Ryker's lips collide with mine, my body still shaking uncontrollably with the rolling aftershocks of the most incredible feeling I've ever experienced as he swallows my moans.

When the quaking subsides, his fingers slow, but he doesn't stop pumping until he's wrung every last spasm of my orgasm from me. I lay there, blissed out of my mind, until his voice cuts through my mental haze.

"You're the most beautiful thing I've ever seen," he whispers, leaning down to brush his nose against mine.

I bring my palm to his cheek, heart thumping wildly when he doesn't flinch. But before I can tell him that *he's* the beautiful one, he's rolling over and repositioning himself between my thighs.

His expression hardens, and then he slides his hand to my ass and squeezes. "Are you done ignoring me?"

I shake my head. "If this is what happens when I do, definitely not."

"*Brat*," he growls, pinning my arms above my head and kissing me again, harder than before. More urgent. I kiss him back, rocking my hips against the straining bulge in his jeans while his belt buckle presses into my stomach.

Releasing my hands, he trails his mouth down my neck, my sternum, and then lower...

I try to sit up, but he stops me with two hands on my hips. I go to reach for his belt, but he stops me again.

"That's not how this works," he says with a dark chuckle.

"But I— I already came." My cheeks heat.

Was I supposed to tell him? I thought it was obvious...

Ryker grins, pushing my shoulders back onto the couch. "Once, Princess. You came *once*." He kisses the skin right below my belly button, and my breath hitches at the mischievous glint in his moss-colored eyes.

"Spread these pretty legs for me," he says with a devilish smirk. "I've been dying to know what you taste like."

A car door slams, and Ryker's head snaps to the window. "*Fuck*," he hisses, scrambling off me to retrieve my shorts from the floor. "Your brother's home early."

Chapter Twenty-Nine

I bolt upright, my adrenaline spiking so violently black specks obscure my vision as I spot the top of my brother's Blazer through the window.

My stomach drops. "Oh my God, he's going to *kill* us."

Ryker shoves my discarded clothes into my hands. "Noah's not going to fucking touch you. Get dressed and I'll go talk to him."

"*Talk to him?*" I choke out. "Absolutely not. You can never tell him about this."

Ryker stares at me, lips turned downward and eyes moving rapidly across my face like he doesn't understand what I'm saying.

Outside, another door slams. *Shit.* If that's Noah getting his bags from the trunk, we have seconds before he walks through the front door. The rapid tempo of my already erratic pulse rises to an even dizzier pace.

"Ryker, we have to hide." Panicked and still only wearing a bra, I shove my arm through the head hole of my shirt and end up getting trapped inside. Footsteps sound on the porch while I desperately try to claw myself free. But then I'm being tossed in the air and thrown over Ryker's shoulder, my bare ass and arousal-drenched inner thighs catching a chilling blast of arctic AC as he starts walking.

"Ryker," I plead, bobbing up and down while trying to escape from this stupid straight jacket of a shirt. "Noah's going to freak—"

"I said I'll handle it." His tone is clipped and hard, but he sets me down gently, and a moment later, the sound of the shower fills the room.

Holy crap. He's a genius.

The second I finally manage to get my shirt on straight, I throw myself against the bathroom door, trapping Ryker in here with me.

"Hello?"

Fear racks my body as Noah calls out to us from the living room.

The steady stream of the shower pounds the tile, the heat of the water making the air dense, humid, and difficult to breathe. Beads of sweat gather on my neck, slowly trickling down my thundering chest.

"Ryker? Wills?" The sound of my brother's chipper voice is so close it scrapes across my already raw nerves.

Ryker's gaze connects with mine, and I shake my head, silently pleading with him to stay quiet. Jaw hard and immobile, his attention strays from me to the door.

"*Please*," I whisper, sliding my shorts back on and nearly falling over in the process. "Noah will never forgive me and he'll kick you out of the house."

Ryker's nostrils flare but his breaths are even, his upper body hard and unmoving.

"*Fuck*. Fine," he finally concedes, the muscle in his jaw feathering so forcefully I'm surprised I don't hear his teeth grinding. "I'll keep my mouth shut on one condition."

"Anything," I breathe.

The corner of his mouth kicks up. "Leave your bedroom door unlocked tonight."

Ryker nearly breaks his ribs shimmying out through the bathroom window, and I spend the next few minutes trying not to vomit as I talk to my brother through the door—repeatedly reassuring him that I have no idea where Ryker is. Even going so far as to suggest he check with Old Man Dan.

I should be relieved when Noah leaves, but when I crawl into the shower and sit fully clothed beneath the spray, all I feel is the massive burden of guilt lodging in my chest. Guilt for betraying my brother's trust. Guilt for asking Ryker to lie to his best friend. And most of all, guilt for knowing, beyond a shadow of a doubt, I'd do it all over again.

This is so stupid. Being around Ryker makes me feel alive, and I'm leaving Deadwood in less than two weeks anyway. Don't I deserve a few happy memories from this horrible place?

Maybe if I came clean about some other secrets, I'd feel less guilty about this one?

Not wanting to lose my courage, I rise to my feet and strip off my soaked shirt and shorts, then throw them against the wall where they drop to the floor with a *splat*. An electric current fans out from my fingertips as I trail them across my lips and between my breasts, reveling in how my body no longer feels like a cage of pain and shame but something beautiful and strong.

I wash my hair and body as quickly as possible, barely wasting time wrapping a towel around myself before heading straight for my brother in the kitchen. Ryker is there, too, leaning against the counter, looking like a sinful dessert with his arms folded over his chest and bulging biceps on full display.

My heart skips a beat, and I quickly avert my gaze.

Noah's smile fades when he sees my exposed shoulders, the water dripping from my hair and the heat from the shower probably making my scars more prominent than he's used to seeing. He closes his eyes tightly and swallows.

A few weeks ago, his reaction would've had me running back to my room. Today, I feel nothing. If my brother has a problem with my scars, that's his burden to bear, not mine.

I tap my wet foot against the worn oak floors. "I need to talk to you."

Ryker shoves off the counter, subtly positioning himself so he's within arm's reach of Noah. I give him the tiniest shake of my head, but not a single muscle in his rigid posture uncoils.

Noah groans. "Do you want to put some clothes on first?"

"This will only take a second and it's important."

"Fine," he laments, eyes locked on the ceiling. "Hurry up, though, because—" His phone rings, and he holds up a finger in my direction when he answers. "Hey, man. Yeah, Ryker's going to shower real quick and then we'll be over. It's just you and your cousin, right?"

My grip on the towel tightens, rivulets of water snaking down my arms and legs to form a tiny puddle on the floor as I furrow my brow. He's been home for all of twenty minutes and he's already going out? I glance around, noting that while he has on clean clothes, there's a trail of mud from the front door to his discarded boots and a massive pile of laundry has been dumped in the hallway.

"Noah," I clip, trying to convey my annoyance so he'll end the call. When the finger he's holding up turns into an open-faced palm gesturing for me to wait, my blood begins to boil.

"Noah Dunn," I screech. "I'm trying to tell you something important here."

He sighs. "I'm going to have to call you back— Yeah, we'll be there in less than thirty." He finally hangs up, mustache twitching as he glares in my direction. "Wills, you can't seriously still be pissed about me picking up more hours on the rig?"

"What? No, of course not." I clutch my towel, head cocking to the side. "Wait, why *are* you home so early?" His normal fourteen-day stint shouldn't be over yet.

"I've been home for ten fucking seconds and you're already interrogating me?" Noah throws his hands into the air, jutting his chin out with an impatient shake of his head. "Can't you just say whatever it is you came out here to say and then go get dressed?"

"Noah, lay off," Ryker interjects. "If you stop jumping down her throat and give her a second, I'm sure she'll tell you."

My brother rolls his eyes, boredom leaking through every pore in his body as he makes a circular motion with his hand for me to get on with it.

My pulse stalls. *Moment of truth.* I take a deep breath. "Dad's been acting a little cagey. I also found a weird note in the garden, and then someone broke into the house and left another one—"

Out of the corner of my eye, Ryker bristles and takes a step toward me, but the seething look I toss his way thankfully stops him in his tracks.

When I glance back to Noah, he's yawning and looking at his phone. "Was that it? We're meeting up with Marco in like thirty minutes and I still need to change and take a shit," he says, not bothering to look up as he types.

Okay, *gross*, and *what the hell?* I just told him a stranger was in our house and *this* is his reaction? Ryker opens his mouth to say something, but I beat him to it. "No, that's not it. I also wanted to tell you I got into the Un—" My voice cracks and my lip starts to quiver, but Noah doesn't notice. He's too busy smiling at something on his screen, not listening to a word I've said.

I lift my chin. "You know what, yeah. That was it."

The front door swings open. "Hey, kiddo. I saw Noah's Blazer in the—"

I stomp off to my room without hearing the rest of Dad's greeting, kicking my door closed and locking it for good measure before remembering what Ryker said in the shower...

Leave your bedroom door unlocked tonight.

A shiver dances up my spine, and without a second thought or an ounce of guilt hanging over my shoulders, I reach for the handle and unlatch the lock.

Chapter Thirty

Sleep is evasive, interrupted by the roar of my father's snores from the opposite side of the house and the low groan of the wind rustling through the pines.

The shadows crawling across my curtains take on the sinister form of the half-man, half-goat cryptid Elanor told me about a few days ago, its spine hunched and horns twisted skyward to skewer the stars. The rational part of my brain knows there's nothing out there, that the dark is playing tricks on me, but legends have to come from somewhere, right? If a cautionary tale about a murderous goat-man stealing virgins from their beds at night exists, something must've occurred to inspire it.

My mind wanders to the day of the eclipse—the way the dying light almost made the hooded figure look like he had horns or antlers... Beneath the comforter, a shiver slides up my legs. This is exactly why I wish there was a way to turn my brain off at night. I just can't help but—

A floorboard creaks on the porch, and this time the silhouette that crosses over the curtains is suspiciously human shaped...

Having tortured myself enough, I roll away from the window, my blood freezing as a looming shadow takes shape on my armchair in the corner of the room. I blink, trying to force the trick of the light into something less sinister, but a flash of silver catches my eye, and the shadow rises.

My muscles tense, and even though I should run and scream, I can't seem to move.

The shadow takes a step closer but—trapped somewhere between fear paralysis and a silent scream—all I can do is draw in a shaky breath. I'm about to die, I know it, and I still can't find the strength to move...

Rain-soaked pine hits my nostrils and my rigid shoulders instantly soften.

"Ryker?" I breathe out in a rush.

"When the *fuck* did someone break into this house?" he growls, stepping into the thin stream of moonlight seeping through a gap in the curtains while flipping the silver trinket in his hand—which I now recognize as his boot-shaped lighter.

"I thought you were at Marco's with Noah?" I whisper, clutching the comforter to my sweat-slick chest. "How long have you been sitting there?"

"Answer the damn question, Willa," he says, voice low and dangerously calm. "When the fuck did this happen? Did someone hurt you?"

My hands shake as I sit up and draw my knees to my chin. "No, of course not. It wasn't like that. There was a noise when I was in the shower, and then I found a note in the living room and an egg carton full of seedlings. It's not that big of a deal. I'm fine."

"When you were in the fucking *shower*?" Ryker's chest heaves, his shadow growing larger with each rapid breath. "When was this and why the hell didn't you tell me?"

"It happened the afternoon Noah left," I stammer, baffled and slightly terrified by the rage radiating off him. "I didn't want my dad to freak out, so I only told Isabel... She still has the note. I swear it's not a big deal. It was just someone messing with me."

He growls again, the sound so deep and threatening my body trembles in response. For some reason, it feels as though I've been caught lying, and all I want to do is kneel at his feet and beg for forgiveness.

What the hell? Where did that thought even come from?

Confused by the unexpected heat stirring in my belly, I look away, only to have Ryker close the distance and force my gaze to his with a hooked finger under my jaw. "Do you have any idea who it was?"

"No." I rise onto my knees to ease the strain in my neck, and the comforter slips from my body. My nipples instantly pebble under the cool rush of AC while the sliver of moonlight perfectly illuminates my thin tank top and lacy boy shorts.

Ryker's breaths turn ragged as he takes me in. "I like you keeping things from me about as much as I like you pretending I don't exist," he says, digging his rough fingers into the soft flesh of my hip and taking a step closer. His mouth is only a centimeter away from mine now, my face still firmly in his grip while the smell of pine curls around me like smoke.

The pulse between my legs gives a painful throb. "Maybe you should remind me what happens when I do something you don't like?"

Ryker rumbles, the sound resonating deep in my stomach before he abruptly drops my chin and storms out of the room.

I stay there, slack-jawed and frozen in place until an engine roars to life in the driveway.

What the hell?

I scramble out of bed, tearing open the curtains in time to see a spray of rocks and dust as Ryker peels onto the dirt road and heads toward town.

Chapter Thirty-One

My bucket list is missing.

I've torn the house apart twice over and have nothing to show for it. I thought maybe I'd find remnants of the disintegrated paper in the shorts that got wet in the shower, but that proved to be wishful thinking.

Throwing the couch cushion back into place, I tug at my hair. The last thing I need is for Noah to find the list and start asking questions about Isabel's lovely addition of *Get Laid*—or worse, have him rat me out to Dad about wanting to leave Deadwood before I get the chance to tell him myself.

Groaning, I bury my face in my hands. *I'm so screwed.*

Gravel crunches outside, followed by two doors slamming in quick succession. My whole body goes on high alert with the sudden realization that Ryker is about to walk in here any second. Apart from his unexpected appearance in my bedroom in the middle of the night, he and Noah never came home from Marco's.

My heart thuds wildly inside my chest. How am I supposed to act normal around the man who had me convulsing around his fingers yesterday when my brother is in the same room with us? How am I supposed to feel after he disappeared into the night when he should have stayed and done it again...

My eyes fly to the door as it creaks open, an odd mixture of disappointment and bitterness crawling into my throat when Noah walks through it alone.

"Hey, Wills," he says sheepishly, eyes darting between me and the floor. I can smell the hangover on him from here, as well as whatever citrusy cologne he borrowed in a half-assed attempt to cover up the sweat, whiskey, and beer leaching off him.

I cross my arms, brows pinching as I take in his appearance.

The collar of his shirt is torn and his lips are pink and swollen, like he got into a fight—*go figure*—but there's something different about him today. He has the same bags under his eyes that he always has after coming off the rig or spending a night out drinking. But he's also tanner with little patches of white skin near his temples and forehead, the type you only get after a bad sunburn...

My head cocks to the side. That sort of coloring doesn't happen overnight. Was I so eager to get my secrets off my chest yesterday that I overlooked it?

Movement in the window catches my eye at the same time Noah clears his throat.

"Listen, I wanted to apologize for being a dick yesterday. You were trying to talk to me, and I was..." His voice trails off as he follows the direction of my gaze to the garden where Ryker is messing with the hose.

I school my features and try to feign indifference to the glorious way the morning light highlights the muscles in Ryker's neck and arms, but that's a *very* difficult thing to do with butterflies fluttering inside your belly and heat creeping into your cheeks.

A small grin curls the corner of my lips before I quickly tuck it away.

When I return my attention to Noah, the severe set of his mouth almost makes me flinch. A moment passes while we stare at one another, then my brother slowly bobs his head, the *too*-controlled movement coating my stomach with icy dread.

"What were you going to tell me yesterday?" he asks calmly, tone flat and inflectionless.

"Do you mean after I mentioned someone broke into the house and you ignored me for your phone?" I scoff.

Neither one of us breaks eye contact, although Noah's mustache flares occasionally, like he's sucking his teeth or flexing his jaw.

"Do you really expect me to believe that someone broke into our house and you didn't immediately tell Dad?" he asks through a sarcastic laugh. "Seems to me like you were mad I left a week early for the rig and didn't want me to go out with *my* best friend, so you made up a story to keep me home."

My head snaps back. "What? I would never—"

"If you didn't make it up, then let's tell Dad right now. He'd want to know if there was a stranger in the house." Noah takes a deep breath. "Hey, Da—"

I clamp my hand over his mouth, his mustache scraping against my palm as he lifts a single smug brow that screams *I knew it.*

"I'm not lying," I whisper-yell, retracting my hand.

"Fine. Let's say you weren't lying about that," he says with so much sickly sweet snark it makes my teeth hurt. "There was something else you wanted to tell me yesterday, right?" He glances out the window toward Ryker. "What was it?"

He waits, blinking slowly while his gaze bores into mine.

My pulse kicks up a notch. *There's no way he knows...*

"I thought you were going to apologize," I croak, and when he says nothing, I take a single step in the direction of the hallway, giving him one last chance to show concern over anything other than his suspicions about my interest in Ryker.

He, of course, does no such thing.

A lump forms in my throat and I take another step backward. "If you're not going to say sorry for being a jerk and you still don't believe me about the break-in, then I have nothing more to say to you."

Noah's eyes stay locked on mine as I retreat, their once familiar soft blue now cold and distant. When I'm safely behind my closed bedroom door, I take a deep, shuddering breath and lean my forehead against the frame—one thought repeating over and over again in my mind.

I can't wait to get the hell out of Deadwood.

I spend the next hour and a half curled up in bed with one of Isabel's books—this one with the perfect amount of darkness and angst about a girl who's been snowed in with her hot step-uncle and two broody step-cousins. But then my grumbling stomach finally forces me to get dressed and leave my hovel.

Reluctantly, I slide into a pair of jean shorts and a black tank top.

All you have to do is pretend like your life isn't a chaotic mess of half-truths and awkward tension long enough to grab some toast and then you can go back to your room.

After shrugging on a long-sleeve sweater that it's way too hot for, I waltz into the living room, my steps faltering when I find Noah and Dad already staring at me expectantly from the breakfast ladened dining room table.

Oh God... They found my bucket list.

Or worse, they know Ryker fingered me on the couch...

For one horrible second, I can't breathe as slicing blades of panic threaten to eviscerate me from within. I scan the room, searching for some sort of clue as to what's about to happen but find nothing. Forcing myself to think this through, I quickly realize there's no way my family would be sitting at the table so calmly if Dad found out about Austin, and no possible way Ryker would be humming in the kitchen if Noah knew anything had happened between us.

Still, the air in the room is so thick and heavy it squeezes my lungs with every inhale.

278

"Have a seat," Dad says solemnly, his words amplifying the cramped feeling in my chest until it sinks into my stomach.

"Is this some sort of weird intervention for Noah's shitty attitude?" I ask, trying to force a note of brevity into my voice that I definitely don't feel.

Noah scoffs. "I wish, but no. I also have no idea why the hell we're sitting here. *Especially* since Ryker and I were trying to go fishing before he leaves for his appointment..." Noah's eyes dart to the kitchen where Ryker is loading up a bowl of what looks and smells like fluffy Nutella-swirled muffins.

Feeling slightly more confident that I'm not the one in trouble and trying my best to act like my insides aren't a nervous mess, I take the seat across from my brother and steal a slice of bacon from his plate. Before he can snatch it back, I lick it and shove the entire thing into my mouth, smiling at the repulsed look he gives me.

That's what you get for accusing me of lying, asshole.

I chew quickly and wait for Noah's verbal lashing, but it never comes. He just stares at his plate, muttering under his breath.

The bacon loses all flavor, and I frown.

"What was that, son?" Dad chimes, oblivious to the tension brewing right under his nose.

Noah snorts humorlessly, refusing to look in my direction. "I was just pointing out how ironic it is that there's a whole plate of bacon on the table and Willa still chose to take mine."

Dad frowns. "Let me get this straight. Your little sister, the person who cooks, cleans, and looks after you, had a bite of your breakfast. The breakfast that was made and served to you by your best friend while you sat here and didn't lift a finger. And you're being pissy about it?" He leans back in his chair, eyes narrowed. "I think you'll live, son."

Noah crosses his arms and angles his body away from our father.

The vindictive part of me wants to grin from ear to ear that he's being called out on his bullshit, but the bitter taste in my mouth stops me.

With Dad and Noah diving into a new round of bickering, I try to catch Ryker's eye when he rounds the table, but he immediately looks away. I frown, taking in his lowered brow and the hard set of his jaw while he places a pot of coffee and the bowl of muffins on the table.

Is he mad at me too?

I keep trying to grab his attention as he refills Dad's mug and pours out three more cups, but he never looks over—not even when he takes the seat between Dad and me.

A bubbling nausea rolls around inside my stomach.

"Where'd you go last night?" I whisper, eyeing my brother to make sure he's not listening.

"It doesn't matter," Ryker replies out of the side of his mouth. He keeps his eyes straight ahead but pushes the plate of muffins in my direction before quickly tucking his hand under the table. Chocolate hazelnutty goodness floods my senses.

"It *does* matter," I insist. "Where did you—"

"Not here, Willa," he bites out through clenched teeth, the sharpness in his tone a clear indication I'm not going to get an answer out of him. Not right now, anyway.

"You'll tell me later, then?" I ask, but he doesn't answer.

My limbs tingle with the sudden urge to flee from the table, but the crushing weight of my spiraling thoughts prevents me from moving. Does he regret what happened between us? Yesterday was amazing, but we were interrupted before I had the chance to reciprocate. Maybe Ryker went out and had someone else take care of his needs—someone more experienced, who already knows what he likes...

Like Jenny.

I shake my head. No, he wouldn't have come back to ask me who broke in if that was the case. But something *has* changed.

Throat tightening, I glance at Ryker. Now that my brother is home, maybe he decided fooling around with me wasn't worth the risk... That *I* wasn't worth the risk.

My shoulders curve inward in a futile attempt to keep the

growing disappointment in my chest at bay while I continue to watch him load up his plate with food, never so much as breathing in my direction. Noah and Dad are still arguing, but I'm no longer hungry. If Ryker's going to spend the rest of breakfast ignoring me, then I should just go back to my damn room and—

Rough knuckles drag up the length of my thigh, leaving a heated wave of shivers in their wake as Ryker shoves his plate in front of me. "Eat something," he says quietly, now running his knuckles in the opposite direction, toward my knee.

Dad taps his palm against the table, and I jump. "Willa? Are you listening?"

I turn my head so fast my neck cracks and my elbow knocks into my coffee mug, but thankfully I catch it before it spills. "Sorry, what?"

Dad sighs, the purple bags under his eyes darker than they were only a minute ago. "I said I've been holding on to this for a while"—he glances at Ryker—"but it was brought to my attention that it was a mistake to keep it from you."

Noah sits up straighter, making nervous eye contact with his plate while sneaking glances in my direction. A coldness settles over my skin. Does he know something I don't?

Before I have the chance to spiral down that rabbit hole, Dad is talking again. "Chief Thompson is retiring, and I've been selected to take over as chief of police."

My shoulders sag in relief.

"I know y'all think I work too much already," he continues, "but with Willa getting her degree and Noah gone half the month, this will be good for me. I can make a difference in this town."

"Congrats, Dad. That's amazing." *It's also about damn time.* I was starting to think he was never going to tell us.

"Thanks, kiddo," he says through a forced smile, meeting my eye for barely a millisecond before looking away.

My brow furrows.

Ryker and Noah offer their congratulations next, and this time Dad's grin seems genuine.

"I won't officially take over until after the next town hall meeting, but one of the first things I plan on doing is getting some new blood in the department. Which means I have one more bit of news," he says, staring across the table at Ryker. "I'd like you all to say hello to Deadwood's newest police cadet."

My brother opens his mouth like he's about to argue, but stops, face twisting from annoyance to something closer to hurt when he realizes who Dad's looking at.

Beneath the table, Ryker grips my thigh. It feels so much like a panic reflex, I'm not even sure he knows he's doing it. "I thought there wasn't going to be an academy opening for six months?" he asks, body eerily still except for his twitching fingers and the pulse in his neck hammering away.

Dad beams at him. "I pulled some strings and got you a spot in the upcoming class. You start next Monday."

My stomach drops. *So soon?*

Ryker's grip on my leg loosens, his expression transforming from tight and disbelieving into something radiant. My heart skips a beat, and after one final squeeze, Ryker lets go of my thigh and rises to his feet.

Dad smiles so wide I can hardly see his eyes. "Fair warning. Our department is small, so we partner with a few of the neighboring towns and train at the Sheriff's Facility in Jonestown. We have the budget to put you up in a hotel Monday through Friday, but you'll need to come stay at the house during the weekends. I figure you can use that time to study."

"I don't know what to say." Ryker shakes his head, voice thick with emotion. "Thank you, sir."

Dad is all smiles. "I also took the liberty of getting your packing list for you—uniforms, gear, boots, everything you'll need." He gets a faraway look in his eye, the same way he always does when he's remembering his early days on the force. "The training can be overwhelming, but once you're sworn in, you'll have great benefits and be an excellent candidate for guardianship or a kinship placement for Charlotte. Everything is going to work out the way it should."

Ryker's eyes brighten, like he's just seen his first sunrise after a decades-long night. "I'm meeting with my attorney this afternoon to go over the plan and fill out some paperwork. What else can I do to be a better candidate in the eyes of the court?"

"We probably need to get you your own apartment. Line up some day care options for when you're on shift, that way you can show you've thought all this through." Dad rubs the stubble on his chin. "You'd look better on paper if you were married, but it's not a requirement. Just the same, you might want to hold off on casual encounters and start going on a few dates," he says with a wink.

My fists ball under the table, the thought of Ryker with another girl curdling my insides so violently I speak without thinking. "I can watch Charlie."

Ryker's smile falters, his brows scrunching together before he closes his eyes.

"That's sweet of you, kiddo," Dad says with a proud laugh that sounds foreign after not hearing it in months, "but Ryker needs reliable childcare if he's awarded guardianship. With classes and commuting, you won't be here during the day, remember?"

Realization coils tightly around my lungs... Dad might've had the specifics wrong, but he's right. I won't be able to help with Charlie because I'll be in Austin...

Ryker glances at me over his shoulder, and even though I'm the one leaving, I can't shake the feeling that Deadwood is once again about to take something from me.

He turns back to Dad, voice chock-full of emotion as he shakes his hand before abruptly pulling Dad up and into a hug. "Thank you again, sir."

Dad freezes, looking momentarily surprised before his shoulders soften and his eyes turn water-lined. "No need to thank me, son. You know I've always thought of you as family."

I catch the briefest flash of red on Ryker's knuckles when he leans away, but he shoves his hand into his pocket before I get the chance to see what it is.

Throughout the exchange, Noah remains silent, staring at the two of them with an expression I've never seen on his face before. It's almost soft, maybe defeated, but after a moment or two, he grits his teeth. "Is there anything else you wanted to talk to us about, *Dad?*"

It's almost the exact same question he asked me earlier, and even though Dad's eyes flash to mine, he's already shaking his head. "Nope, nothing I can think of."

Something in my stomach hardens as I look between them, their stern expressions locked in an unspoken exchange I can't even begin to decipher except for two glaringly obvious facts:

Taking over as chief wasn't Dad's only secret, and whatever it is he's keeping from me, Noah already knows.

Chapter Thirty-Two

Isabel climbs into my truck and trails French-tipped fingers appreciatively over the dashboard. "Damn, look how much room there is in here. A girl could get used to this."

Without power steering, it takes all my concentration and strength to back out of her parents' curved driveway, but I'm smiling when I pull onto the main road. "Is that your subtle way of saying I'll be our designated driver next semester?"

She laughs, but the sound is dry and flat. "Yeah, maybe."

My brow furrows at the sudden shift in her tone. "I was *kidding*. You've been driving us around for years, I'm excited I finally get to repay the favor."

"I know," she says with a forced laugh, but there's a strain in her voice. When I glance over, she's fidgeting with the hem of her pale-yellow dress.

"Hey," I nudge her with my elbow. "Everything okay?"

"Yeah, I'm fine." Isabel waves me off with a shrug, her lip trembling slightly as she turns toward the window. "Cross my heart." She draws an X over her chest instead of her usual T for trust.

"Okay, what's going on?" I ask gently before putting all my strength into making a wide right turn.

"It's just..." She lets go of a heavy sigh that sounds like it's been bottled up for quite a while. "I've been talking to some of the patrons at Rib Cage and... I don't know. Do you ever wonder what the point of it all is?" She gestures around her and sighs again when I shake my head.

"I mean, is *this* all there is?" Her voice pitches an octave higher. "Like, why are we going to school in the first place? So we can get a job that makes some rich guy even richer? Just to pay off the degree we didn't want to begin with? Why? Because it's expected of us?"

Out of breath, she scoffs and reaches for my hand on the shifter, curling her fingers so tightly around mine her nails threaten to break the skin. "There has to be more," she says, eyes wild and brimming with unspent tears. "Life has to *mean* more. I'm not here by accident, and you didn't survive that fire just to leave this place and never look back, right?"

Her statement lingers in the air between us, the shock waves reverberating through my skull like an unexpected slap to the face. I rip my hand out of hers, and the second I do, the spark in her gaze fades. She blinks and then the look is gone entirely.

"Sorry," she mumbles. "I don't know what's wrong with me. I think I'm just tired."

I eye her skeptically as her jasmine perfume swirls around the inside of the truck, the familiar scent laced with the light hint of something musky and foreign.

"Who have you been talking to at the bar?" It's not the most sensitive question to ask, considering she's obviously feeling out of sorts, but it's the most pertinent. "Was it one of the Blackthornes?"

This time, she really does laugh. "God no. Honestly, forget I said anything. Jenny and I hung out at my brother's place after I got off work last night and I'm exhausted." She pauses, and I feel her heavy gaze caress my cheek.

"Noah and Ryker were there," she prompts when I don't respond.

286

"Ryker disappeared for a couple hours after everyone passed out. You wouldn't know anything about that, would you?"

My muscles tense. I want to keep pushing her on the previous topic, but of course she'd go and bring up the one subject I'd find more interesting.

"No, ma'am." Keeping my facial expression as neutral as possible, I take a left turn, stopping at a crosswalk to let a sour-faced Dorothy Blackthorne cross the street. It takes her a second to realize who's driving the truck, but when she does, she promptly makes the sign of the cross over her upper torso with a pasty white finger and quickly waddles away.

I roll my eyes. *Damn Blackthornes.*

"So, Ryker disappeared in the middle of the night? Where do you think he went?" I do my best to sound uninterested, but the question comes out a little too high-pitched.

"Yep. He asked me what I knew about the break in and got all broody when I suggested he talk to the person who was there. I thought for sure he'd snuck off to do just that," she says with a disappointed huff, thankfully not noticing how I'm hanging on to her every word. "But if he wasn't at your house, then I have no idea where he ran off to. He and Noah were already leaving when I woke up, so I didn't get a chance to ask."

I scrunch my mouth to the side and shrug. "Weird."

Still mulling over where he could have gone after leaving my bedroom last night, I pull into a parking spot in front of Benny's Ice Cream Parlor. After throwing the truck into park, I stare blankly ahead at the picture frame windows while a nervous churning bubbles to life inside my stomach. One that has nothing to do with Ryker.

Isabel must sense the shift in my mood because her soft hand lands on my forearm. "It looks *really* crowded in there. Why don't I just grab the cones and bring them out like I normally do?"

I glance down at my outfit. Black boots, jean skirt, and a tight black cap-sleeve T-shirt that I changed into after work today. I have my little red bandana tied loosely around my neck, but no jacket... Which means the scars on my shoulders and neck are readily visible for anyone who looks hard enough.

I shake my head. "No. I'm going in so I can officially cross off number seven on my bucket list."

Stop hiding. Go out more.

I might've misplaced the list itself, but I need to finish it and I'm running out of time. I take a deep breath and crack my door, flinching when two hands slam onto the hood of my truck.

"Nice wheels," Cooper Blackthorne sneers, picking at a rusted section of metal as a dark cloud momentarily blocks out the sweltering sun. "Looks like you *and* your truck have damage no amount of paint or makeup could cover. Fitting."

My grip on the handle becomes crushing. *Maybe now would be a good time to cross off another bucket list item...*

I look Cooper up and down, scowling at the rolled-up sleeves of his Deadwood Fire Department T-shirt and the disgusting way his overly suntanned skin and Blackthorne-brown hair are soaked in sweat. I scan the street to see if his friends are close by, noticing three more sweaty firefighters jogging into the station a block away—clearly just finishing up some sort of group run.

"I know what you're thinking," Isabel whines, "but he's not worth it. Let's just go."

"Sure as hell seems worth it to me," I say through gritted teeth. "And since when did you start trying to talk me out of doing something unhinged?"

Annoyed, I go to shut my door, only to have Cooper rip it all the way open, my grip on the handle yanking me out of my seat and onto the pavement. I land *hard* on my hands and knees, barely stopping myself from face-planting into the blacktop.

Before I can pop back up, tires are squealing on the road behind me, the nauseating scent of burnt rubber suffocating as it crawls inside my lungs and squeezes. Eyes watering, I cough, and a door slams a few feet away, followed by thudding bootsteps.

"Back the fuck off, Blackthorne," a smoky male voice says from my left.

Ryker.

My body exhales a sigh of relief, only to start choking on the tire fumes all over again.

"I'm just repaying Willa for your little visit last night," Cooper sneers. "You're lucky you didn't land that punch or I'd be doing a lot fucking worse. That being said," a hissing sound fills the air, "this might not be *your* truck, but payback is payback."

Isabel shrieks, and my head snaps to the right where Cooper is removing a pocketknife from my rapidly deflating front left tire. My fingers flex on the pavement.

What the hell? Where was he even keeping that thing?

Ryker's massive hand wraps around my bicep, steadying me while I scramble to my feet. The second I'm upright, I lunge for Cooper, but Ryker's fierce grip stops me.

"There are about a dozen gawking idiots staring at us right now," he growls against my ear. "If he fucking touches you, I won't be able to stop myself from laying him out. It was hard enough to pull back last night..."

A flicker of understanding bleeds through my anger. *Getting into a fight would lose him his spot at the academy...* But what does he mean last night? His fingers tighten around my bicep. Glancing down, I spot the angry red abrasions on his knuckles.

My throat dries out, and I slowly lift my chin to meet his stormy green eyes. "Ryker, what did you do?"

Cooper belts out a laugh. "Your fucking guard dog ambushed me in the middle of the night and accused me of breaking into your house. Then he punched my truck like a goddamn animal and cracked the fucking window." Slow jogging backward, he points an aggressive finger at Ryker. "You're lucky I'm at work right now. If you *ever* come at me again, it won't be her truck I sink my knife into next."

"*Motherfucker*," Ryker says through gritted teeth, shoving me aside to go after Cooper who's thankfully already a half a block away.

I reach for his shoulder. "Don't. It's not worth it."

Ryker stops mid-step, a bead of sweat rolling down his temple as we watch Cooper disappear inside the station. Fists clenched at his sides, he glances toward the peaked stone arches of the police station on the other side of the Old Town Square and then roughly rakes his fingers through his hair.

"We're leaving," he says, grabbing my elbow and dragging me to his truck before unceremoniously throwing me inside. "Isabel, do you need a ride?"

"Nope, I can walk," she says with a smile, already locking up my Chevy and tossing him the keys. The second he turns to close the door, she gives me a little wink and mouths, "*Go get 'em, girl!*" before pantomiming a small explosion with her hand.

"*Traitor,*" I mouth through the dirty, half-open window.

Ryker doesn't say a word to me as he climbs in and takes off, speeding down the road in the opposite direction of my house.

Chapter Thirty-Three

Hair lashing at my cheeks, I shift uncomfortably on the wool blanket. "You showed up in the nick of time back there. You stalking me, Bennett?"

My smile is bright and playful, but he doesn't even acknowledge that I've spoken as he turns us onto a dirt road. My insides shrivel. "What," I say with a strained laugh, "no comment about how good I look on my knees this time?"

Eyes hard, he glances over at me but still doesn't say a word.

A gust of wind kicks up the dirt in the nearby field, giving the sun a deep burnt-orange hue and filling the air with an earthy metallic scent that makes me a little queasy.

My stomach flips, and after several minutes of excruciating silence, I ask, "How'd it go with your lawyer?"

"Not great." He grinds his teeth, apparently annoyed with my constant questions, but at least he responded.

"Why, what hap—"

He slams on the brakes, barely shooting out a hand in time to keep me from banging my head against the dashboard.

"Can you stop talking for a fucking second?" he huffs, roughly dragging his fingers through his hair. "I've had a shit fucking day. I'm a shit fucking friend. And it's taking all my willpower not to bend you over my knee and punish that perfect little ass of yours for not telling me that someone broke into your goddamn house. For making me lie to Noah..."

Biting his lip, he grunts and hits the steering wheel.

Sounds like we've both had a shit day, and while he's not responsible for mine, I'm partially to blame for his. My pulse kicks up a notch, heat pooling between my legs as an idea takes root.

"Would that make you feel better?" I ask, surprised by my boldness as I rise onto my knees and slowly inch my skirt up.

"Would *what* make me feel better?" Ryker growls, sucking in a sharp breath at the sight of my see-through lace thong. A second later, he's scooting to the middle of the bench seat, jaw hard as he uses his calloused palm to slide the denim up and over my hip until it's bunched around my waist.

Eyes zeroed on my barely covered pussy, his chest rumbles—the sound so similar to a predator zeroing in on prey that it makes my belly quiver.

Leaving my skirt hiked up, I crawl forward, draping myself across his lap with my ass in the air. "Last night, you risked your position at the police academy to go after Cooper for me. I also asked you to lie to your best friend *and* shoved you out the window like a dirty secret," I rasp, looking over my shoulder at him. "What are you gonna do about it?"

With a dangerously low growl, he slides his palm up the back of my thigh, stopping right below the crease where my butt meets my leg.

Shivers pebble across my exposed skin and knots coil in my stomach.

"You want to know what I'm going to do about it?" His hand lifts, and before I can rethink this brazen decision, his palm strikes my ass with a loud *smack*.

I gasp as the warm sting spreads through my body.

"Is this what you wanted, Princess?" he asks, chest rising and falling in quick succession.

I nod, unable to form words as an intoxicating heat courses through my veins like a drug. He smacks my ass again, the sharp bite untwisting those tightly coiled knots in my stomach until I'm putty in his lap. All thoughts of the secrets Noah and Dad are keeping, of Isabel's awkwardness, even my hurt over Cooper's stupid comments about my truck and my scars slowly melt away.

"Do it again," I mewl. "Please."

Ryker's hard cock presses into my stomach, twitching beneath his jeans. "*Fuck,*" he groans, hand coming down hard over and over again until I'm a whimpering mess and the pulse between my thighs is so wild it demands attention.

God, what is he doing to me? And why do I hope he never stops?

He spanks me again, the loud *crack* echoing through the truck and out into the adjacent field. A soft moan escapes my lips, and I squeeze my legs together, desperate for more friction between them.

He growls, stilling his palm mid-swing and sending a rush of air sliding across the inflamed cheeks of my ass like a smooth caress.

"Arch your back and keep those pretty thighs spread for me, Princess."

I comply, opening my legs and curving my spine until the strain is nearly unbearable. He rewards me by trailing his fingers over my pussy and giving my clit a few light slaps that have me seeing stars. My clit throbs, craving more of his touch in whatever form he's willing to give it.

I open my legs wider, and this time when he smacks my ass, he gets my pussy too, sending molten waves of heat coursing through my belly. My brain goes numb as he does it again and again, praising me with each swipe of his hand.

"Look at you, taking your punishment like such a good fucking girl." My chest buzzes with warm contentment. "Are you going to stop keeping things from me?" Ryker asks, dipping his fingers between my legs, teasing me with painstakingly slow circles around my clit.

"*Yes,*" I gasp, already so close to coming I can barely keep my eyes open.

He hums appreciatively and spanks me again, the momentum of his palm propelling me a few inches forward so that my clit is now pressed against his knee.

I squirm and electricity shoots up my spine like a bolt of lightning across a stormy sky.

Oh God... I'm almost there.

"Ryker," I whine, desperate for more. "*Please.*"

"You're about to come, aren't you?" His voice is low and full of dark amusement that only heightens my arousal.

I nod, tears threatening to spill from my eyes with the intensity of my need for him. One more touch and I'll—

Ryker removes his hands from my body entirely. "Are you leaving Deadwood?"

"What?" I try to look back at him, but he spanks me so hard all I can do is close my eyes tightly, my insides fluttering.

"Number two on your fucking list," he growls. "It said to tell your dad and Noah that you want to leave Deadwood. I'd like to know where the hell you think you're going."

Holy shit.

He's the one who found my bucket list?

I barely have time to react before two hands trail up the inside of my leg—one inching my thighs further apart while the other slides my underwear to the side.

I clench, waiting for the relief of his touch, but it never comes.

"I asked you a question, *Princess,*" he says, voice seductive and threateningly low as he drags a knuckle down my center, teasing the swollen lips of my pussy while avoiding my clit entirely.

"Austin! I'm moving to Austin to go to UT," I cry out, arching my back and wiggling my hips to bring him closer to where I so desperately need his touch. *Jesus,* it's like he's turned me into a needy monster. I'd say anything, *do* anything to have his fingers inside me—for him to bring me to the edge...

Ryker stills and then, in one fluid motion, he's flipping me over and taking my jaw into his large hand. *"When?"* he demands, tone full of gravel and smoke.

I stare up at him, my heart beating so fast it feels like it'll explode. "Orientation is in less than two weeks. The Sunday after next," I pant as he holds me in place.

Ryker's eyes widen, his mouth forming into a tight line. "And I start the fucking academy on Monday..." His grip becomes crushing. "I want those two weeks. But if I can't have that, I want every damn second you'll give me," he growls.

I search his stony face, unsure exactly what he means but wanting to give it to him just the same.

"They're all yours," I whisper.

Gaze locked on mine, he trails his thumb across my bottom lip before forging a slow path down my sternum and over my stomach, then lower until he's cupping me between my legs. "I want this pussy too."

Pulse pounding in my ears, my belly flutters. "It's yours."

"Damn right it is." His chest rumbles with approval. "Take off your underwear so I can taste what's mine."

Holy hell, that's hot. Hands shaking, I slide backward off Ryker's lap into the driver's seat and shimmy out of my thong as he kicks open the passenger door. I let out a squeal when he grabs my boots and drags me across the seat. At the last second, I grip the steering wheel with both hands, baring myself to him entirely.

"You have the prettiest pussy I've ever seen," Ryker says, eyes rolling into the back of his head as he crouches over and slides his palms beneath my hips. I shiver when his nose trails up my inner thigh. He kisses and licks his way north until his tongue meets my center, and I let out a sound I've never made before—carnal, needy, and half feral.

My head tilts back as he licks again and again, increasing the pressure on my clit with each stroke until I go still, lungs emptying on a gasp while my belly floods with heat. Unable to stop myself, I writhe against his lips and tongue, still holding on to the steering wheel like my life depends on it.

"Fucking hell, you taste like heaven," Ryker pants, shoving my knees further apart to lap up every ounce of the wetness he wrung out of me with the spanking.

A bolt of pleasure shoots through me, and I nearly lose my grip on the wheel.

God, I want to run my fingers through his hair and draw him closer, but even though Ryker let me touch him yesterday, I don't want to push him too far. Especially when he said he needs to be able to move his head.

With only his bright green eyes visible above the mound of my pussy, he glances up at me while his tongue continues to work my swollen clit, brow furrowing when he notices my hands over my head on the wheel. With a growl, he abruptly rises to his feet, pushing his hips between my legs and leaning over to reach for the bandana around my neck.

Body aching with the sudden loss of his heat on my clit, I whimper as the lemony scent of the bandana swirls around me. Then my wrists are pinned together and Ryker's using the worn red cloth to tie them to the steering wheel.

"You like putting yourself at my mercy, Princess?" he asks darkly, tugging on the bandana to see if it's secure.

Hands above my head, I nod, heart racing as I pull against the restraint to see if it'll slip. It doesn't. I yank harder, a mixture of nerves and excitement causing my stomach to corkscrew and tremble.

Ryker grins, quirking a brow. "Do you want me to untie you?"

I immediately shake my head, unable to verbalize how the loss of control has molten exhilaration coursing through my bloodstream, heightening all my senses.

"Good, because you look so goddamn beautiful like this." He

slowly inches up my shirt to expose my thin bra, pinching my peaked nipples through the fabric.

My pussy clenches and I moan, grinding my hips against nothing. He leans forward and kisses my belly before dropping down to bite my inner thigh, not quite hard enough to leave a mark, but hard enough that the pain travels straight to my throbbing center.

I whimper and then gasp when he wraps his mouth around my clit, flicking his tongue until every inch of my skin is tingling. I'm already close again, still teetering on the edge from the spanking.

"*Ryker*," I whine, and thankfully he keeps going, sliding his hands under my ass and feasting on me with long, delicious strokes.

I buck my hips, chasing the rippling warmth spreading from my center into my legs. It feels so good, *too good*, so much so that I'm writhing uncontrollably while my cowboy boots dig into the dashboard and the bench seat. That doesn't deter him, though. He just pins my hips and keeps at it, adding two fingers that send me careening straight into an orgasm with such force it blurs my vision.

My whole body is spasming, but he keeps sucking my clit and pumping his fingers, drawing out the ecstasy. I can't breathe. I can barely see as I'm tossed about in the eye of the storm. All I know for sure is that rain-soaked pine and the sweet-and-salty scent of Ryker's sweat is everywhere—*he* is everywhere, the low groan of his approval seeping into every corner of my being.

"Fuck," he says once my body finally stops quivering. He slides both hands up and down my inner thighs until one moves to the very obvious bulge in his jeans. I bite my lip when he reaches down to adjust himself, shifting his length to the side so it rests against his thigh before stroking himself over the denim.

My mouth salivates. I want his cock. I want him to feel as good as I do, and I want him to fuck me right here in the middle of this road where anyone could drive by and see.

Jesus. What's gotten into me? Was this depravity always lurking beneath the surface? Or is this just what Ryker does to me...

Still stroking himself, he leans forward, his hot breath ghosting over my soaked center. "Less than two fucking weeks and I'm not even here for half of it..." Squeezing my inner thigh, he shakes his head. "It's not enough time. I want to paint you with my fucking cum. Brand myself on your goddamned soul."

"Ry— Ryker," I pant, volts of electricity shooting up my spine as he draws my clit into his mouth once again. "Oh, God. Please, don't stop."

He looks up from between my legs, pulling away just long enough to say, "I fucking love it when you beg, Princess," before diving right back in.

Chapter Thirty-Four

Sometime after my third orgasm, Ryker unties the bandana from around my wrists, kissing the slightly pink skin beneath before sliding my clothes back into place. I am boneless and drenched in sweat, but I've never been more content.

"You were right," he says with a massive grin, throwing the spare shirt he cleaned me up with onto the floor before buckling my seat belt. "I feel a whole hell of a lot better."

Chest buzzing and brain fuzzy, I wiggle in my seat, wincing while I struggle to find a position that doesn't hurt my butt.

Ryker's grin falters, then he reaches over to gently cup my jaw. "Was I too rough?"

"No, you were perfect," I say honestly, because he was. There's something about putting myself entirely at his mercy that's freeing and powerful. Something about the sharp sting of his hand against my bare ass that makes my head quiet and calm. I feel incredible... *Burdenless.*

...Until I realize that once again Ryker's pants never came off. If he hadn't been dry humping the bench seat as he tongue- and finger-fucked me, I might doubt how into it he was, but each time I came, the sounds he made had me falling apart all over again.

A pronounced frown settles across my lips. I don't want to dwell on this but, thanks to Isabel and *Jenny*, I'm well aware of Ryker's reputation at college. Now, all I can think about is why he'd be holding back with me...

"Why are you making that face?" Ryker asks, expression drawn as he gestures to my closed-off posture.

"What about you? Shouldn't we have..." My eyes drop pointedly to his groin.

Ryker laughs, the sound deep and infectious when he leans over and kisses my temple. "That *was* about me. This was the best afternoon of my entire fucking life, even if this morning was one of the worst, so you can go on ahead and tuck that pouty lip away."

Heart twisting inside my chest, I set aside my insecurities and unbuckle myself to scoot closer. "What happened?"

Above us, dark clouds blot out large portions of the previously blue sky, casting Ryker in a kaleidoscope of shadow and light as he hangs his head.

"My lawyer's not sure there's anything I can do to prevent Beau from getting Charlie back. He's got a job, he's got a support system with his family, he's attending his parole meetings—"

"He's an alcoholic abuser," I say incredulously.

"Not in the eyes of the system. He's her father and I'm just the half brother who dropped out of college. It doesn't help that I'll be stuck in training for the next six months." Ryker can't even pick his eyes up off the floor, and while I know there's nothing I can say to make this better, I still want to offer him some sort of comfort.

I put my hand on his, and to my surprise, he turns it over and kisses my palm before intertwining our fingers and resting them on my thigh.

My heart gallops painfully against my rib cage.

"It'll work out," I say, squeezing his hand. "Beau will fuck up at work or get a DUI."

Ryker's jaw hardens. "I won't let him hurt her. I'll kill him before I let that happen."

My lips tug down at the sides. People say all sorts of things when they're angry, but there is no question in my mind that Ryker meant what he said. He'd kill Beau to protect his sister.

A shiver runs up my spine, followed by the low *thump, thump, thump* of blood rushing through my ears, growing louder with each beat of my heart until it feels like the whole truck is vibrating.

Ryker leans forward to glance out my window. "Is that a helicopter?"

I turn, bringing my hand to my brow to shield my eyes. Cold dread settles across my shoulders when I spot the red helicopter in the distance, the one Dad only calls in for serious accidents our local hospital can't handle.

"That's an air ambulance," I say, voice trembling as I realize whose property it's hovering over. "They're landing at Crowe Ranch."

Dad is already waiting on the porch of the big house at the ranch when Ryker skids to a halt in the driveway. I immediately throw open the door and pile out.

"What happened?" I screech, tripping over my feet as I bound up the steps. "Is it Elanor or Old Man Dan?"

Several of the ranch hands mulling about eye me cautiously before removing their hats and making themselves scarce. My stomach sinks, my hands shaking while a thousand possibilities filter through my mind.

Dad scuffs his boots, waiting until the porch is empty before clearing his throat. "There was an accident. Old Man Dan's in a bad way." His blue eyes are bloodshot, his voice low and thick as he drives a fence post straight into my gut.

"What happened? Where's Elanor? Is she okay?" I scan the

living room windows, taking a single step toward the door, but Dad stops me with an outstretched hand.

"Dan had to be transported to a specialty hospital in Austin for a head injury. Elanor went with him." His eyes drop to the floor.

"I don't understand. What kind of accident? How did he hurt his head?" Stomach twisting painfully, I wrap my arms around my middle to quell the ache. "What aren't you telling me?"

Dad takes a deep breath, averting his gaze. "We're not sure, kiddo. Dan and a few others were out rounding up cattle for the sale. He went after a stray calf and one of the ranch hands found him in a field about an hour later. He was unconscious and unresponsive. By the time the air ambulance took him, he still hadn't woken up. It looks like his horse might have gotten spooked and thrown him..."

Shaking my head, I take a step backward.

When my father finally meets my eye, the growing pit of dread in my gut nearly swallows me whole as my own skepticism is reflected back at me in his blue-gray gaze. His lips thin, and he slowly nods, like he's thinking the same thing I am.

In all his years of riding, Old Man Dan has *never* been thrown from his horse.

Chapter Thirty-Five

Emotions high, I sprint back to my house, change, grab my pistol, and then spend the next few hours out in the fields, looking for any sign of what might've spooked Old Man Dan's horse.

The site of the accident is far enough away from the main property that no one saw or heard anything, but I really thought I'd be able to find a clue that would help me piece together what happened. Unfortunately, the tire tracks, flattened grass, and ridiculous amount of bootprints left by the first responders covered up any usable evidence in the immediate area.

I keep looking anyway, but beyond some coyote tracks about half a mile away, my search comes up empty. Maybe he really did fall? However good he is on a horse, Old Man Dan *is* aging and accidents *do* happen...

With a sigh, I reluctantly leave the field, feeling useless and defeated. By the time I get home, Noah is playing video games in the living room, Ryker is nowhere to be found, and Dad is already back at work, which is absolutely unfathomable to me. How can they just go on about their lives when our neighbor, a man who's practically family, is in the hospital?

I grab my phone, a fraction of my anger dissipating when I see a text from Ryker.

TROUBLE

> I'm at the station filling out paperwork for the academy with your dad, but I wanted to remind you that Old Man Dan is one tough son of a bitch. He'll pull through.

> I also got the phone number for the hospital.

There's a third text with a screenshot of the hospital's contact information.

Still restless, I click on the number to call Elanor.

I thought the purpose of technology was to make our lives easier, but every time I call, I'm barely able to say my name before the auto-mated operator transfers me to the same wrong room. Each time, the rather surly man who answers gets more and more frustrated by my frantic requests for updates.

"Officer Kelp," he says for the fourth time.

"Dammit. It's me again, sorry."

On my fifth attempt, I'm so frustrated I just yell "Elanor Crowe" into the automated system instead of my name. By some miracle it actually works, and I sigh in relief when Elanor's voice answers the phone.

"Hello?" she says weakly, and my small feeling of victory is immediately eclipsed by the sadness dripping from her tone.

"Mrs. Crowe, it's Willa. How are you? How's Old Man Dan?"

My lips tremble as she explains that her husband is in a medically induced coma and will be for the foreseeable future—at least until the swelling in his brain goes down.

"When he does wake up," she continues, "the doctors suspect he'll need months of rehab. I'm so sorry to do this to you, sweetie, but I've spoken to my lawyer, and we've accepted one of the offers for the ranch *and* the house. We need the money for Daniel's care. The truck is yours, and if you don't mind stoppin' by every now and then to make sure the house isn't falling apart until the sale goes through, I'd be more than happy to pay you."

"Of course I can do that." My voice cracks, and I have to clear my throat before continuing. "You don't need to pay me either."

"You're too sweet." She sniffles into the phone. "Don't be surprised if you see a lot of traffic at the ranch. We're moving fast, so the next few days are going to be jam-packed with activity."

I bob my head. "Mrs. Crowe?"

"Yes, dear?"

"Who are you selling the property to?"

She sucks in a sharp breath. "Kane Bennett."

Ice prickles across my skin. Once the sale goes through, Kane will own each and every square inch of land surrounding my house...

Sometime around midnight, Ryker crawls into my bed. He doesn't say a word, just wraps his arms around my middle and tucks me against his chest. I want to ask him what he's doing. I want to demand he go convince his brother not to buy the ranch because once he does, that will mean the Crowes are really gone...

But I don't say a word because the warmth of his body pressed against mine and his comforting smell keeps the deep sadness at bay, preventing me from drowning, at least for one more night.

Unfortunately, I wake the next morning to Ryker packing for an unplanned trip to Denton after receiving an email from his lawyer asking to meet with him and Charlie's foster parents. He apologizes profusely while spreading Nutella over toast and forcing me to eat before he leaves, but that only makes me feel more guilty about wanting him to stay.

Noah disappears shortly after Ryker's departure to do God knows what.

Then I'm alone.

Later that day, I watch from the window as a brigade of semi-trucks cart off each and every single animal from Crowe Ranch. Their attorney also stops by my house with the pink slip for the truck and a note from Elanor saying it's officially mine.

Sleep is fitful and sparse, and the next day, the noonday sun has barely settled in the sky when the ranch hands load up and head out, leaving a cloud of dust in their wake that I choke on while trying to garden.

There's no bleating livestock. No pounding of hooves. No shouts or laughter.

The atmosphere is eerie and desolate.

The following day, not even a full seventy-two hours after all this chaos started, I watch as a crew of movers pack up and cart off the Crowes' belongings for storage.

It's all so sudden...and permanent. I'd love nothing more than to crawl back into bed and pretend this isn't happening, but then a case-worker from CPS rings my doorbell.

For thirty minutes, I try to explain that Beau Blackthorne is the absolute scum of the earth and shouldn't be allowed within a mile of his daughter, but she won't have any of it.

"Miss Dunn," the exasperated caseworker huffs as little beads of bronzer-coated sweat run down the sides of her pale cheeks. "For the last time, I stopped by to speak with your *father* as part of the reunification protocol, not *you*. Now, if I can just be on my—"

I sidestep, once again blocking her from leaving the porch. "You've seen the report, right? Tell me someone at your office has seen the documentation of how violent Beau is."

She hugs the clipboard to her chest, puffing her cheeks to blow her yellow-blonde hair out of her eyes, sending a powerful wave of plumeria and diet coke in my direction in the process. "I'm not at liberty to disclose that information."

"He tore my favorite jacket!" I turn, putting my shoulder in front of her face. But then I hear how dumb that must sound and realize she's going to need to see what's *under* the ripped fabric for it to have any effect.

Sighing, I pull the sleeve down, pointing to the fading remnants of the pale green-and-yellow bruise. "Beau hit me with a baseball bat after attacking his stepson. This bruise is *weeks* old. How is that a safe environment for a nine-year-old little girl?"

She eyes the fist-sized discoloration, briefly glancing at the scars on my shoulder and then down to her clipboard. Her expression softens the tiniest bit. "It's been documented. That's all I can say. Now, can I please go?"

Unsure what else I can do, I drop my head and move out of her way. She leaves without another word, her car tires filling the air with the nauseating scent of exhaust as she spins out onto the dirt road.

"Dammit!" I scream into the wind, repeating the phrase until my throat is raw.

I hate everything.

I hate that Charlie's father is a piece of shit. I hate that Old Man Dan got hurt. I hate that all of a sudden Isabel is too busy entertaining her cousin to hang out with me. I hate that she's being secretive about what they're doing and that she's not inviting me to tag along. I hate that Noah has dragged Ryker off to fish every day since he got back from Denton and that the only time I see Ryker is when he sneaks into my bed to hold me in the middle of the night.

I also hate myself for being upset about that last one in the first place. I'm leaving soon, I shouldn't get attached to anyone or anything I can't keep.

Collapsing into a heap on the rocking bench, I cross my arms and pout, the chair creaking from my forceful rocking. The cicadas and crickets sing their manic songs as the breeze shifts my hair while poor, unsuspecting mosquitos and flies get electrocuted by the stupid bug zapper.

Then everything goes still and quiet, the steady hum of the electric insect killer the only sound in my ears. I stop rocking, uneasiness seeping into my pores and the hairs on the back of my neck standing on end. Slowly, I rise to my feet, and unplug the death machine.

Wind tousles my hair and rips through the nearby trees, drawing a low groan from their dead branches. But there are no birds chirping. No cicadas singing their eerie songs.

Just silence.

Something is out there...

Movement to my left catches my attention... A crouching shadow, barely noticeable in the tree line, but it's definitely there. Watching me.

I lift my arms up over my head, pretending to stretch to see if I can get a better look. Whatever it is, it's cloaked beneath the thick shade canopy not too far away from the path my mom and I used to take on our walks to the Cartwright Estate—the one I like to pretend doesn't exist.

Sweat pools on my lower back and I shudder.

My first instinct is that it must be a coyote or a stray dog, but when a stream of sunlight breaks through the clouds, I swear I see two curling horns. My gut tightens, adrenaline pounding in my veins.

All the animals from the ranch are gone...

"Willa?" a deep, melodic voice calls from my right.

I jump two feet into the air, my soul temporarily leaving my body when Kane Bennett appears at the bottom of the porch. "Jesus Christ!"

"Alas, I am but merely his servant." Kane half bows, peering up at me over those ridiculous wire-rimmed glasses as the sun beats down on his raven hair. "Is my brother around?"

I fold my arms across my chest. "Why, so you can drug him again?"

"That's actually why I'm here," Kane laments, his entire countenance changing from playful to serious in the blink of an eye. "Another member of our collective fell ill shortly after the two of you left. She was hallucinating, and at one point may have even had a seizure." He drops his eyes to the concrete walkway, shoulders slumping, like it hurts to relive the memory.

I lift a single brow but unfurl my arms. "Is she okay?"

"Yes, thankfully." He breathes out a heavy sigh and climbs up the stairs, the silver cicada bolo tie around his neck swaying as he stands before me.

"Turns out our property has a meadow full of a rather poisonous flower called hemlock. Not knowing what it was, I'd asked Ryker and a few others to clear it out so we could make room for a garden." His lips thin as he looks away from me. "Our resident healer said it could have been fatal. I came to see if he was doing alright and beg for his forgiveness."

I purse my lips. If I hadn't seen the field of flowers for myself, I might say the whole story sounded a little outlandish, but Elanor *did* mention that was a possibility when she warned me away from the same plant out in her pasture...

"Why are you just now stopping by to check on him?" I ask, back straight and brow still raised. "It's been weeks."

"Our healer made the connection yesterday. I came as soon as we confirmed." Kane stares up at me through thick lashes with green eyes so much darker than his brother's—emerald instead of moss.

My posture softens. I can't begin to imagine the guilt he must be feeling right now.

"Ryker's fine. I think he's more worried about Charlie right now than anything else." I reach out, gently patting Kane's forearm. "He's out fishing with Noah, but you should still explain to him what happened as soon as you get the chance."

Kane's gaze drops to my hand on his arm, his lip twitching up at the corner ever so slightly before he asks, "He doesn't remember anything?"

My spine stiffens, but I force myself to shrug. "No, not really."

Kane's brow furrows, and he gets a far-off look in his eye until a passing delivery truck shifts gears, the sharp grating noise cutting through the silence and snapping him from his reverie.

"Kane?" My brow furrows as I lean to the side and glance at the empty driveway.

"Yes?"

"Where's your car? Did you walk here?"

A satisfied gleam sparks in his eye. "I just met with the Crowes' attorney next door. We're in the process of renegotiating some of the smaller details of my previous offer now that it includes the house. My car is parked over there."

I follow Kane's hand, spotting his boat-sized white Cadillac in the Crowes' driveway. After sucking down a painful breath, I press my palm to my chest to ease the growing ache.

This is all happening too fast. *I was supposed to be the one leaving...*

"Old Man Crowe is going to be just fine." I startle when Kane's dry hand cups my face, his fingers like weathered paper against my cheek. He smells like old parchment and something earthy and green.

I should pull away, but I'm such an emotional mess right now that when he tugs me in for a hug, I tense, but don't fight him.

"We're told that God will never test us beyond our limits," Kane says, holding me so tightly I have to adjust my cheek to keep the cicada bolo tie from digging into my flesh. "But the truth is, we are tested to weed out the weak. You are not weak. You've already survived so much worse than this."

Tilting my chin up, I stare up at him, confusion rippling across my brow as I breathe in his musty tweed jacket. Beyond Ryker's brief text, that's the only comforting thing anyone's said to me in the past few days.

The tightness in my chest lessens.

Maybe I was wrong about Kane the same way I was about Ryker...

Chapter Thirty-Six

"Rummy!" Noah yells, shifting the entire kitchen table as he slaps his palm over the card Ryker just tossed out.

Clutching the book I've been pretending to read, I eye Dad's closed bedroom door from my spot on the couch and pray he has earplugs in. If he doesn't, there's no way he's sleeping through Noah's antics and we're seconds away from getting a lecture.

"My guy," Noah sighs, mock disappointment heavy in his tone. "You *really* suck at this. What's going on in that big, handsome head of yours?"

Ryker's eyes flash to mine from across the room. "Guess I'm just distracted."

"Birthday boy blues?" Jenny coos, her sparkly crop top dipping almost low enough for a nip slip as another waft of her cotton candy perfume accosts my senses.

My ears perk up, stomach plummeting to the floor. I knew Ryker's birthday was coming up, but I've been in such a slump over Old Man Dan I didn't realize it was *today*.

Jenny leans forward, like she's trying to catch Ryker's eye with her cleavage. "We could fix that with some birthday shots?"

Ryker taps his cowboy boot-shaped lighter against the table. "I'll pass."

"Oh, come on," she pouts, bouncing in her seat like a petulant child. "The whole reason we're celebrating your birthday a day early is so you have time to recover before you start your training. Do a shot with us, *please?*"

Even through my scowl, my shoulders relax a little. *At least I didn't miss his actual birthday.*

Ryker lets loose an exasperated sigh. "I already told you, no. I'm going to visit my sister tomorrow, and I can't be hungover."

I bite my lip, covering my face with the book to hide my smile from Isabel, who I can feel staring at me from the other end of the couch.

Since Ryker got back from Denton, Noah has filled each and every hour of his day dragging him around to visit friends and hit up old fishing spots. Which means that although Ryker's snuck into my bed as soon as everyone is asleep, we haven't actually talked. So it's hard to tell if he's shutting Jenny down or just pissed off in general.

Even though I'm leaving soon and have no right to claim ownership of his attention, the vindictive part of me likes to imagine it's the first option. To her credit, Jenny takes the whole thing in stride.

"Fine, the rest of us will drink double on your behalf." She turns away from him to face her cousin. "Marco, what's our poison tonight? Please don't say whiskey."

"Wait," Noah interjects, right eyebrow arched. "Why not?"

"Because," Jenny drawls, "whiskey and Castillos don't mix. Marco gets slutty, Isabel gets emotional, and I suddenly think I'm the world's best dancer."

"Well, I'll be damned," Noah shouts, slapping his knee and nearly upending the table as he rises to his feet. "Looks like we're drinking whiskey tonight!"

After rummaging through the kitchen cabinets, he returns with an amber bottle of booze and shot glasses. Jenny throws her head back and groans while Marco smiles, unfazed by the chaoticians around him.

Normally, I'd be worried about my brother pouring his first drink before five when he's going to be boozing all night, but we're not exactly on good enough terms for me to say anything. I'm also struggling to think about anything other than how *painfully* obvious it is that Jenny isn't wearing a bra and how good she looks in those expensive, barely there clothes while I'm covered head to toe like a damn nun.

I jump as the book is ripped from my hands to reveal Isabel staring daggers at me. "What crawled up your butt and died today?" she asks, tossing the book onto the table.

It's her property to do with as she pleases, but I still cringe at the new dent on the spine... *Damn.* I was going to ask her if I can keep that one, too. I've really been enjoying the story about a traumatized female serial killer and the hot FBI guy assigned to bring her down.

"I don't know what you're talking about." I cross my arms over my chest, doing my best to sound nonchalant, but her quirked eyebrow tells me she's not buying it.

"Jenny's done messing around with Ryker. You can ease up on the death glares." Isabel purses her lips and glances to the table.

"Sorry." My cheeks heat, and her expression instantly softens.

"I wasn't trying to pressure you into something you're not ready for by adding 'get laid' to your bucket list, and Ryker doesn't sound like a beginner-friendly type of guy anyway. The whole forbidden-fruit thing is hot, but maybe you should let it go?"

After quickly glancing around the room, I fight the urge to roll my eyes.

I don't think anyone heard her, but with my brother pouring shots barely fifteen feet away, now isn't the best time to continue this conversation. And it's definitely not the time to tell her Ryker sure seemed "beginner-friendly" enough a few days ago with his face buried between my thighs.

I quash down the smile threatening to spread over my lips.

"It's not about the list," I assure her—and I mean it.

For so long, the relationships in my life have felt transactional. However irrational it might seem, I think I've had this idea in my head that if I didn't make myself absolutely essential to someone—like I have to Dad and Noah and even the Crowes—they would discard me the same way my mother did and I'd end up alone.

At the end of the day, my family might depend on me to keep their lives in order, but do they actually want me around? With Ryker... I don't have anything to offer him, yet he still wants to give without requiring something in return. Spending the last few nights in my bed without a hint of anything physical happening between us has made that more than clear.

Whatever this thing is between us, it has nothing to do with my bucket list and everything to do with how I feel about myself when he's around. I like being close to him. I like the comfort of his quiet warmth. And most of all, I like the way the chaos in my head settles when we touch.

"Then what's going on?" Isabel asks. "I came over because I need to talk to you, but you've barely looked at me. Are you having second thoughts about leaving Deadwood?"

The question is a bucket of ice over my head. "Of course not," I assure her. "I just have a lot going on right now."

"Like what?"

"Well, for starters, my dad's still hiding something from me. My brother's being an absolute dick. I haven't told either of them I'm moving to Austin. And there's also what happened to Old Man Dan—"

"That's not an excuse," she says, the bite in her tone accosting me like a slap. "We all have a lot going on right now."

Okay, ouch. But I guess she's not wrong. She *was* the one struggling the last time we hung out, and I haven't even asked her about it...

"Sorry," I whisper. "I didn't mean to get all in my head. What is it you wanted to talk about?"

She quickly glances at her brother and lowers her voice. "I met Kane. You were right, he's not creepy at all."

Her declaration is so unexpected, I can't find the words to respond. Turns out, I don't need to because the faraway, glazed-over look in her eyes has me questioning if she still remembers I'm here in the first place.

"There's just something about him," she says dreamily. "He knows exactly who he is and what he wants out of life. His way of viewing the world... It really makes you wonder what we've been brainwashed into prioritizing. He's kind of incredible."

My muscles tense. That sounds eerily similar to what she said on the way to Benny's the other day...

"And Willa, you should hear the things he says about you."

My stomach churns and I shift away from her. "What does he say about me?" I have a brief flash of Noah saying something similar a few weeks back, but Kane talking to people outside of my direct family about me is even more off-putting.

Isabel's olive cheeks flush pink as she reaches out to brush a white strand of hair away from my shoulder. "I wouldn't do his words justice. You're so much stronger than anyone gives you credit for. If you are having second thoughts about leaving Deadwood...maybe it's a sign?"

"Isabel, I already told you I wasn't. What are you—"

A sharp peal of laughter rings out from the dining room, and Isabel looks away, smiling sadly to herself. "We can talk about this another time, okay?"

"Sure?" I lean away, following the direction of her gaze to where Jenny is attempting to throw popcorn into my brother's mouth. Despite the copious amounts of kernels littering the floor marking his previous failures, he keeps backing farther away to try again until he finally catches one.

"Did you decide what you want to do tonight, Ryker?" he asks, chomping on his victory. "I already invited a few people over. I was thinking we'd have a pregame party here and then hit up a bar closer to midnight. But are there any games you want to play or anything else you had in mind?"

My stomach sinks. *Guess I'm not invited to the second part of the evening.*

Ryker spins his lighter between his finger and thumb and then taps it against the table.

"I'd rather not have people over." *Tap. Spin. Tap. Spin. Tap.* His eyes flash to mine. "We could go to Honky Tonk and play darts?"

My ears perk back up. Honky Tonk Junction is an eighteen and up bar. Excitement bubbles in my chest, threatening to force its way out as a high-pitched squeal.

But then Noah snorts. "You're fucking kidding, right? You know I'm banned. Wait, why don't you want to have people over?"

A muscle in Ryker's jaw ticks as he shifts in his seat. "Because I'm visiting Charlie tomorrow and it doesn't feel right to trash the place knowing Willa will have to clean it up on her own. She does enough around here without adding a stupid fucking party for me to her list of burdens."

Tucking his chin into his chest, Noah furrows his brow like he doesn't see the connection. "Willa doesn't care. She likes doing that stuff."

Ryker slams the lighter onto the table. "I care, and *no*, she doesn't."

The air turns heavy.

"Then I'll help clean—" Noah starts, but Ryker doesn't let him finish.

"We both know you won't."

A thick silence falls over the room, pressing down on my lungs as I hold my breath.

Out of the corner of my eye, Jenny and Marco shoot a glance in my direction, but my heart is too fluttery for me to care. Not only did Ryker stand up for me, but with the same sentence he also called out Noah—the way I've been dying to for years.

The two of them stare at each other without blinking until Marco rises from the table, gently tossing an arm across my brother's tense shoulders.

"We could have the party at my place?" he suggests, tone light. "I don't mind doing the prep or clean up."

Noah glances up at Marco for a millisecond, but it's enough for me to catch a glimpse of something I've never seen in his expression before—something soft and almost peaceful.

Ryker nods once. "That would be awesome, thank you."

"Fine," Noah grumbles, but his attention is on me, a clear warning in the depths of his blue eyes.

Chapter Thirty-Seven

This might be the cutest outfit I've ever worn. The black micro miniskirt barely covers my butt and the silver concho chain belt I paired with it is nearly as big. My hair is also so perfectly curled that the white streaks almost look like expensive highlights.

I'll be damned if I don't feel like a y'allternative goddess.

I'm digging my vibe so much I'm tempted to wear a camisole with no cover up... Then again, maybe not. This is a Deadwood party, after all, and I don't need the extra attention.

After a minute or two of searching my closet, I go with a tight semi-sheer top with a Queen Anne neckline that covers all my scars except the ones at my collarbone, and I cover those with a cute little black handkerchief that ties at the side. The shirt is black, *obviously*, and goes perfectly with the black knee-high cowboy boots I'm wearing.

My brother and the others left earlier to set up for the party, which means I've been blasting music since Dad left for work. I'd thought some tunes might help with my nerves, but now that it's almost time to leave, my stomach is queasy as I shrug on my green fringe jacket for an extra layer of armor.

After tonight, I've given myself permission to officially check off number seven on my bucket list. While Benny's Ice Cream might've been a bust, going to a birthday party *on top* of the eclipse party *and* the night I went to Rib Cage definitely qualifies as going out more.

My phone chimes, and I disconnect from Bluetooth before bringing up the new text.

NOAH

Is Ryker there?

My brow wrinkles. I glance out my window to see if Ryker's truck is parked outside, but the driveway is empty.

WILLA

No? Should he be?

NOAH

K good

Pls grab the bottle of whiskey on the counter before you head over

That doesn't exactly clear up my question... And also, what a dick. He's seen me struggling with the news about Old Man Dan, but the only thing he wants to know is if I'm alone with his best friend?

Screw that.

I close out of the text and give myself a once-over in the mirror before heading for the kitchen. The sun won't be setting for at least another hour, but it's already much cooler outside, the warm summer breeze carrying the fresh scent of wildflowers and greenery through my open screens. It's the perfect weather for a drive with the windows down and the music up, which—thanks to Dad—is still possible.

Not wanting to draw attention to the fact that Ryker threatened Cooper, I'd lied and told my dad my tire was flat because I'd run over a screwdriver. Thankfully, not only did he buy the excuse, he even changed my tire and brought my truck home for me.

Hopefully the party will be in Marco's backyard so I can enjoy this strangely tolerable weather. We never get nights like this so close to the end of summer, and I'd love to not be cooped up indoors with a bunch of people who don't want me there in the first place.

Pushing aside that last unhelpful thought, I close up the house, grab the bottle of whiskey Noah asked for, and head outside. The glass bottle *clinks* against the doorframe as I double check the lock, and then I turn, grinning when I spot a familiar brown truck idling at the end of the driveway, my nervousness suddenly replaced by a giddy sense of excitement.

Not only is Ryker alone, but his smile is visible from here, the sight of it lifting some of the heaviness of the past few days off my chest and replacing it with a warm, fluttery feeling.

Using the bottle, I gesture toward the garage to see if he wants me to drive, but he shakes his head and points to his passenger seat in what looks like a silent command for me to get in. I try not to smile like an idiot as I skip down the gravel, failing the moment he slides across the seat to open the door for me.

"Fuck," he murmurs, gaze dragging over my body as I climb in.

My insides go liquid at the borderline obscene desire etched into his expression. It's like he's undressing me with his eyes. My toes curl in my boots while I fight the urge to climb onto his lap and ask him to strip me bare.

"Hi," he says with a wicked smirk.

Ears on fire, I drop my eyes to the wool blanket covering the seat, waiting for my flush to clear before trying to respond.

"Are you really going to ignore me, *Princess*? You know how I hate that..." he warns, waiting for me to lift my chin and look at him before throwing the truck into drive.

The emphasis he places on the dumb nickname is playful, like he's challenging me to push his buttons. "I'd *never* dream of ignoring you on your *birthday*."

His eyes roll and he groans, shifting the truck into another gear as we speed down the dusty road. "It's *not* my fucking birthday."

320

Biting my lip to keep from grinning, I scoot an inch closer, reveling in how much easier and comfortable life feels when it's just the two of us.

"In that case, do you want to bail and go do something else?"

Ryker quirks a brow. "Don't tempt me. Your brother's already pissed enough that I didn't want people over."

"Thanks for that." My heart *thumps* at the memory of how he stood up for me earlier. "I thought you were going to Marco's with Noah? Where are you coming from?"

No matter how much I'd like to flatter myself by pretending he came back just to get me, the way his truck was facing when I walked outside means he drove in from the opposite direction.

"I met up with Kane to work out a deal for me to rent the big house once he takes ownership of the ranch," Ryker says, turning onto the main road leading into town.

A jolt of pain rips through my heart at the thought of anyone living next door except for Elanor and Old Man Dan, but if it has to happen, I'm glad it's Ryker.

"That's awesome, especially since you'll be so close to Charlie if she does end up back in Deadwood. But won't renting the ranch be way more expensive than an apartment?"

Ryker's lips curve downward. "It's a *when* at this point. I spoke with her foster parents this morning. As of yesterday, all the paperwork's been filed. The only thing Beau needs to officially have his rights reinstated is a court hearing."

Anger sizzles so fiercely in my veins that my fists coil. *I should have hogtied that caseworker and forced her to listen to me.*

"As far as the cost," Ryker continues, "Kane's actually going to pay me to stay there as long as I help maintain the property."

There's a long pause while Ryker gnashes his teeth, and I can almost see his mind asking the same question I am. Not wanting to put an additional damper on his mood, I offer up a neutral response instead of voicing the question aloud.

"That's interesting."

Ryker snorts and glances at me out of the corner of his eye. "Just say what you're really thinking."

"Your brother bought the Cartwright Estate *and* he's buying the ranch. Now he's going to pay you to live there? How can he afford all that? Where's he getting all this money from?"

Ryker lets go of a long sigh as he breaks at a four-way stop. "I have no fucking clue."

I scoot closer. "Do we believe him about the flowers being the reason you got sick?"

The corner of Ryker's mouth kicks up and then flattens, like he's holding back a smile.

"What?" I ask.

"It's not important," he says, still fighting back a grin when he eases off the brake and accelerates through the intersection. "But no, *we* don't believe him. General rule of thumb with Kane is not to trust a single word that comes out of his mouth."

My head tilts to the side and I purse my lips. Maybe I shouldn't have believed Kane so easily, but he seemed genuinely upset about the whole ordeal... I lean back in my seat, moving just a tiny bit closer to Ryker's thigh.

"I think that's the first bad thing I've heard you say about your brother."

"Yeah, well, it won't be the last," he scoffs. "The fucker is family, but sometimes I wonder if he really has gone off the deep end." We turn onto Marco's tree-lined street and he sighs. "Do you mind if we don't talk about Kane? He already took up my entire afternoon."

I bob my head. "Sure thing. Actually, how about we pretend like neither of our brothers exist for the rest of the night?"

Ryker smiles and gives my thigh a playful squeeze. "Sounds like a good plan to me."

After deciding to park a few blocks away so Noah won't notice that we drove in together, Ryker makes no move to get out of the truck. Instead, he shuts off the engine and leans back in his seat, like he's in no rush to get to his own party.

"You doing okay with the news about Old Man Dan?"

"I've been better," I admit, because I'm not afraid that he'll try to overcorrect the situation or make it worse like Dad or Noah would.

"Dan's a tough son of a bitch. So is Elanor." Ryker's eyes drop briefly to the last three inches of space between our legs before he threads an arm around my waist and tugs me against his side.

Body humming, I melt into him. "What about you? How's all that fishing with Noah been going? Have you had any time to relax before the academy starts?"

Mindlessly, he rubs his thumb back and forth across my hip, soothing some of my restlessness. "Considering how I hate fishing almost as much as I hate this fucking town, it was pretty damn awful."

I lift a quizzical brow. Growing up, Ryker used to weasel his way onto every single one of our family fishing trips. It didn't matter if it was an afternoon or an entire weekend, without fail he was there, secondhand rod in hand. Even when Noah was grounded, Ryker would insist on coming out with me and Dad.

"Since when do you hate fishing?"

Climbing out of the truck, he chuckles humorlessly, like I asked him a loaded question. "Princess, there hasn't been a day of my life I haven't absolutely fucking despised fishing."

I scramble out after him. "Don't let Noah or Dad hear you say that. It would literally send them into cardiac arrest."

This time, Ryker's laugh is genuine, and my heart flutters at the beautiful sound.

We round the bed of the truck, a smile on my face and barely any space between us as we take our first few steps down the car-lined street toward Marco's.

Crickets chirp along with the steady beat of my heart, and the light evening breeze rustles through my hair and the surrounding trees. Who knows, maybe I'll actually enjoy myself tonight. A soft smile spreads across my lips, and I take a deep breath, only to be assaulted by the potent scent of liquor and body odor.

My spine stiffens.

"You evil bitch," a rough voice slurs from our left. "Did you really think I wouldn't find out what you were up to?"

Chapter Thirty-Eight

Ryker throws out an arm, stopping me dead in my tracks as Beau stumbles down his mother's driveway with a bottle of beer clenched in his fist. "I should kill you for this."

I glance back toward the truck. *Dammit.* I'd been so distracted I hadn't realized we'd parked near Dorothy freaking Blackthorne's house.

"Go home, Beau," Ryker says dryly, already positioning me slightly behind his body.

"Shut up, *boy*. Did you r-really think I wouldn't find out? Come on now, I thought you were smarter than that. I know everythin' that happens in this town. My uncle's a damn judge!" Beau hiccups and then shrugs, stumbling a few steps as the motion throws him off balance. "She sure did stir the shit, though, I'll give you that."

"What the hell are you talking about?" Ryker growls.

"You gonna pretend like you didn't convince this abomination to file a report"—*hiccup*—"with the county sheriff instead of the local police? You gonna act like it wasn't *your* idea for her to tell the CPS caseworker I'm an unfit parent?" He takes a swig from the bottle, fizzy-liquid leaking from the corner of his mouth and dripping down his chin as he shakes his head. "Lettin' a woman do your dirty work" —*hiccup*—"now? Same way you let your brother take your beatin's. You're a coward. Always fuckin' have been."

Shit. If Ryker was barely able to restrain himself around Cooper the other day, there's no way he'll be able to control his temper around Beau. Especially not when he's already clenching and unclenching the fist not holding on to my hip.

"Don't let him bait you," I whisper, dropping my voice so Beau won't hear. "If the police academy finds out you got in a fight, they'll rescind your acceptance."

"I'm aware," Ryker says through gritted teeth.

Beau wipes his mouth with his forearm and takes a step into the street. He's at least fifteen feet away, but it's close enough that his rancid body odor and the stale cigarettes on his breath twist my stomach.

"Come on over here, Willa Dunn," he taunts with a crook of his finger. "If my stepson wants you to"—*hiccup*—"take the blame, I'm more than happy to teach you not to mess with a Blackthorne. Maybe I'll finish what your mama started."

Every muscle in Ryker's body tenses as he curves forward, readying himself to strike. I glance back and forth between them, pulse thudding against my temples. Beau knows exactly what to say to piss Ryker off. If this goes any further, I doubt I'll be able to prevent the two of them from going at it.

A flash of metal near Ryker's belt catches my eye, and I glance down to see his phone sticking out of his pocket. Cautiously, I step forward, tucking myself halfway between his back and arm.

"Why do you want custody of Charlotte in the first place? Won't taking care of a kid cut into your drinking time?" I call out over Ryker's shoulder, hoping my question will distract Beau while I delicately extract the phone.

"It's not about *want*," Beau sneers, right as I press Record. "It's about takin' back what was stolen from me. What's"—*hiccup*—" rightfully *mine*."

Ryker glances down as I slide the phone into his front pocket. "*It's recording*," I whisper.

Without missing a beat, he rotates his body for a better camera angle. "Do you really think I'm going to stand by and let Charlie become your new punching bag?"

Beau stops walking but doesn't respond.

"Keep going," I whisper.

"I know all too well what you do to the people dependent on you, the people you're *supposed* to protect, because I fucking lived through it," Ryker seethes. "I won't let that happen to my sister. I won't let you fucking touch her."

Beau's face contorts into a sinister grin, shadows crossing his features when he turns away from the fading rays of the dying sun.

A chill skitters up my spine.

Come on, just say anything incriminating we can use...

Beau laughs, and my face contorts in revulsion. I can't even imagine how terrifying it must've been for Ryker and Kane to grow up under his roof.

"Try again," I whisper, grabbing onto the back of Ryker's belt so he knows I'm here with him. Ryker straightens, which Beau seems to take as a challenge.

"You"—*hiccup*—"you're the one who made this 'bout me and her. Step aside, boy." Beau laughs, taking a few more stumbling steps toward us while another potent wave of his atrocious body odor hits my nose.

"If he gets any closer, I'm going to fucking kill him," Ryker seethes, and I still, unnerved by the conviction in his voice. *How am I going to stop him if*—

Across the street, a door clatters open, and Dorothy Blackthorne steps onto the crumbling stoop of her once stately house.

"Get back inside this instant," she shrieks. Beau grumbles inaudibly, and I barely register what's happening before his mother marches over and grabs him by the ear. He roars in pain, and Dorothy rewards him with a hard smack across the mouth, her bracelets jingling from the impact.

Generational violence. I guess that explains a lot...

"But, *Ma*," the late-forty-something-year-old man-child whines as he's dragged across the street by his earlobe. "You heard what Uncle Abbott said."

Dorothy slaps him upside the head. "Yes, I remember. And I'm perfectly aware of what the Dunn girl tried to do, but Abbott already took care of it. That's the benefit of havin' a judge in the family instead of a small-town cop."

She slaps him again. "Did you ever stop and consider that this was all part of her plan? That she was hoping you'd do exactly what you're doin' now? No, of course you didn't, because I apparently raised a moron. So help me God, Beaumont Benedict Blackthorne, if you mess up me getting my granddaughter back, I'll end you."

Still holding on to her son's ear, Dorothy turns and points a scathing finger at me. "Stay out of our business. Charlotte deserves to grow up with her family."

"She deserves to grow up *safe*," I hiss, something inside me snapping as I attempt to maneuver around Ryker. "That disgusting son of yours killed his wife and beat his stepchildren. How can you put a helpless little girl at risk like that?"

Dorothy's sharp hazel eyes flash to Ryker, softening for a second, like clouds parting to reveal a single ray of sunlight, before the look fades, blotted out by deep shadows of guilt.

My mouth falls open, bile rising up my throat. "You knew he was hurting them?"

The heat in my veins turns molten, the rage coursing through my bloodstream making the undeniable urge to slap Dorothy so strong that I'm charging toward her without consciously deciding to move my feet. I only take three steps before Ryker snakes an arm around my waist.

"You're just as pathetic as your son," I shout, feet coming off the ground as Ryker holds me back. "No wonder Beau's such an abusive piece of shit. He's exactly like you!"

I struggle to free myself, but Ryker holds me in place, keeping me pinned against his chest until Beau and Dorothy disappear back into their dark house.

My body slumps and eventually I stop fighting. "She knew and she didn't help you?"

"It doesn't matter," he whispers, turning off his phone and then spinning me to face him.

A single tear rolls down my cheek before he tilts my chin up to wipe it away.

I want to tell him that it does matter. That *he* matters. That he's incredible and I respect the hell out of him for how hard he's fighting for his sister. I don't know anyone who would change their entire life for a sibling like he has. Most people would have given up by now.

Noah would've.

But I don't say any of that because if I try to, I'll start crying in earnest and that will scare him off. I sniffle, tamping down my emotions and blinking my eyes dry.

"Willa, I need to know what Beau was talking about. What did you do?" Ryker asks, voice choked and almost pleading as a gust of wind whips through my hair. I try to look away, but he places both hands on my face, forcing my gaze to his. "Tell me."

"A caseworker stopped by to interview Dad. I wouldn't let her leave until I'd said my piece about how horrible Beau is. It doesn't matter, though. She wouldn't listen."

He widens his stance so that his face sits just a little closer to mine. "What about the sheriff?"

I wipe my nose on the back of my hand, inhaling a deep breath to keep my voice steady. "On the morning of the eclipse, I filed a report with the sheriff's department about Beau hitting me with the bat."

Ryker's brow pinches together. "Their office is two towns over.

Why go that far? And how did you even get there without your dad finding out?"

"I hitched a ride with Isabel." I try to move my head, but he's holding my cheeks so firmly I can't. "I was nervous about Dad kicking Noah out if he knew I got hurt, but I had to do something so your sister wouldn't end up with Beau. I figured if I filed with a different department, there was less of a chance Dad would find out. Isabel doesn't know what I did. I made her swear not to ask me any questions. It's not like it worked anyway..."

Ryker's grip becomes crushing, his breathing so fast I can't tell if he's mad or having a panic attack. "They take pictures when you file a report like that..." he says, making my stomach twist because he knows that from firsthand experience with Kane. "You let them see your scars?"

A wave of nausea racks through me as I remember the low whistle the female officer let loose when she saw my shoulder and back. "I had to."

He leans forward, thumb brushing gently across my cheek. "You did that for me?"

I search his eyes, trying to find the hidden meaning behind the question, but there's only confusion and maybe a little pain. I place my hand over his wrist. "For Charlie, and it wasn't a big deal. It was the least I could do."

He shakes his head like he can't wrap his brain around what I'm saying. "But why would you do that? You hadn't seen her in years and you've always hated me."

My chest pinches. "I didn't *hate* you."

"You most definitely did," he says through a laugh, eyes scrunching. "Do you even remember what you said to me when I left town, the day CPS came for me and Charlie?"

I shake my head, holding back a new onslaught of tears threatening to spill over. I can only imagine how awful it was if he still remembers.

Ryker rests his forehead against mine, his soft, shallow breaths and the scent of rain-soaked pine dancing across my nose and cheeks. "You grabbed my shirt like a little brat and told me that getting out of Deadwood was a gift that was wasted on a shithead like me."

My eyes widen. "That's horrible. I told you I was jealous, but that's not an excuse. Ryker, I'm so sorry."

"Don't be," he says, low and gruff. "You were the only person who asked for more of me. The only person who didn't give me a hall pass because of the shitty way I grew up. I could see in your eyes how angry you were that I was getting out when you were stuck here, and that drove me to push myself harder in everything I did. It pushed me to be better for Charlie."

"Ryker—"

"Wait." Loosening his grip, he caresses my cheeks with his thumbs. "I have one more question," he says, brows pinching together like he's in pain. "Why did you change your mind about me?"

"Who says I have?" I whisper through a watery smile.

"Answer the question," he demands, voice clipped and rough. "I know you're leaving, but I'm lying to my best friend. My *best* fucking friend, Willa. I have to understand why." He closes his eyes tightly. "Are you trying to check off number nine on your bucket list before you leave for school? I'm not saying I won't do it, I just need to know."

My stomach bottoms out. *Jesus.* Is that why he kept his pants on when we were making out on the couch and in his truck? Because he thought I was trying to *use* him?

I grab his wrists, gently squeezing until his eyes pop back open. "Ryker, I'd never do that to you. Isabel added that to the list, not me."

I rise up onto my tippy-toes and touch my nose to his. "And I changed my mind about you because you're everything I'm not. You were hurt by the people who were supposed to protect you, and instead of hiding like I did, you're out here *living* and doing your best to prevent it from happening to your sister."

His eyes move rapidly across my face, like he's not sure if he can believe me or not.

"I didn't really know you when we were kids," I say, clutching his wrists tighter so he can feel how much I mean this. "But I wish I did. We've lost out on so much time."

Ryker's lips slam into mine, frantic and desperate, like he's dying of thirst and only I can save him. I moan as the kiss intensifies, grabbing onto his shirt to keep my hands from wandering.

"You think you know me now, Princess?" he rasps, pausing his assault on my lips just long enough to walk me backward and press me against the tailgate of his truck.

"I want to," I say between kisses, leaning my body against his.

After a moment, he grabs my arms and wraps them around his shoulders. Desperate to be closer and delighted with clear permission to touch him, I drag my fingers through his hair, my chest exploding in a rush of heat when he groans.

Then his hands are everywhere—on my waist, my hips, in my hair, electrifying every inch of my skin. Without breaking the kiss, he shifts his body and slides his palm to my inner thigh, where he slowly inches up my skirt until my bare ass is smashed against the sun-warmed metal of his truck.

His mouth slows, and I moan again as he kisses my neck and cups my pussy. Every surface of my skin is tingling like a live wire. And although I'm vaguely aware that we're in the middle of the street across from Dorothy Blackthorne's house, I just don't care.

I need more. I need *him.*

We're blocks away from Marco's...no one would notice if we climbed into the truck and—

Something vibrates against my hip, and I gasp for air. "Ryker."

He trails kisses down my throat, licking and nipping as he goes. "Yes, Princess?"

"Your phone," I pant.

Cursing under his breath, he pulls his mouth away from my neck and retrieves the cell from his front pocket. "*Shit.* It's Noah wondering where I am. We better grab the whiskey and head to the party."

My elation quickly fades.

But then Ryker grabs my chin. "Come find me in an hour and we'll get the hell out of here," he says, lifting my hand to his cheek and leaving a soft kiss on my inner wrist.

A slow smile spreads over my lips. "Deal."

Chapter Thirty-Nine

After two and a half agonizing hours at this stupid party, I—much like Bella Swan—now know two things with absolute certainty.

One, I hate people.

And two, my bucket list was the stupidest idea ever.

If the definition of insanity is doing the same thing over and over again while expecting different results, then I must be absolutely deranged. What other explanation is there for why I keep forcing myself out of my comfort zone when time after time the people of Deadwood have shown me that they're incapable of treating me like a normal human being?

Taking a swig of a mixed drink I swiped from the kitchen after finally working up the courage to venture out of the dark corner I've been lurking in, I scan Marco's crowded living room in search of Isabel so I can convince her to bail with me.

I considered finding Ryker and sneaking away like he'd suggested, but he's been surrounded since the second we walked through the door and is currently winning his beer pong game. It doesn't feel right to ask him to come with me when I've never seen him smile this much before. Just because I'm having a bad time doesn't mean he needs to leave his own party. He deserves to let loose, especially after that awful encounter with his stepfather.

I let go of a long exhale and blow my bangs out of my eyes.

Once I spot Isabel on the opposite side of the crowded living room, I begin the delicate process of weaving my way through the throng of people while trying not to spill my drink or draw attention to myself. I've taken about three steps when the first person notices me and nudges his friend. A moment later, Coraline Parker, a girl I used to go to school with, makes eye contact with me before kissing the dainty gold cross around her neck.

She must say something because more heads turn in my direction.

That's when the pointing starts.

The bass from the stereo system pounds in time with my pulse, rattling my brain and ricocheting off my rib cage as they stare and whisper. No one smiles or waves or asks me how I'm doing—but then again, neither do I.

Having seen enough, I keep my head down the rest of the way, letting the strobing red, green, and blue lights from a wall-mounted projector illuminate my path. It doesn't stop the trail of whispers in my wake, but at least the music is loud enough to drown out the specifics.

I'm so done with this place and these damn people.

By the time I make it to the hallway where Isabel and Jenny are chatting, I'm nauseous and dizzy from the cloud of alcohol fumes and cheap perfume. Unwilling to barf on the carpet and not wanting to interrupt what looks like a serious discussion between cousins, I lean against the wall a few feet away, breathing in the lemon oil on my bandana while I wait for an opening.

"I know it happened weeks ago, but I still can't believe he gave you the brush-off like that," Isabel says in a rush. "What a dick. We can leave anytime you want if this is too awkward."

"I'm fine," Jenny says. "I promise. It's not like I actually wanted to date him. I knew when I got involved with Ryker that he's not a relationship guy." Jenny shakes her head before taking a long sip from her pink Solo cup. "Besides, the orgasms might have been incredible, but they were costing me a fortune."

"I'm sorry, *what?*" Isabel screeches over the thudding base of the music.

Her cousin leans forward conspiratorially and bats her feathery lashes. "Getting your cheeks clapped with your hands tied behind your back wreaks absolute havoc on eyelash extensions. It's nice not having to get a fill every week."

My hand contracts involuntarily, my plastic cup cracking as everything around me turns an awful shade of red.

"Seriously, though," Jenny continues, "Ryker was *very* up front with what he wanted from me. At the time, it was fun. But now that the orgasm-induced dopamine has faded, it's a lot easier to see how unhealthy the whole thing was."

"What do you mean?" Isabel asks, concern etched into her manicured brow.

"For starters, he hates kissing and he *never* let me touch him. I wasn't even allowed to give the man a blow job unless my hands were behind my back and I was blindfolded. He always had to be in complete control." She sighs and shakes her head. "This isn't worth diving into right now. I just hope your friend knows what she's doing. Ryker can be...*a lot.*"

"Willa will be okay," Isabel says confidently. "She's stronger than she looks." My chest swells, but then she grimaces. "I'm really counting on her to remember that when she finds out I'm taking a year off school..."

Jaw clenched so tightly my teeth creak, I fight back the bitter mix of shock and betrayal crawling up my throat. *What the hell does she mean she's taking a year off school?*

Sure, she was acting a little cagey on the way to Benny's, and the stuff she said this afternoon about Kane and knowing what you want out of life was slightly unsettling... But never in my wildest dreams did I imagine she'd bail on me. Not when *she* was the one who encouraged me to apply to UT in the first place so she could have a friend there.

The muscles in my forearm twitch, causing the cup in my hand to crack further.

I'll be alone now...

I bring the drink to my mouth, my throat burning and my stomach churning as I gulp down the rest of the contents in one go. How could Isabel keep this from me?

"I'm sure Willa will understand," Jenny offers with a comforting side hug. "You have to do what's right for *you*. If that means taking some time off to figure out who you are and what you want in life, then do it. A good friend will understand that you've been struggling and want the best for you. College will always be there when you're ready."

A cold wave of uncertainty washes over my indignation.

Clearly, I was too caught up in my own bullshit to see that Isabel was going through something, but she still should've warned me...

Caught between a storm of self-pity and self-doubt, I set my cup on a nearby table and quietly slip away through the backdoor in search of fresh air.

There are far fewer people out here, which makes zero sense because the night air is still abnormally cool and Marco's backyard is incredible. Not only is it massive, but it backs right up to the forest, creating a thick canopy over the grass that I bet would be amazing for shade. I squint, peering into the darkness. It looks like he even has a little seating area near the tree line.

My skin prickles when the smell of musty old paper and oak drifts toward me on the breeze a second before boots *click* on the concrete patio behind me. I whirl around, irrationally expecting Beau to be there even though that's not what he smells like. Instead, I find

Kane dressed to the nines in a 1970s western tweed suit, half his hair pulled into a bun.

"Jesus," I hiss, clutching my chest to keep my heart from bursting.

"You're going to give me a God complex if you keep calling me that," he says, a dark grin spreading over his full mouth. "What are you doing out here all on your own?"

I turn toward the window where the beer pong game has managed to attract an even larger crowd. Noah has girls climbing all over him, his hand around the waist of a particularly beautiful blonde I went to school with. No one is touching Ryker, but more than a few of his old female classmates are close by—all of them positioning themselves in his line of sight with a significant amount of their perfect skin on display.

"I needed some air," I supply dryly.

Kane moves to my side, leaving about a foot of space between us while he follows my gaze to where our brothers are now high-fiving, their boisterous spectators clapping and spilling beer as they cheer for the shot Noah just made.

Jealousy worms its way beneath my skin, uprooting deep-seated feelings of inadequacy.

After spending so much of my life despising Ryker, it's easy to forget how much everyone else in this town loves him.

I wrap my hands around my middle and rub my palms over my forearms. Ryker and I have a connection, of that much I'm absolutely sure. But what could I ever offer a man like that—someone so welcomed and admired by the same people who've scorned me?

"I used to think that being on the outside looking in was a punishment," Kane says, not tearing his gaze away from the scene unfolding inside. "Now I understand that they tried to silence us because we're different. Society may have pushed us away, but being ostracized is a blessing. It allows us to see people like the ones in that house for who they really are."

"Who are they?" I ask, unable to help myself.

"Sheep," Kane says simply. "Easily influenced. Do as they're told.

338

Most of them incapable of independent thought. *They* are the reason the human race will annihilate itself." He steps in front of me, the new position cloaking his face in shadow and blocking the window from view.

I swallow the lump in my throat. "If they're sheep, then what are we?"

Kane grins, his eyes glinting in the moonlight like I've said something amusing.

"*We* are the lions who care little for the existence of sheep until it's time to eat. We are the dogs the livestock cast aside until they realize too late they can't survive without us." He lifts his hand, hesitating for a single moment before dragging the pad of his index finger over a scar on my collar bone. "*We*, Willa Dunn, survived the fire. We are gods among men, and this world is ours for the taking."

I shiver.

However ridiculous and outlandish that statement might be, there's a part of me that's desperate to believe him—the same dark part that would rather burn this entire town to the ground than forgive them for the way they've treated me. Maybe then they'd finally understand what it's been like...the way Kane seems to.

I might hate the way my skin crawls around him, but there's something almost familiar about Kane Bennett, like a reflection in a warped mirror showing me an alternate version of myself.

"Why would you ever come back to Deadwood?" I ask, taking a single step into the already minuscule space between us.

He tenses, the air around him shifting as clouds momentarily block out the light of the moon. "Children of Salvation was a joke," he spits, full of wrath and sounding more like his brother than he ever has before. "The idiot running the place was a weak liar obsessed with personal gain."

I take a step backward, and Kane pauses his rant to follow the movement.

When he speaks again, the anger is gone, replaced by the lofty air

I've grown accustomed to. "As for why I came back... We all have a role to play in the path ahead."

"I won't come back," I whisper, more to myself than to him.

A multitude of Edison-bulb string lights flare to life around the patio, followed by a few notes of eerie piano as "Run From Me" by Timber Timbre crackles through the outdoor speaker system before quickly cutting out for an upbeat dance number.

"I thought the same thing when I left," Kane says, looking over his shoulder at the gaggle of partygoers pouring through the back door, his brother's raven hair visible among them. "But the truth never stays buried. And no matter how far you run, Deadwood always calls you home."

I frown, grasping at a tiny spark of recognition in the recesses of my mind. "Why does that sound familiar?" I ask, but Kane's already gone, swallowed up by the growing tide of people he called sheep.

Rain-soaked pine hits my nose a second before strong arms snake around my waist.

"Where've you been?" Ryker whispers against the shell of my ear, the warmth of his chest seeping through my jacket like a calming salve. "Was that my brother?"

"Sure was." I turn into his arms, brow furrowing as I take in his rigid posture and narrowed eyes while he scans the crowd. "What's wrong?"

Without answering, he grabs my hand, leading me away from prying eyes to the shadows of the side yard where no one can see us before once again pulling me against his chest.

The music isn't quite as loud over here, allowing the gentle whir of locusts in the nearby brush to serenade us. But even now, he keeps glancing around like he half expects someone to have followed.

"You need to start making sure all the doors and windows are locked in the house," he growls, grip on my waist tightening possessively. "And I don't want you anywhere near my brother when I'm not around."

Grabbing onto his biceps for leverage, I rise onto my tiptoes to catch his eye. "Did something happen when you guys talked earlier?"

After weeks of defending Kane, that's twice in one day Ryker's said something less than favorable about his half brother...

His gaze drops to mine, lips thinning as he lets go of my waist and reaches into his pocket. "Isabel brought me the note you found in your house," he says, holding up the folded piece of paper between us. "This is my brother's handwriting."

My eyes widen as I stare at the scrawling black ink barely visible between his index and middle finger. "Are you sure?"

"Fucking positive," he growls.

There's a part of me that wants to be relieved it wasn't Cooper or some drifter, but then I picture Kane skulking through my house while I was in the shower and shudder. If it had been Cooper, at least I'd know he was just trying to scare me, but I have no idea what Kane wants, and that makes the whole thing that much more unsettling.

Unlike me, Ryker doesn't seem to have any confusion over how he feels about finding out who broke in, his agitation so palpable it's vibrating through his body into mine.

I give his tense biceps a gentle squeeze. "At least we know who it was now, right?"

"Yeah. I guess. I'm just glad you're getting the fuck away from here." He glowers before cracking his neck and shrugging. "*Fuck*, could I use a smoke..."

Not willing to acknowledge the way my heart just shriveled and dropped into my stomach at the mention of me leaving next week, I force an uneasy smile. "We're outside, go ahead."

"My pack is in the goddamn truck." He grumbles something under his breath as he reaches into his pocket and pops a piece of gum into his mouth.

"I could go grab it for you?" I rub my palms up and down the length of his arms, pausing when I snag on something square and plasticky beneath the sleeve of his T-shirt.

"Ryker," I ask, brows pinching together. "What is this?"

"A nicotine patch."

I lean away to look him in the eye. "Why are you wearing a nicotine patch?"

After chewing a few times, he spits the gum onto the grass and exhales, his muscles softening beneath my palms as he brings his nose to mine. "Strong smells and fire bother you."

My eyes narrow in disbelief. "So you quit smoking?"

"I didn't *quit*, I cut back."

"Why would you do that?" I inhale deeply, finding no trace of tobacco on him, just rain and pine and the light smell of my honeysuckle body wash mixed with the salty scent of his skin.

I hadn't thought about it until now, but he hasn't smelled like tobacco in weeks, and I haven't seen him smoking in that same time either. I'm also fairly certain I felt the nicotine patch a few days ago when he was telling me how much he hated being ignored...

My heart flutters, warmth spreading out from my chest before it quickly cools. Ryker has more than enough going on without adding worrying about me to the mix. "You didn't have to do that. I'm not as weak as people think I am—"

"Don't put words in my mouth," he growls. "I've never once thought of you as weak. Sheltered? Definitely. Babied? Sure. But weak? Not fucking once."

I blink, mouth dry and eyes watering. I drop my head, but he grabs my chin, forcing my eyes to his. "Listen, Princess. Putting aside the logical reason that I can't be chain smoking if I want to pass the physical fitness test at the academy, how does it make you feel if I flinch when you touch me?"

"Like pond scum," I admit, noticing for the first time how the reflection of the string lights look like tiny fireflies flittering in his eyes.

"It's the same for me. We can't help the way our bodies react, but when I see fear in your eyes because of something I did, it makes me feel like a fucking monster." He grinds his teeth. "It makes me feel like *Beau*, and I can't fucking handle that."

I stare at him, a million different emotions running through my head at once.

On the outside, Dad grumbling about not having a barbecue in the backyard or Noah complaining about the scent-free detergent I use might seem small, but over time, their repeated complaints about the sacrifices they've made to accommodate my quirks add up, culminating in me feeling like a constant burden who needs to earn their keep to be tolerated.

Then there's the man in front of me. He not only eased my fears but did so by being open about his own...

Regret for wasting so much time not seeing Ryker for the incredible man he is weighs down on my shoulders, followed shortly by a crushing longing for the time we no longer have. Their combined weight presses down on me until my eyes are watering and I can't breathe.

Ryker's brow pinches as he cups my cheek. "It's not a big deal. They're just cigarettes. I never do anything I don't want to."

I link my fingers behind his neck, watching his face carefully for any sign of discomfort and finding none. "Don't do anything you don't want to, huh?" I say through a watery smile. "This coming from the man who claimed he didn't want a party and proceeded to have the night of his life."

"That was for Noah," he says with an eye roll. "I could've left thirty seconds after we walked through the door."

The corners of my mouth slip into a frown. "You really love him, don't you?"

"He's my best friend. The brother I should've had." Ryker pauses, a heavy sigh escaping his full lips. "I have to tell Noah about us. I know he's been a real jackass to you lately and he might never talk to me again, but it's fucking killing me to sneak around behind his back like this."

I want to remind him that I'm leaving and ask *what* he's going to say to my brother, since I barely understand what's happening between us myself... Instead, I nod. He's right. My family is drowning in enough secrets as it is. We don't need to add this one to the mix.

"Really?" Ryker sounds so relieved, I can't help but smile.

"Yeah. We should tell him. It's the right thing to do. I'm slightly terrified, but at this point, it's not like my relationship with Noah could get any worse."

Ryker grins at me, stepping into my space like he's trying to guide me toward the patio.

"Wait." My voice is high-pitched and squeaky. "You're going to tell him *right now*?"

"God no," Ryker chuckles. "Let him have fun. We can talk to him in the morning." After a quick look over his shoulder, he walks me backward until I'm pressed against the brick siding of the house. "I've got a much better way for us to spend the night."

Heat blossoms in my cheeks. "Oh, yeah? Tell me about this idea of yours."

"Words are cheap," Ryker says, hoisting me up by my ass with a cocky grin. "How 'bout I show you instead?"

Grinning from ear to ear, I wrap my legs around his waist, freezing when footsteps echo down the narrow walkway, followed by the sound of two angry voices—one of which I'd know anywhere.

My head snaps toward the driveway, time slowing to a skittering halt as my brother and Marco stride into the side yard.

Chapter Forty

Heart racing, I cling to Ryker's shoulders as he slowly lowers my feet to the ground. It's dark enough that I don't think Noah or Marco have seen us yet, but the bright-yellow headlights of a passing car illuminate them with perfect clarity.

Every muscle in my body screams for me to run, but that would only draw more attention to the fact that we're here in the first place.

"Come on," my brother sighs, throwing his hands in the air. "Why are we still talking about this? I don't need *another* fucking babysitter policing my actions."

Stomach twisting, I take my first cautious step backward, tripping over my feet when Marco grabs Noah by the throat and slams him against the brick house.

"Fuck you, Noah Dunn," he sneers, palm pressing into my brother's windpipe.

I stop on a dime. *Oh, hell no.* Spitting mad and ready to tear Marco a new asshole for daring to lay hands on *my* brother, I take one seething step forward before Ryker grabs me by the waist and yanks me backward.

"*Wait*," he hisses, tugging me to his chest and clamping a hand over my mouth. Unable to move my head, I can only stare straight ahead as Marco leans forward and brushes his lips against my brother's with surprising tenderness.

Dumbfounded and slightly in shock, my body goes limp when Noah melts into Marco's touch, smiling into the kiss as he runs his hands through Marco's hair to pull him closer. The act is gentle and intimate—a far cry from the unpracticed movements of a fumbling first kiss.

"I hate seeing women draped all over you," Marco says, nipping at Noah's nose playfully. "If you don't behave yourself at the bar, you'll be looking for a new boyfriend in the morning."

Boyfriend?

A jolt of pain stabs through my heart. Marco is his *boyfriend?*

The rational part of my brain knows that who Noah loves and who he chooses to tell about it is nobody's business but his. But the irrational part feels sucker punched by the idea that my own brother trusts me so little he thought he had to hide his relationship from me...

"We need to get out of here," Ryker whispers against my ear, waiting for me to bob my head before removing his palm from my mouth.

Heart in my throat, I allow him to lead me toward the back patio, dragging my boots through the dead grass until we're out of earshot. When my steps falter, Ryker turns to face me.

"You already knew?" My voice is small and quivers slightly.

"I did."

"How long?"

Ryker's lips press into a thin line as he clamps a hand on the back of his neck. "I've already fucked up so bad by not telling Noah about us. I'm sorry, Princess, but this is really a conversation you should have with him."

I drop my chin. First Isabel, now my brother. Do none of the people I love trust me?

As if reading my thoughts, Ryker reaches out to cup my cheek.

"Noah not telling you has more to do with this small-minded fucking town than anything else. Give him time. Let him do this his way."

A truck door slams in the driveway, and I turn as another dark figure enters the side yard, my blood chilling when his sharp voice cuts through the air like a blade.

"Well, well, well. What do we have here?" Cooper Blackthorne spins his keyring on his pointer finger, his taunting laugh menacing and maniacal. "Looks like I might have some fun tonight after all."

Heart thudding against my ribs, my entire body goes on high alert. Cooper rarely travels alone, which means any second now the rest of his idiot friends will emerge from the shadows and we'll be outnumbered...

"Listen, Coop. This is getting sad," Noah says, interrupting my doom-planning for how to keep Ryker out of this fight while also protecting my brother. Noah pushes off the wall, smoothing down his mustache. "I know you miss my cock, but that doesn't mean you can show up here whenever you want."

I blink, brain short-circuiting as I struggle to comprehend what I just heard.

"Why the hell not?" Cooper asks, taking a step closer to my brother while gesturing to Marco. "Because you're with this asshole now? That's bullshit and you know it."

"I happen to be *dating* that asshole," Noah bites back, his voice lower than I've ever heard it.

Behind him, Marco rolls his eyes, mumbling something under his breath that sounds a lot like *"thanks, babe."* Then he pinches his nose and sighs. "Looks like you two need to have a conversation. Noah, I'll be in the kitchen when you're done." He squeezes my brother's shoulder before disappearing around the opposite corner.

Brows knit, I duck out of Ryker's grip, keeping to the shadows near the wall while I inch forward.

Once Marco is out of earshot, Cooper shifts from one foot to the other, a hint of hesitation lacing his tone, almost like he's embarrassed. "That asshole comes back to town and suddenly you're done with me? After eight fucking years?"

Fire replaces the ice in my veins, immediate and all-consuming. *Eight years... They've been hooking up for eight years?*

"Coop, come on, man," Noah says, softening his tone. "I've finally got something good going for me and I won't mess it up. You could have that too if you'd just—"

"Don't," Cooper snorts. "I don't need *you* or your advice. Especially when we both know you'll come crawling back to me like you always do." Cooper's grin is calculating and malicious. "In the meantime, I heard Willa's here tonight. Maybe I'll go find out if she sucks dick as well as you do."

Noah's jaw flexes. "Don't you fucking dare—"

"Don't *what?*" Cooper sneers. I'm only ten feet away now, but with the two of them breathing down each other's throats, neither seems to notice. "Don't press you up against this wall and fuck you? Don't shove my cock so far down your throat you can't breathe? You like it rough. Always have. We both know no matter how hard Marco tries, he'll never fill that need. I bet he's still giving you shit every time you look at a girl, isn't he? He'll never fully trust you because he doesn't understand how we can be attracted to both. He'll never understand *you*, not the way I do." Cooper's voice cracks.

"*Coop,*" Noah warns, but then he brings his hand to Cooper's neck, thumb rubbing his jaw with so much intimate familiarity it makes my chest hurt. "Come on, man. We were fucking toxic together. Sometimes love just isn't enough."

A hailstorm of emotions crosses over Cooper's face. Then he clicks his tongue and slowly nods his head. "Fine," he says coolly, ducking out of my brother's grip before rolling up his long sleeves. "You don't want to remember how good we were, let's settle this like we used to when it was *bad...*"

Having heard more than enough, I close the distance in three long strides. Cooper's eyes widen in surprise a millisecond before I ram my fist into his groin, throwing my full body weight into the punch.

He doubles over, a *whoosh* of air escaping his lungs in a soundless howl of agony at the same time bolts of white-hot pain shoot up my wrist—because of course I forgot to keep my damn thumb on the outside.

"Don't *ever* threaten my brother," I spit, bouncing from foot to foot while shaking out my hand to ease the sting.

Unable to stand straight, Cooper gives me the finger.

I stop bouncing, my head cocking to the side a split second before I bring my leg back and slam my knee into his face. A disgusting *crunch* echoes through the side yard and Cooper collapses to the floor, flailing in blind agony as bootsteps sound from behind me.

"God-*fucking*-dammit, Willa. That was even worse than the first time!" Ryker huffs, snatching up my hand and gently palpating my knuckles and bones to make sure they're not broken. "This is exactly why you should have let me teach you how to throw a punch."

I must pass inspection because his jaw hardens. "And you." Ryker's raven hair juts forward as he releases my hand to point a raging finger at my brother. "It's fucking criminal that you haven't taught her to fight. What's wrong with you?"

Noah blinks. "Are you serious right now?"

"Fucking Dunns," Ryker mumbles. "Y'all are gonna get me kicked out of the academy before I even start."

He leans down to grab a whimpering Cooper by the collar, effortlessly maneuvering him up and over his shoulder before his gaze bounces between me and Noah. "I'm going to toss this asshole in his truck and call one of his buddies from the station to come pick him up. Figure your shit out by the time I get back."

The moment Ryker disappears around the corner of the house, I ball my aching fist, pausing the tiniest fraction of a second to make sure my thumb is positioned correctly, and slam my knuckles into my brother's nose.

His head snaps back, a delicious *crunch* cutting through the night air.

Wow. That really did hurt way less...

"What the hell was that for?" Noah snivels, blood leaking from his nostrils and dripping onto his shirt while he clutches his face.

"You've been sleeping with Cooper Blackthorne for *eight fucking years*?" I jam my fingers into his shoulder. "You said you fucking *loved* him. After the way he's treated me? How could you?" I seethe, chest heaving as I contemplate hitting him again.

Noah peers at me through his bloody fingers, eyes wide and horrified while the sharp tang of iron swirls in the air around us. "What are you talking about? I haven't— I'm not—"

I cross my arms, trying to keep my anger from dissipating at the slight way his voice wobbles—like he's afraid of what I'll think or say. "Noah, I heard your entire conversation."

His jaw drops, eyes rapidly searching my face in the darkness. "Whatever you think—"

"Save it." I hold up a hand. "As far as I'm concerned, you can sleep with and date anyone you want to—anyone *except* the asshole who stole my first kiss, locked me in an incinerator, and basically told me to kill myself."

"Willa, I..." His words trail off, his mouth opening and closing like a fish out of water.

Even though I'm riled up, there's a small part of my brain that registers that outside of the Cooper betrayal, this is an important moment for us. No matter how mad I am, I need my brother to understand that my feelings about this situation are based entirely on Cooper being a monster.

"Please hear me when I say this: If I wasn't so mad at you right now, I'd be telling you how excited I am for you and Marco. I will love and support you to the ends of the earth. I will destroy anyone who tries to stand in the way of you being happy with whomever you want to be with—as long as that person isn't Cooper fucking Blackthorne." Trying to keep my voice even, I take a deep breath. "Do you understand me? Anyone but him."

My word choice hovers in the air between us like a line in the sand.

A beat passes. And then another.

Until, in slow motion, Noah's blue-gray eyes meet mine. "Anyone but him?" he repeats, eye twitching and voice hard as iron. "Why does that sound so familiar?"

Shit.

A sticky coating of guilt threatens to extinguish the anger raging in my chest, but it quickly turns to ash. While he's not exactly wrong, it's not the same thing. Ryker was never his tormentor. And Noah doesn't *actually* know that anything happened between us. Instead of apologizing and taking ownership of what a betrayal this is, he's just looking to spin it on me.

What a joke.

"That's what you have to say?" I shake my head. "You know what, Noah? Go fuck yourself."

Chapter Forty-One

I stomp toward the patio, my thoughts a flurrying storm of warring emotions as the heels of my boots sink into the brittle grass.

Yes, I'm hurt Noah didn't trust me enough to tell me that he and Marco are dating, but the revelation that my brother's been sleeping with my arch nemesis for years is threatening the entire foundation of our relationship.

We're family. We're supposed to protect and trust one another...

A bitter laugh escapes my lips at the hypocrisy of my anger, since I've been fooling around with his best friend after he explicitly asked me not to. But unlike Noah, I was going to tell him... And this thing with Ryker doesn't feel like *just* fooling around.

Not anymore. Not for me.

Being with him is like finding a soft, cool place to lay my head after a day of toiling under the sun. Like stepping into a pair of perfectly broken-in boots after stumbling through life in unstable high heels.

And now I'm leaving...

I stop dead in my tracks, body jolting as if I'd walked into an electric livestock fence. I'm leaving Deadwood next Sunday, and Ryker has no choice but to stay.

I glance around the yard like I might find him there, noticing for the first time that the crowd that filed out earlier is gone and the music is off. Through the window, I spot Marco as he scurries about inside, collecting discarded bottles and cups in the living room.

Everyone else must've left for the bar.

The front door opens and Noah trudges in, heading straight for the kitchen where he sticks his entire bloodied face under the faucet. With a frown, Marco sets down the trash and grabs something from a drawer. Then he taps Noah's shoulder before delicately placing a towel against his bleeding nose. When my brother nods, Marco pulls him into a fierce hug.

A tiny pang of guilt needles at my stomach, and I quickly turn away. I might've busted up Noah's nose, but the trust he shattered between us will take a lot longer to mend than broken bones.

Movement has my head snapping left to where a small group is gathered in the tree line. There are only about ten of them, but I spot Isabel's glossy dark hair gleaming in the moonlight near the back.

The wind picks up, and I fold my arms across my middle. It might be the breeze rattling the chain-link fence or the owl screeching from its high perch in the dense trees, but all around me, the shadows seem to shift and move, almost as if they're reaching out to grab me.

My pulse drums in my ears as I step off the concrete patio and into the grass, my body making the unconscious decision to head closer to the group. I hadn't realized it at first, but there's a man standing in the center of their circle. His back is turned to me, body cloaked in darkness, but even from thirty feet away, it's easy to see how captivated these people are by whatever he's saying.

A few more steps, and his voice hits my ears, the cadence low and even. No one around him speaks, no one smiles or laughs. They just hang on to his every word as he turns, arms stretched out and palms facing skyward.

I freeze mid-step as Kane's sharp features come into focus. An unsettling tingle crawls up my spine. *Sheep. Easily influenced. Do as they're told. Most of them incapable of independent thought.* Isn't that what he just said about these same people?

Rain-soaked pine and a faint hint of honeysuckle flood my senses. "Did you and Noah work things out?"

"Not even close," I huff, rage pouring back into my bloodstream full force. "I still can't believe that out of everyone my brother could've been screwing around with, he picked Cooper *fucking* Blackthorne."

I turn and lift my gaze to Ryker's, my shoulders curving forward as I brace myself for the question I have to ask. "Did you know?"

"No, I didn't." He wraps an arm around my waist, fingers digging into my hip when he tucks me against his side. "Which is why Noah and I are about to have some words that will probably end with him eating my fist."

A weight lifts from my shoulders, the corner of my mouth twitching up. "There's a good chance I already broke his nose. And I kept my thumb in the right position this time."

"Sure you did, Princess." Soft light twinkles in the reflection of Ryker's eyes, his expression full of amusement as he brushes the white strands of hair away from my face. A twig snaps in the tree line, and he scowls when he looks over and spots Kane. "Do you want to get out of here and go back to the plan where we pretend we're only children for the rest of the night?"

I glance toward the window where Noah is still holding his nose, his free arm waving around animatedly while I assume he rants about what happened between us. Just looking at him makes the knife of betrayal sticking out of my back sink deeper.

I nod, letting Ryker lead me away from the party without ever looking backward.

Our walk to the truck is cloaked in darkness and serenaded by various insects and other creatures of the night. A warm wind whips across the slanted roofs of the crumbling Victorian mansions on one side of the street and through the narrow alleys and side yards of the Colonial Revival homes on the other, lacing the air with delicate notes of maple and birch with just a hint of mildew and rotting timber.

The night is quiet and calm, and with only a few inches of space between Ryker and me, the silence is comfortable instead of unnerving.

Even so, a slight churn of nervousness flutters inside my stomach. I'm determined to turn this night around for both of us, and since we'll have the house to ourselves, I have a good idea of how I can accomplish that...

"All the lights in the Blackthorne house are off and Beau's car is gone," Ryker announces when we get to the truck. He glances up and down the quiet street before exhaling and reaching into his jeans for the keys.

Something falls out of his pocket, clattering to the pavement before bouncing beneath the truck. Ryker curses, and I spring into action, my skirt riding up as I hastily drop onto my hands and knees to retrieve the item from under the carriage. "I'll get it."

As quickly as I can, I grab the silver lighter and crawl back out.

I'm still on the ground when Ryker steps into my space and cups my chin, forcing my eyes to his. "Fuck, Princess," he sighs, running his thumb over my bottom lip. "You really do look so goddamn good on your knees."

My heart gives an excited thud, heat flooding to my inner thighs.
Be daring, Willa.

"You keep saying that," I murmur, staring up at him through veiled lashes with my heart in my throat. "Maybe you should show me *why* you think so?" I hand him the lighter, which he swiftly pockets, but I stay on my knees, slowly reaching for his belt. "Or maybe I could show you?"

Ryker's breaths quicken, his gaze homed on mine as his buckle clatters to the side and I start in on the top button of his jeans. Eyes black in the low light of the moon, he clenches his jaw. "You don't know what you're asking for…"

I take a deep breath. *Here goes nothing.* "Really? Because I'm pretty sure I'm asking you to fuck my mouth…"

"*Fucking hell,*" he hisses, already undoing his zipper. "Put your jacket under your knees."

Giddy, I scramble out of my coat and place it on the asphalt, the relief on my kneecaps instantaneous as I climb atop it. When I glance up, Ryker is fisting himself, the head of his enormous cock glistening in the moonlight.

Jesus. How the hell is that thing supposed to fit in my mouth?

Eyes wide, I swallow down the tightness in my throat. "You'll show me what to do?"

Leaning over, Ryker grabs my face with one hand and tucks a loose strand of hair behind my ear with the other. "Anything you do will be perfect," he says, the tip of his nose brushing against my own. "Just no hands, okay?" He waits until I nod before kissing my forehead and standing back up.

The air shifts, and I swear Ryker's voice drops three octaves. "Open your mouth and stick out your tongue for me."

The pulse between my thighs goes wild from the memory of him saying those exact words on the water tower. Adrenaline coursing through my veins, I push up off my toes to make myself taller and grab onto his jean-clad thighs for balance. Keeping my eyes locked on his, I slowly open my mouth, salivating as he strokes himself—this time mere inches away from my face.

"Perfect, just like that." Breathing heavily, he angles himself forward, threading his fingers in my hair with one hand while tapping the thick head of his cock against my waiting tongue with the other. My clit throbs at the taste of him.

"*Fuck,*" he moans, thighs tensing beneath my palms. "You have no idea how long I've wanted to fuck this smart mouth of yours."

Body buzzing, I let go of a keening groan when he slides his cock a few inches into my mouth before sliding back out. The hand in my hair tightens and then he's dragging his shaft across my parted lips.

"These pink lips of yours are so goddamn beautiful," he whispers as he sweeps his cock over them, repeating the same process on my cheeks and then my chin—like he's marking me. Every time his dick touches my skin, it sends an electric zap straight to my clit.

"*Hmm.* Too fucking perfect," Ryker growls. "Open wider so I can fuck that pretty mouth."

God, yes. Straining my neck, I take down as much of him as I can before wrapping my lips around his shaft and flicking my tongue. I moan, my eyes fluttering open and closed in delight at the slightly salty taste of his skin. I do it again, this time rotating my tongue to explore the feel of him.

For a second, I'm nervous I'm not doing it right, but then Ryker tilts his chin skyward and lets out the sexiest breathy sigh, causing my belly to erupt into a flurry of need.

I'd do literally *anything* to hear that sound again, but his grip is so tight in my hair, I can't actually move anything besides my tongue. So that's what I do, swirl my tongue and draw him as deep as I can, devouring him with the same enthusiasm I would a popsicle in the heat of summer.

Ryker glances down at me, biting the corner of his lip as he pushes in farther. My jaw struggles to hinge wider and accommodate his length. "That's it, Princess. Look at you. So fucking beautiful with my cock in your mouth."

Chest so warm I wouldn't be surprised if I was glowing like a firefly, I let Ryker gently guide my head up and down his thick length. He never takes his eyes off me, not for a single second. Not even when he adds his other hand to my hair and starts thrusting into my mouth in earnest.

My pussy throbs, and I'm a mess. Not only is there drool dripping down my chin and moisture soaking through my thong from how turned on I am, but every time Ryker grunts and pants as he pumps against my tongue, it awakens something wild in me. Something feral and desperate for more.

I work my tongue faster, drawing on every smutty book I've ever read and every filthy porn I've ever streamed to bring him closer to the edge.

"Fuck, Princess. A little deeper." His nails dig into my scalp as he takes full control of my head. "Yeah, that's it— Jesus— *Fuck*." Ryker tenses beneath me, and a proud warmth pulses through my torso.

He's close.

Laughter sounds from down the street. "Fuck," Ryker hisses before abruptly pulling out of my mouth and dragging me to my feet. Dazed and slightly disappointed, I follow the direction of his stare to where I can just make out a group of ten or so people filing out of Marco's backyard.

There are no streetlights over here, so I'm not exactly worried about anyone seeing us...

But then I notice the single dark silhouette standing in the road.

Chapter Forty-Two

Ripping open the door of the truck, Ryker grabs my jacket off the road and gives my ass a playful pat, urging me inside. "Keep an eye out," he says, climbing in after me and turning over the engine. "I'm about to break every speed limit in Deadwood so we can finish what we started, and the last thing we need is to get pulled over."

Unconcerned by the last few people we saw leaving the party, I place my hand over his on the shifter. "Why do we have to go anywhere?"

"What do you mean—" Ryker quirks a brow, then widens his eyes when I lay down on the seat, shifting my hair to the side to take his dick between my lips. His body shudders, hand automatically threading back into the hair at the nape of my neck.

"Jesus, *fuck*. How are you so good at this already?" He thrusts into my mouth, panting as I flatten my tongue and take him deeper. With a groan, he increases the pressure on my head, gently forcing me farther down his cock. "God, *yes*. Just like that, Princess. Keep going. *Fuck*."

My cheeks flush with heat and my core throbs. Ryker controlling the motion of my mouth is one of the sexiest feelings ever. But there's something about his fierce grip on my scalp, his slow movements, and the way his body trembles beneath mine that's almost *too* controlled —like he's struggling to restrain himself.

My brows furrow, and I'm about to ask him to stop holding back when he stills.

"*Shit*," he grunts, already breathless. "Someone's coming over. He's still a ways off but— Fuck. I think it's Kane."

My eyes bug out of their sockets, and I scramble to sit up, but Ryker's devilish grin stops me dead in my tracks. "I didn't tell you to stop," he all but growls, sending an electric thrill up my spine.

Unable to keep the smile from my lips, I sink as low as possible, resting the side of my head against his stomach so that I'm looking at the steering wheel and face-to-face with his raging hard-on. Without his hand guiding me, I have a little more room to explore, so I grip his thigh and tentatively lick up the length of his shaft, mapping each ridge and groove before taking the tip of him into my mouth.

He sighs, nails scraping against my scalp as he slides his fingers into my hair. I bob up and down, and when I reach the crown of his cock again, I swirl my tongue, reveling in his breathless moans.

"*Fuck*, that feels good. Don't stop," he groans, filling my chest with a pleasant warmth.

I shiver when Ryker leans over and slowly inches my skirt up around my waist. Mouth full but needing him to touch me, I whimper and wiggle my hips, doing everything I can to encourage him to keep going. Thankfully, I don't have to wait long before he's tracing the thin fabric of my thong between my ass all the way to the apex of my thighs. I moan around his shaft when he grazes my clit, and then he roughly shoves my underwear aside and plunges two fingers into my soaked pussy.

I gasp and grind against his hand, each movement impaling my mouth on his dick as I chase the rapturous sensation between my thighs while struggling not to choke on him.

"That's it, Princess, take my cock down your throat," he grunts, thrusting against my tongue in time with the fingers he's sliding in and out of me. "Show me what a little slut you are."

My pussy clenches around him, his filthy words flooding my entire body with heat. *Okay...slight degradation kink officially unlocked, along with an insatiable desire to do exactly as he asked.*

Jesus. Why is this so hot? The feel of Ryker in my mouth. Those little gasps and moans he makes when I do something he really likes. It's enough for anyone to lose their mind to lust. If I thought my jaw could take it, I'd do this all day without any care for who saw us.

Hollowing my cheeks, I flick my tongue again, paying special attention to the divot where Ryker's shaft meets the head of his cock, and delighting in the way he abruptly pumps into my mouth in response, like his control is finally slipping.

But then he stills.

"Fucking hell. It's definitely my goddamn brother out there," he says, voice strained as I continue to bob up and down. "I'm going to roll down the window. I don't want you to stop and I *don't* want you to be quiet. *Fuck—*" He uses the hand on my head to force me into a slower pace before taking a deep, shuddering breath. "I need Kane to understand who you belong to. I want him to know you're in here with *my* cock in your mouth and *my* fingers in your perfect, wet cunt..."

Holy shit. My pussy throbs, flooding my thighs with moisture.

"Do you understand me, Willa?"

"*Mm-hmm,*" I reply, lips still stretched around him and absolutely loving the way his body quakes in response to the vibration of my muffled voice.

"Fucking *hell,*" Ryker says under his breath, fingers sliding out of my pussy when he sits up straighter. My head jostles slightly as he cranks open the window, and then the sound of crickets chirping and boots crunching through the nearby grass pours inside the truck.

"What do you want, Kane?" Ryker barks, continuing to guide my head up and down his cock. "Don't you have people to brainwash or creepy notes to leave inside someone's house?"

361

"You're such an asshole," his half brother says, his casual, modern tone shattering the numinous façade he normally tries so hard to keep in place. Honestly, it's the first time he's ever sounded like the twenty-three-year-old he really is.

My heart races. Judging by the volume of Kane's voice, he can't be more than a few feet from the window. While I don't know if he can see me or not, I really don't care. This guy broke into my house *and* I'm fairly positive he has something to do with why Isabel is bailing on me for school.

There's also a sick part of me that wants someone to see me like this—to bear witness to Willa Dunn actually *living* her life instead of just letting it happen around her.

Emboldened, I increase the suction of my mouth, delighting in the hint of salty precum on my tongue and the sharp intake of air from Ryker.

"Say what you came here to say, Kane," he grits out, pushing my head down a bit too quickly as he slams into the back of my throat. My eyes water as I struggle not to cough.

"What the hell is wrong with you?" Kane hisses, but there's a note of confusion tacked on to the anger.

"What's wrong with *me*?" Ryker lets go of a humorless laugh. "You're kidding, right? I've been trying to give you the benefit of the doubt here, but did you seriously break into the Dunn's house the day after I left town? What the actual fuck?"

Ryker's body tenses, the contraction of his arm forcing his cock deeper down my throat until my eyes are watering and I have to tap his thigh to remind him I'm still down here. He immediately eases up, allowing me to take a single breath before resuming his previous pace. My belly coils and heats when he subtly leans over and dips his fingers back inside my pussy in what feels like an apology for being too rough—which is unnecessary because I love the way he's using my mouth.

"I've done no such thing," Kane replies, his lofty, pious tone firmly back in place.

"*Bullshit*," Ryker says through gritted teeth as he drags his fingers across my scalp. "Did you come here for a reason? I'm sort of in the middle of something right now." One hand still in my hair, he teases my clit with the other, forcing me to moan around his cock as pleasure ripples up my spine.

Ryker curses, thrusting his hips at the same time he pushes my head down. My nose smashes into his hip and I gag—*very* audibly.

Kane goes suspiciously quiet, and even though I can't see him, I imagine his eye twitching before he says, "I saw you leave with Willa. Where is she?"

"Right here." Ryker slips a finger under my chin, guiding me off his cock with a trail of spit still connecting the crown of his dick to my swollen lips.

Kane's eyes lock on mine as I sit up, a murderous shadow crossing over his features as his brother wipes the drool from my chin. Then Ryker surprises the hell out of me by capturing my mouth with his. The kiss is hungry, possessive and claiming... I lose myself in the feeling and fuse my lips with his.

When he pulls away, I'm breathless and so dizzy that I have to brace myself with one hand on his chest and the other in his lap to keep from falling over.

"I'll be done with Kane in a minute, Princess. Then we can pick up where we left off," he says, rubbing his thumb back and forth on my hip as he tucks me against his side.

I feel Kane's resulting rage burning a hole in my cheek, but I couldn't care less.

"I thought we had an agreement?" he fumes.

"We do," Ryker responds firmly. "I signed the rental *agreement*, and we *agreed* to stay out of each other's way. I'll continue looking out for Charlie, and you'll continue using those fancy public speaking skills you learned in New Mexico to save the town—or whatever the hell it is you think you're doing. Willa's not a part of that."

Kane doesn't say a word, but that doesn't stop me from noticing the subtle shift in his posture or how his eyes narrow in the darkness.

Ryker revs the engine, silencing the nearby crickets as he moves his hand from my hip to the shifter. "If that was all you needed…"

Kane's shadowed gaze lands on mine, hard and unrelenting while moonlight glints off his cicada bolo tie. "By all means." He extends a palm toward the road. "Happy birthday, *brother*."

After Ryker tucks himself inside his jeans, we peel out of there so fast that if he didn't reach out an arm to stop me, I'd have impaled myself on the gearshift. My hair whips across my face, pulse pounding as we speed through the night.

That might've been the hottest thing ever, but there was a lot more going on in that exchange than meets the eye.

"What agreement was Kane talking about?" I ask once we're back on the main road and his silhouette is just a speck in the rearview mirror.

"My brother has a problem with letting things go," Ryker scoffs, grabbing a pack of cigarettes off the dash and quickly shoving one between his teeth. "Once Kane gets something in his head, he becomes obsessive."

He brings the lighter up and then hesitates, his jaw flexing as he glances at me.

I take it from his hand, wincing when I strike the starter, but no flame appears. "And that something he's obsessive about *is*?"

With a humorless laugh, Ryker rips the unlit cigarette from his lips and tosses it out the window. "You want the truth?"

I bob my head, moths fluttering inside my stomach in nervous anticipation when he cracks a half smile that flickers in and out of view under the passing amber streetlights.

"I had a thing for you growing up," Ryker says, and I swear a blush creeps into his cheeks. "I made the mistake of telling my brother, and he made it *very* clear that under no circumstances was I allowed to go after you."

My face scrunches. "What? Why not?"

Frowning slightly, Ryker glances at me from the corner of his eye. "Kane's always felt a weird connection to what happened to you.

And since Noah and your dad would have killed me anyway, I promised him that I wouldn't touch you... No matter how badly I wanted to."

Warmth blossoms inside my chest. "You've sure got a funny way of showing a girl you're harboring a secret soft spot for her. I mean, honestly, jump scares and crickets? How could I have resisted?"

The coy smile on his lips widens into a cocky grin. "What can I say? I guess I've always liked making you scream."

My lips pull into a grin. If I'd known how he felt back then, would things be different between us now? Could we have had this—whatever *this* is—sooner?

The air between us is thick, and I'm finding it difficult to sort through all of the chaotic thoughts in my foggy mind except for one: I'm done wasting time. If I have to leave Deadwood without Ryker, I want to give him as much of myself as humanly possible.

"You're awfully quiet over there," he says, keeping his attention straight ahead as we pull up to a stop sign. "Did I take things too far by making you—"

"You didn't *make* me do anything." I lift my skirt, grabbing his hand and placing it between my thighs so he can feel how wet I am. "If your brother really does have some sort of weird obsession with me, then hopefully seeing your dick shoved down my throat was more than enough to break it."

An animal-like sound rumbles in his chest as he glances down, sliding his fingers over my soaked panties. "Seems like someone enjoyed having their mouth used like a fuck toy."

I turn to face him, waiting until he meets my eye before responding. "I loved it."

Ryker's eyes light up, my declaration somehow casting out the dark shadows left by his brother. "Good, because I'm not even close to being done with you."

Chapter Forty-Three

Ryker slams the front door closed, never removing his mouth from mine as he carries me into the dark house. My knee scrapes against a doorframe—or maybe it's a wall—but my legs are wrapped tightly enough around his waist that it barely registers. I drag my nails through his hair, kissing him back like my life depends on it.

I'm vaguely aware that we almost died at least a hundred times on the drive home because we couldn't keep our hands off one another, but I can't find it in myself to care. Hell, the world could be crumbling down around us and I wouldn't even notice.

"Is your dad working tonight?" Ryker breathes against my neck.

"I think so," I reply between kisses that I trail across his temple and forehead.

My ass hits a cold, hard surface, and then Ryker's ripping my blouse up and over my head.

"Wait, why are we in the bathroom?" Heart racing, I unhook my bra with one hand and reach for Ryker's shirt with the other, silently pleading for him to remove it because I can't from this position.

"Seemed like the safest place to be if anyone came home." He shrugs off his own shirt and leans down to kiss me deeply, shivering when I drag my fingers across the hard surface of his scarred abdomen. "Spread your legs, Princess."

When I don't move fast enough, he does it for me, wrenching my knees apart with two rough hands. There's a loud *thunk*, and a second later, his head is between my thighs, his mouth devouring my still-covered pussy through the thin lace. Grasping at his shoulders for balance, I arch my spine and squirm while his tongue dances across the soaked fabric with languid strokes.

"Ryker," I pant, writhing against his mouth. "*Please*, take them off."

My pulse races when the distinctive metallic *clicks* of his zipper unfurling fill the small bathroom, and then I'm gasping as he slips beneath my underwear.

Cupping my face with two hands, he kisses me again, all the while continuing to tease my pussy with an urgent yet gentle pressure. God, it feels good—*different*, but incredible—almost like he's using two thick knuckles instead of the pads of his fingers...

Heat pulses up my spine each time he slides back and forth across my clit, the feeling only intensified by the hand cupping my cheek and the other dragging across my scalp—

Wait...

My breath hitches, brain tripping over itself as I try to make sense of what's happening. *If Ryker's hands are on my face, then how is he—*

Oh my God. That's his cock.

I bring a hand to his waist, moaning into his mouth when he thrusts forward, the ridge of his dick gliding over my clit with glorious friction as he grinds against my pussy. *Holy shit*. Is this dry fucking? A pussy job? Should I even care when it feels so good?

He picks up the pace, one of his hands leaving my cheek to press his dick more firmly against the outside of my pussy while he continues to rut. "Listen to how wet you are. *Fuck*. I need to be inside you," he pants, the desperation in his voice making my stomach coil.

"I'm on birth control," I breathe out. "Please, Ryker."

He laughs, the sound deep and strained. "Jesus Christ, Willa, I'm not gonna fuck you on the bathroom counter in the goddamn dark. Not the first time, anyway."

He bends to kiss me, but I lean away.

"Then turn on a light," I say matter-of-factly, and before he can come up with another excuse, I use my forearm and the counter as leverage to lift my hips and slide my pussy along his thick length. "You start training the day after tomorrow and I leave next weekend. What if right now is all we get? What if this is it?"

Ryker stills, his body trembling as he leans over and switches on the light. "Are you sure?" he asks, the moss-green of his eyes swirling with a storm of uncertainty.

My heart drums against my ribs like furious hummingbird wings.

"I've never been more sure of anyone in my life," I say with absolute confidence. But that doesn't really answer his question, so I keep going. "I might not know what's going to happen tomorrow or the day after, but I know I want this. I want *you*."

Ryker presses his mouth to mine, and then he's shoving my underwear and skirt down my hips. I think he does the same thing with his jeans, but I'm too consumed by the intoxicating feel of his lips and tongue to break the kiss and see for myself.

Then he steps closer, his pulse nearly bounding out of his chest as he slides my ass to the edge of the counter and notches himself against my entrance. Heart racing, I wrap my arms around his shoulders, but he hesitates. "This isn't how your first time is supposed to go. A better man would wait and make this perfect for you, but I'm not a good man, Willa. I've waited too long not to—"

I silence him with a kiss, gasping into his mouth when he pushes inside me with one steady stroke. My body tenses at the intrusion, and I cry out at the same time Ryker's mouth drops open to swallow my scream.

Keeping his hips still, he kisses me through the shock of the stretch, only stopping when I pull away to come up for air.

There's so much of him... Too much of him. I can't— How am I supposed to—

"Holy fuck, Willa," he whispers, breath trembling and muscles quaking beneath my grip. I want to respond, but all I can think about is the burn as I struggle to acclimate to his size.

There's too much of him. He's too big...and yet I still want *more*. Desperate to relieve the pressure and quench the ache, I try to rock my hips against him, but Ryker pins me in place and brings his forehead to mine.

"Are you okay?" he asks on a ragged breath, shaking as he plants delicate kisses along my brow and down my temple.

Unable to find my voice, all I can do is nod.

"Then I need you to relax, Princess. I'm not even halfway in yet..."

My eyes go wide, but I nod, sucking in a sudden breath as he brings his thumb between us to circle my clit. My muscles slowly uncoil, and I let loose a relieved exhale when he sinks in another inch, and then another with shallow thrusts.

Heat prickles beneath my skin and I moan, eyelids fluttering as my body melds with his.

"That's it, Princess. You're taking me so fucking well," he whispers against my lips before continuing his trail of kisses down my jaw. "God, you're perfect. You're the most beautiful thing I've ever seen."

My head drops back, warmth spreading from the apex of my thighs to my low stomach as my muscles uncoil further. There's still so much of him, but each thrust and word of praise melts away the slight discomfort until there is only pleasure.

"Ryker, please don't stop," I pant into the crook of his neck, rocking my hips to meet his.

With a shaky breath, he slowly pulls out before sinking back into me. Then he does it again, each time getting just a little bit deeper and working my clit a little bit faster. Sweat beads on his brow, and while I'm almost positive he's still holding back, there's no question in my mind about whether or not he wants this as bad as I do. Not with the way his grip tightens on my hip with each *slap* of our sweat-soaked bodies, and not with the way his blown pupils keep volleying between my face and the bounce of my breasts every time he thrusts.

"I need to be deeper," he breathes, eyes returning to mine as he slides the hand on my hip up my scarred back to draw me against his chest. "God, Willa. You feel so fucking good."

Ryker slides my ass off the counter and sinks himself to the hilt inside of me. Bursts of pleasure prickle across my skin as he fucks me faster and faster, slamming my lower back into the granite with the fervor of a wild animal until we somehow end up on the floor.

Eyes locked on one another and sharing the same ragged breaths, he keeps one hand on the back of my head, the other on my ass to keep us firmly locked in place, then he's pushing my knees wider and pounding into me with absolute abandon. The new angle is intoxicating and mind-numbingly perfect, each thrust now grinding directly against my clit.

We are drenched in each other's sweat, our moans and groans entwined in one another's as we move together on the floor. With each thrust, it feels like Ryker is laying claim to a piece of my soul—unraveling the very essence of who I am and threading himself into the fabric as he knits us back together. When his movements become frantic, I wrap my arms tighter around his shoulders, the pressure in my low stomach building as he drives me into the tile.

The lights flicker above us.

"Ryker, I'm going to—"

"I know," he groans, face flushed and eyes full of such a deep longing that it tugs at something inside my chest. He drops his forehead to mine. "I'm right there with you, Princess."

I dig my nails into his back, and he slams into me. "Ryker, I—"

I can't even finish my thought before I explode, shattering into a million pieces as wave after wave of euphoria washes over me—the feeling amplified tenfold when Ryker swells and spills into me in a rush of heat.

"Oh *fuck*," he grunts, jerking his hips and drawing out our orgasms until he collapses on top of me. Chest heaving against mine, he breathes me in, his cock still pulsing while my body twitches with the aftershocks of pleasure. Then he smiles and brings his mouth to mine, kissing me long and hard.

The lights flicker again, and I flinch when Ryker slowly pulls out.

"Fucking hell," he says, trailing his rough palm up my inner leg to the apex of my thighs. "I thought watching you come undone beneath me was the hottest thing I've ever seen, but watching my cum drip out of that sweet pussy—"

I gasp as he shoves two fingers into my center, pushing his cum back inside. Every inch of my skin is swollen and oversensitive, but that doesn't stop my moan or the little tremors of pleasure when he slides them back out and drags me into his lap.

"Open your mouth," he says against my ear, voice low and husky.

Pulse racing, I part my lips, allowing Ryker to slip his cum-drenched fingers between them. He groans when I flick my tongue and lick them clean, the salty, almost metallic taste of our combined arousal making my stomach flutter all over again.

"I've never done that before," he says, voice strained and full of wonder while he leans his forehead against my temple and nestles his nose behind my ear. "Not without a condom."

"It was always going to be me, wasn't it?" I say playfully, but the smile falls from my lips when he looks up, a turbulent storm brewing behind his moss-green eyes.

Brow lowered and jaw hard, his expression twists into something that's halfway between adoration and agony. "Always."

There's a tug inside my chest and then a sudden drop, sort of similar to when you startle awake from a dream after tripping or plunging from a cliff—the weightless feeling as you anticipate the endless fall.

How can I leave this behind?

How can I leave *him*?

Don't I owe it to the both of us to give this thing between us a chance?

"Ryker, what if—"

"*Don't*," he says, fingers digging almost painfully into my waist. "*Please*, Willa. Whatever you're about to say, just don't."

"Why not?" My voice is small and watery as Ryker brushes his thumb over my quivering lower lip.

"Because you're finally getting out of Deadwood and I can never leave. Not without Charlie." He plants a soft kiss in my hair. "I'm a selfish prick for taking it this far to begin with, but I won't be the reason you question leaving this hellhole. I won't hold you back. Not ever."

I close my eyes against the gut-wrenching sensation clawing at my insides. It's too late. I'm *already* questioning if leaving is still the right choice. And Ryker's statement just confirms that he's the only person worth staying for.

Chapter Forty-Four

The next morning, Ryker's warm, solid body is wrapped around me like a cocoon. The house is dark and silent, my heart is full, and my mind is quiet and content as the soft-gray light of early dawn filters in through the curtains.

I yawn and stretch beneath the rust-brown comforter, a delicate smile spreading across my face at the gentle soreness between my legs. My hips ache from accommodating Ryker's tree trunk of a body, my lips are swollen and bruised, even my shoulders are tender from the fervid way he fucked me into the bathroom floor, and yet I've never felt so alive. Never felt so strong and beautiful. So comfortable in my own skin.

My relationships with my brother and Isabel might be falling apart, and there might be a growing mountain of lies between me and my father, but the day still seems bright and full of possibility. Maybe I'll stay like this forever, tucked away from the rest of the world in the shelter of Ryker's strong arms where nothing else exists except for this moment...

The croon of a mourning dove drifts in through the window, her sad song an unwelcome reminder of the real world carrying on outside these walls. The world where Ryker and I can't have forever because we don't even have today...

In less than an hour, he'll head to Denton to visit Charlie and tomorrow he starts the police academy. We might see each other for a day or two next weekend, but I leave for Austin on Sunday. An emptiness slowly replaces the warmth in my stomach. The longer I stay here, the harder it'll be to disentangle myself from Ryker, but the urge to soak up every last second, even if he's asleep for it, is almost stronger than my common sense.

Almost.

Wanting to let him rest for a bit longer but needing to escape the sharp twinge of pain radiating down the center of my chest, I attempt to slip out from the covers—barely making it a few inches before Ryker's arm snakes around my waist and he yanks me backward.

"Get back here," he grumbles, and a shiver dances across my skin as his smoky voice ghosts over the nape of my neck.

A second ticks by, my head at war with my heart until Ryker's cock twitches, hardening against my *very* naked ass and sending heat pulsing up my spine. Now that he's awake... I might as well give him a proper birthday-morning hello—

My phone vibrates.

With an annoyed huff, I reach for it, barely managing to knock it off the charger into my waiting hands.

DAD

You up? Need to talk ASAP.

My heart skips a beat.

"Fuck," Ryker groans, tensing behind me as he reads the text over my shoulder.

Stomach knotting, I turn to face him. "What do you think he knows? It has to be about UT, right? Or do you think it's about my fight with Noah?" My voice is shrill as I run out of oxygen.

"It's probably nothing," Ryker assures me, but he's already sitting up and swinging his legs off the bed. The *B*-shaped burn scar on his ribs flexes as he curses and rakes his fingers through his hair. "Let me shower and get dressed before you reply, just in case." He rises from the bed, grabs a change of clothes from the living room, and heads to the bathroom.

After quickly scanning my phone for any other missed calls or texts and finding none, I throw on a pair of underwear and an oversized Johnny Cash T-shirt before dragging my feet to the kitchen. A terrifying thought lodges in my throat, threatening to suffocate me as the coffee machine gurgles and spits beside me. What if Dad's text has nothing to do with UT and Austin? What if he came home during the night and saw—

My head snaps toward the sound of footsteps on the porch a second before the door swings open, and I gag at the god-awful smell that pours into the house.

"Jesus Christ, kiddo. Put some pants on, would ya?" Dad says, closing the front door way too loudly before dropping his Stetson onto the entryway table.

Scrunching my nose, I forget every other thought in my head so I can concentrate on not puking. "What is that horrendous smell?" I screech, covering the lower half of my face as I dry heave. "Why do you smell like literal shit?"

"*Language*," he chastises, but his voice is too tired for there to be any real bite.

"She's right, Mr. Dunn. You smell like manure," Ryker says, face contorted in disgust as he strolls into the living room and gives me a curt nod, like he didn't just spend the night in my bed.

"Joel, son. I've already told you to just call me Joel." Dad's worn expression sags further when he drops into a seat at the table. "And judging by those statements, I'm guessing neither of you have looked outside this morning?"

My eyes dart to the window where a small fleet of vans and trucks are lined up in the Crowes' half-circle driveway. There are several men in jumpsuits milling about, as well as a backhoe and other digging equipment being unloaded off a trailer.

"What happened?" I ask, nausea abating as I inhale the decadent, steamy tendrils of the breakfast blend coffee I pour into three mugs. It's not quite strong enough to cover up Dad's smell, but it does take the bite off.

"The Crowes' plumbing took a dive," Dad says with a shudder. "I'm not sure if the septic tank or the water heater went first, but either way, sewage backed up through the sinks and toilets and the flooding made the damage ten times worse."

My steps are heavy as I walk to the table. "This is the last thing Elanor needs to be dealing with right now. How did that even happen? Is there anything we can do to help?"

Dad shakes his head, avoiding eye contact with me as he takes the cup from my outstretched hand. "Unfortunately, by the time I drove by and saw water streaming down their driveway, it was already too late. I managed to get the main valve shut off, but the damage was done."

He lifts the mug to his face and blows on the liquid gold. "As far as how it happened," he says into the rim of his coffee, "that's what I wanted to talk to you about. The Crowes had flood sensors, but not a single one of them went off. Did y'all hear or see anything odd at the ranch last night?"

Warmth creeps into my cheeks as images of me and Ryker flash through my mind like a smutty montage, but the flush quickly abates when one memory stands out in particular.

"The lights were flickering on and off. Did anyone in town report a power issue?"

"No," Dad says, taking an obnoxiously loud slurp from his cup. "But they wouldn't have. Beau's house, the Crowes' Ranch, and our place are the only three properties on this section of the grid. Well, us and the Cartwright Estate."

Ryker's jaw flexes, his eyes darting out the window and then back to Dad as he takes the coffee from my outstretched hand. "Does the electric company have a record of outages?" he says, brows furrowed.

"Would that show if someone interfered or cut the power to the ranch?"

"You really are going to make a great cop," Dad says with a pleased snort. "Keep up that line of thinking and you'll be just fine at the academy."

Ryker's gaze drops to the floor, and a small smile spreads across my lips at the light-pink blush staining his cheeks.

God, he's awful at taking compliments, but he's so damn cute about it.

"I'll call the electric company and see what I can dig up," Dad continues with a yawn. "I'd hate to think someone in town was capable of sabotaging the plumbing, but I wouldn't put it past any of the Blackthornes to try to steal the place out from under Kane. That being said, things like this do happen with old houses..."

His voice trails off, like he's talking more to himself than to us, and I clear my throat. "Was that all you wanted to talk to me about?"

"It was. If neither of you saw anything else, then I'm going to hit the shower." Dad rises to his feet and stretches his hands up over his head, sending another potent wave of sewage in my direction. "Do you have everything you need for tomorrow, son?"

"Yes, sir, I'm all set. I'm hitting the road soon to see Charlie, and then I'll be staying at a hotel near the training center until Friday. I'm not sure what Noah's plans are, but you and Willa will probably have the house to yourselves this week." Ryker steps closer, nudging his shoulder against my back to urge me forward. "Depending on your work schedule, maybe the two of you could go fishing?"

Dad pauses in the hallway to glance between the two of us, his lips curving downward before hardening into a tight line. Much to my surprise, his blue-gray gaze meets mine. "Guess we haven't seen much of each other lately, have we, kiddo?"

I shake my head and he nods, the creases near his eyes softening into something sorrowful that almost looks like regret. "Alright, then. Let's plan a date at the range, maybe a little fishing followed by lunch at Rib Cage?"

"I'd like that," I say through a forced smile, only drawing in a full breath when he leaves.

The shower starts up a few seconds later and Ryker wraps his arms around my waist, refusing to let go when I swat him away.

"*Uh, maybe the two of you could go fishing,*" I say in a mockingly deep voice while trying to peel his fingers off of me. "What the hell was that?"

"I don't want you alone in this house, and it'll be a good opportunity for you to tell your dad that you're leaving next week," Ryker replies with a gentle bite to my earlobe that instantly has my anger melting away. "Imagine how hurt he'll be if he finds out on his own— the way you did with the Noah-Cooper shit."

My throat bobs. I should be ashamed that I haven't told my dad I'm leaving, but the sensation curled around my neck feels a lot more like fear.

"What if he says I can't go?"

Ryker stills, his audible swallow filling the room. "Would that stop you?"

"Shouldn't it? If my need to get away from this place hurts someone I love..." My voice is so thick I trip over the words.

"Willa, I thought you wanted to get out of Deadwood more than anything? Has that changed? Do you not want to leave anymore?" Ryker's voice is ragged, rising up at the end with an odd quality I've never heard from him before.

My lungs strain with the effort it takes not to scream that yes, it *has* changed because now I also want *him*. But what would that accomplish other than distracting him during training or torturing me when he tells me he doesn't feel the same way?

"That's what I thought," he says when I don't respond, wrapping his arms around me just a little bit tighter. "Go after what you want, Princess. Leave this shithole in the dust where it belongs."

Desperate not to acknowledge the gnawing ache beneath my ribs, I lean into his chest, staring out the window as a tractor begins excavating what I assume to be the septic tank at Crowe Ranch.

With only the quiet hum of the shower down the hall and the gentle *thump* of Ryker's heart against my back, we stay like that for a good minute or two. Then Ryker pulls his phone out to check the time. The air shifts, and a frantic pounding takes over my pulse.

I'd almost forgotten he needs to leave soon...

"I saw the look on your face when Dad was talking," I say in a rush. "Do you really think the Blackthornes did that to the Crowes' plumbing?"

The muscles in his forearms stiffen. "No. I think it was Kane."

"You can't be serious," I say, incredulity heavy on my furrowed brow. But when I tilt my head to glance up at him, my insides shrivel at the rage painted across his chiseled cheeks.

"It makes sense, doesn't it? If the house is unlivable, Elanor will have to cut Kane a deal on the price." Ryker sucks his teeth and lets go of a humorless laugh. "The question is, did he have me sign that rental agreement because he had this planned and needed plausible deniability? Or is this his retaliation for last night?"

Ice coats my stomach.

Kane knows what Beau's capable of, would he really do something this malicious when Ryker's applying for guardianship of their sister? There's no way. No matter how mad I was at Noah—and I'm pretty damn mad at him right now—I'd never sabotage his living situation or do something that would put another family member at risk. Yes, Ryker and I might've pissed Kane off with our blow job stunt in the truck last night, but he's not evil enough to do *this*... Is he?

I turn into Ryker, my breath catching in my throat at the way the morning sun shining through the window kisses his cheeks and brow with a golden glow. There has to be a trace of Ryker's goodness in his half brother. "Are you sure he'd—"

"I'm sure." Ryker tucks a lock of hair behind my ear, holding on to one of the white strands between his thumb and forefinger. "Kane had a dark side long before Beau fucked with his head. I was reluctant to admit it when I first came back, but I think whatever happened in New Mexico changed him... Or maybe it just set free some of the darkness he always kept caged."

I bite my lip, unsure how sensitive this topic is. "You mentioned New Mexico last night. Why was he there in the first place?"

"He found his dad," Ryker says lowly. "A few weeks before Mom died, Kane found our birth certificates in one of her suitcases."

Gaze zeroed in on my mouth, Ryker lets go of my hair and slides one hand down to my ass. "Once we had that, it only took a two-second internet search to find out Kane's dad was the leader of a doomsday megachurch operating out of the southwest. You might have seen him on the news a few times lately. Josiah Koresh? I think he's being investigated for embezzling church funds or some shit like that."

I let out a low whistle.

"Yep," he says through a sigh. "Kane took off the day after Mom died to go find Koresh. I didn't realize he wasn't coming back until I got a postcard from New Mexico two weeks later. He's been out there with his dad ever since. At least he *was* until he showed up here a few months ago. He won't say shit about what happened, but every time I bring it up, I swear to God his eyes turn black and he—"

Ryker's phone goes off with an alert. "Shit, I need to hit the road."

I want to ask more about Kane, but really I just want a few extra minutes with Ryker. "Do you have time for breakfast before you leave?"

He shakes his head. "I'm not hungry."

"What about for a birthday present?" I inquire with a lifted brow before guilt has me backpedaling. "I'll go grab it so you can take it with you. It's kinda for Charlie anyway."

The next thing I know, Ryker's lips are on mine and he's backing me up against the table.

"The only thing I want for my birthday is more time," he says breathlessly, hands sliding into my hair to keep my face close to his. "Are you sore from last night?"

I bite my lip and shake my head.

"Are you lying?" he asks, pushing into me so that my back arches over the table as he positions himself between my legs. "I could lick it better before I go..."

The shower shuts off, and he pulls away, keeping his palm on my neck until the bathroom door *clicks* open, like the thought of letting me go a moment before he needed to was as unbearable to him as it was to me.

Dad doesn't look at us as he walks to his bedroom, but it's not until he speaks that I realize it's because he's on the phone. "I already signed and emailed the paperwork," he says, head hung low as he listens to the person on the other end of the line. "I understand that, but terminal or not, we're still not requesting clemency *or* a reprieve from the governor. This is on the state to figure out. I can't keep—"

The conversation cuts out when he closes his door.

I shake my head. "That's going to be your life here in a few months. Pretty soon, you'll be so consumed with the job you won't even notice when I'm around."

Ryker roughly grabs my face with one hand, cupping my jaw with his thumb and fingers on either side of my mouth as he forces me to meet his gaze. "I've never been within a hundred yards of you and not known exactly where you were. You're the first person I look for when I walk into a room, even when I know you won't be there. I'd notice you if I was deaf and blind because you're branded on my goddamned soul, Willa."

His chest heaves and then he's kissing me again, his mouth and tongue merciless, like he's trying to sear those words into my lips to make sure I don't forget them. We're both breathless when he pulls away.

"Don't you ever tell yourself something different. Got it, Princess?" I nod, heart overflowing with emotion. "Good. Then I'll see you on Friday."

With one more rough kiss, he turns, grabs his bags, and heads for the door, never giving me the chance to give him his birthday present.

Chapter Forty-Five

Five and a half days in Deadwood without work or Ryker to distract me is a good reminder of how much I hate this place.

A trip to the grocery store resulted in a run-in with one of my mom's old friends who barely looked at me before she turned and ran away, bawling her eyes out. I then ran into Isabel in the produce aisle where she'd asked if I had time to meet up and talk, to which I told her I already knew she was taking a year off of school and there wasn't any reason to. She's called several times since, but I send each one to voicemail.

At the gas station a day later, a clerk asked me if he could pray for me and then proceeded to do so anyway after I politely said no. The words "cleanse the evil from this young woman's soul" and "heal her broken body" weren't exactly encouraging. The day only got worse when I ran over a stray spray paint bottle on my way home. The small explosion covered two of my new tires and the front left bumper of my truck in bright-red paint splatter that too closely resembled blood after a gory accident.

A pressure washer and a few hours of elbow grease took care of most of the mess, but the experience was enough to convince me to stay home for the rest of the week.

At least Dad followed through on his promise to spend some time together this morning. I'm pretty sure he would have held out longer, but apparently the stack of dirty dishes and clothes piled throughout the house combined with the sight of me binge eating Nutella in front of the TV for sixteen hours a day was concerning enough that he finally broke down and took me fishing...where he proceeded to take one work call after another about the upcoming quarterly town hall meeting.

For as long as I can remember, Dad's discussed his job without inhibition or filter. His "Ignorance isn't a shield, it's a blindfold" motto means I've overheard the gruesome details of decomposing bodies, horrifying accounts of domestic abuse, and the particulars of everything from Deadwood's ongoing feud between the police and fire departments to the town drunk getting caught naked in the fountain in the Old Town Square.

He's never held anything back. At least he never used to...until today.

Out of all the calls Dad took while he should've been fishing, there was only one he excused himself for, taking special care to move out of my range of hearing on the opposite end of the dock while throwing tentative glances in my direction.

I've been working up the courage to tell him about Austin all morning, but between the constant phone calls and sidelong glances, there just hasn't been an opening. I peer over to the passenger seat, but Dad's too busy scouring the glove compartment to see my pensive gaze.

"It's not a bad truck, kiddo," he says, closing the glove box and leaning back in his seat. "I hate that it doesn't have airbags, but at least the engine is only a few years old and you have seat belts now. Do you remember when I helped Old Man Dan put that engine in?"

I bob my head. "The oil stains ruined two loads of laundry. How could I forget?"

Outside, something red catches my eye, but I'm driving too fast to see what it is.

"Never thought my daughter's first car would be a beast like this, but at least I know she runs well." His phone chimes with an alert, a smile spreading over his lips as he reads the message. "Looks like our boy's already making a name for himself at the academy."

Our boy...

I doubt it's the first time he's used that phrase, but it's the first time it's ever made my stomach feel all fluttery.

Dad's phone goes off again, the sound of cheering and his hardy chuckle filling the truck a moment later. "Apparently, Ryker put everyone on their asses during their first Ground Defense class yesterday." He turns his screen and I catch a brief glimpse of Ryker slamming someone onto a dark-blue wrestling mat before returning my eyes to the road. "He also got the top score on their first test. Even their guest lecturer was asking the cadre about him."

Dad's phone goes off again.

"Damn," he mumbles. "I forgot I wanted to sit in on that lecture. The commandant got someone from the FBI's white-collar crime unit to come and—"

"They already had a test?" I interrupt, attempting to redirect him back to the previous topic for more information about Ryker without being too obvious. Grunting, I use both hands to make a wide left turn. The lack of power steering took a hot minute to get used to, but I'm finally getting the hang of it.

"Two tests, actually," Dad replies. "The first few weeks are jam-packed with opportunities to weed out cadets who shouldn't be in law enforcement."

My brows pinch. I'd never considered that Ryker might not graduate. I assumed once you got in, it was a sure thing.

"Hey, that reminds me," Dad says, tearing me from my thoughts. "Where's your brother been? If he's not going to be around this week-end, I want Ryker to take his room so he can get some rest and have a quiet place to study."

I shrug. "Who knows. Staying with one of his friends, if I had to guess."

A heaviness settles over my shoulders. Noah hasn't been home since the party. He hasn't responded to any of my texts asking if he wants to meet up and work things out either.

The thing that really pisses me off is how badly I *want* to forgive him about the whole Cooper bullshit before I leave. But in order to do that, I need him to explain himself and admit how messed up his actions were. If he does that, then I'll come clean about Ryker. Maybe once all our cards are on the table, Noah and I can start earning each other's trust back.

"You really don't know where he is?"

"*Nope*," I say, popping the *p* to signal I'd like to be done with this line of conversation as I pull into an empty parking spot at Rib Cage.

Judging by the scrunched-up expression Dad makes, it doesn't work. "Is there something going on between you and your brother I should know about?"

My stomach lurches. *No, Dad, I just found out Noah's been screwing my arch nemesis for the past eight years and apparently trusts me so little that he's been hiding who he is from me our entire lives. Oh, and I also lost my virginity to his best friend...*

I don't actually say that, though, because no matter how hurt I am, I'd never out Noah. I'll just add this secret to the ever-growing pile of Dunn deceptions.

"Everything's great," I say, throwing the car into park. I press my lips together, reaching for the door handle, but Dad stops me with an outstretched arm.

"You know," he says after letting me stew in my own guilt for another agonizing twenty seconds, "not being able to look someone in the eye isn't an issue when you're being truthful."

I force myself to meet his gaze, catching the tail end of the circular motion he's making with his index finger to point at my mouth.

"And that thing you just did with your lips?" he continues.

"That's called a tell. It's an unconscious mannerism someone makes when they're lying."

"Good to know," I sass. Blood boiling, I fold my arms. How dare he demand honesty when he refuses to give me the same. "I'd have thought someone with all that useful knowledge would be better at hiding secrets from their daughter."

He sucks in a sharp breath, dropping his head as he rubs his calloused palms on his faded blue jeans. "Fair enough."

Silence surrounds us like a suffocating blanket.

A minute goes by. And then another.

"Seriously, Dad? That's all you're going to say?" An incredulous laugh bubbles out of my throat. "Well, one of us needs to start being honest, so I guess now's as good a time as any to tell you I got accepted into UT and I'm going."

"No, you're not." His tone is relaxed and slightly annoyed, like he thinks I'm saying this just to get a rise out of him.

With a huff, I whip out my phone and scroll to the documents in my admissions portal. I turn the screen to show him, a sick wave of satisfaction rolling through me as his eyes widen before realizing too late that he's not even looking at me...

"Dad?" I lean forward, trying to catch his eye, but his attention is fixed on the front of Rib Cage.

"Who the fuck drew that?" he growls.

"Dad," I say again, this time much more forcefully. "I'm trying to talk to you—

"Dammit, Willa, you're not going to UT and you're not leaving Deadwood. End of discussion."

He doesn't even give me time to respond before he jumps out of the truck and stomps toward the front door of Rib Cage where the bright-red outline of a cross is painted on the bar door. I move to follow, the strong chemical scent of spray paint stinging my nostrils the second I step outside. I'd been so entrenched in our conversation I hadn't realized the parking lot was empty...

Where the hell is everyone?

Bringing my hand to my brow, I squint against the bright sun and scan the parking lot, spotting the same red cross adorning the trunk of a nearby oak tree, a flapping sheet of paper stapled to its center. Dirt crunches beneath my boots as I close the distance and tear the parchment off the bark.

"It's a note from Kane," I call out after skimming the flyer. "He's inviting the town to Divine Mercy for an open house so people can check out the renovations this weekend."

Dad rushes over and rips the paper from my hand, his face contorting with rage as he reads it for himself. Tossing it on the ground, he laughs, the sound dry and hollow. "You think you're ready to go out into the world on your own? How could you be when you don't even recognize danger staring you in the face?"

His eyes are wild, his chest rising and falling so fast he's almost hyperventilating. I jump when he throws his hand in the direction of the cross. "Look at it, Willa. Don't you think that looks a little *familiar*?"

Body trembling, I glance at the tree again, but I don't notice anything different. Sure, the way the red paint dripped on one side kind of looks like blood, but otherwise there's nothing unique about it. I take a step away from him. I've never seen my dad react this fervently before. It's...unsettling.

I shrug. "It just looks like a cross."

"Look *again*," he says adamantly, sweat dripping down his temples. "Kane also put a neon-red cross up at Divine Mercy *exactly* like that. The sick bastard is toying with us."

I glance at the red paint, cold recognition crawling up my spine as I hesitantly reach under my shirt, grazing my thumb over the raised outline my mother carved into my back fourteen years ago.

My muscles tighten uncomfortably, but I shake my head. Kane's never seen my scars. And, despite what Ryker said about his brother's odd fascination with what happened to me, the thought that Kane would model the symbol of his church after what my mother did to me is too morose to consider.

"Every church for a thousand miles has something similar," I mumble, but the wobble in my voice makes my declaration less than convincing. So I try again, unsure whether I'm attempting to persuade him or me. "It's just a coincidence."

Knuckles blanched, my father points toward the bar door. "The hell it is. The image of your tiny burned and bleeding body is scarred into my retina. I see it every time I close my eyes and every time I catch a glimpse of your hair or scars. I don't know what sick game Kane's playing at, but I'm damn sure goin' to find out. Get in the truck, I'm taking you home."

"Dad, we still need to talk about Austin and—"

"For once in your life can you do as you're told, Willa?" A vein appears in his forehead, the tendons in his neck straining as his skin flushes and little beads of sweat pop up on his temple.

Every cell in my body tries to refuse, but Dad using the condescending-rage tone he normally reserves for my brother has my shoulders slumping and feet moving of their own accord.

I don't protest when he snatches the keys out of my hand, and I don't bother arguing when he drops me off at home without saying another word. I'm still not entirely convinced that cross has anything to do with me, but his reaction made it more than clear that I'm not the only one with lasting marks from what happened fourteen years ago.

The difference is, while my injuries have scarred over, my father's wounds are still open and festering. He'll never move on with the constant reminder of what happened staring him in the face, and unfortunately for the both of us...that constant reminder is *me*.

Chapter Forty-Six

Dad returns to the house a few hours later, barely staying long enough to change into his uniform and grab his work bag. He doesn't look me in the eye, and for once I don't bother trying to talk to him. Not even when he hovers in the doorway on the way out to his cruiser.

"I'm sorry I lost my temper earlier." He sighs, long and heavy. "But everything I've ever done is to protect you—to make up for the way I failed you when you were little. How can I keep you safe if you're not in Deadwood?"

"You didn't fail me," I say, turning back toward the TV and ignoring the rest of his statement. I don't have the energy to fight with him, and it's not like he'd hear me anyway. I'm not mad anymore. Not even hurt—just resigned to my decision to leave. The way Dad spoke to me today made it more than clear that he will never see me as anything other than a broken child.

The floorboards creak as he shifts from one foot to another. "Maybe I should've handled this differently..."

He's not really asking, but I nod anyway. "Yeah, maybe you should've."

I hear the *tap, tap, tap* of his finger drumming across the door-frame, followed by another long exhale and the soft *click* of the door closing behind him.

The second he's clear of the driveway, I rise to my feet and walk to my bedroom. It takes me an hour to pack up all my clothes. Another to collect everything else and shove it into the duffle bag I stole from Noah's room. I'd had to dump a bundle of what looked like journals onto the floor, but I didn't bother picking them up or putting them away because, again, I just don't care.

Why would I when I'll be gone in less than forty-eight hours?

Once packed, I glance around my sparse room, struggling to remember how I was considering staying a few days ago.

After showering, I change into pajamas, grab the last jar of Nutella from the pantry, and settle back down on the couch to watch Vampire Bill deep in the throes of his corruption arc before promptly falling asleep.

The house is dark when a set of strong arms gently lifts me from the cushions. Rain-soaked pine and an unfamiliar leathery scent surround me as I bury my face against Ryker's warm shirt.

"What time is it?" I ask through a yawn while he maneuvers us through my bedroom door.

"Late," he whispers, laying me on the bed and removing the single sock that's already hanging halfway off my foot. "Or early, depending on how you look at it."

I watch his dark silhouette kick off his boots and shrug out of his shirt and pants before crawling into bed beside me. Face-to-face, he tugs me against his torso and kisses my forehead. My body softens as I breathe him in, his scent a calming balm for my soul.

He shudders when I place my palm on his chest, but relaxes a millisecond later, grabbing my hand and resting it on his cheek. We stay like that for a moment, his eyes closed as he leans into my touch, and then he kisses my palm and settles against the pillows.

Tilting my chin up, I kiss his jaw, trailing my lips down the column of his throat until he wraps a second arm around me and shivers. Just like that, the reason I considered staying crashes back into me with the ferocity of a hurricane.

"Fuck, I missed you," he says into my hair, fumbling in the darkness until his mouth captures mine. The kiss is slow and unhurried, but that persistent ache at the apex of my thighs awakens just the same, amplifying when Ryker rolls me onto my back and settles between my legs.

"You taste like chocolate and hazelnut," he whispers, nuzzling his nose against mine before kissing a trail half-way down my chest and laying his head atop the spot between my belly and sternum. He sighs contentedly when I drag my fingers through his hair, and the trust and comfort wrapped into that single sound pierces my heart.

"God, that feels good," he says after another minute. "Is anyone else home? There weren't any cars in the driveway, but I parked at the ranch just in case."

The wings inside my stomach flutter. "It's only you and me."

"Good." He continues to make little noises of appreciation as I massage his scalp.

Content in his arms, I spend each pass of my fingers trying to get used to the shorter length of his hair, conjuring up an image of what feels like a high-fade. At least the academy let him keep a few inches up top, although I suppose Ryker would look good with any hair style.

"Sorry I'm late," he says after another minute. "One of the guest lecturers wanted to meet with me after class." He hesitates, his jaw ticking against my stomach. "I think I found a way to make it all work... A way for me to keep Charlie safe *and* get us the hell out of Deadwood within a year."

My heart stutters.

I'm aware that the *us* he's referring to is him and his sister, but for one brief second, it felt like it included me too. A hollow feeling opens in my center, but knowing Charlie might not have to live with Beau is enough to keep the emptiness at bay.

"That's great news."

"It is." His tone is heavy, burdened with a thousand unsaid thoughts.

The room goes silent beneath the weight of whatever it is Ryker's not saying. "This is what you've been working toward all summer," I prompt, unsure why I suddenly feel like I missed something. "Why don't you sound more excited?"

"Because in order to keep my sister out of Beau's clutches, I'll have to—" He sighs and shakes his head, the rough stubble on his jaw grating against the bare skin of my stomach when my tank top rides up. "*Fuck*, I can't even bring myself to say it."

He slides his hand under my shirt, clinging to my waist in a way that feels possessive and needy, like he's searching for reassurance.

Confusion ripples across my brow. "You don't need to tell me if you're not ready to. But, Ryker," I say, imbuing as much strength into my voice as possible, "whatever it is, if it keeps Charlie away from Beau, it's worth the cost. You have to do it."

"You're right." His voice is calmer, his head lighter as he tilts his chin to look at me in the dark. He plants a small kiss against my sternum, trailing his lips upward while sliding his hand to my breast and grazing his thumb across my nipple. "How was your week, Princess?"

"It was fine. I—" A gasp escapes my lips when he replaces his thumb with his tongue, drawing my peaked flesh into his warm mouth. I arch into him, trying to stay focused but quickly losing my train of thought as his other hand trails to my hip.

"What was I saying?" I pant.

"You were about to lie and tell me you had a good week," he growls, tugging my shirt up over my head and rising onto his knees to secure my wrists to the headboard with it. It's not a tight knot, and I could probably break it easily, but I don't want to.

Breasts heaving, my nipples pebble under the silver moonlight seeping in through the window. Adrenaline floods my veins, washing away every memory of hurt and annoyance from the last few days until the only thing I feel is excitement and Ryker.

Always Ryker.

"I wasn't going to lie—"

"You were," he breathes, capturing my needy moan with his mouth as his fingers dip below the hem of my shorts and sink into the wet heat between my thighs, thrusting in and out of me at a tortuously perfect pace. "Do you want to come, Princess?"

"God *yes*." My belly coils as he moves faster, palm grinding into my clit with each stroke of his thick fingers.

"Then don't fucking lie to me when I ask you how you're doing."

"I won't," I whimper, the T-shirt restraint digging into my wrists as I arch my back.

"Good girl. And is this pussy still mine?" Ryker growls, lips hovering millimeters away from my own, fingers curling and pumping.

My mouth falls open in a silent moan.

"Answer me, Willa," he says, tone gravel and smoke as he moves faster. "Who does this pussy belong to?"

"You," I gasp out through the ecstasy building in my center. "It's yours. *I'm* yours."

Ryker stills above me, his head tilting to the side as footsteps pound down the hallway.

The door bursts open, neither of us having time to react as shards of wood explode into the bedroom and my brother barrels in through the door.

Chapter Forty-Seven

Red-faced and seething, Noah crosses the room, grabs Ryker by the hair, and throws him to the floor. "Get the fuck off my sister!"

Freeing my wrists from the headboard, I scramble for the comforter to cover myself, but Ryker beats me to it, tossing me his shirt and taking Noah's fist to the face in the process. I scream when a mixture of spit and blood fly from his mouth onto the hardwood floor.

"I fucking knew it!" my brother roars, already rearing his arm back to strike again.

After haphazardly shoving my arms through the oversized sleeves of Ryker's shirt, I throw myself between him and Noah, giving Ryker just enough time to wipe the blood from his lips and slide his jeans on while my brother's chest pushes against my open palm.

"Noah, please—"

"Please what? Pretend like I didn't walk in on you fucking my best friend?" He scoffs as somewhere behind me, Ryker flips on the light. "What a joke. I can't believe I actually came here to say sorry."

Glancing at my phone on the dresser, my fear and guilt from moments before slowly bleeds into skepticism. "It's almost five in the morning... You didn't come here to apologize."

"Yes, I fucking did!" Noah closes the distance until he's practically screaming in my face, his mustache puffing up angrily. "Dad told me you've been moping on the couch all week and that I needed to make things right with you." Noah snorts and shakes his head. "I thought I'd come by early and we could air our shit out on the lake. I even loaded up the fucking truck before coming inside, so don't you dare try to tell me what I came here to do."

I glance toward the dark driveway where a stream of light from my window illuminates the fishing rods sticking out of his tailgate. Guilt slices down my throat. "We can still go to the lake—"

"No, we can't." His eyes dart from Ryker to the bed and then back to me, his face falling into an expression so devastating he might as well have slapped me. "You couldn't just let me have one thing, could you, Willa?"

Noah bends over, tugging at his dirty-blond hair. "I've given up everything for *you*. Pushed aside all of my own shit to protect *you* and be a good fucking brother. There was one person who understood me —one person who got what it was like to be the less-damaged sibling. One fucking person who didn't see me as a fuckup, and you couldn't even let me have that!"

Jaw hard, he straightens his posture. "Maybe Mom was right and you really are—"

"Don't fucking say it," Ryker growls, moving to my side. "If you're mad, be mad at me."

"You're even worse," Noah sneers. "First you stole my dad, now my little sister? I let you into my home and this is how you repay me? What the fuck is wrong with you?"

Ryker winces and puts up two hands. "I get how this looks, but let's all just take a breath and I'll explain." He takes a tiny step forward, but my brother retreats three.

"There's *nothing* you could say to make this okay." Noah scoffs. "She's going to destroy you, man, the same way she destroyed our mother and our father."

I stumble back a step, his verbal sucker punch making the room spin. "You don't really believe that, do you?"

"You destroy everything you touch." Noah shrugs. "I don't think you can help it."

This time, it's me who scoffs. "Let me get this straight. You can fuck the man who literally suggested I kill myself, the same man who's continued to torment me for years, but somehow *I'm* the one who's not good enough for your best friend?"

Noah laughs, the sound cruel and unfamiliar. "Cooper never gave a fuck about you. He only asked you out because he and I got caught fooling around in the locker room. I was scared Coach was going to tell someone and Cooper got pissed when I broke things off. He knew going on a date with you would hurt me and figured it might make it seem like Coach was lying if he ratted us out."

I blink. And then blink again. "You knew it was fake and you still let Cooper humiliate me anyway? You let that disgusting excuse of a man lock me in an incinerator just so no one would know you liked each other?"

Noah has the good sense to drop his eyes to the floor and soften his tone. "Of course not. I had no idea he was going to pull that shit, which is why I beat the living daylights out of him when I found out. Willa, he's not a bad guy. He's just...lost. Like everyone else in this fucking town."

"You're still defending him," I say, tone cold and flat. "If you really can't see what a betrayal fucking around with Cooper Blackthorne was, then there's nothing left for us to talk about."

Ryker presses a comforting hand to the small of my back, a move that only pisses my brother off further. He balls his fists and shifts his weight.

"Why are we even talking about me when you've been fucking my best friend behind my back? You promised you'd stay away from him. I practically begged you—" His blue-gray eyes darken, the water line near the corners filling before he wipes the moisture away with his sleeve.

His nostrils flare, brow lowering as he slowly shakes his head. "You don't know what it's been like for me here. How hard it's been living in your shadow while pretending I didn't have shit of my own to deal with. I had one person I could be myself with—one person I didn't have to pretend around. Now I have nothing."

No matter how angry I am, it doesn't stop the guilt from constricting around my lungs.

Ryker must feel the same way because he drags a hand through his hair and sighs. "That's not true, Noah. You have Marco and you have a great job—"

"A great job?" My brother snorts. "I got fired from the rig when Marco and I went to Corpus Christi a few weeks ago."

"*What?*" Ryker and I screech at once.

"Yep." Noah laughs bitterly. "I told Willa I was picking up extra hours, but I was at the beach. I was so fucking hungover I missed the boat out to the rig, and they fired me." He shrugs and laughs again. "Guess I really am a fuckup. Right, *Wills?*"

My chest tightens at the sarcastic, almost spiteful way he says my nickname.

Ryker steps forward. "Listen, I'm sorry about the job, and I'm even more sorry you had to find out about me and Willa this way. I messed up, but you're still my best fucking friend. If you give me a minute to explain—"

"No." Noah's voice is hard and final as he squares his shoulders. "Willa can't get over Cooper, and I can't be your friend if you're fucking my sister."

"Noah, come on." There's an edge to Ryker's voice that wasn't there a second ago, a subtle shift in his shoulders when he crosses his arms. "This doesn't need to be an ultimatum. I fucked up, but we can make it work. You're like a brother to me. Let's just talk for a second."

Noah shakes his head. "No. It's me or her."

"Then it's her," Ryker says without an ounce of hesitation. My heart thumps wildly. "It's always been her. It's always going to *be* her. I think a part of you has known that since we were kids."

Spit particles fly into the air as Noah laughs. "I hope she's fucking worth it."

Without so much as a glance in my direction, he turns and storms off into the night with Ryker hot on his heels.

Alone, I collapse onto the bed, hugging my knees to my chest in an attempt to stave off the impending emotional breakdown...but it never comes. I might have just lost my brother forever, but instead of feeling distraught, I feel even more resigned to leave—the same way I did after the argument with my dad.

Noah thinks he's been living in my shadow? Fine. There's no way for me to block out his sun if we never see each other again.

A slightly unhinged, slightly pathetic high-pitched laugh barrels out of me.

A moment later, Ryker appears in the doorway, his shoulders slumped and brow heavy. "Your brother's gone," he grits out, clutching the frame with an iron grip. "Wouldn't let me explain or apologize... Fifteen years of friendship and he's just done."

"Ryker, I'm so sorry." A stabbing sensation pierces my heart. "You were right, we should have told him sooner. I just wasn't sure what we were doing or how you felt about me, and I didn't want to blow up either of our lives if—"

"You weren't sure how I fucking felt about you?" He stares back at me, eyes blazing with heat. "Are you fucking kidding me?"

I open my mouth, shaking my head and shrugging when no words come out.

Ryker works his jaw. "You're saying you didn't know that I'm in love with you?" he rasps, closing the distance between us in three strides. "That I've *always* been in love with you?"

My heart swells as I slowly rise to my feet. "How could I—"

Something he said to Noah filters through my memory.

It's always been her. It's always going to be her... A part of you has known that since we were kids.

"Noah knew?"

Ryker laughs. "Noah, Kane—hell, I'm pretty sure your dad has a good idea. Everyone but you, apparently."

I shake my head. "There's no way."

His jaw tightens, and then—almost as if making a decision—he closes the last foot of distance between us and grabs my wrist, gently placing my palm against his cheek. "Willa, I've never willingly let anyone put their hands on me before. Not once. But when you touch me..." He closes his eyes, leaning into my palm. "When *you* touch me, I feel fucking whole. I feel...quiet. Like there's—"

"No more noise or chaos," I finish for him, struggling to keep my heart from exploding.

"It's not just me, then?" He takes my face between his hands, moss-green eyes pleading for me to agree. "God, Willa. Tell me I didn't destroy my best friend's trust for nothing. *Please*, tell me it's not just me."

"It's not just you," I choke out.

A small puff of air escapes my lips at the devastatingly beautiful smile that takes over his face—like a beacon in the dark. I swallow the lump in my throat. "But, Ryker, I can't stay in Deadwood... I can't be here, not when—"

"I know, Princess." He kisses me softly, and I melt into him, my body relaxing and my mind stilling. "You're going to get out of Deadwood, and we'll make this work."

Grabbing onto his wrists, I bob my head. "Okay."

He makes a satisfied grunting noise. "I need a year. It'll take me six months to graduate from the academy, and I'll need another six months to get guardianship of my sister."

"I can help," I say, nodding. "I'll get a job and move closer—"

"No. I want Charlie away from Deadwood. Austin is as good a place as any. We can handle a year of long distance." He brings his nose to mine. "Say you can handle a year. Please fucking tell me you can wait for me to get all my shit figured out."

My heart feels so light, I'm almost floating. "I'll wait."

"Thank *fuck*," Ryker says, pulling me to his chest and exhaling with a shudder.

He holds me like that for a while, neither of us saying a single word. I listen to his breathing even out and concentrate on the way our heartbeats slowly sync with one another. In the past, my brain might have used this quiet moment to replay every horrible thing Noah said to me. But right now, the only thing I keep thinking about is how lucky I am to have found this incredible man.

We can definitely handle a year of long distance, and Austin will be the perfect fresh start for all three of us.

"Hey," I lean back just far enough to catch his eye, "I know it's a ways off, but there's a dinosaur park thirty minutes outside of Austin we could take Charlie to. She'd like that, right?"

Ryker grabs a white lock of my hair, his grin so beautiful my chest aches. "She'll love it."

Chapter Forty-Eight

Every house has a smell. It might be the spices a person cooks with, an air freshener, or maybe that tiny leak in the attic feeding the black mold hidden within the walls of the guest bathroom, but it's there.

Over time, our brains tune out the common scents of our home so we can better identify when something new and potentially dangerous enters our environment. It's called olfactory adaptation, or nose blindness. Unfortunately for me, my hyperosmia only amplifies this phenomenon any time there's even a slight shift in my surroundings.

It's why I know I'm alone in bed without having to open my eyes, and how I know Ryker's already showered and that he's cooking Nutella pancakes in the kitchen. It's why I can immediately conjure up an image of the cardboard boxes full of my belongings stacked in the corner, and the bottle of chemical astringent Ryker must have used to clean something.

What I can't smell is the gnawing feeling in my stomach as snippets of the argument with my dad and brother come flooding back to me with perfect clarity, or the nervous trembling in my limbs

Emmerson Hoyt

knowing this is my last full day with Ryker for who knows how many weeks...

I can't smell the hole in my heart or the weight on my chest that makes me want to stay in bed all day, but even if I could, I refuse to let Dad or Noah take anything else from me. I'm leaving tomorrow with or without Noah's apology or Dad's permission.

Not wanting to waste any more time wallowing beneath my comforter, I rise from the bed, quickly tiptoeing my way across the creaky wooden floors into the kitchen.

My steps falter when I spot Ryker at the griddle. There's a full pot of coffee on the counter next to him and every surface of the kitchen is once again spotless. There's also a load of laundry tumbling around in the machine down the hall, an in-progress grocery list on the fridge, and my favorite pair of cowboy boots are propped up next to Ryker's new tactical ones, looking like they've been recently shined.

Overwhelmed with gratitude, I rush to him, wrapping my arms around his middle from behind and kissing a spot on his shirt where a circular scar makes a small bump in the fabric.

"How am I ever going to outgrow the princess moniker if you keep treating me like one?" I ask, pressing my cheek against his warm pine-and-rain scented T-shirt.

My body jostles with his hardy laugh. "I don't have a problem with you being a princess, as long as I'm the one doing the spoiling."

Stepping out of my embrace, he reaches for the biggest mug in the pantry, giving me an eyeful of the deep-purple bruise on his cheek where Noah punched him as he pours me a cup.

"Your dad stopped by this morning," he says, quietly assessing my face for a reaction. "I've never seen him that worked up before. Apparently, he spent all night trying to get the mayor to cancel the reopening of Divine Mercy. Did I miss something?"

I take a gulp of my coffee before telling him about Dad's freak-out over the spray-painted crosses at Rib Cage yesterday, making sure to

402

leave out the part where I told him I was going to UT and he forbade me from leaving.

Ryker's face pales, his fingers lifting to trace the scars peeking out of my shirt near my collarbone. "I never put that together..."

My body stills. I'd thought Ryker would laugh off Dad's reaction, but the look on his face is anything but skeptical. He almost looks... scared. Which immediately has my hackles rising.

"You don't really think Kane's using the cross on my back as the symbol for his new church, do you?"

Ryker blinks and shakes his head. "No, of course not. Have you seen the journal he carries around?"

I bite my lip and try to think. "Maybe? He might've had it the day Elanor and I ran into him after the fires, but that was so long ago, it's hard to remember."

Ryker's lips thin. "Our mom got him a set of journals with a red cross etched into the cover long before you had that scar. That's probably the symbol he modeled the one on his church after, but I'm tempted to confront the fucker about it when I see him today anyway."

"You're going to see your brother?"

"I have to," Ryker says with a grimace, turning away to pour the last of the pancake batter onto the griddle. "Kane is a fucking liability. If I'm going to fight for guardianship of Charlie, then I have to make sure he's on my side when he's interviewed by the court. And like I started telling you last night, I'll need him to trust me if I'm going to—"

Ryker glances over his shoulder at me, pausing like he's still struggling to explain the new plan he's come up with.

"Do whatever it takes," I say with a small, unconfident smile, echoing the same words I spoke last night. "The sooner you get guardianship of Charlie, the sooner we can all get away from this hellhole." I place my hand on his shoulder as the other details of the flyer Kane posted at Rib Cage come back to me. "Does that mean you'll be at the open house today?"

"Unfortunately, it does." He takes a deep breath, his broad back expanding beneath my palm. "I stopped by last night to bury the hatchet before coming here, and he asked if I could help set up and stand behind him when he makes the announcement about his new church. I think the fucker likes the optics of having a future cop in the family," he says with an eye roll. "But all this bullshit will be worth it if Charlie is safe."

After he figured out it was Kane who broke into my house and after basically accusing him of sabotaging the sale price of the ranch, I thought Ryker was finally done with his brother for good.

I frown and draw my lower lip between my teeth.

Ryker might not be able to verbalize the full extent of the plan he's come up with, but the fact that he's willing to make peace with Kane at all *and* is so clearly torn up about it tells me all I need to know: In order to stop Beau Blackthorne from getting custody of Charlie, he needs to convince Kane to press charges against their stepfather.

That seems like too much pressure for one man to bear alone, especially when Kane might not be ready to revisit his trauma, but at this point, what other choice does Ryker have but to try?

Still, something about this has me feeling on edge.

"Please be careful. I know Kane's been through hell, but he's the one who should be bending over backward to get on *your* good side. I just don't trust the guy," I say, changing my tone as Ryker's mouth tugs into a deep frown and it dawns on me that I'm not making this any easier on him. "Want me to break his nose for you? I'm getting pretty good at the whole punching thing." I ball my fist and wiggle my eyebrows.

"That's a tempting offer." Ryker turns and kisses my forehead, the shit-eating grin spreading over his lips my only warning before he smacks my butt and gives it a rough squeeze. "But no matter how much I'd love to see you knock Kane out cold, if I'm going to pacify my brother, then we can't keep rubbing this in his face. Even if he does deserve it."

A stabbing sensation in my chest momentarily takes my breath away. He's talking about his own brother...but he might as well have said the same thing for me and Noah.

Not wanting to go down that rabbit hole, I hop onto the counter, biting my lip and choosing my next words carefully. "Just to clarify... what are we not rubbing in Kane's face?"

The low sizzle of the griddle in the otherwise quiet kitchen feels ten times louder when Ryker stiffens. "That you're mine."

My heart gives a stupid little flutter. "Which makes you..."

"Which makes *me* your goddamn boyfriend." He flips a pancake, shaking his head as he grumbles to himself. "The only one you'll ever have if I have anything to say about it."

Giddy, I kick my feet. "Sounds good to me."

I catch the tiniest hint of a smile on his side profile while he finishes stacking the last of the pancakes onto a plate. "It's that simple, Princess?"

"*Mm-hmm.*" I set my coffee aside and make a *gimme* motion with my hands. "Breakfast will definitely seal the deal, though."

With a devilish grin, he scoops out a heaping dollop of Nutella onto the stack of fluffy pancakes and hands me the plate. "Do you have any deal-breakers or rules? Because I do."

I almost crack a joke, but Ryker's flat expression quickly makes me realize he's serious. I've never thought about what boundaries I'd have in a relationship, but I can see the value in laying out clear expectations early. I'm just not sure where to begin. "Can you go first?"

"Sure. For starters, I don't share well. I hate the idea of another man touching you for any reason. *Ever.*" His eyes darken as he says it, and even though my rational brain knows that level of possessiveness is probably a massive red flag, it feels like this is Ryker's way of laying claim to me...which has the pulse between my legs throbbing.

I've been reading too many of Isabel's books if the alpha male *"mine"* thing is suddenly a turn on. Even so, I can't help but admit that it most definitely *is*.

"Okay, I can live with that. But I'd like that rule to go both ways. I don't want you touching other girls or them touching you."

"That won't be an issue, but I'm glad you said it. Is there anything else? Anything you're worried about that we can address now?"

I blink a few times, thrown slightly by this side of Ryker and even more surprised to find that I like it. He's trying to take the guesswork out of things, which will hopefully keep my ever-active mind from dwelling over these issues later.

I take a chocolaty, delicious bite, using my chew time to think over my answer. "You're going to be busy, and even though I know that, I'm going to overthink whether or not I'm bothering you by texting too much..."

My face scrunches up because that's not really a rule, it's more of a problem without a solution.

Ryker shakes his head. "You can't text me too much. But since we're not allowed to use our phones during training, I don't want you to think I'm blowing you off when I'm slow to respond. What if I send you my schedule for the week ahead of time? That way you'll know when I'm in class and won't have my phone. I can also text when I'm back at the hotel?"

I hate how nice that sounds. But if I had that knowledge ahead of time, I think it'd help quiet the voice in my head when I don't hear from him for a while and assume the worst—like I did when he was at the Cartwright Estate for three days.

"That won't be an inconvenience for you?"

"Would it give you peace of mind so you can concentrate on school?" He takes one look at my face and nods, apparently seeing my answer without me needing to verbalize it. "Then it's no trouble. It's going to be hard enough doing the long-distance thing right off the bat. Anything I can do to make it easier on us is a no-brainer. I'm not willing to let anything fuck this up, Princess."

He grabs a steaming mug off the counter and takes a long sip of his coffee before resurfacing. "That does bring me to my next rule, though. If and when a misunderstanding occurs, we have to promise to keep a cool head and hear the other person out. I can't lose you the same way I lost..."

My gut twists when his head drops. "Of course. I can do that."

"Thank you." Jaw hardening, he glances down the hall toward Noah's room, and a wave of guilt washes over me for the rift I caused between him and my brother.

"You guys will patch this up, even if he and I never do."

Ryker shakes his head and sets down his coffee. "No. Noah did exactly what my last boss did. He wrote me off without giving me a chance to explain. If someone can do that, then they never really valued or respected you in the first place. Besides, I don't like the way he handled the Cooper situation. Your battles are mine now, and that's beyond fucked up. *Shit*, that reminds me." He pulls out my bucket list from his back pocket, unfolding it before spreading it out on the counter.

Deadwood Bucket List

1. ~~Buy a cheap car~~
2. Tell Dad and Noah you can't stay in Deadwood ↘
3. ~~**Punch Cooper Blackthorne**~~   (MOVE TO AUSTIN!)
4. ~~Go to the solar eclipse party~~
5. ~~Explore the Cartwright mansion~~
6. ~~Hang out with Dad and Noah as much as possible~~
7. ~~Stop hiding. Go out more.~~   → (AND ISABEL!)
8. ~~Be daring and live a little~~
9. ~~GET LAID !!!~~
10. Stop Beau from getting custody of Charlie

He slides the pad of his pointer finger over number ten before returning to the top of the list.

"I took the liberty of crossing off a few more for you. The last one on the list is my responsibility, and I think we both know I more than took care of number nine." He winks, and my stomach flip-flops with a flood of heat. "So that leaves number two. Did you get a chance to tell your dad about UT?"

And now the heat is gone...

"I did, and it didn't go well. Honestly, after Noah's fun visit this morning, I don't want to talk about anything involving my family..." I run my foot up the inside seam of his pants. "Especially when there are much better ways for us to spend my last full day in Deadwood."

Ryker's answering grin does all sorts of things to my insides. "Easy now, Princess. Don't start something we don't have time to finish."

"But I'm leaving tomorrow. Who knows when we'll—"

"That's another thing I wanted to talk to you about," he says, squeezing my thigh. "Can we meet up in Buffalo for your birthday? I'll have a four-day weekend over Labor Day and it's about halfway for the both of us. I'd offer to make the whole trip, but if Charlie is back with Beau by then, I don't want to be too far away."

"Halfway will be perfect. Oh, wait!" I hop off the counter and scurry to my room, returning a minute later with a sparkly pink parcel in tow. "I never gave you your birthday present."

"You didn't have to..." Ryker peels open the ridiculous glittery princess wrapping paper and looks up at me, utter confusion etched into his wrinkled brow.

"They're two-way radios," I explain with a hesitant smile, suddenly far less confident in the awesomeness of this present than I was when I bought it at an Army surplus store. "They're for you and Charlie." I point to the description on the packaging. "They connect to Wi-Fi, so you can send texts even when you're out of town for training. And you also need a code to access them, so Beau won't be able to see what you're saying even if he finds them. They work like regular walkie talkies, too, with a range of up to ten miles for when you are in town."

Ryker makes a choking noise. "God, I love you." He grabs me by the neck, dragging me in for a rough kiss. "These are perfect. Thank you."

Fisting his shirt to keep him from pulling away, I tug him down for another kiss, running my tongue along his lips until he deepens the kiss and we're both breathless.

A buzzing sounds from the counter, and he reluctantly checks his phone. "Shit, I've gotta get to the estate to meet my brother. I'll clean the griddle and do the dishes when I get back tonight."

"I'll do them."

"Don't you dare touch a fucking thing," he warns, roughly palming my ass while nipping at my nose. "I know I said we shouldn't rub our relationship in Kane's face, but will I see you there?"

"I don't think so." However curious I am about the open house, I'm not ready to go back to Divine Mercy just yet. Even so, I can't shake the tugging feeling of unease that ripples through me at the thought of Ryker going alone.

Especially considering what happened last time.

Ryker places my hand on his cheek and turns to kiss my wrist before heading for the door. I open my mouth to remind him to be careful, but he's gone before I get the words out.

Chapter Forty-Nine

I spend the rest of the morning clearing out my garden, taking special care to keep my back to the Crowes' house in a mediocre attempt to make this slightly less depressing. Unfortunately, all that ends up doing is giving me an unobstructed line of sight to the overgrown path leading to the Cartwright Estate and Divine Mercy.

No matter how much I try to throw myself into gardening, my eyes stray back to the path every few minutes, almost like an unseen force is beckoning me from the shadows of the forest.

When the last of my plants are pulled and added to the compost heap, I wipe the sweat from my brow, throw my gardening gloves in the dirt, and head for the tree line.

My steps slow and my brow furrows as I approach. Dad and Noah rarely spend time out here and I haven't dared venture this far into the yard for fourteen years, so why are there so many broken branches and crushed weeds on the path? It almost looks like someone's been walking up and down this route...

A shiver skitters up my sweat-soaked spine.

It's probably a game trail now, but I can't help imagining there's a skinwalker lurking in the shadows.

Shielding my eyes from the blaring sun with my forearm, I stare up at the hillside. *God, I hope Ryker is okay.* It's been hours since he left, and I still can't shake the gnawing feeling that I should have gone with him.

To hell with it...

Without stopping to overthink, I take off up the trail. It's a solid mile to the church, most of it uphill, but it only takes me about ten minutes before I spot the ancient fence separating the Cartwright property from ours. Thankfully, a large section of the wrought iron is down, the rusted metal in the decaying leaves crumbling beneath my boots as I step across.

This deep into the woods, there's no breeze, which means despite the tree cover, it's sweltering in here. Sweat pours from every surface of my skin, and I might be losing my mind, but I'd swear it's getting hotter the farther I travel into the trees.

With only the crunch of my bootsteps and the shrill cry of unseen cicadas overhead, I stumble over downed trees and through a thicket of branches until I wander into the strip of lifeless forest this town was named after.

The Dead Wood.

I pause on the threshold of desolation, horrified at the way the trees' skeletal fingers claw at the sky in a vain attempt to free themselves from the cursed ground below.

Sweat beads down my spine and temples, an uneasy tension racking through my body while I fight the urge to run home. I force myself to take one step, my breath quickening as the faintest trace of rotten eggs tickles my nose before traversing the necropolis as quickly as possible.

After a quarter mile, the foliage thickens, the landscape bleeding from brown to green as the trees fill out once again. Realizing I must be close, I pick up my pace, breathing out a sigh of relief when the murmur of a large crowd finally reaches my ears.

I emerge from the wood near the south end of the cemetery,

slowing my steps when I spot the enormous crowd gathered in the adjacent field separating me from Divine Mercy.

All of Deadwood must be here, the low groan of their prattling echoing off the nearby tombstones like a phantom song. The urge to disappear back into the trees pounds inside my chest, but my need to see Ryker and make sure he's okay is stronger, and I refuse to continue allowing fear to make my choices.

I've barely taken three steps when the chatter of the assembly dies out all at once. My head snaps up just in time to see Kane taking the stage. His microphone picks up each *clack* of his boots, his steps vibrating over the speakers and through the ground beneath my feet, giving his walk an almost unearthly quality.

"Welcome, citizens of Deadwood," Kane beckons, arms extended, as he stands center stage behind an oak podium. Something is stamped into the front of the worn wood, but the crowd is packed so tightly I can't see anything but a flash of red each time they undulate to compete for a better position.

Not that anyone has an issue seeing Kane. By placing the slanted stage on the high ground of a natural depression in the field, he's given everyone in attendance—including myself—an unencumbered view. Even the noon-thirty sun seems to be strategically placed in his favor, hitting the back of his head at just the right angle to give the impression of a golden halo.

His tweed sport coat, white western-style shirt, and black slacks are clean and pressed, held in place by a pair of smart black suspenders and his signature cicada bolo tie. Even his tiny man bun is perched a little higher on his head than usual, making him appear even taller and feeding into the vibe that he's orchestrated every minute detail of this shindig.

But I can't see Ryker...

Using the graveyard wall for cover, I slink closer, noticing the rest of the changes to the property as I try to avoid being seen.

The burnt debris from the church is gone, the broken windows exchanged for new ones, and the destroyed sections of wall replaced with brand-new siding that's been painted a muted shade of white to match the existing exterior of the church. The shrubs and vines are now neatly pruned, and all the weeds on this side of the road have been cleared out, including the patch of poisonous hemlock. In their place, a row of greenhouses made from what looks like recycled windowpanes stand like silent sentinels on the edge of the forest.

Without the remnants of the fire readily visible, my stomach doesn't lurch the way it did the last time I was here. But not even the restorations can change the fact that there's still a presence about the place—a quiet foreboding that crawls up my neck, like the church itself is watching me.

Kane clears his throat. "Many of you have asked what we've been doing up here these past few months. I thought it was high time I let you all in on the plan."

Over three hundred voices erupt in low, excited whispers. Even my pulse picks up with my piqued curiosity.

"There's a sickness plaguing our nation," Kane laments, a satisfied grin tugging at the somber set of his lips when the chatter promptly quiets down. "This sickness has wormed its way into our homes and houses of worship. It haunts our schools and festers in our hospitals, feeding off the desiccated remains of our once great democracy. Brothers and Sisters, our nation is on the brink of a civil war, and yet we continue to elect men so ancient and senile they require special procedures to renew their driver's license. How can we trust these men to lead our nation when our own laws don't even trust them to operate a vehicle?"

Kane places two hands on the podium in front of him, scanning the crowd as his last words echo through the valley. "Is it not time we took our future into our own hands?"

The assembly shifts forward, and like everyone else present, I find myself leaning in, too, enraptured by the impassioned cadence of his voice despite the way my skin crawls.

"Across the planet, crops are failing and livestock are dying. There are fires and earthquakes, droughts and famines. Floods decimate entire regions while disease runs rampant in our communities. Are these not clear signs that we've strayed too far from God's path? That our current way of living is no longer sustainable? And yet our leaders do not act."

"So how do we change that?" a man shouts while pockets of townsfolk nod their agreement.

"I'm glad you asked." Kane smiles, and the crowd shifts again, giving me the briefest glimpse of my father's Stetson standing beside the mayor near the front left of the stage. I lean back against the cemetery wall, praying he doesn't look this way.

"Buckle up," Mayor García calls out in a mocking lilt. "This is where he passes around the collection plate."

To Kane's credit, he doesn't take the mayor's bait. "We are not interested in your money," he says, like the notion disgusts him. "What we're interested in is your time and investment in our community's future. We want leaders and freethinkers. We want a better tomorrow for our children."

A small group of people break away from the larger crowd, two of them continuing on to the stage. My body sags with relief as Ryker's familiar head of raven hair takes a position behind his brother, but then I notice the hard, unreadable expression etched into his face and my stomach immediately tightens.

The uneasy feeling triples when I spot Isabel's shining black hair in the middle of the group that broke away, all of whom are now standing beside the stage.

"A war is coming," Kane says ominously. "Every year it draws closer. Deadwood is my home. I will not abandon you as every leader has done before, and I will not use you for selfish gain. This town, much like our country, is falling apart. But starting with this old church, I'm going to transform Deadwood into a safe haven where we can weather the storm."

Kane scans the crowd, making eye contact with each and every person. When he sees me, I'd swear his lips spread into a dark grin before he subtly looks back at his brother.

"Thank you all for coming," he says after a pause "We have food and refreshments over by the church. If you are interested in learning more about our plans for the future, services will be held every Sunday at six in the evening. I'll see you all at the next town hall meeting where we'll be asking Mayor García to account for the poor management of Deadwood's resources."

One person starts clapping, and then another, until soon more than half the town is putting their hands together while the other half glances around like they've missed something.

Now that I've confirmed Ryker's okay, I need to get out of here before anyone else sees me. I take three steps back toward the forest, freezing mid-step when a strong black-peppery whiff of men's after-shave assaults my nose.

My eyes fly to my dad's Stetson across the field.

How—

"Looks like I'm not the only uninvited guest today," a cool voice drawls from behind me.

I whirl around and find Beau Blackthorne leaning against the stone wall.

Not only has he showered, but he's wearing a collared shirt *and* his hazel eyes are clear, which means he might actually be sober for once. I take a step away, far enough that I'm out of arm's reach, and scrutinize the rest of his nearly unrecognizable appearance.

I've always had a hard time imagining Beau as anything other than my piece-of-shit drunk neighbor, but with his clean clothes and gray-flecked nutmeg-brown hair tamed, I can almost see a glimpse of the man he could have been without the drink—and it somehow makes him feel more dangerous.

"There's somethin' dark in that boy," Beau says, jutting his chin toward the stage and what I assume is Kane. "His mama knew there was somethin' wrong with him ever since he was a baby. Same way Annalee did with you."

The casual mention of my mother's name catches me so off guard that the muscles in my calves lock up when I try to take another step

415

away, causing me to tumble backward, where I scrape my palm against the rock wall before landing flat on my ass. I quickly scramble to my feet, wincing when I spot the slow trickle of blood dripping down my forearm.

Beau's smile is sickly sweet as he looks from my red-stained palm to my face, the tilt of his head casting deep shadows beneath his eyes. "Did your daddy ever tell you Annalee flatlined twice bringing you into this world?"

I don't have to say a word for him to read the horror etched into my scrunched brow.

"Didn't think so." He laughs, the low sound rumbling deep in his chest and belly. "That would lend too much credence to the idea that your momma might've been right about you all along, wouldn't it?"

I continue backing up, and Beau keeps advancing.

"What do you want?" I manage to squeak out. "Why are you here?"

"Same reason as you." He glowers as he glances over my shoulder. "I wanted to know what that boy was up to. Then I saw you skulking about and thought I'd come tell you the news."

"And w-what news is that?" I ask, silently cursing myself for the way my voice shakes.

Beau's answering grin sends a chill through my blood.

"Take a look for yourself." He points to his beat-up truck on the opposite end of the graveyard, and my stomach plummets when I see a ponytailed little head peeking over the edge of the tailgate.

I try to keep my voice inflectionless, but my brain is too busy screaming for me to grab Charlie and get her the hell away from Beau. "How long is she in town for this time?"

"Just a day visit," Beau says dismissively, and the hackles on my neck rise at the underlying tone of annoyance buried beneath it. "After the hearing on Wednesday, though, my parental rights will officially be reinstated. I'll get my daughter back, then who knows... maybe I'll rectify a few of my other shortcomings and past transgressions."

It sounds like a threat, and even though I don't understand why...
the feeling only grows as he scans me up and down, the corners of his
lips pulling into a pronounced scowl.

Then his attention flickers to something behind me, the predatory spark lighting up his eyes sending a shiver down my spine.
"Looks like Charlotte and I are about to have a little family
reunion..."

Chapter Fifty

Following the direction of Beau's glare, I spot Ryker and Kane charging across the field, my father and Mayor García trailing behind them—Dad in full uniform, his hand extended as he shouts something I'm too far away to hear.

Hundreds of eyes stare at the unfolding scene, each of their faces cast in various degrees of light and shadow, like a baroque painting, while a storm brews above them, the sun barely peeking through the purple-gray sky.

Beau laughs, muttering something under his rancid breath about what an idiot Ryker is to think he can be a cop, and that's when it dawns on me what my dad is shouting.

"Get Charlie out of here," I hiss at Beau, the sound of my father bellowing for Ryker not to do anything stupid finally reaching my ears, growing louder by the second. "Beau, please. You've already won. Just take her and leave. She doesn't need to see her dad and brothers fight."

"And miss all the fun?" Beau clicks his tongue. "No, I don't think I will. You and those boys need to learn what happens when you fuck with the Blackthornes, and my daughter needs to understand that no one comes for us and walks away. Even if that someone is her own half brother or...*you*."

Movement catches my attention when another group breaks away from the larger crowd, this one with Cooper and his cousin Houston at their lead. My pulse stutters. If this turns into a brawl, Ryker will never get guardianship of Charlie and he and his sister will be stuck in this cursed fucking town forever.

"Excuse me, Mr. Beau?"

My head whips toward the small voice weaving its way through the weathered tombstones.

The tendons in Beau's neck strain. "How many times do I have to tell you to call me *papa*?"

"*Papa*," Charlie says, the tiniest hint of sass leaking through as she climbs up onto the stone wall and takes a seat. "When are we going to Grandma Dorothy's? I'm *really* hungry."

Beau's nostrils flare, his fists opening and closing at his sides in a way that has my stomach trembling on his daughter's behalf. "You can wait until my business here is done."

"Oh," Charlie says, eyes connecting with mine before she removes a notepad from the pocket of her pink jean shorts that have adorable little green dinosaurs embroidered into them.

"What are you writing?" Beau snaps, attention flitting from his daughter to the angry mob headed our way.

She kicks her feet and releases her lower lip from her teeth to respond. "The caseworker lady told me to write down everything that happens. She wanted to know when I was happy or sad...or *hungry*. She also told me to write down why I felt that way." Charlie gets a very serious look on her face as she sounds out each word she's transcribing. "*Papa* and a teenage girl were arguing. The girl fell. She was bleeding, and I was so hungry, but *Papa* said..."

I have to bite my lip from smiling. *She is definitely Ryker's sister, the sneaky little shit.*

But then my insides sour. She'll be alone with Beau after this, and now he'll be even more pissed.

"Fuckin' hell, girl. Get in the damn truck. I'll take you to Grandma Dorothy's in a minute."

As soon as Charlie is out of earshot, he whirls on me, mouth contorted like he's about to start yelling, but then the clouds clear overhead and a bright stream of sun beats down on us so fiercely through the patch of open sky that I can feel the heat radiating off the crown of my head.

Beau's chin tilts to the side as his gaze bounces between my mouth and hair before he abruptly turns to stare at his daughter. There's a flash of something in his side profile, the look only intensifying when his gaze lands back on me, his eyes so big there's white visible around his entire iris.

I take another tentative step away. "Why are you looking at me like that?"

Beau doesn't answer, already halfway to his truck by the time I finish asking. Without a single glance backward, he throws himself into the cab and peels off down the dirt road as a little hand waves at me from the passenger window.

My shoulders slump, knees nearly buckling as the overwhelming weight of impending doom weighs down on me. Charlie's quick thinking might have gotten Beau out of here before Ryker had the chance to ruin his future, but now she's alone with him...and I just let them go.

"What the hell was Charlie doing here?" Ryker pants, a note of confusion clinging to his unchecked anger as he skitters to a stop behind me. "Where the fuck is Beau taking her?"

I can't bring myself to look at him, not even when a soft cloth is pressed to the bloody scrapes on my palm. Unsure what to say, I keep my eyes on the road and don't answer.

Ryker brushes past me, his forearm held above his brow while he peers down the dusty road. I take a single step to follow, but a tug on my hand stops me.

What the hell...

Old parchment and something earthy floods my senses as I

420

attempt to extricate myself from the person holding onto me—the person I *thought* was Ryker. When I whip around, Kane increases the pressure of the cloth on my palm until little stabs of pain shoot into my fingertips and forearm.

My instinct is to lash out and push him off, but I'm almost certain Ryker will escalate the situation if he sees that I'm uncomfortable. Since I already screwed up by letting Charlie leave with Beau, I refuse to make this any worse.

"Kane, let go," I hiss, keeping my voice low as I pry his fingers off. "You're hurting me."

Much to my surprise, he loosens his grip, gently peeling back the fabric from my palm. "Look at that," he murmurs, voice full of wonder as he examines the bloody handprint I left on his stark white handkerchief.

Bile rises in my throat as I rub my wrist and take a step away from him, smashing into something hard. "Did Beau do that?" Ryker's chest rumbles against my spine, his shoulders encasing mine when he wraps his arms around me to inspect the scrapes.

I shake my head. "Beau didn't touch me."

"Did he say why my sister was here?"

I bite my lip, terrified of how he'll react.

"Say it," he grits through clenched teeth.

"Beau said the custody hearing is Wednesday."

Ryker drops my hand and backs away, the devastation in his expression a knife to my heart.

It's not like we didn't know that's where all this was headed, but —like me leaving Deadwood—it always seemed so far off. Time is funny like that. The more you're looking forward to something, the slower the days trickle by. But when you're dreading an event, it has a way of sneaking up from the shadows and dragging you into the abyss long before you're ready.

"Fuck." Ryker's hands fly to his hair as he doubles over. "*Fuck!*"

Kane tucks the blood-stained handkerchief into his lapel and moves to Ryker's side. "I already told you, Beau will never get custody of Charlotte. You need to have faith, brother."

A muscle in Ryker's jaw ticks. "I'm here, aren't I?"

"Being present isn't enough. You need to prove yourself." Kane turns a disdainful eye to my father, who's only twenty feet away with what looks like the whole town behind him. "You'll be tested. The same way I've been tested. If you make it through the trial, you'll need to pick a side."

Ryker catches my eye, his flat expression and slow blink telling me how much he despises this.

"Dammit, son," Dad calls out. "What were you thinking running after Beau like that? And, Willa, what the hell are you doing here?"

"*Joel,*" Mayor García chastises, flashing him a disappointed look that would knock lesser men off their feet.

I lift my foot to move closer to Ryker, but Kane drops to my side, placing a wool-clad arm around my shoulder as the low murmur of the approaching crowd reaches my ear.

"Your daughter is more than welcome here, Officer Dunn. Our collective is open to all." I don't even have to look up to know there's a smile on Kane's face. His fingers dig into my sleeve, but when I try to shrug him off, he tightens his grip. "Unless, of course, there's another reason you don't want her here?"

My initial inclination is to brush the statement off as another one of Kane's cryptic ramblings, but then I see the sweat pouring from beneath my father's Stetson and the shifty way his gaze keeps dropping to the ground. I glance at Ryker for an answer, but he's too busy staring at his brother's arm slung over my shoulder to notice.

"Go on, tell your daughter what you've been hiding. Tell her where you really go on your so-called *business trips to Austin.*"

Acid bubbles up my throat, a newfound queasiness making my insides churn and twist.

"Dad? What's he talking about?"

My father's eyes soften as he shifts his weight to his opposite foot. "Please, go home, kiddo."

Kane leans over, the painful bite of his fingertips in my shoulder preventing me from moving as his sweat-slicked upper lip grazes the shell of my ear. "You don't have to listen to your father anymore. You don't even have to listen to me," he whispers, low and seductive, like my own personal shoulder devil. "I think you're going to want to hear what I have to say, though."

A chill rakes down my spine when the crowd approaches, a familiar head of blond hair detaching from the mass to jog over and stand by our dad.

I hadn't even realized Noah was here...

"Your father's been lying to you, Willa. He's been lying to all of us," Kane says, raising his voice loud enough for everyone to hear. "Go on, Joel. Tell her where you go. Tell her what you've been hiding or I will."

"Not like this." My father's pleading tone turns the contents of my stomach rancid, fear churning in my belly the likes of which I've never felt before. It's in my blood and in my sweat, coursing through every fiber of my being until my knees shake.

"I'm sorry," Kane laments, "but your daughter deserves to know the truth." Keeping his arm around me, he shifts his attention to the assembly. "At the next town hall, Mayor García will announce that she's appointed Officer Dunn as Deadwood's next chief of police."

My shoulders relax. I already knew that. Why would Dad be nervous about—

"What Mayor García won't tell you," Kane continues, a poorly suppressed smirk tugging at the corner of his lips, "is that she's been sleeping with Joel Dunn for years."

My eyes fly to my father right as he takes a step away from the equally guilty looking mayor. I want to be mad that he didn't tell me, but the only feeling in my chest is relief.

Apparently, all three of the Dunns were keeping our romantic lives a secret. But unless Dad also had an affair with Cooper fucking Blackthorne, I don't really care one way or another who he dates. If I wasn't so frustrated, I might be happy for him. Luciana García is a badass.

Kane gives my shoulder an excited little shake. Confused, I glance up at him, sour dread filling my stomach again at his amused grin.

"Regardless of the legal concerns, there may be some who don't take issue with the mayor appointing her lover as chief of police. They're both *single* consenting adults after all, right?" He pauses, brow lowering dramatically as he stares out at the crowd. "But what if one of them isn't as single as they claim? What if one of them has told everyone in this town his wife died in a fire when in reality, Annalee Dunn has been rotting in a prison cell for the past fourteen years?"

Chapter Fifty-One

A gasp ripples through the crowd, their accusing stares landing on my father in a mirror image of my own.

Dad only has eyes for me, but all I can do is shake my head. My mother died in the fire at Divine Mercy. Everyone knows that. Kane is wrong. There's no possible way she's been alive this entire time.

"Willa, please..." Dad rasps, eyes pleading and expression ghostly white as he takes the tiniest step toward me and extends his hand.

Dread drops into my stomach like a boulder. "Tell me he's lying. Tell me you didn't keep this from me."

"*Willa*," Dad says again, tone so thick it sticks to my skin.

The hairs on the back of my neck rise at the same time a shiver rakes down my spine. I stare at him, silently pleading for him to contradict Kane, but he doesn't.

"Mom's alive?" My voice is barely a whisper, but much like the broken jukebox at Rib Cage, the phrase is now stuck on repeat as it echoes inside my skull.

My mom's alive.

My mom's alive.

My. Mom's. Alive.

The truth of that statement presses down on me so heavily my knees give out.

Before I can hit the grass, Ryker catches me by the elbow, maneuvering me away from Kane and tucking me against his side in one fluid motion.

"You're okay," he soothes against my ear. "I've got you. I'm right here."

My legs are rendered immobile by the wall of flame dancing in my memory and the blood-curdling scream that fills my ears. There is something else there, too. A shadow shifting in the curtain of red and orange before everything turns black.

Kane's chest rumbles with a low, almost pleased sound that only Ryker and I hear, and then he's speaking again. "I told you why I came back to Deadwood," he bellows beside us. "But how can I make this place a safe haven if our leadership cuts my legs out from under me every time I file for a permit? Just last night, the mayor and Officer Dunn were trying to put a stop to this open house because they didn't want any of you up here. Mayor García can't be allowed to install her puppets in positions of power—"

Kane keeps droning on, but the second I regain feeling in my legs, I drown him out and shrug out from under Ryker's arm.

Seeing red, I march straight up to my dad. "How dare you keep this from me!"

"Let's talk about this at home, kiddo," he says softly with a brief glance over his shoulder to the restless mob at his back. "I promise I'll tell you whatever you want to know. Let's just—"

"No." My vision blurs with hot, angry tears that I refuse to let fall. No part of me wants to have this conversation here with so many spectators, but the second we leave this field, Dad will find another excuse not to talk to me. "Tell me now or I swear you'll never see me again."

I've barely gotten the words out when Noah grabs me by the

upper arm and drags me over to the shade near the cemetery with our father trailing behind us.

"Let go of me," I squawk, struggling to free myself.

"Calm the hell down," he grunts, batting away my hand as I attempt to pry his fingers loose, flooding my senses with his citrus and sage cologne—a smell that once felt like safety and now reeks of betrayal. "Come on, Willa. You're making a scene. Just give us a chance to explain."

Humid wind rips through the trees while an involuntary stillness takes hold of my body.

"*Us?*" I shriek. "*You knew?*"

Noah's eyes widen, the rise and fall of his chest rapid enough that he might as well have just finished a sprint. "Not until I was older." His lips slip into a frown, the set of his eyes softening until he almost looks like the brother I grew up with instead of the stranger he's become these past few weeks. "It fucking killed me to keep this from you, but I didn't know how to tell you."

My heart throbs so painfully I glance down to see if there's a knife sticking out of it. When there's not, I resume attempting to escape Noah's hold.

"Let me go, you fucking traitor," I lash out, startling when Ryker appears out of nowhere and roughly slams his palm into my brother's shoulder. He lets go of me as he stumbles backward, barely catching himself before he hits the dirt.

"Touch me again," Noah pants through gritted teeth, "and I'll knock you the fuck out."

"Then have this conversation like a man and keep your fucking hands off your sister," Ryker spits, snaking an arm around my waist to hold me back when I try to push past him.

"You knew and didn't tell me?" I scream at Noah, balling my fists so tightly my nails bite into my flesh.

"Not at first," he says, voice wavering as his eyes drop to the dirt.

Dad takes up a position at my brother's side, his hands open and palms facing outward like I'm a spooked horse in need of soothing. "Kiddo, please. You used to wake up every night in the hospital screaming that your mom was going to come back for you. You were tearing open your wounds each time you had a nightmare. You were so young and in so much pain... I did the only thing I could think of and told you she was gone. The nightmares stopped and you finally started to heal. You have to understand, I was trying to make you feel safe."

"Dad," I say incredulously, "even if that's true, I'm eighteen now. You've had plenty of time to come clean. And it wasn't just me you lied to, it was the entire town!"

He hangs his head. "Annalee was so sick after the fire, I never even considered she'd survive. When people asked, it was easier to just lie and say she'd passed."

"Why?" I shout, sounding a bit hysterical now. "Because no one asks about a dead woman? Because you thought no one would bring her up in the presence of the daughter she tried to kill? Well, they did, Dad. Each and every single time they saw me."

Slack-jawed, I take a step backward, staring at the two men I once trusted most with new eyes. *I've been living with strangers.*

The shock of their betrayal reverberates through my bones, shaking the foundation of everything I thought I knew about my life.

"Is she still in jail? How long is her sentence?" Another question lodges in my throat, but I can't find the strength to ask it aloud... *Does she regret what she did?*

Dad removes his Stetson, rotating the brim in a full circle before answering. "Twenty-five years. Ten years for what she did to you, fifteen for burning down Divine Mercy."

I can't decide if I want to laugh or scream. She got more time for destroying a church than she did for trying to kill me...

That's fucking Texas for you.

Inwardly, rage courses through my veins so violently my muscles twitch with the force of it. Outwardly, all I can do is nod. It all makes so much sense now... Dad's lack of eye contact, Noah asking if there was *anything* else Dad wanted to tell me after his promotion announcement... Mayor García's confused expression when I mentioned that Dad had been traveling a lot for work on the Fourth of July.

I scoff, the sound thick and unamused. "So that's what you're doing when you say you're going on a work trip to Austin? Visiting your murderous wife?"

Dad winces. "I divorced your mother years ago, when Lucy and I started to get serious. We've kept things private for the sake of her position." His mouth pulls into a tight line. "As far as why I've been going to Austin, your mother's been in and out of the hospital, and up until a few weeks ago, I still had medical power of attorney."

Dad lets go of a long, exhaustion-drenched sigh. "It was a mistake not to tell you, but let's go home and talk about this away from prying eyes." Shoulders slumped but brows slanted optimistically upward, he extends a hand.

I glance at his open palm and laugh. "Ignorance isn't a shield, Dad. All you did by keeping me in the dark was take away my autonomy and ability to fight back. I feel like I don't know you anymore." My eyes dart to Noah. "Either of you."

With a frown, Dad drops his hand and slowly puts his Stetson back on. "Don't blame your brother. This is on me."

I press my lips together and shake my head. As far as I'm concerned, Noah is just as complicit as Dad, but at this point in our crumbling relationship, it's not like it matters.

Rage burns through me so ferociously my senses go into overdrive.

The light breeze becomes a howling gale as the smell of the dirt beneath my boots and the sweaty bodies of the nearby crowd become so accosting I might be sick... My head swims, and then all at once, the chaotic drum of my pulse slows while my eyes heat and glaze over.

"I'm leaving for UT tomorrow," I say with zero inflection, staring absently into the vacant space between my father and brother, not making eye contact with either of them. "I'd appreciate it if you both kept your distance until I leave."

Dad says something, but I can't even hear it. Like everything else, the words are empty.

Peering over my shoulder, I nod at Ryker, who's kept a healthy distance but never strayed more than a few feet from my side. "I'm assuming you have to stay or go check on Charlie?"

"I do." He slides his hands into his pockets, casting tentative glances between my father and Kane, who's still droning on about the future to an enraptured crowd. He returns his gaze to me. "But I can at least give you a ride."

I hold up a hand. "No. I want to walk and clear my head. Take as long as you need, but I'd like to see you before I leave in the morning."

Ryker's eyes stay locked on mine, his brow creasing as he dips his chin. "I need to wrap up a few things here and then I'll be over." The way his jaw works makes me think there's more he wants to say, but I'm glad he keeps it to himself.

"Kiddo," Dad pleads, but I ignore him, heading for the path buried in the trees.

"*Willa*," he says more firmly. "You can't leave. I'm your father and we're going to talk about this whether you want to or not. Austin is too far. I can't look out for you there."

My steps slow as an unhinged laugh escapes my lips. *Now he wants to talk?* I force myself to meet his eye.

"Look out for me? Dad, I haven't seen you in *months*. I'm the one who's been looking out for you and Noah for *years*." Still laughing, I shake my head. "There's nothing left for us to talk about. I'm eighteen, you can't stop me from leaving."

I take a single step before another voice slams into my back.

"Figures you'd walk away," Noah calls out. "It's not like Dad and I have set aside our entire lives to take care of you—to cater to your every whim and fear. God forbid you actually talk to us when we make a mistake, since you're so fucking perfect."

I whirl around, strands of my hair lashing at my cheeks as the wind picks up. "You know what? I didn't see it before, but you've been using what Mom did to me as an excuse for your lack of drive and laziness for so long I think you've convinced yourself *I'm* the reason you're a fuckup. But you did that *all* on your own. If I never see you again, Noah Dunn, it'll be too damn soon."

Chapter Fifty-Two

Emerging from the path into my backyard, I swat away the mosquitos circling my head like buzzards locked on a juicy carcass and start the arduous process of removing twigs from my hair. I'd been in such a numb daze on the walk back that I'd run into several low-lying branches as I stumbled my way home.

I'm still so out of it that I've already dragged myself up my porch steps before I notice that my front door is cracked open. I must've forgotten to close and lock it before setting off for Divine Mercy... Not that it matters. There are no creepy notes or egg cartons full of seedlings inside. No Dad. No brother. No signs of life. The house is cold and empty, like it always is.

It takes me thirty minutes to load the back of my truck with my belongings, and another thirty to shower and put on clean clothes. When a light rain starts, I stop in the kitchen to make a sandwich but end up just staring at it until a fly lands on the crust.

I'm not hungry. Or sad. Or angry. I'm not anything.

In a way, I feel like the withered pepper plants I tore out of my garden this morning. After a summer of neglect, their leaves were brown, their branches shriveled inward in a last-ditch effort to stay alive—but the truth of the matter is they've been dying for weeks. Me ripping them from the earth only solidified the inevitable. Today's revelation about my mother didn't kill my relationship with my dad and brother, it was just the final nail in the coffin.

Sluggishly, I turn toward my vibrating phone on the counter, my eyes widening when I read the caller ID and swipe right.

"Mrs. Crowe?" I breathe out. "What's wrong? Is Old Man Dan okay?"

"Hello to you too, sweet pea. That's actually what I was calling about." She sucks in a wet breath, and my broken heart drops onto the floor. I close my eyes, bracing myself for more bad news.

"Daniel woke up today," she says, voice cracking as a relieved sob escapes her lips.

"That's fantastic," I choke out. "Is he—" I hesitate, unsure how to phrase the question. "Is he *himself*?"

"I think so. Talking is a little difficult, and he doesn't quite have control of his motor skills yet. But he's been demanding to be released from the hospital, so I'm taking that as a good sign." I can almost hear her smile through the phone, and that eases something deep in my soul—at least until she adds, "Your dad called me."

"I don't want to talk about it," I reply automatically, throwing my internal shutters back into place now that I know Old Man Dan is alright.

"Then you can listen," Elanor spits hotly. "I didn't know about Annalee, but you can best believe I laid into Joel for keeping that from us. I also want you to know that I support you going to UT. It's a major accomplishment to get into a school like that, and I'll expect you at the house I'm renting at least once a week for dinner. If your grades start slipping, it will be five times a week."

My body trembles. "You're staying in Austin?"

"Yes, sweet pea. I am. The specialized care Daniel will need once he's medically cleared is only available here, and I want to be as close as possible. It's why I expedited the sale of the ranch—so we could afford his treatment and I could get a little place of my own." There's a beep on the other end of the line that sounds like hospital equipment and some rustling. Then she says, "The place is small, but there's a guest bed with your name on it. Feel free to be at the house as often as you please."

A dry sob escapes my lips, bringing a little life back into my stiff limbs. "I'll be there every day."

"Now, now. Maybe not *every day*," Elanor chides. "A woman needs her space, after all."

"Okay, every other day, then," I say through a wet laugh. "God, I'm so relieved. I thought you were going to say I should stay in Deadwood."

There's a long pause before she clears her throat. "No, dear. Unlike your father, I'm not sure that's a good idea."

The hackles on my neck rise. "Why do you say that?"

"Well... When Daniel woke up, he said the last thing he remembered was a man-sized figure with horns emerging from the woods. Then *BAM*, lights out. I'm not sure how much credence we can give to the ravings of a concussed man, but if that's what caused him to fall from his saddle, I don't think it's safe in Deadwood anymore."

I swallow the lump in my throat. "Maybe it never was."

After hanging up with Elanor, I leave my phone on my bed and wait for the rain to stop before grabbing my pistol and heading out to the ranch. I don't bother holstering the gun, instead keeping it at the low ready, muzzle aimed at the ground the way Dad taught me.

My chest hollows at the memories of all the hours we tooled around at the gun range. After today's revelations, I doubt we'll ever have another carefree afternoon under the sun again...

As quickly as the hollow feeling rises, it drifts away on the humid wind, replaced by the cathartic numbness currently keeping me upright.

It takes me an hour to walk to where Old Man Dan fell, and by the time I've finished scouring the surrounding woods for this mysterious horned creature, the sun is low in the sky and the cicadas are so loud I can barely hear myself think.

Sweat drips down my back as I listen to their oppressive shrill, the pulse in my ears falling in step with their erratic song until I think my head will explode. Holstering my weapon, I untie the bandana from around my neck and wipe my forehead and chest.

What the hell was I thinking coming out here? Did I really think I was going to shoot whatever this thing is? What if it turned out to be a person? I can only imagine how that'd go over in court.

"Well, you see, Your Honor, I came out here to kill a wild beast and accidentally killed a man..."

Thank *God* I didn't actually find anything.

Groaning, I retie the bandana around my neck and head home as the sun bleeds out on the horizon. Darkness falls quickly, and the walk back takes twice as long, the ghosts of the once bustling ranch haunting my every step with their silence. When my house finally comes into view, there are two shadows in the driveway. I recognize the broad shoulders of the first as Ryker and the Stetson on the second as my father.

"Of course I still have the original report," Dad says as I inch along the fence line. "I'd always hoped your brother would change his mind. But this is a bad idea, son. It's not going to go the way you think. Seeing you up there with Kane today has me questioning your ability to be rational right now."

"Doesn't matter," Ryker replies with a shake of his head. "I'm out of options and it's too late to turn back now."

Dad reaches for the cuffs on his utility belt, the unsaid threat clear as day.

My brow creases. Why would he have a problem with Ryker convincing Kane to press charges against Beau? Wouldn't he want to help?

Ryker leans forward, fists clenched and voice dangerously low. "Mr. Dunn, I came to you because there is not a man alive I respect more, but so help me God, if you get in the way of me protecting my sister, I *will* go through you. No matter the cost."

Dad sucks his teeth. "I'd like to see you try, *son*."

Tension vibrates through the air like a rubber band about to snap. And even though I can see what's about to happen, I can't find the motivation to stop it... Then again, maybe there's a part of me that wants to see Ryker put my father on his ass.

A low rumbling sound emanates from Dad's chest before he turns on his heel and heads for the cruiser.

"Mr. Dunn," Ryker calls out. "Where are you going? I need an answer."

"I don't have time for this," Dad tosses over his shoulder. "I'll be at the fucking office when you come to your senses."

The door slams and the cruiser speeds off toward town, the red glow of its tail lights disappearing into the night, leaving Ryker standing alone in the driveway.

"Fuck!" he shouts into the blue-black sky, then he's ripping out a pack of smokes from his pocket and lighting one up.

I flinch when the flame sparks in the darkness, but in addition to my vision swimming and my knees locking up, there's an inexplicable urge to chase that tiny ember of trepidation flaring to life inside my chest. After the day I've had, this pulse-pounding, sweat-dripping-down-my-back rush of terror almost feels *good*.

Apparently, when you're afraid, there's no room to feel anything else.

I take a step forward, breath hitching as the tip of Ryker's cigarette glows bright orange, surprised to find that instead of running, my first instinct is to draw closer.

"I thought you said you were quitting?" I ask from only a few feet away.

"Fucking hell." Ryker jumps, the contents of his hands spilling onto the gravel.

I shuffle over, tobacco flooding my senses as I scoop up his silver boot-shaped lighter and the lit cigarette. Again, fear flickers to life inside me, warm and alluring as I place one in his hand and the other between his waiting fingers.

"I told you I was cutting back, not quitting." He takes a long drag before stomping it out on the ground. "Sorry."

I shrug, but with my pulse already slowing, the movement is limp. "Is Charlie still here?"

Ryker shakes his head. "Left with a social worker an hour ago." I think he tries to force a smile, but it's too dark to tell. "Should we go inside?"

When I glance over my shoulder to the vacant house, my vision is warped, almost like everything is underwater. "I don't want to be here if my dad or brother decide to come back."

Ryker grabs my hand, his rough palm scraping against mine as he leads me across the yard and says, "I know a place."

I should ask where we're going, especially since that's the exact phrase he used before taking Noah and me to the water tower on the Fourth of July, but why bother when anywhere is better than going home?

Neither of us speaks while we make our way onto the Crowes' property, and he doesn't let go of my hand until we're standing in front of the dark, empty bunkhouse. I swallow the lump in my throat at the unfamiliar sight before me. No matter the time of day, this building was always full of music, chaos, and laughter, now it's cold and silent. A vacant shell.

Crouching down, Ryker turns over several rocks I can barely see next to the door.

"*Ah-ha,*" he exhales, rising to his feet to shove a dirt-caked key into the lock.

After a brief struggle, the door swings open and he leads me inside by the small of my back. My nose wrinkles as I breathe in the stale air that still reeks of musky cologne and sweat-stiffened Wranglers.

It takes a second for my eyes to adjust after Ryker flips on a light, but when they do, I'm greeted by a yellow oak kitchen on my left and a decent sized living room off to the right, where the faint outline of couches and recliners are still imprinted on the faded-red wool rug someone forgot to pack with the rest of the Crowes' belongings.

Confusion creases my brow, and it takes me a second to realize why. "There wasn't any flooding in here?"

"Nope. All the buildings on the property are connected to the same water and sewage line, but *only* the big house was affected," Ryker says with disgust. He gestures to a hallway with several doors on the opposite end of the living room. "Kane plans on moving some of his people into the bunk rooms as soon as he takes ownership of the ranch. You do the math."

The implication of his statement hangs heavily in the air between us until he clears his throat and points to a single door off the far end of the kitchen. "The foreman's quarters are through there. There's also access to a little room in the attic that way."

I lift a quizzical brow.

"I spent a few nights here when I was a teenager," he offers by way of explanation before reaching out and sliding his palm up and down my arm. "Are you alright?"

I stare at him, a sliver of guilt worming its way through my numbness at the worry in his moss-green eyes. "No, not really. Are you?"

"No," he says with a far-off look. "Definitely not. I'm so close to getting everything I've ever wanted, but I feel like I'm free-falling. I've got one chance to pull the cord and get this right, but one wrong move, one *tiny* fuck up, and I'll lose everything."

My head jerks back as I stare at him. I've grown so used to Dad and Noah bottling everything up, I didn't actually expect him to answer.

"What?" he asks, narrowing his eyes with a small tilt of his chin.

"Nothing," I reply after a moment or two. "That's just eerily similar to how I'm feeling."

"Is that right? You fallin' right alongside me, Princess?" Ryker's mouth quirks up on the side. "In that case, want to hold hands on the way down? I hear it's an awfully nice view..."

Despite the pressure on my chest, I can't help but roll my eyes. "I said I feel *similar*, not exactly the same. You're afraid of losing the people you love. I'm afraid of losing myself."

"What do you mean?" His thumb brushes over my hip bone as he reaches for me.

"All summer, I've been teetering on the edge of a cliff with all these lies and secrets pushing me closer and closer to the precipice. I'm terrified I'm about to topple over and take you down with me."

"I'd go willingly." The corner of his mouth ticks up again. "But I'd never let you fall."

The crazy thing is, I believe him. Ryker has an uncanny ability of knowing what I need and where my limits are. If I plummeted over the edge, I have every confidence he'd be right there to drag me back up. The problem is, he has more than enough to worry about without adding my issues to the mix.

I fold my arms across my chest and glance toward the door. *Maybe I should leave for Austin before I ruin his life the same way I apparently did my family's.*

Before he has a chance to let me down like everyone else...

"Don't," Ryker says gruffly, snaking his arm around my waist. "Whatever you're thinking right now... Don't. You're the only thing in my life that makes sense. I won't let you fall, Princess. I promise. Just tell me what you need."

My lip quivers. "Just don't do what they did—don't lie or keep things from me. Not to protect my feelings. Not because you're scared of what I might think... I can handle anything except that."

"I won't," he says earnestly, eyes clinging to mine.

I want to believe him, I *do* believe him, but I'm also so brittle right now I need to make sure he fully understands. "I'm serious. Even a lie of omission—"

Before I can finish, Ryker's lips crash into mine, soft yet possessive, as he forces a breath of life back into my dormant lungs. "I promise I won't lie to you," he whispers. "But you can't shut me out when you don't like the answer. No matter what happens, it's you and me."

"I won't shut you out. I promise."

I sigh when his fingers thread through my hair, my pulse picking up as he walks me backward and abruptly spins me around so that my ass is pressed against his groin.

A shiver rakes up my spine as he slowly drags my shirt over my head before wrapping his arm around my waist. "Good, because there's something else we need to talk about," he whispers against the soft skin behind my ear.

Chapter Fifty-Three

"You broke one of our rules today," Ryker says darkly, trailing his lips up the column of my throat. Then he's undoing the button on my shorts with one hand and pushing down on the space between my shoulder blades with the other.

"What rule?" My body quakes with anticipation as the cold counter presses against my chest and upper stomach.

"The one where you don't let another man touch you," he says so dangerously low that my thighs clench. "Especially not my fucking *brother*."

Ryker shoves my shorts down to my ankles and then whips off my bra, leaving me in just my boots, thong, and red bandana. A soft gasp escapes my lips when he slides a palm across my ass, squeezing and kneading until suddenly he rears back and spanks my right cheek with a loud *smack.*

"Every time you wiggle in your seat because you can't get comfortable on your drive tomorrow, I want you to think of me. I want you to picture my handprint on this perfect ass."

Crack.

He spanks me again, same cheek, same spot, but twice as hard. I moan through the sting, my pussy throbbing as need soaks my under-wear. "No one touches you except me. Got it, Princess?"

"Yes," I pant, voice rising when he strikes again. The sting sends sparks tingling up my spine, my brain humming with quiet satisfac-tion while I fight the urge to rub my thighs together.

"That night at Rib Cage, when you spread your legs for me as I spanked you..." He shifts his palm to the opposite cheek and gives it the tiniest *smack*. "I've beat off to that memory so many fucking times, imagining what it would have been like if I'd slid my fingers into your wet cunt. Wondering if I could've made you come draped over my shoulder like that."

With one of his hands still on my ass, he slides the other around my hip to my belly, dipping inside my panties to circle my swollen clit. A tremor of pleasure racks through my core, and I struggle to keep my eyes open.

"I should have kissed you on that water tower like you wanted me to. Should have tasted you. Bent you over and..." His fingers plunge inside me, retreating the second I moan.

I rotate my hips, desperately searching for his touch. "I didn't want you—"

Crack.

He spanks me full force, so hard that I cry out, but the pain barely lasts a second before my brain goes fuzzy again, heat coursing through my center until my body buzzes with the singular desire to be filled by him.

"You *did*. Admit it." Ryker grabs my thong, pulling it so far up my ass the fabric grinds against my clit. My eyes flutter open and closed from the delicious friction, and then he's spanking me again in quick succession.

Crack. Crack. Crack.

My back arches as everything outside of this room fades away until there is only me and him. "I wanted you," I admit on a breathy moan when I can finally think again.

Ryker hums in approval. "I fucking knew it." His hands drop to my hips and then he uses his foot to spread my legs apart. My body trembles when his fingers slide beneath my underwear, teasing me with painstakingly slow circles around my drenched opening.

His belt clatters to the floor, and my pulse goes wild. "Should I take my boots off?"

"No, Princess." A sharp sting slices across my hip, followed by a tearing sound as he rips my thong clean off. "The boots stay on."

Ryker nudging the crown of his cock against my entrance is my only warning before he grabs my hips and yanks me backward, sheathing himself inside me with a single thrust. I cry out, my eyes rolling backward while heat thrums up my spine. His cock pulses, and then he's fisting my hair, tugging me upward and tilting my head to the side so he can capture my mouth with his.

With our tongues entwined, he angles his hips back and thrusts inside me again and again—slow at first as I stretch around him, then faster until we're both sweaty and moaning. My breasts bounce in time with each punishing movement of his cock. I lift my arm, grasping him behind the neck as he trails kisses across my jaw and buries his nose in my hair.

Ryker's chest heaves against my back, the heat of his body seeping into mine as he breathes me in. "You're the only good thing in my life, Willa."

He drives into me with long strokes, harder and faster, until he's bottoming out and the pressure building in my belly is near explosive. "Fuck, Princess, I love the way your pussy clenches around my cock. I love every fucking thing about you. You're fucking perfect."

Heat blooms in my chest, my heart so full I can't hold it back any longer... "Ryker, I—"

"Come for me, Princess," he demands.

"No," I pant, brain fuzzy as his thick cock plows into me from behind. "That's not it. *Ryker, I—*"

Taking my entire jaw in his hand, he tilts my head back and to the side so that our noses are touching and I'm forced to look him in the eye.

"Say it," he grunts against my lips as he continues to move inside me.

My eyes water as the tension between my thighs builds until I can barely stand. But he needs to know. I need to tell him. Even if it gives him the power to hurt me. Even if my world will never be the same...

"Say it, Willa," he growls, rolling his hips. "Fucking *say* it."

"I love you," I cry out as my orgasm barrels through me in a flurry of heat and light so vibrant I forget to breathe.

Ryker's lips curve into a soft, radiant smile. "Goddamn right you do. I love you, too, Willa Dunn. Always fucking have."

Hours later, tucked against Ryker's chest on a nest of blankets we piled on the floor, a deep sense of calm settles over me. Every other relationship in my life might be in shambles, but if I have this—if I have *him*—that's all I need.

I wake with a start, pulse thudding and nose twitching at the horrifyingly familiar scent of smoke in the air.

Something's burning.

Sitting up abruptly, I reach for the light switch before realizing I'm still on the rug in the bunkhouse. Only now, I'm alone.

"Ryker?" I call out, voice shrill as I draw in a smoke-laced breath.

Besides the rattle of my lungs, the bunkhouse remains quiet. My head whips from left to right, panic making my breaths come too quickly while I clutch the unfamiliar blanket wrapped around my body and wait for him to round a corner.

He doesn't.

Unease slithering up my spine, I scramble to my feet and throw on my clothes.

Ryker wouldn't have left me here without telling me where he was going, would he? He must be getting something from the house or taking a phone call outside...

Another whiff of smoke hits my nose, and my body tremors.

Breathe, Willa. Find Ryker and then you can figure out what's going on together.

I dash to the door and rip it open, skittering to a halt when I'm greeted by an ominous ocher glow illuminating the otherwise black sky to the south. *Holy hell.* It's so bright it almost looks like the first light of dawn...except the sun doesn't rise in that direction, and it definitely doesn't create those thick billowing clouds.

I break into a cold sweat, my vision narrowing when I turn my back on the fire and sprint on quivering knees toward my house. The driveway is empty, but I still manage to trip three times before bursting through the door.

"Ryker?"

Once again, there's no response. No sound at all. Even the crickets and cicadas outside are silent, as if they, too, sense that something is horribly wrong.

I stumble to my bedroom, hands shaking violently as I grab my phone and call Ryker.

It goes straight to voicemail.

I try again, but the same thing happens.

Pulse thudding in my temples, I stare at Dad's contact info next before deciding this isn't worth putting my anger aside for. If I call him the first time I get scared, I'll be proving him right that I'm not ready to move out and be on my own.

Breathe, Willa. Just breathe. The fire is nowhere near your house. If anything, it looks like the smoke is coming from downtown—

My heart skips a beat and then another as I rush to my bedroom window for a better view.

My brain hiccups, ice crystallizing up my spine when I realize that not only is the orange glow even brighter now, but that it's coming from the Old Town Square...

Near the police station.

I drop my phone twice before successfully clicking on my dad's contact info. It rings and rings and rings, the tempo of my pulse rising with each passing second he doesn't answer. I explicitly heard him say he was headed to the office. It's almost four o'clock in the morning, there's no reason for him not to pick up his phone. Unless...

Hyperventilating, I dial my brother.

I tap my foot as it rings once. Twice. Three times.

"Willa? What's wrong?" Noah's voice is sleep-drenched, but he doesn't sound annoyed. If anything, he sounds worried, which throws me more than it should.

I force myself to suck down a ragged breath. "Dad won't answer his phone...a-and I think there's a fire downtown."

A mattress groans on the other end of the line before Noah's thudding footsteps echo loud enough through the speaker that it feels like he's in the room with me.

"*Shit.* I see it," he mutters. Then more footsteps sound through the phone, far faster, like he's running, until a door slams. "Holy fuck..."

"What?" My heart crawls into my throat and then drops into my stomach when he doesn't answer. "Noah? What is it? What do you see?"

I pull the phone away from my ear to look at the screen.

The line is dead.

He hung up on me.

Not knowing what else to do, I stare vacantly out the window at the undulating gray-and-orange clouds in the distance, every muscle in my body trembling as the unnatural shape continues to grow.

I try Dad again, and then Noah, neither of them answering. But then I remember that emergency calls go straight to the police station. Hope takes root inside my terrified heart, blotting out the fear as I dial 911 and imagine Dad's voice on the other end of the line. But it slowly withers when the phone just rings and rings.

The call is eventually transferred to the fire station, where a frantic Mandy Cromwell answers and shouts, "We're aware of the second fire and are working on getting the crew there," before abruptly ending the call.

A second fire? Body trembling, I stand there like a helpless child. I consider crawling into bed and pulling the covers over my head. I even think about getting into my Chevy and driving in the opposite direction, but I need to prove to myself that Dad's fine.

Wrapping my arms around my middle to control the shaking, I stumble into the garage and climb into my truck. Staggered breaths rattle inside my chest as I throw my phone onto the passenger seat and start the engine, keeping one hand braced on my queasy stomach while I open the garage and head out into the night.

My windows are up, but the smell of smoke still permeates through the ancient air conditioning, getting stronger and stronger with each revolution of my tires—my pulse ramping up right alongside the atrocious scent. I take one squealing turn after another, adrenaline making my hands shake when the glow of the fire intensifies. By the time I turn onto Main Street, the smoke is so thick and acrid that I'm already coughing.

Almost there... One more turn...

Every fiber of my being tells me to turn this truck around, but I'm almost there now. I just need to drive by, see what's on fire, and then I can get the hell out of there...

I turn left, slamming on my brakes as the flame-engulfed police station comes into view.

A violent bout of nausea racks my body as I stare unblinking at the inferno.

This has to be a nightmare... This can't be real...

Clamping my hand over my mouth, I barely swing the door open in time to spill my guts onto the pavement. When I'm finished, I wipe my chin and stumble forward. Where is everyone? Why aren't the firetrucks here? I whip around, a sob escaping my lips when I spot Dad's cruiser parked in front of the blazing station.

Oh God...

Flames dance in my memory at the same time they slither through gaps in the roof and out the busted-up first-floor windows of the stone building in front of me. A siren wails from somewhere in the distance, and when the heat of the blaze licks at my cheeks, I can't tell if it's in my mind or in real time.

Another round of nausea forces me to empty the remaining contents of my stomach onto the sidewalk, but still, I can't tear my eyes away from the flames. Not even when I fall to my knees, the scars on my back tightening as the ghost of a memory whispers that *the fire is a cleansing...*

My teeth chatter, and then I'm wrenched upright, my brother's blurry face coming into view as he spins me to face him.

"What are you doing here?" Forehead etched with deep lines of worry, Noah shakes me forcefully enough that my brain rattles against my skull. "Willa, why are you here?"

"D-Dad's inside," I choke out, grabbing his hand so tightly my nails sink into his flesh.

"What?" he gasps, head whipping to the station as his face drains of blood. "No, he's not. He can't be. Are you sure?"

A choked sob escapes my throat when I try to answer him, but instead of screaming at me, Noah wraps his arms around my shoulders and draws me to his chest. "You're okay, Wills. I promise I won't let anything happen to you." He places his hands on either side of my face and pulls back a few inches. "You're safe out here. Don't look at the station. Focus on me."

Reluctantly, I tear my eyes away from the flames and meet his blue-gray gaze. My breath hitches when instead of the anger I've grown so accustomed to over the past few weeks, I see love and concern. He looks like himself, like the Noah I grew up with.

For one second, I allow myself to pretend it's just another day. That we're running errands and it's the sun casting that perfect golden glow over his face.

"You're okay, Wills. Take a breath and tell me why you think Dad's inside." He nods encouragingly, the same way he did when he was trying to convince me to get back on my bicycle after my first big wipeout when I was ten.

Gripping his wrists with both hands, I force myself to swallow my fear. "D-Dad isn't answering my calls. He said he was going into work, and—" My voice cracks. "And look, his car's here." I raise a shaky hand to point at the cruiser.

Following the direction of my finger, Noah's eyes widen, the muscles in his arms going impossibly rigid. "*Shit.*" He swallows once and then turns to face me. "Stay here, Wills. Keep your back to the fire and wait for help."

Brow pinched, I stare at him as ash rains down around us. Then, without warning, he kisses my cheek and turns, sprinting for the flame-engulfed door where he disappears behind a veil of smoke like a ship beneath the sea.

I blink once, twice, waiting for him to reappear, but he doesn't.

I call his name. Scream it. But my only answer is the roar of the fire.

He's okay, I tell myself as my pulse hammers inside my chest. *They both are. Noah will find Dad and they'll be just fi—*

Several of the second-floor windows of the police station crack and then shatter. My arm rises up instinctively to shield my eyes when the influx of oxygen makes the fire blaze ten times brighter. Heart in my throat, I watch in horror as flames lick up the sides of the ancient building, the crackling groan of the inferno intensifying until the ground itself seems to sway and shift.

"Noah!" I scream, taking three steps forward until my legs give out and I fall to my knees. I tell myself to get up and go help him, but my muscles won't work.

I scream his name again, unable to look away as the god-awful truth burns my retinas.

There's no way anyone can survive that...

The realization flays my insides open with a serrated blade.

I just sent my brother to his death...

Chapter Fifty-Four

A siren wails, and I think someone screams my name. But I hardly react when Cooper Blackthorne kneels beside me, his half-donned fire kit making his already imposing frame twice as large.

"Willa," he says, placing a gentle hand on my shoulder. "What are you doing here?"

Unable to find the strength to shrug him off, I slowly turn to face him. Even then, I can still see the flames dancing in the reflection of his sweat-soaked cheeks. "Dad and Noah are... Noah went..."

I can't even bring myself to say it, so I point toward the door.

"Your brother's inside?" There's a note of alarm clinging to the otherwise calm cadence of Cooper's tone as he rises to his feet.

I nod in confirmation, barely catching the glimpse of true terror that flashes across the whites of his eyes before he bounds for the station. The other members of his crew scream for him to wait and put on his respirator and helmet, but Cooper ignores them, never slowing his pace as he barrels through the blazing door.

The world around me explodes in a flurry of sound and motion. To my right, firefighters hook up a hose to the nearby hydrant while several more fully kitted firemen rush into the burning building after

Cooper. Someone on my left shouts orders when more of Dead-wood's volunteer forces arrive behind me.

A minute goes by.

Another.

Noah hasn't come out and Dad is still nowhere to be seen. Every second feels like hours. I've never been so useless in my entire life. My family is inside that smoldering station and all I can do is stare, unable to move or speak.

My vision swims as an ambulance comes to a screeching halt on the grass beside me.

The wind picks up, my hair lashing across my face and neck while the first embers of the smoldering roof rain down from the sky. The smell of burning hair fills my nostrils, and I close my eyes. For one horrible moment, I am four years old again, screaming and bleeding as I'm dragged across the rough-hewn floors of Divine Mercy while flames dance around my broken body.

When I force my eyes open, a helmetless firefighter is silhouetted in the doorway with a limp body clutched in his arms.

I scramble to my feet, a sob splitting me in two as my brother's blackened head flops to the side, revealing pink flesh peeling up and down his neck and chest.

My world tilts and I stagger toward him, stumbling over my own two feet when I see the tattered remnants of his clothes clinging to his badly burnt torso and legs. I'm almost there when someone grabs my wrist and yanks me backward. Desperate to help my brother, I thrash against their hold until my elbow collides with a nose and I finally break free.

Breathless, I make it to Noah and Cooper at the same time the paramedics do.

"Is he alive?" I shriek, but Cooper collapses onto the pavement with my brother still in his arms before he can answer.

The paramedics grab my brother while several firefighters rush to Cooper's aide, stripping him of his jacket and pants while combing over his body for injuries. Cooper's nose and mouth are stained with soot, his hands and half his face burned and blistering. I recoil, my chest shriveling at the sight.

He knew the risks of charging inside without his gear, but he did it anyway—*he did it for Noah.*

Despite my hatred for this man, my heart throbs with gratitude before faltering when I catch a glimpse of a B-shaped scar on his lower abdomen.

Unable to confront the storm of conflicting emotions thundering inside my skull, I turn my attention back to my brother, eyes widening in horror at the state of his motionless body.

"He's not breathing and there's still no pulse," the paramedic doing compressions says breathlessly. "If you don't get that defibrillator going, this'll be over before it starts."

"I'm trying, but his skin keeps sloughing off and I can't get the pads to stick," snaps the red-faced paramedic kneeling on the other side of my brother's chest, his words battering against my insides.

"What do you mean he's not breathing?" I shriek, taking a step closer before clutching my stomach and doubling over as the smell of burnt flesh and singed hair hits my nose. Blood pounds in my temples, the roar of the fire now deafening. "Noah, get up!"

Two more paramedics rush to my brother's side, but no one responds. They don't even look in my direction, too busy starting an IV and messing with some sort of contraption that looks like a massive radio.

Two paddles are placed on Noah's chest and then someone shouts, "Clear!"

All at once, everyone's hands shoot into the air as they echo, "Clear!" The machine beeps and Noah's body goes rigid before going limp once more.

"Did it work?" I sob, tears streaming down my face while I claw at my throat. *It had to have worked. Any second, Noah will sit up and make a joke about how we both have scars now—*

I flinch when they shock him again, beads of sweat dripping down my back as I hold my breath and wait for Noah's eyes to open.

"Still no pulse. Resuming compressions," one of the paramedics shouts before he grunts. "Someone get his fucking sister out of here."

I stagger backward, falling into the grass as they continue to work on my brother. At one point, someone tries to make me leave, but I refuse, eyes locked on the EMTs as they shove tubes down my brother's throat and shock his burnt body again, switching out the person doing compressions every few minutes or so in a frantic flurry—

Until all at once, they stop.

"I'm calling it," a faceless man in gray scrubs says. "Time of Death: 0437 hours."

Clambering onto my hands and knees, I scream. "What are you doing? Keep going! You have to help him," I plead, icy numbness spreading from my chest to my fingertips. One by one, they remove their pale-blue gloves and back away from my brother. "*Please*. You can't stop—"

Noah's head lolls to the side. His charred and peeling chest unnaturally still while ash and ember rain down around us. His beautiful blue eyes are closed, an unsightly bloodied tube protruding from the corner of his lips. I crawl to him, dirt and soot stuck to my shaking palm as I wipe the blood from his mustache.

"Noah, wake up." A single tear rolls down my cheek when I give him one more chance to open his eyes and smile at me—to proclaim that this was all a joke with that obnoxiously boisterous laugh of his...

But he doesn't.

He just lays there, still as death.

Vision blurry with tears, I brush my fingers through the unmarred side of Noah's hair, vaguely aware of the paramedics arguing about whether or not they should stop me until one of them taps my arm.

"Don't touch me," I hiss over my shoulder, feral as a barn cat until I notice the folded white blanket in the middle-aged man's hands.

"I thought maybe we should protect your brother from the ash," he says softly. There's something vaguely familiar about his smile, and I try not to look at the blood staining his light-gray scrubs as I take the outstretched cloth from his hand.

Delicately, I cover Noah, ignoring the surrounding whispers and the crackling fire behind me as I fold down the excess blanket so only his face is visible. White-hot anger floods my veins when I notice that ash and scorch marks have already soiled the pristine fabric. I brush them away as best I can and smooth out my brother's hair before grabbing his hand over the blanket.

The man clears his throat. "You might not remember me, but my name's Dr. Peterson. I work in the emergency department."

I don't bother acknowledging him. Not as I'm struggling to understand why Noah's hand is so cold while the rest of his body seems to be radiating heat.

The doctor clears his throat again. "With your permission, I'd like to clean your brother up at the hospital. The thing is, I've also got a firefighter who needs to be treated and there's not a lot of room in the ambulance. If you'd like to come with us, I can have one of the paramedics drive your truck?"

My breathing slows, and I blink away the tears welling in my lower lids. "I can't go with you," I rasp, welcoming the coldness in my limbs that's slowly creeping up my neck and into my skull. "My dad's still inside."

Dr. Peterson's mouth tugs into a pronounced frown. "Are you sure?"

"Yeah," I say through a sniffle before hardening my tone. "Once they get him out, we'll meet you there." My eyes burn, lips trembling while I struggle to keep the tears at bay. "If for some reason he finds you before I do, please don't let him see Noah like this..."

The doctor's expression softens, and he gives me a subtle dip of his chin before waving over the paramedics hovering near a gurney.

As the squeaky wheels approach, I lean down to kiss my brother's forehead, where just the tiniest hint of cedar and sage still lingers on his skin. "I'm so sorry, Noah," I whisper for only him to hear. "Please forgive me. You were the best brother. I'm so sorry I didn't tell you more often. I'm so sorry for everything..."

After leaving one final kiss on his temple, I rise to my feet and square my shoulders.

The doctor whispers something about me being in shock, giving orders for someone to watch me until the second ambulance arrives. I ignore him and turn away, focusing instead on how to get my father out of the station.

I've only made it a few steps when an anguished, guttural cry slices through the night.

Even though I shouldn't, I look over my shoulder to the ambulance where Cooper Blackthorne is kneeling next to my brother's gurney, soot-stained tears streaming down his face as he collapses to his knees, screaming into the night sky.

My chest cracks, but before I can fully process the image, the sound of the chaos around me comes flooding back all at once. There are three hoses pouring water into the police station, firefighters scampering about in every direction, and a slowly growing crowd of townsfolk gathering in the square who can't stop shrieking as they point at the horror unfolding before them.

My head snaps toward the station where smoke pours from the windows instead of flames. I thought that would be a good thing, but there's an underlying franticness to the rapid movements of the firefighters scurrying about that makes me think I'm wrong.

"The roof's not going to last and we've still got men in there," the fire chief barks from his perch atop the firetruck.

The building creaks and groans, and everyone present—including the spectators—duck and gasp when a large section of roof bows and buckles.

"Find him," I chant. "*Please,* find my dad."

Two firefighters stumble out of the police station doors, one of them with a severe limp. My heart swells. *If they made it out, Dad can too...*

Something inside the building snaps, and a plume of smoke billows out one of the third-floor windows along with a flare of flame.

The order to evacuate goes out a second later, rippling through the first responders as the word is passed along.

My stomach plummets.

"What are you doing? My dad's still in there and we're running out of time!" I cry out, but no one listens. They're too busy taking a count of their personnel and moving their equipment away from the building.

My hands fly to my ears when a loud crash cracks through the night and a large beam collapses near the door, blocking the exit for anyone still trapped inside.

I stare into the flames, allowing the heat to dry the last of the tears still clinging to my cheeks. *I can't let Dad die... I won't. Not when Noah gave up everything to save him.*

Bolstered by my brother's strength, I draw in a deep breath and run, sprinting around the building as I check the windows for any sign of my father while looking for another way in.

"Dad?" I shriek, peering through one of the broken windows into the smoke-filled basement below. No one makes a sound.

Desperate, but undeterred, I remove my bandana from around my neck and retie it over my nose and mouth before moving on to the next window, and then the next. Most of the glass is shattered from the heat, with more windows cracking and exploding every minute on the upper floors, but through the cacophony of chaos, I swear I hear faint coughing.

Rounding the corner, I barely make it three steps before my shin bashes into something hard and metallic, sending me toppling to the ground. I throw my hands up a millisecond before I slam into the asphalt, scratching my forearms and palms on the pavement as whatever I ran into rolls away.

Scrambling to my feet, I brush myself off, freezing when the coughing starts again.

My spirit soars. *I'm not too late.*

A backpack lands on the ground in front of me, kicking up the ever-growing layer of ash at my feet. Brows pinched, I follow its trajectory back to a broken basement window on my left. I blink, shielding my eyes as I stare into the darkness where the head of a man in a black hood is just visible. He grunts like he's struggling with a heavy load, pausing only to hack up a lung before the grunting starts all over again.

"*Fucking hell,*" a deep voice bellows, the grating sound sending a chill of recognition rippling up my scarred spine.

In slow motion, I watch dirt-caked hands appear on the windowsill a few inches above ground level. A broad body follows soon after, the hood of the man's sweatshirt falling back as he hoists himself up, giving me a clear shot of his profile.

As if caught in an electric current, every muscle in my body seizes.

Even covered in soot with his hair singed and clothes burnt, I'd know that man anywhere...and it's not my father.

Chapter Fifty-Five

"Ryker?" I tug the bandana away from my face, head tilting to the side as my brain fumbles over the shock of seeing him here.

"*Help me*," he croaks, biceps and neck straining as he struggles to lift something out of the basement. "*Willa*, help me get him up."

My heart gallops inside my chest.

I rush to the window and drop to my knees, crying out in relief as I grab onto my father's uniformed arm, only to immediately lose my grip. Dad's blond hair slips out of sight, and Ryker grunts, the dead-weight pulling him several inches back inside the window. Panicked, I brace a scraped and sweaty palm against the stone exterior and hook my opposite wrist beneath Dad's armpit, dragging him upward with every ounce of my strength. My pulse riots as inch by painstaking inch he rises until finally we get him onto the pavement.

"What happened?" I cry out, dropping my ear to Dad's sternum where the steady rise and fall of his chest soothes my ragged nerves. He's soaking wet but breathing, and besides a few ashy smudges and a bump on his temple, I can't find anything else wrong with him. "What happened to his head? Why isn't he awake?"

Ryker flops onto his ass, head hung low and forearms resting on his knees as he falls into another coughing fit before answering. "Got knocked out," he says through a wheeze, "but I think he's going to be fine."

As if on cue, Dad groans and slowly brings his wobbly hand to the lump on his temple.

I let go of a choked laugh, my shoulders slumping as a watery smile stretches over my lips. *He's okay...he's really okay.*

Wiping at my eyes, I grab hold of his upper arm and glance at Ryker. "Can you help me get him to a safer spot?"

He nods and rises to his feet, looking a little worse for wear as we drag my father from the building. My hamstrings burn with every step, and the awkward angle I'm hunched has my lower back seconds away from spasming, but there's something cathartic about the pain, so I bear it in silence and keep going.

Ryker, on the other hand, can't stop huffing or gritting his teeth as we backpedal Dad across the pavement toward the grass. Not only is he limping, but there are angry scorch marks seared into the flesh of his knuckles, forearms, and neck—the unfamiliar black hoodie he's wearing burned in so many places I don't know how it's still on him. But what's even more concerning is the way he constantly looks around us, his movements jerky and erratic—like he's on high alert or waiting for someone to pop out of the shadows. The little hairs on my arms stand on end, but that's probably just my adrenaline wearing off, so I concentrate on channeling all my energy into putting one foot behind the other. If I can get us far enough away, I'll go grab one of the paramedics for Dad and have them look at Ryker, too.

Once we're a safe distance from the building, we lay Dad in the grass. He grumbles something about his head hurting, and even though I know that's a good sign, it's not enough to ease my worry.

Swiping my arm across my forehead to keep the soot-stained sweat from dripping into my eyes, I turn toward Ryker. "I'm gonna go get help."

"Don't," he rasps, lunging to stop me before quickly pulling back his hand. "Just—" He rakes his fingers through his hair. "Just let me get the backpack first."

"What the hell are you talking about?" Smoke and ash billow around us like a vortex, singeing my nostrils and drying out my throat. "The building is literally about to collapse," I say with a furrowed brow, "and you want me to wait until you get your *backpack?*"

"Please, Willa. Just let me go grab the bag," Ryker insists through clenched teeth. His eyes are pleading, but there's something else hidden beneath their green depths. Something hard and unfamiliar that sends a ripple of goose bumps cascading down my arms and up my neck.

A knot forms in my stomach as the building groans and shudders.

More sirens wail in the distance, and someone near the front of the station shouts, "The roof's gonna go! Get everyone back!"

"*Fuck,*" Ryker curses, eyes darting from the smoking building to something on the ground behind me.

Following the direction of his gaze, I spot the backpack he threw out of the basement window. But that's not what has nausea surging through my gut. No, that would be the rusty red fuel cans lying discarded by the corner of the building—one of them tipped on its side a few feet apart from the others.

Blood draining from my face, I turn toward Ryker.

"*Willa...*" My name is a warning on his lips as he extends his soot-stained palm in my direction while gray flecks of ash swirl around us like desiccated snowflakes.

All I can do is shake my head, a thousand panicked thoughts threatening to buckle my knees. Why is Ryker here in the first place? Why was he inside the station...

A pit opens in my stomach. I take a step backward, and then another, slowly inching away from him until something crunches beneath my shoe. I pause, eyes dropping to the concrete as I rotate my heel, revealing a silver boot-shaped lighter glinting up at me from the ground.

My head cocks to the side, and half in a daze, I stoop to pick it up, blinking over and over again as I glance from the lighter to the gas canisters, then back to Ryker. My hair whips around my face, lashing at my cheeks while an invisible hand constricts around my heart.

Ryker reaches for me again, but I rip my arm away. "What have you done..." I rasp, voice barely audible over the mind-numbing roar inside my head.

His throat bobs. "Willa, it's not what you think."

"Really?" My voice cracks as the world tilts on its axis. "Because from where I'm standing, it looks like you started the fire that killed my brother!" I chuck the lighter as hard as I can at him, but he doesn't even flinch when it bounces off his shoulder and clatters to the pavement.

"What are you talking about? Noah isn't—" Ryker's jaw gapes as he spots the tears streaming down my cheeks. "Willa...what happened?"

"Dad wasn't picking up his phone. Noah went inside—" My voice breaks, and I ball my fists, fighting back the burning tears blurring my vision. "Noah went inside to find him," I sob, chest heaving uncontrollably, "and now he's dead. My brother is dead—because of *you.*"

Ryker pales, his eyes darting back and forth across my face. He takes a stumbling step backward, expression slipping into something I can only describe as absolute devastation. "No. He can't be..."

A monstrous crash sounds from inside the burned-out station, the ground shuddering as the support beams for the roof finally give way.

My hands fly to my head and Ryker dives for me at the same time the roof bows and then collapses, taking each floor beneath it out on its descent and sending a plume of glowing embers into the black-and-gray sky. Ryker pins me to the asphalt, covering my body with his as glass and debris rain down on us from above. He keeps saying something, but I can't hear him over the rubble crashing onto the pavement and the sound of my own screaming.

After what feels like an eternity, everything goes eerily quiet—even the bits and pieces of noise I can actually hear sound muffled.

461

For one second, I think I've gone deaf, but then I realize Ryker's arms are still wrapped around my head in a protective cocoon.

I cough, struggling to draw in a full breath with his weight on top of me, until he finally lifts up, slowly unfurling his arms from around my head. I try to look away from him, but he grabs my chin, gently turning me so I'm forced to meet his eyes.

My body trembles at the sight of his nearly white hair and the slow trickle of blood sliding over his soot-stained brow onto my cheek and neck. My eyes flutter open and closed as the pain in my chest becomes unbearable.

"Tell me you didn't start the fire," I plead, choking on the words while my sanity teeters on the edge of a cliff. It's not just my sanity either, it's me dangling over the edge, barely hanging on by my fingertips.

"Ryker!" I scream into his face. "*Please*, just tell me you didn't do this..."

Jaw clenched, he releases my chin to brush the loose strands of hair away from my eyes, holding on to one of the white locks and sliding it between his thumb and forefinger. I want him to explain himself, I *need* him to keep me from falling into the abyss like he said he would, but the second his throat bobs, I already know what's coming.

"I can't do that," he says, voice low and rough.

My lip quivers. "Why not?"

"Because I promised I wouldn't lie to you."

For a second, all I can do is stare at him as I plummet from the cliff—the endless fall stealing my breath as my world comes crashing down around me. The future I saw for myself with Ryker, the loss of my brother, my mother being alive—all of it hits me at once, battering against my psyche until I'm broken and bloodied.

"But, Willa," Ryker continues, "it's not what you—"

Before he can finish, he's ripped off of me and thrown to the pavement, a loud *thunk* reverberating through the air when his skull bounces off the hard ground. I lunge forward to see if he's okay, but my father grabs me by the bicep and yanks me backward.

"*Willa*," he seethes, chest heaving as he towers over me. "Get away from him."

"But—" I scramble for Ryker when Dad grabs me again, shoving me to the ground.

"Willa, *goddammit*, look around you." His arm waves wildly toward the destroyed building. "Ryker's not the man we thought he was."

"Mr. Dunn...*please*," Ryker rasps.

My father brings his hand to the large lump on his temple and turns to stare at Ryker on the ground. "After everything I've done for you..." He shakes his head, blinking slowly, like it's an effort to form words. "This is how you repay me? By ambushing me and burning down the goddamn station? All because I wasn't willing to break the law for you?"

The last trace of air is ripped from my lungs. It's true, then. Ryker started the fire...

He's responsible for killing my brother.

My pulse pounds violently while my gaze volleys between Ryker's agonized face and my father's furious one. My vision swims, and for one second, I think I might pass out as Dad uses the radio barely hanging on to his uniform to call for backup.

Ryker is so close, three feet at most, but it feels as though there's an entire continent between us. And still, I can't help but try to make sense of this madness one more time.

"Did you do that to Dad's head?" I ask softly.

Casting a tentative glance over his shoulder toward the tree line, he grits his teeth. "I can't do this here—"

"You can't do this here?" I repeat, voice cracking as I gesture to the ruins of the burned-out police station and then to my father. "You already did it. How could you have possibly thought *this* would keep your sister safe?"

I scoot a few more inches away from him.

463

"Willa," he says, brow lowered and jaw etched in stone. "You *promised* you wouldn't shut me out. You *promised* you'd give me the chance to explain."

My lungs seize and I flounder for a moment, questioning whether or not I should grab Ryker and make a run for it so I can hear him out. But no matter how reluctant I am to accept it, the truth is there's nothing to explain...

I wipe the angry tears from my eyes and rise to my feet. "What could you possibly say that would fix this, Ryker? Noah is dead and you started the fire that killed him."

Dad's hand lands hard on my shoulder, my ash-flecked hair fanning out as he whips me around to face him. "What did you say? What happened to Noah?" There's a franticness in his tone that feels like it's ripping me in two. But I can't fall apart...*not yet.*

"Dad—" I sob through the tears blurring my surroundings.

"Answer me." He shakes my shoulders the same way Noah did when he found me staring at the flames. "Willa! What happened to your brother?"

For the third and most painful time, I explain what happened—my voice cracking on every other syllable. "They didn't... They couldn't get him out in time... Noah's *gone.*"

The sound that rips from my father's throat is nothing short of pure agony. It is the lament of someone's heart being shredded to pieces. Their soul being torn from their body.

And then he's on top of Ryker, pummeling his face until two officers round the corner and peel him away.

"Get off of me," Dad growls, his eyes full of animalistic rage. "He killed my son!"

The officers pivot so quickly I barely see them pin Ryker to the ground. He tries to shrug out of their hold, but the second one of them slaps a cuff over his wrist, it's like a switch flips and Ryker stops fighting.

Eyes wild, like a fox caught in a snare, his gaze lands on mine. Every fiber of my being aches to reach for him, to blink and wake us both up from this horrible nightmare, but the next thing I know, he's yanked to his feet and his hands are roughly forced behind his back as one of the officers finishes cuffing him.

Ryker stares at me, his jaw hard and bottom lip quivering almost imperceptibly—not with sadness, but with something bitter and tangy I can almost taste on the smoky breeze.

"*Willa,*" he says, my name a plea on his lips. But then the officer gives the cuffs a rough tug, and Ryker stumbles, struggling to keep his footing as he's dragged to a nearby cruiser.

Ash kicks up in their wake, the red-and-blue lights of the emergency vehicles bouncing off every surface until I'm dizzy and half blind. Dad is shouting directions from somewhere on my right, and I glance over my shoulder in time to see an officer placing Ryker's boot-shaped lighter into an evidence bag.

Time is warped. I can't tell if it's moving too fast or two slow, or if it's moving at all. The only thing I know is that I can't seem to tear my attention away from Ryker, who's peering at me from the back seat of the cruiser, eyes dark and hollow.

Like a moth to a flame, my legs move of their own accord, but when I'm only a few feet away, Dad's voice stops me. "Willa, I need you to come fill out a witness statement."

I glance from my father to Ryker, who's so close now I can hear the ragged sounds of his breathing through the open front window. He continues to stare at me, green eyes narrowed and sharp as a blade, but he doesn't say a word.

I shake my head. "Dad, please don't make me do this. I just want to go home—"

He shoves the pen into my hand, drags me to the tail end of the cruiser, and slams the paper onto the trunk. "This isn't a request. Write down everything he said to you about the fire."

Eyes filled with tears, I glance into the patrol car's rearview mirror at Ryker's silhouette. There's so much ash on the window I can't see his eyes, but that doesn't stop the invisible tug in my chest—

"Excuse me, Officer Dunn?"

"What is it?" Dad snaps, eyes red and glassy. "Oh, you're the IT guy, right? Tell me you have the footage."

"Yes and no," a gangly man in a baggy white polo says as he approaches, laptop clutched in his spindly fingers. "The interior cameras weren't hooked up to the network yet, but the back camera—the one that's already synced to the cloud—did manage to get something."

"Show me," Dad demands, rage radiating off him in pulsing waves.

The IT guy's black-rimmed glasses slide down the bridge of his nose as he places the computer on the trunk next to where I'm standing. I chew on my inner cheek, not daring to breathe while he queues the video up and presses Play.

The footage is grainy and I have to squint to sort out what I'm seeing, but when a man with a black hoodie enters the frame, my heart shatters. The hood is up, and although he never looks directly at the camera during the three trips he makes to lower gas canisters into a basement window, you'd have to be an idiot not to recognize those broad shoulders.

That familiar coldness creeps back into my gut, steadily crawling into my extremities until my eyes glaze over and my pulse becomes all but nonexistent...

The IT guy shuffles his feet. "There's no movement for about an hour and a half, which Chief Thompson said is probably when he lit the diversion fire on the outskirts of town. I'm going to fast forward through the gap."

When he presses Play again, the hooded man stops to stare at my dad's cruiser before looking directly at the camera. It's Ryker's face, clear as day. Then he sneaks into one of the station's first-floor windows. My body stiffens, the last shards of my disbelief obliterated when the words Ryker spoke to my father in the driveway come back to me.

If you get in the way of me protecting my sister, I will go through you. No matter the cost.

Apparently, that cost included my brother's life...

I grit my teeth and close my eyes. All the other men in my life lied and let me down, why did I think Ryker would be any different?

"Fill out your statement, Willa," Dad says, tone clipped and miserable. "We can't let him get away with what he's done to our family—what he did to my *son*."

Ash swirls around us, smoke settling so deep in my lungs I don't think I'll ever smell anything else ever again. Without blinking or even breathing, I pick up the pen and write down every single detail of what I saw.

When I'm done, my legs are shaking, but I can't feel them. My heart is hammering inside my chest, but I can't hear it.

When the patrol car holding Ryker speeds off into the night, I can't even watch it go.

I don't consciously make the decision to leave, but all of a sudden, my feet are moving.

"Willa, where are you going?" Dad calls out as my boots *click* on the pavement, but there's no way I'm stopping now.

With every tie binding me to this godforsaken town irreparably severed, I don't bother looking back or responding.

Chapter Fifty-Six

Figuring that as long as I keep my mind occupied I won't have to feel anything, I spend the first hour of my drive making funeral arrangements for Noah with almost clinical detachment.

For the most part, it works.

When all is said and done, not only can I attend my first week of college orientation *and* my brother's service next Saturday, but all Dad needs to do is show up.

After that, I occupy my time with a few other calls, one to Elanor and one to the prison my mother is incarcerated at, only to be told that the latter is currently hospitalized. That piece of news is enough to send me spiraling.

For a hundred miles, I oscillate between banging my fists against the steering wheel until my knuckles are raw and crying my eyes out until I can barely see. Then, about halfway to my destination, I'm so submerged beneath my grief and rage, every inhale feels as though I'm filling my lungs with water and I have to pull over to dry heave on the side of the road.

Sweat-drenched and trembling, I kneel in the dirt, the sun beating down on me as it all comes crashing back. The secrets Dad kept, the emptiness of losing Noah, the outrage over Ryker's betrayal...

How could the one person I still trusted do this? How could he take my brother from me? I'll never get to apologize to Noah...

A sob racks my body as I dig my fingers into the dirt and tilt my chin skyward.

How do I come back from this? How do I live with myself...

Sweat pours from my skin while semitrucks amble down the highway, shaking the earth beneath my knees while tears stream across my cheeks.

Above me, a turkey vulture circles in the cloudless sky, waiting for the opportunity to swoop in and pick my bones clean... I fist a handful of dry dirt, the painful bite of little stones tearing at my nails.

My jaw hardens, and I slowly rise to my feet. "I'm not dead yet, you bastard!" I scream, throwing the dirt into the sky. "Not by a long shot."

Wiping the tears from my eyes, I climb back into my truck. If *she* couldn't kill me, then neither will this.

My knees shake as I gawk at the massive white limestone hospital in the middle of downtown Austin. The Crowes are in there somewhere, but so is the woman who tried to murder me.

I put one ash-caked boot in front of the other until a blast of arctic air conditioning and the stringent smell of antiseptic nearly mows me over. The sparkling floor-to-ceiling windows lining the walls make the space bright and cheery—such a stark contrast to the way I'm feeling that I wince when I catch sight of myself in their reflection.

I'd changed my clothes and washed my face in a rest stop bathroom, but my hair is singed and there are deep-purple bags under my eyes no amount of makeup could hide. I'm sure I also reek of smoke, but I've gone nose blind to it.

Averting my gaze, I head for the directory on the wall to locate the Intensive Care Unit. Thankfully, the halls are clearly marked. If I had to stop and ask for directions, I might lose my nerve and turn around.

The elevator rattles as the doors open to the ICU, where instead of antiseptic, I'm slapped by the pungent odor of bleach and something musky and rotten that reminds me of the dead opossum Noah and I found under the porch last summer.

My heart lurches painfully at the memory of my brother chasing me around the yard with that dead rodent on a shovel while I screamed. Noah laughed so hard he fell over and accidentally threw the disgusting thing at me, then he'd spent the next week apologizing by bringing me donuts every day.

I'll never hear his laugh again.

I fucked his best friend and sent him to his death...

My fists clench at my sides. Now is not the time. I'm here to confront the last of my demons before putting Deadwood in my rearview mirror for good. After this, I'll never have to think about that town or anything that happened there ever again.

I look up, realizing that I've made it halfway down the hallway without paying attention to the rooms I'm passing. Not that I need to. There's only one with a corrections officer stationed out front.

With my stomach tangled in knots, I drag my boots to the end of the hallway, hesitating when I spot the name of the burly officer embroidered into his gray-and-blue uniform.

Kelp...

"Can I help you, miss?" Officer Kelp asks, one dark brow raised as he eyes my ratty appearance.

There's only a thin sliding-glass door separating me from my mother, but I still can't find the strength to look past the officer's brawny chest. "I-I'm here to see my mom," I say after an awkward pause, silently cursing myself for stammering.

The tawny skin near his eyes crinkles when he points toward the nurses' station. "I'm sure one of the staff members can help. Unfortunately, my partner's on break and I'm unable to leave—"

"No, you don't understand." I shake my head, hoping it covers the wobbly quality of my voice. "My name's Willa Dunn, I think we spoke on the phone the other day? I was trying to get a hold of my neighbor, but the hospital's automated system kept connecting me to this room. My mother's in there..."

Officer Kelp's eyes widen. "I'm sorry, Miss Dunn," he says after smoothing away his horrified expression. "Your mother's not allowed to have visitors. Once we're back at the prison hospital, our chief medical officer can clear you for a visit." He smiles, but it's forced.

I bite my inner cheek, shifting my weight onto my opposite heel to keep myself from turning around and leaving. "You've let my dad visit."

Officer Kelp's grin drops abruptly. "Your father had medical power of attorney. He also never actually went into the room. Well —" He tilts his head to the side. "He went in once about six months ago, but that was authorized and he'll never make that mistake again. Sorry, kid. I can't let you in."

My hands tremble as I shove them into my pockets. "I just found out she was alive yesterday," I say softly, trying to keep my voice even. "What if this is my only chance for closure?" Tears well in my lower lids, but I quickly blink them away. "*Please.* I have to put this behind me, and I can't do that without talking to her, and—"

My voice cracks, the rest of the thought lodging in my throat.

Officer Kelp stares at me for a long moment, the deep brown of his eyes soft and contemplative until he sighs and turns to slide the door open. "My partner will be back in twenty minutes. If anyone asks, I thought you were hospital staff."

Knees trembling, I murmur a soft thank you and take a step forward—only to hesitate on the threshold of the dark room.

Every person I've ever loved has betrayed my trust, but my mother was the first. The woman in that room should have loved me unconditionally, but was instead the source of all the horrible moments in my life.

Does she regret trying to kill me? Could I ever forgive her if she does?

Will I forgive myself for my part in my brother's death?

...Can any of us come back from our biggest mistakes?

I'll never know if I can't find the courage to walk into this damn room. With a deep breath, I steel my spine and step inside.

Chapter Fifty-Seven

The room is dark and quiet except for the gentle whir of the infusion machine perched next to the drawn blinds. But light from the hallway and the gaps in the window coverings illuminate enough of the room for me to see the faint outline of a tiny, frail body in the hospital bed before an overhead light abruptly switches on.

"Who's in here?" my mother snaps, voice raspy and unfamiliar as she clutches the bedside remote.

My arm flies up to shield my eyes from the shockingly bright light, and I have to blink a few times before I can acclimate.

"I said who's in here?" She's staring right at me when she says it, but her eyes are cloudy, one of them barely cracked open as she peers out through the shiny pink-and-white skin covering her face and neck.

When the room spins, I reach out to brace myself against the wall, spotting the whiteboard beside her bed.

**PATIENT IS LEGALLY BLIND.
SHE CAN SEE BLURRED IMAGES AND GENERAL SHAPES.
PLEASE IDENTIFY YOURSELF UPON ENTERING THE ROOM AND
PRIOR TO ADMINISTERING PATIENT CARE.**

"Mrs. Dunn," I croak, unable to bring myself to look directly at her. *She was burned so much worse than I was...*

Somewhere deep down, I'd been expecting to confront a monster, not a feeble woman with patchy hair and a broken body. My stomach does an uncomfortable flip when my eyes drop to her restrained wrists.

I mean, *Jesus*, she's got tubes and wires sticking out from every available surface of her body and she's struggling to hold up her own head, but they've got her handcuffed to the fucking bed like an animal?

"It's Ms. Dunn now," she says, voice low and grated as she takes a wheezy breath. "I'm here often enough, you think y'all would've caught on by now."

"I— I don't work for the hospital."

God, I sound like a scared little girl... Where is all my rage and anger? Why am I letting her have this effect on me?

"Who are you, then? Did Joel send you? Does he finally believe me?" She breathes in an excited rush. The monitoring machine mounted on the wall alarms before shutting itself off when her heart rate drops back below one hundred.

"Believe you about wh-what?" *Dammit, Willa, pull yourself together.*

"Beau Blackthorne." My mother yanks her cuffed wrist against the bed frame. "Joel has to believe me. It wasn't my fault! Beau put that abomination inside me against my will!"

Goose bumps ripple across my flesh. The ticking of the hospital equipment is so astronomically loud it feels as though it's banging against the inside of my skull as I stumble backward. My spine collides with the wall, and even though I can't possibly move farther away, I keep trying to.

"Beau raped you?" I ask with a shaky voice as bile claws up my throat. "He's the father of your daughter, not Joel?"

My skin crawls because I already know the answer. I saw it in the way Beau looked at me in the graveyard at Divine Mercy yesterday. *Jesus*, that's why Charlie and I have the same color hair, why Cooper and I have the same eyes. It's why I look so different from Noah, and it's the real reason why Dad has barely looked me in the eye since he visited my mom six months ago...

I blink once.

I'm not a Dunn, I'm a fucking *Blackthorne*.

"Yes," my mother says, voice cracking. "That wicked man *forced* himself on me. It's not my fault. He—"

Folding over, I clutch my stomach to stop myself from being sick all over the floor while my mother keeps droning on. I try to listen to what she's saying, but with my head such a jumbled mess of emotions, I only catch fragmented chunks.

She'd caught Beau touching one of his nephews at the park...

He pinned her against a picnic table...

She was too terrified to admit the child wasn't her husband's.

She believed God would heal her of the *abomination* growing in her belly.

Then the abomination tried to kill her...

She prayed and prayed for an answer until one day, God revealed that fire was the only way to cleanse her and her daughter's souls...

Rage quickens my blood, proliferating inside of me until I'm seconds away from exploding. I want to scream and curl up on the floor, but even more pressing is my desire to smash everything in this room and burn the world down for what Beau did to her...

For what he did to *us*.

This information in no way excuses her actions, but this woman is sick. Beau Blackthorne is the clear monster here. Now the only question is, what the hell am I going to do about it?

Standing up straight, I whip out my phone and point it at my mother. "Ms. Dunn, you were right. Joel did send me."

Joel... Because he's not really my father...

I wipe an angry tear from my eye and bring up the video app before hitting Record. "Joel wants to believe you about what happened, but he said he needs more details. Would you mind starting from the beginning and telling me what happened so I can record it for him?"

My mother goes off on an even more detailed recollection of what Beau did. How he raped her and threatened to kill Noah if she told anyone. How when she told Beau the child was his, he accused her of being possessed by the Devil.

"Who else in Deadwood knows?" I ask once she's done.

"No one," she whispers, her opaque eyes blinking in the bright fluorescent lights. "I didn't say a single word at my trial, but the doctors are telling me I won't see the new year." She adjusts the oxygen tubes near her nose with her uncuffed, shiny-scarred hand and shakes her head. "Joel already divorced me, and my son won't visit. I just want my husband to understand I didn't betray him. I want to keep him safe from the abomination Beau created. That girl's not right."

She keeps talking, but I interrupt her. "Thank you," I say, adrenaline helping the insults roll right off my skin. "I'll make sure the right person sees this."

Without another word, I leave the room and skitter right past the corrections officer into the hallway. My thoughts are frantic, my heartbeat uneven, but it takes me less than two minutes to track down the number I need from the Town Council directory, and only three seconds to queue up the video and send it.

The read receipt pops up a few seconds later, and not long after, I get a phone call.

"*She's lying,*" Dorothy Blackthorne hisses, her voice so loud and full of hatred I have to pull the phone away from my ear.

"We both know she's telling the truth, and I can prove it with a court ordered DNA test if you'd prefer I make this video public."

"What's your price, *girl?*"

Knowing I have one shot to make this work, I draw in a shaky breath and steel my spine. "I want Beau to stop trying to have his parental rights reinstated and sign off on Charlie's foster parents adopting her. If he does that, then this video will never see the light of day."

I can hear Dorothy's mouth twisting into a snarl through her exhale. "That's my only granddaughter—"

"No," I say firmly, "she's your *youngest* granddaughter. *I* was your first. And I'd rather die than let Charlie spend a single second in your rapist son's house. If you care for her at all, you'll convince him." I let that simmer for a second before continuing. "Otherwise, I'll release this video to the public and my mother will take Beau to court."

Dorothy doesn't say a single word, but her breathing on the other end of the line lets me know she's still there.

"I need an answer, Dorothy."

"Fine," she spits. "I'll talk to him."

If there's one thing the Blackthornes are good for, it's protecting their family name, but it's not enough. I need to make sure she understands. "I'll post this on social media if you don't send confirmation that Beau's officially withdrawn his petition for custody within twenty-four hours." I take a deep, sobering breath. "And Dorothy, I need you to make one more thing *very* clear to your son. If he ever comes after me or Charlie, I *will* kill him. And then I'll release the video anyway."

"I said I'll take care of it," she hisses.

Relief washes over my shoulders like a cool wave. The rest of my world might be on fire, but at least I know Charlie is safe...

The line goes dead and I'm forced to stare at my own reflection on the screen. My stomach churns. Nutmeg-brown hair. Hazel eyes. Soul dead and empty. Turns out, Willa Blackthorne is a more fitting name than Willa Dunn ever was.

Maybe I belong in Deadwood with the rest of my cursed blood-line, but I don't fucking care. After my brother's funeral, I'll never step foot in that godforsaken town again.

Epilogue

Ryker, Age 21

Six months later

The fluorescent lights flicker overhead, buzzing like they're on their last breath before they burn out. There are three dead moth carcasses in the plastic casing of that same light, and a hundred other insect bodies crammed into the corners.

I glance down at the moth tattoo on my forearm, its wings barely visible beneath the rolled sleeve of my beige—soon to be bright-orange—uniform.

Some fucking warning that turned out to be.

Another black suit walks into the courthouse holding room. I don't bother looking up, but I can tell from the slow *tap* of his footsteps that it's not my lawyer.

"You fucked up," he says flatly, metal chair squealing against the concrete floor as he takes the seat across from me. "You fucked up *bad.*"

Grinding my teeth, I strain against the handcuffs until the bite of pain cuts through my rage. "I did exactly what you asked. Maybe if you'd hired a better attorney, I wouldn't have been sentenced to *seven* fucking years."

"With a manslaughter conviction, you're lucky it wasn't twenty," he sneers, sending a white jolt of pain slicing through my chest at the reminder that my best friend—*my only fucking friend*—is no longer breathing. "Don't forget, *you're* the one who told me you could get what we needed from Kane. You also said you could keep the Dunn girl from testifying against you. If anyone's responsible for you going to prison, it's her."

Willa's soot-covered face cuts through my memory from the night of the fire, quickly replaced by her stone-cold expression and lifeless eyes when she testified against me in court this morning. She kept her attention on the ground the entire trial, refusing to speak with anyone, including her own father as she sat silently in the back corner.

Being in the same room with her already felt like repeatedly taking a dagger to the heart, but it wasn't a death blow until they called her to the stand and she wouldn't even look at me...

Hatred leaks from my pores, hot and vicious with the weight of her betrayal.

I've been let down before, but this is the first time it's felt like I was fucking dying. I thought Willa saw me—that it was us against all these other fucks. But she was so damn ready to believe the worst about me. So eager to blame someone for Noah's death... Completely unwilling to let me fucking explain myself.

My blood curdles, and I tighten my fists.

I'll never forget the way she looked at me on the night of the fire. Like I was a fucking monster... *Like I was Beau.*

"She wouldn't answer my calls or take my fucking letters. What the hell else was I supposed to do?" I say through gritted teeth, tugging against the metal restraints. "I did everything you asked. It's not my fault everything went south. You can't go back on our deal."

"Our deal still stands," he says, eyes darting upward before he scoots his chair closer to the table. "Thanks to *me*, Charlotte remains with her foster parents in protective custody." He pauses. "That being said, how long she remains there is entirely dependent on *you*."

I glance at the security camera above us, unsurprised to find the red recording light no longer blinking. "Explain."

The man smiles, drawing out the moment like he gets off on making me suffer.

I knew he was pissed about how things went down, but whatever he's feeling right now, it's nothing compared to the fucking shitstorm brewing inside my skull. Yes, I might've started the fire, but it was *contained*. Everything was going to plan...until it wasn't.

This guy's career might be on the line, but my stakes were ten times higher. My best friend is dead and the person I trusted most in the world sold me down the fucking river. For six months, I waited for her to visit—to come to her senses and let me explain. But she never did. Now I've lost everything and Charlie's going to pay the price—unless this asshole's found a way to salvage the situation.

"Well?" I prompt through clenched teeth. "Are you going to explain or not?"

"Kane came to your sentencing today," he finally says. "He's still here, actually. Brought a fancy lawyer with him and everything."

I can't help but laugh at the demoralizing irony. "A little too goddamn late to matter, but I guess I got him to trust me after all."

Grinning, he taps his knuckle against the metal table, causing the odd mole on his inner wrist to shift into something that resembles a kidney bean. "Keeping you off the witness stand played in our favor. There's a chance you can still get the information we need."

I snort. This bastard made it more than clear that if I breathed a single word about why I was at the police station that night, not only would I spend the next twenty years of my life locked up, but he'd personally ensure Beau's parental rights would be reinstated.

"What can I possibly do from prison?" I spit through a humorless laugh that echoes off the barren walls.

A devious spark flares in his eye. "Like you said, Kane trusts you now, he might be willing to testify against Josiah Koresh to knock a few years off your sentence."

My pulse picks up and I sit a little straighter.

"The thing is..." he continues, "even if he does, five years is still a long time for me to look after your sister while you rot behind bars. But depending on what cell block you end up on, you might be a useful informant on a few of my other cases. If I could call on your services from time to time, I think I could keep Charlotte out of Deadwood *indefinitely*. That would also look great for the parole board in, say...two years?

I dip my chin.

If it keeps Charlie away from Beau, I'll do my time and whatever else he asks. But when I get out of here, I'm going to make damn fucking sure Willa Dunn regrets the day she turned her back on me.

End of book one.

The journey continues in book two of the Deadwood Duet.

Acknowledgments

Thank you for reading!

The idea for the Deadwood Duet came to me after listening to "Country Song" by Seether. I loved how gritty and passionate the song was, and by the end of my third listen, I was imagining a creepy small town, cultish mischief, and two characters who absolutely hated each other but used to be in love.
Before I could tell that story, I had to know what drove these two people apart in the first place.
Thus, *The Endless Fall* was born.

To the readers–thank you for going on this journey with me. None of this would be possible without you and I can't wait to get the second installment of this duet in your hands.

To the bookstagram community–y'all are the BEST! Thank you for sharing your excitement for my books with the world and for getting the word out. I see your posts, tags, and DMs, and I am so appreciative!

To my husband–I'm obsessed with you. Thank you for putting up with my chaos.

To my editor–you are amazing and I honestly don't know what I would do without you. Thank you for lending me your brain and constantly pushing me to be a better storyteller.

To my critique partners, Lauren, Larissa, and Adrian–thank you for your patience and incredible input. You helped me keep my sanity while writing this book and I am crazy grateful for all of you.

To my beta readers–this was a short turn around and you guys are rockstars, thank you!

Extra special thank you to Angelique, Alex, Jasmine, and Sam–your feedback was invaluable to me. Thank you for going above and beyond and helping me make sure what was in my head was on the page with the rewrites.

To Lois–I am so thankful for you and your attention to detail. You once again saved my butt!

To Joy–I adore you! Thank you for all your support and for lending me your eyes on this project.

To my street team members–you guys are incredible and you kept me afloat this past year! Thank you for your support and general awesomeness.

Gratefully yours, Emmerson

About the Author

Emmerson Hoyt lives in Austin, Texas with her husband and a small horde of animals. When she's not writing, she's playing video games or finding an excuse to get another floral tattoo.

Check out her website for the latest news!
www.emmersonhoyt.com

Also by Emmerson Hoyt

Content Warnings

The following list may contain spoilers.

Consensual sexual activity, spankings & light bondage, light bullying (MMC), bullying (antagonist), brief descriptions of dismembered livestock, religious indoctrination, attempted filicide (historical/off page), homophobia & biphobia (antagonist), homophobic slur (antagonist), child abuse (historical/off page), sexual assault and childhood sexual abuse (referenced/historical/off page), underage drinking, drugging (hallucinogens), PTSD & CPTSD, murder, death, violence, graphic injury, fire.

Made in the USA
Columbia, SC
31 March 2025

55975311R00297